TAKING A CHANCE IN DEADWOOD

A WILD DEADWOOD READS ANTHOLOGY

A. L. LONG

TAM DE RUDDER JACKSON

STEPHANIE WEBB DILLON

LACY CHANTELL   HALEY RHOADES

VIA MARI   JULIEN BRADLEY

CICI CORDELIA

BETTY BRANDT PASSICK

TINA SUSEDIK

Twisted Teacup
PUBLISHING

TAKE A CHANCE... YOU WON'T REGRET IT!

BEFORE I FALL BY A.L. LONG

Life is full of unexpected challenges, and for Lana Porter, taking over Porter Vineyards was one she never could have prepared for. It had always been her father's dream to make the vineyard the number one in all of South Dakota, and when he passed away, Lana made a vow to make that dream come true. Her first step was securing a big account with Jaden Edwards, a wealthy businessman in Sioux Falls. But it wasn't just his business that she wanted; she also craved his presence in her life. As she delved deeper into their negotiations, she couldn't help but feel a pull towards him, like he was the missing piece to her puzzle. However, things took a turn for the worst when she discovered that his interest in stocking his exclusive nightclub with Porter wines was simply a front for his ulterior motive - gaining control of Porter Vineyards.

A CHANCE ENCOUNTER BY TAM DERUDDER JACKSON

Sadie Bennet doesn't gamble, but then a friend convinces her to play some games in Deadwood. The stakes are high when she meets a hot Blackjack player who dares her to take a chance on love.

FINDING OUR WAY IN DEADWOOD BY STEPHANIE WEBB DILLON

Clay Wheeler grew up in Deadwood. He had always been a lady's man until he met Jillian. He knew she was it for him from their first dance. They got married and started a business. Things were going great until a huge misunderstanding came between them.

Jillian Lewis Wheeler fell hard for the handsome cowboy. They had chemistry from their first meeting and being married to and working with her best friend seemed like a dream come true; so when a woman came in claiming he had fathered her child, Jillian felt her world crumble from under her feet.

Will the truth come out and will Clay and Jillian be able to put the pieces of their marriage back together again?

DREAMING OF DAHLIAS BY LACY CHANTELL

Dahlia has terrible luck with men and pours all her energy in her flower shop. When a mysterious cowboy, Hunter Haynes, buys a secluded ranch and turns it into a wedding venue, they end up working side by side to make brides' dreams come true. It isn't until she gets stranded during a snowstorm that she learns the truth about his past and realizes what it is she feels for him.

BACKROADS & BONFIRES #2 BY HALEY RHOADES

Amy's an all-around tough nut to crack. With a little help from Amy's best friend, Lucas persists in bumping into Amy every chance he gets. Will her long work trip to Deadwood end with more than luggage in her car?

FEARLESS PROTECTOR BY VIA MARI

Mason

The wedding of one of our own in Deadwood, South Dakota should be a special time, especially for the bride and groom.

The sexy little bartender serving drinks at the bachelor party and I will get to know each other a whole lot better before this night is through. At least that was the plan.

But the sassy dark-haired beauty wants nothing to do with a crime boss bodyguard like me.

When the Chicago boys strike, it's up to me to find her before they can use her for what they want in exchange.

Priscilla Jean is going to belong to me whether she has agreed to take a chance on love or not. She'll see now that when someone messes with her, this town, and her friends, they'll end of dealing with me.

BLUE DOG BLACK DRAGON BY JULIEN BRADLEY

April sets out for her first bike ride of the season. After inflating the tires, and checking the brakes and gears, she begins her assent out of Deadwood gulch via the George Mikelson bike trail, a trek as familiar to her as her own name. The trip is uneventful until an unexpected storm forces her to seek refuge in one of the trail shelters. Hunkered down near the foot of an abandoned gold mine, April encounters a mythical deity setting her on a supernatural journey from which she may not return.

GUNSLINGERS AND HEARTSTRINGS BY CICI CORDELIA

In the spring of 1876, gold is discovered in the Black Hills of Dakota Territory, drawing miners and fortune-seekers from far and wide to the new town of Deadwood. Among them are carpenter Dewey Bower, wagon train entrepreneur Colorado Charlie Utter, and the legendary James "Wild Bill" Hickok, all hoping to leave their mark on the growing town. Other, more dissolute souls flock to the mining camps, seeking to make their fortunes by any means necessary.

Dewey, determined to better himself and his circumstances, finds love when he meets Melanie Hayes, a newcomer to Deadwood and part of Charlie Utter's wagon train. Hired by her father for his carpentry skills, Dewey also befriends Wild Bill, who offers to mentor him in the ways of the law. But amidst self-discovery, a budding romance, and the promise of a bright future, tragedy strikes. Dewey and Melanie bear witness to a despicable murder and suffer the loss of a good friend and mentor.

In the aftermath, they will find a way to honor his memory as they reach for their own happiness.

A THOUSAND MILES FROM BOYHOOD BY BETTY BRANDT PASSICK

In May 1876 "Wild Bill" Hickok departs for the goldfields of South Dakota, hoping to find the fortune that thus far had alluded him as gunslinger and gambler. Along the banks of Deadwood Creek, with the help of a young boy panning for gold, he discovers the kind of riches his mother had spoken of, a thousand miles earlier in his boyhood home of LaSalle County, Illinois.

BATTY FOR LOVE BY TINA SUSEDIK

When Nella Cambien decides to stay at an historic haunted brothel in Deadwood, she never imagines herself being transported back to 1880 to solve a murder that's remained a mystery for a hundred and forty years. Now, faced with the daunting task of proving she isn't the murderer, she must navigate the past to uncover the truth.

Deputy Stuart Adams had hoped for a peaceful day off in the woods, but a sudden murder and a fleeing suspect disrupt his plans. As he tries to piece together the events unfolding before him, he can't shake the image of a woman escaping from the brothel. Could she be the key to unraveling the mystery?

Together, Stuart and Nella must work against the odds to solve the murder and ensure Nella's safe return to the present day. But with time running out and secrets buried deep in Deadwood's history, the truth may be more elusive than they ever imagined.

BEFORE I FALL

A. L. LONG

1

This was my father's vision—to build and elevate Porter Vineyards into the most prestigious winery in all of South Dakota. The rolling hills, once barren and dry, were now adorned with neat rows of grapevines, extending as far as the eye could see. Amidst all this natural beauty, surrounded by endless rows of grapevines crawling up trellises toward the bright blue sky, I couldn't help but reflect on how this wasn't the life I had ever imagined for myself. My father had always dreamed of creating a thriving vineyard, and now his dream had become a reality. If only he was here to see it. As the warm sun beat down on my skin and the sweet scent of ripening grapes filled the air, memories of my father flooded my mind. How I longed to share this breathtaking view with him once again, to hear his voice and feel his presence beside me. Today marked the one-year anniversary of his passing, and as bittersweet tears welled up in my eyes, I knew he would always be with me through every harvest and every bottle of wine produced from these very vines.

"Here's to you, Dad," I said as I lifted my glass of Porter Merlot in the air in celebration of the success we had achieved. "We finally did it."

I held the Decanter plaque, naming Porter Vineyards one of the top vineyards in the US, against my chest. If it hadn't been for my father teaching me everything he knew about grapes, I wouldn't be holding his dream against my heart.

With a faint sigh, I drained the last drops of rich red wine from my glass. The smooth, rich flavors lingered on my tongue, tempting me to pour another glass and relax. But duty called, so I turned on my heels, leaving the grape orchards and heading back to the house. As the owner and vintner of a successful winery in Deadwood, I had a full schedule of appointments lined up for the day. There were always new clients to meet and deals to negotiate. But before I could dive into my work, there was one important task that needed my attention. Before retreating to my home office, I made a quick detour to check on the progress of the new shipment. I was the sole supplier of wine for every hotel in Deadwood, and it was my responsibility to ensure that their orders were fulfilled on time. That meant overseeing the transportation of bulk wine from our cellar to the bottling warehouse in Rapid City.

Making my way through the sprawling property, I took a detour to the spacious cellar where rows upon rows of oak barrels held our prized product. The cool stone walls and earthy scent of aging wine enveloped me as soon as I stepped inside. I spotted James conversing with the driver who would transport the tanks. The earthy scent of fermenting grapes filled the air, mingling with the smell of oak and aging spirits as I approached them. A sense of pride filled my heart, knowing every hour of hard work had paid off.

"Good morning, Lana," James smiled.

"Good morning, James," I replied. "Is everything ready for shipment?"

"Everything is ready," the driver chimed in. "The tanks are filled and secured. I should arrive in Rapid City around 3:00 p.m."

"Wonderful." In a short time, the tanks of Porter Chardonnay would be bottled and ready for distribution.

I gave James a hearty pat on the shoulder and left the dimly lit cellar. My first appointment of the day was less than an hour away, and I needed to make sure every detail was perfect. Wooing a potential customer was no easy task—it required finesse and careful planning. Jaden Edwards had agreed to meet me at the prestigious Franklin Hotel and Casino. It was not only a grand establishment, but also one of my biggest clients. As I headed toward the house to get ready, my mind raced with thoughts of how to impress Mr. Edwards and secure his business. The Franklin was known for its luxurious atmosphere and impeccable service, making it the perfect setting for what I had planned for him. I could almost taste the smooth, rich Porter wine that we would share as we discussed business. Though my wine spoke for itself, I knew I still had to work my charm and convince Mr. Edwards to stock his exclusive nightclub with it. Sioux Falls was a prime location for expanding my product, and securing Mr. Edwards as a client would be crucial in making that happen.

———

As I approached the elegant entrance of the Franklin, I felt a surge of determination—this meeting could be the turning point for my business. I couldn't wait to see where this meeting would take me and my brand in the future. The vibe inside the hotel was excitement. Every time I entered this hotel, it was always the same—packed with guests wagering on luck. Even though I loved the sound of the slot machines, I could never bring myself to play them.

I walked past the dimly lit gaming areas, their flashing lights and ringing bells enticing passersby to try their luck. I made my way toward the grand staircase, which led up to the elegant restaurant on the second floor. Jaden Edwards had given me a vague description of himself—tall with dark hair, a beard, and a great smile. Those were his words, but in this upscale hotel that could have described many men. As I ascended the stairs, I couldn't help but feel a sense of anxiety at the thought of meeting him.

As soon as I reached the top of the stairs and entered the restaurant, it was easy to spot Jaden Edwards. He stood out from the other patrons in his crisp, tailored suit. I couldn't help but compare my own outfit—dark blue jeans paired with stiletto boots and a blue silk blouse—feeling underdressed in comparison. I cursed myself for not choosing one of the few dresses hanging in the back of my closet.

Gathering my composure, I made my way toward his table with as much confidence as I could muster. In my head, I rehearsed my pitch to him over and over again, determined to make a good impression and win him over.

I held my head high, projecting confidence as I extended my hand toward the man seated across from where I stood. "Hello," I said firmly, "I presume you are Jadan Edwards."

"You presumed correctly, Ms. Porter," he replied, pushing his chair back from the table and rising to his feet. "It's a pleasure to finally meet you."

As our hands met in a firm handshake, I couldn't help but notice the warmth of his touch and the charm in his smile. He was right about one thing—he did have a great smile. I wondered how many women he had seduced with it. I needed to remember that this was strictly business, and I had to keep my focus on that.

Taking a seat across from him, I couldn't hide my satisfaction when I saw a bottle of Porter wine displayed proudly on the table. His wineglass was nearly empty, signaling that he had already taken a taste of my signature Merlot. I knew the rich flavor alone would make an impression on him, but there was still a lingering doubt in the back of my mind.

"I see you've ordered a bottle of Porter Merlot. How do you like it?" I asked hesitantly.

"I can't deny its exquisite taste. It's no wonder it received the Decanter Award," he replied, raising his glass in a small salute to me. "May I pour you a glass, Ms. Porter?"

"Yes, please. And please, call me Lana."

He smiled at my request and reached for the bottle on the table. The rich aroma of berries and oak filled my senses as soon as he uncorked the bottle. He expertly poured just enough wine into my glass before setting it down in front of me. Already, I could sense all the hard work and dedication that went into producing this particular vintage of Porter Merlot.

We settled into our seats, the warmth of the bottle of wine spreading through us as we exchanged light banter. The bottle of wine sat between us, a rich burgundy liquid enticing us with its aroma. As we sipped and chatted, our conversation drifted away from business and into personal anecdotes. With each question Jaden asked about the winery and its origins, I felt a swell of pride in my chest. He was genuinely interested in learning about my family's legacy.

He offered his condolences for my father's passing, understanding the pain of losing a loved one all too well. His own father had also passed unexpectedly, leaving him with a void that could never be filled. And like me, he had grown up without a mother by his side. She, too, had left when he was very young. We shared a bond in the loss of loved ones at a young age, and in a strange but comforting way, it brought us closer.

I leaned in closer, resting my elbows on the table. "So, tell me, Mr. Edwards. What can Porter Winery do for you?"

"Please, call me Jaden," he said with a warm smile as he refilled our glasses with the last drops of the second bottle. "Honestly, I believe you've already done everything possible. Here's to a great business relationship and much success."

My heart skipped a beat as I realized what had just happened. I had successfully landed the biggest account that Porter Winery had ever seen. Trying to contain my excitement, I lifted my glass and returned Jaden's smile. "Here's to a great business relationship."

2

I found Lana Porter to be a remarkable woman. I could hardly contain myself whenever she spoke. All I could think about was capturing her soft pink lips with mine. I knew exactly what I needed to do. Seducing her was going to be a pleasure, and I was looking forward to it. By the end of the month, she would be eating out of my hands. I wouldn't be surprised if she offered Portor Winery to me on a gold platter. The best thing about patience was the reward. I no longer had to deal with her father, Neil Porter.

As I settled into my seat on the flight back to Sioux Falls, I couldn't help but feel a sense of anticipation and nervousness wash over me. This was my chance to finally present my proposal for the Deadwood Project to the board members of Dynasty Development. Despite being President and CEO, there were still hoops I had to jump through to get all my projects approved.

The enormity of the Deadwood Project weighed heavily on my mind. Thirty million dollars would be poured into this venture, one that could potentially make or break our company. The Porter Winery, sitting on a sprawling 15 acres, was the perfect location for our plans—a luxurious hotel, resort, and casino with enough space left over for a nine-hole golf course.

I reached for my cell phone on the small table next to me, feeling the weight of the glass of Scotch the flight attendant had brought me in my hand. Taking a sip, I dialed Benjamin Tate, my trusted VP. "Ben, I need you to schedule a meeting with the board members for tomorrow morning. It's time for me to present my proposal for the Deadwood Project."

There was a pause on the other end before Ben spoke again. "So, does this mean the Porter family has agreed to sell their winery to us?"

"Not exactly," I replied cryptically. "But let's just say by the end of this month, Ms. Porter won't know what hit her."

"I hope you're right," Ben chuckled. "Remember how Neil Porter wasn't exactly gracious toward us? If it weren't for his untimely death, that restraining order he filed against you might still be in place."

A grimace formed on my face as memories from that tumultuous week flooded back. "How could I forget about that damn restraining order?" I muttered. "It was one of the worst weeks of my life trying to fight it off."

Thankfully, I had never had the pleasure of meeting Lana Porter in person until now. If she had any inkling of who I really was, she would surely have filed a restraining order against me, just as her father did a year ago.

I ended my call with Ben just as the captain announced we would be landing at Sioux Falls Regional Airport soon. I settled back into my seat and enjoyed the rest of the flight, with only tomorrow's board meeting on my mind. One thing I had going for me was that I could be very convincing when it came to getting what I wanted. The Deadwood Project was no exception. This project had been in the works for over two years and I wasn't about to lose what I had worked so hard for. One way or another, Lana Porter would agree to sell Dynasty Development her winery.

———

The clock read 2:00 a.m. and I was still poring over the proposal that would guarantee the approval of the Deadwood Project by the board members. Exhausted, but unable to find any respite in sleep, I decided to release some of this pent-up tension by going for an early morning run. It was an unconventional choice, to say the least, as most people wouldn't even consider going out for a jog at this ungodly hour. But then again, I had never been one to conform to societal norms. Running was my personal remedy for insomnia, and it never failed me.

After shedding my shirt and trousers, I slipped into my comfortable jogging clothes and left my apartment. One thing I loved about living in the heart of Sioux Falls was its rich history. It was what prompted me to purchase this old building and transform it into a thriving nightclub establishment—Club Ten. It was my prized possession and also my first successful venture in renovating a rundown structure into something spectacular. The upper floor of the nightclub served as my home, and though some may have deemed it unusual for a businessman like myself to live above his own establishment rather than in a swanky mansion in an upscale neighborhood, I took great pride in where I lived. With over 3,000 square feet of living space, I had all the room I needed and more. And with the high-tech security system I had installed, curious patrons wouldn't have access to the elevator, which, other than the fire escape, was the only entrance to my home.

The brisk early morning air felt good against my skin as I picked up my pace to a slow jog. There wasn't a soul in sight as I jogged down the sidewalk toward the city park. The night was silent except for my heart-beat and the sound of my Nikes hitting the pavement. Even the sound of stray cats fighting was absent—too early to claim their territories, evidently.

The city slowly came to life as I ran through the streets, my feet pounding rhythmically on the pavement. A Ford van pulled up in front of the local bookstore, its engine rumbling to a stop as the delivery driver hopped out and retrieved a bundle of newspapers from the back. This routine was familiar to me—running in the early hours of the morning to clear my mind and relieve tension. My father's words echoed in my head as they always did when I ran, reminding me to take time to relax and enjoy life.

My father's dream had been Dynasty Development, and when he passed, I took over as CEO, determined to make it the best development company in South Dakota. The Deadwood Project was my latest challenge, and I refused to let it fail before it even began.

As I reached the nightclub, my legs burned and my body begged for rest. I made my way inside through the alley door and quickly disarmed the alarm before heading up to my apartment. Despite being exhausted, I couldn't resist taking a moment to appreciate the quiet stillness of my living space. It served as a reminder of how mundane my single life could be at times.

But as much as I enjoyed the freedom and independence that came with being single, deep down, settling down with a woman was something I yearned for more than anything else in this world. It would be nice to come home after a long day of work and be greeted by the warmth of a woman's body pressed against mine, or to spend lazy weekends with her. Maybe someday soon that would become a reality for me. Until then, I had to keep my focus on Dynasty Development and push forward toward success.

The warm water cascaded over my body, washing away the stress of the day. Every muscle in my body seemed to relax as I stood under the showerhead, letting the steam fill the small bathroom. But even after a long, hot shower, my mind was still cluttered and my body drained. As I crawled into bed and closed my eyes, hoping for a peaceful slumber, I was met with frustration. Sleep eluded me, no matter how much I tried to focus on it.

I turned and twisted for what felt like hours, willing my mind to shut down and my body to relax. The Deadwood Project that had consumed my thoughts during the day was now replaced by Lana Porter, her image seared into my mind like a brand. The soft sound of rain and waves crashing from my iPod only provided temporary relief before being engulfed once again by racing thoughts.

After four restless hours, I gave up on the idea of sleep and instead dragged my exhausted body out of bed and shuffled toward the kitchen. Maybe a strong cup of coffee would give me the energy I needed to make it through the day ahead, despite the lack of restful sleep.

———

Ben was already hard at work when I arrived at Dynasty. I had a funny feeling he had a touch of insomnia himself. In the five years that he had been VP, never had I seen him here earlier than 8:00 a.m.

"You're here early," I said as I stepped into his office.

"Yeah. Looks like we both had a hard time sleeping." Ben replied. "Are you ready for the meeting?"

"As ready as ever." My confidence in my proposal was high, but facing the board with it was another story. "When is the meeting?"

"Nine o'clock."

"Good. I'm going to get the Power Point ready and make sure it is up and running."

I left Ben's office and navigated my way through the bustling hallways of the Premier Card office building to reach the conference room. Dynasty Development occupied the third and fourth floors, a symbol of our success and our ambitions for even greater growth. We dreamed of expanding to a larger, more efficient location, but for now, this building was the heart of our operations.

Before setting up my presentation, I made a quick detour to my office. Working on two cups of coffee and less than an hour of sleep, I had neglected to check my emails. Glancing at my watch, I saw it was only six o'clock, leaving me plenty of time to catch up on my emails before working on my presentation. As much as I relied on my cell phone for the convenience of quick email checks, nothing beat responding to messages on my laptop. The small cell phone keypad wasn't ideal for typing out lengthy responses. Logging into my email provider, I saw that I had thirty new messages. But there was only one that caught my attention—an invitation from Porter Vineyards.

My heart quickened as I read through the message. It was an invitation to stay at the prestigious winery for the entire weekend and to attend their highly anticipated annual wine tasting event. What better way to sample their exquisite selection of wines than by attending the event? But my motivation for accepting this offer extended far beyond simply stocking my nightclub with Lana's coveted wines. No, this was my chance to win her over, to charm and seduce her until she agreed to sell Porter Vineyards to me. As I read on, my mind drifted back to our first encounter. Not only was Lana the brilliant owner of Porter Vineyards, but she was also a vision of beauty and charm. The thought of spending time with her again filled me with eager anticipation. And I knew deep down that nothing would make me happier than successfully winning her over and securing the Porter Vineyards property.

With excitement bubbling inside me, I quickly typed out a response, accepting her invitation and expressing my eagerness to taste the wines that could potentially grace the shelves of my establishment. Once my proposal for the Deadwood Project was sealed with the board's blessing, I would take the next flight to personally thank her for her generosity. By the time I left, she would not only be shipping her wine to my nightclub, she wouldn't want me to leave.

3

LANA

I sat in my home office, nervously tapping my fingers on the wooden desk as I second guessed the email I had just sent to Jaden Edwards. It was a bold move, inviting a client to stay at the Porter house as my personal guest, something I had never done before. But there was something about him that drew me in. Something different and alluring that sparked a fire within me. In my defense, this weekend was special. The annual wine tasting event had been planned for months and there was no better way to show Jaden how successful the vineyard was than at the event. Two hundred people were expected to attend. Hopefully, the attendance turnout alone would impress him. Maybe even more than just the wine.

As I thought about him, my mind drifted back to our meeting and the way his touch made me feel, igniting long dormant emotions and desires. And yet, amidst all of this uncertainty and doubt, one thing remained clear. I was undeniably attracted to him. But did he feel the same? Had I misread his signals? These thoughts swirled around in my mind as I grappled with taking the first step in a potential relationship, also something I had never done before.

The faint chime of the notification bell jolted me out of my thoughts, signaling a new email. With a quick movement of my hand, I directed my mouse toward Jaden Edwards' name and clicked open his message. As I read his response, a mix of emotions flooded through me, replacing the initial anticipation of receiving an acceptance. Excitement and fear tugged at my heart, knowing that this reply could lead to something more. Yes, the main reason for his invitation was to secure some Porter wines for his establishment. However, I couldn't deny the other motive behind my invitation—a burning desire to get to know this man on a deeper level. Despite our strictly business interactions, there was something about him that beckoned me closer, tempting me with the possibility of more than just a professional relationship.

I stopped analyzing my motive and turned my thoughts to making sure everything was ready for Jaden's arrival. Pushing from my desk, I headed outside to find James. I hired James a year ago, just after my father's passing. Even though there were other guys who worked for Porter Vineyards, I felt the need to hire another guy. With my additional responsibilities, I needed an extra hand to take charge of shipping and distribution of our wine. He was a good hand, and I was glad I hired him. At first, I was hesitant, since he was only a couple of years older than me. His charm and good looks won me over. It certainly wasn't his experience. It was crazy how far he had come in such a short time.

"James," I yelled across the plush green grass in front of the house.

"Hey, Lana," he responded as he walked toward me. "What's up?"

"Jaden Edwards has agreed to be my personal guest for the weekend. We needed to make sure everything is in pristine condition. We need to impress this guy. It could be a big win for the winery."

"I could have sworn you said it wasn't ethical to have clients stay at the Porter house," James snickered. "Are you sure you're making the right decision?"

"I don't know if it is the right decision or not, but we need this client and if it means breaking the rules, so be it."

"In that case, everything will be to your approval before the weekend."

The tension in James' voice was palpable as he expressed his dissatisfaction with my decision. He strode past me, his steps heavy and filled with animosity toward me. This behavior was unlike him; I had never seen him act this way before. A pang of unease settled in my chest as I wondered if James held some underlying jealousy toward Jadan Edwards. But that seemed irrational. How could James be jealous of a man he had never met?

———

Over the next few days, James' attitude had become unbearable, a constant storm cloud looming over our team and poisoning every conversation with his snide remarks and cutting sarcasm. It was a miracle that no one had quit yet, but I knew it was only a matter of time before his toxic behavior drove someone away.

Determined to put an end to this before it destroyed us all, I stormed toward the west building where James was supposed to be stocking the wine fridges and racks. The sound of blaring rock music assaulted my ears as I approached, the bass so loud I feared it would shatter the delicate wine glasses. With a clenched jaw, I pushed open the door and marched over to the stereo system, turning down the volume knob with a sharp twist.

James emerged from behind one of the towering wine racks, his eyes dark with anger as he walked toward me. "What? You don't like my music?" he sneered.

I met his hostile gaze with a hard stare of my own. "I like rock music just fine," I retorted, "But how can you even think straight with it blasting at ear-splitting levels?"

The tension between us hung thick in the air, ready to explode at any moment. Something needed to change before it destroyed not only our work but also our relationship. "What is your problem? Ever since I told you about Jaden Edwards staying the weekend, you have been unbearable to deal with."

"I don't understand you," James growled back, his voice laced with anger. "You had one meeting with this guy and now you're inviting him to spend the weekend with you?"

"Are you jealous?"

"I'm concerned," James corrected me. "You barely know this guy. What could he possibly have that would make lose yourself and risk everything we've worked so hard for?"

"Oh, my God. You are jealous." I scoffed.

As soon as the words left my mouth, I realized there was truth in them. Despite our working relationship, there had always been an undercurrent of something more between us in the way we joked with each other and played games with one another. I never thought of him as more than a friend, but it was clear he saw more. And now, with Jaden in the picture, he was becoming overly protective and hard to deal with. He was pissing me off.

"For your information, I have lost nothing to Jaden Edwards," I spat out angrily. "He is a client and nothing more. And another thing. Porter Vineyards belongs to me. Not to you or anyone else. You are my employee and nothing more. If you got the impression that there was something more between us, I'm sorry, but that's on you."

James' expression softened as he reached out to touch my arms lightly. "I know that," he said softly. "I just don't want to see you get hurt." He pulled me into a hug, trying to appease the tension between us before it exploded into something we would both regret. "Let's forget about this and focus on making this year's event the best one yet."

Even as he spoke, I could see the resentment burning in his eyes. It was then I knew things would never be the same between us again. Having his body pressed against mine didn't feel right. James was an attractive man, but not one that I was attracted to. I felt nothing more than friendship with him.

Making sure that he understood that, I pulled away from his embrace and held out my hand. "Friends."

"Friends," he replied as he placed his hand in mine and gave it a gentle shake.

The way he continued to hold on to my hand without releasing it told me something different. He wanted to be friends—friends with benefits. *Not happening.*

4

"There you have it. The Deadwood Project is something we shouldn't pass up." With a good feeling inside, I concluded my persuasive pitch. The boardroom was filled with tense silence as all eyes turned to George Holmes, the notorious Board Chair known for shooting down every proposal brought before him.

"I must say, this is quite a monumental investment for Dynasty Development," he finally spoke up, his voice carrying weight and authority. "I think it's best if we sleep on it and reconvene in the morning to make our decision."

My heart sank. This was far from the positive response I had hoped for. But Holmes always held the final say, no matter how much effort and preparation I put into my projects.

As the other board members filed out of the conference room, Ben and I stood at attention, ready to shake their hands and thank them for their time. Holmes was the last one to leave, but before he did, he turned back to us with a surprising statement.

"You have done an impeccable job presenting this project," he complimented, his gaze shifting between Ben and me. "Deadwood is a truly fantastic location to build upon. All you need is a majority vote to move forward, and I want you to know that you already have mine."

My jaw dropped in shock. *Had I heard him correctly?*

"Thank you, George," I managed to stammer out, grasping his outstretched hand in gratitude. "Your support means everything to me."

With a firm nod of his head, Holmes gave us both a knowing smile before exiting the room. Ben and I were left standing at the doorway, stunned by his sudden change of heart toward our proposal. It seemed like a dream come true—but only time would tell if this unexpected show of support would be enough to secure our project's approval.

I left the conference room feeling like soon we would be moving forward with the project. Tomorrow I would be on a flight to Deadwood to attend Porter Vineyards' annual wine tasting event. I just hoped the board wouldn't take all day with their decision to approve the project. The sooner I got to Deadwood, the more time I would have with Lana. This weekend would no doubt be a challenge, and would definitely test my skills at seduction.

———

It was a unanimous decision to move forward with the Deadwood Project under one condition—a signed deed by the end of the month. Was I surprised—not in the least. I killed the presentation. Just as I had every other. George Holmes, for once, saw things my way even with this minor stipulation. Maybe he knew he would be up for re-election and couldn't jeopardize a win. Whatever the reason, the only thing holding us back now was the land.

The hour flight to Deadwood was uneventful, making the flight seem much longer. Maybe it was because I knew what waited for me once I landed. Lana agreed to pick me up at the Sturgis Regional Airport so I wouldn't have to rent a car. When I got off the private jet and walked inside the small airport, the first thing I did was search for Lana. It wasn't hard to see that she wasn't among the people seated to wait for their flight. I walked past the row of chairs and toward the entrance. As soon as I swung the door open, I saw Lana leaning against the passenger door of her vehicle, greeting me with a beautiful smile.

"How was your flight?" she asked as she pushed away from her vehicle.

"Much too long," I replied. "Thank you for offering to pick me up. I really wouldn't have minded renting a car."

"I know. But if you need to go anywhere, Porter Vineyards has several vehicles you can use," she smiled. "Besides, it will give me the chance to tell you more about tomorrow's wine tasting event."

"I can't wait to hear all about it."

As we pulled out of the airport parking lot, Lana couldn't contain her excitement about the upcoming event. Her fervent descriptions of what awaited us tomorrow were infectious, and I couldn't help but feel a pang of guilt knowing that Porter Vineyards would soon be no more. Generations of Porters had poured their heart and soul into this place, watching it grow and expand with each passing year.

Under normal circumstances, I would have turned down an invitation to a wine tasting event. I have found that it wasn't the best use of my time. As a businessman, I preferred getting direct feedback from my customers on the quality of our wines. But this event wasn't like the others. I had an agenda—get Lana to fall head-over-heels with me and sell me her land.

"Did you know that certain wines can take one to two years, or even longer, to fully integrate and mature?" Lana asked, changing the subject from the event.

"I believe I read something about the aging process of different wines," I replied.

"It's a highly complex process. We spare no expense and only use the best oak barrels, imported directly from Europe. We are constantly replacing them as they lose their signature flavor components over time."

When we reached the vineyard, I had enough information on having a successful winery to last me a lifetime. As uninterested as I was, I knew I had to continue the charade of being interested.

"Come on, I want to show you something," Lana said as she put the vehicle into park and turned off the engine.

I unfastened my seatbelt and swung open the passenger door. As I looked around, visions of the proposed hotel surfaced immediately. The acres and acres of grapevines would soon be replaced with a 180,000 sq. ft. hotel. It was hard to believe I was only a signature away from the biggest project I had ever taken on.

"Are you coming?" Lana asked, breaking me from my thoughts.

Before I could respond, she took hold of my hand and pulled me away from the sweeping view I was admiring. The hills rolled out before me with shades of green, dotted with clusters of grapevines as far as the eye could see. But my focus was quickly redirected as she attempted to pull me away. There was a sense of urgency in her touch, a determination to get me to go with her.

I pulled her body close to mine and wrapped my arms around her waist, and pressed my lips to hers. They were like velvet, soft and yielding beneath mine. It was a bold move on my part. To my surprise, instead of slapping me away, she melted into the kiss, her body molding to mine in submission. When we finally broke apart, there were no words exchanged. Our eyes met, and it was clear there was an undeniable attraction between us. I couldn't deny it—she was beautiful.

I gently swiped the back of my hand against her flushed cheek before taking hold of her smaller hand in mine. "Now I'm ready to see what you wanted to show me," I said with a smile.

Hand in hand, she led me away from the vehicle and past her residence. The architecture of the home was truly remarkable, a fusion of rustic log and stone that blended seamlessly with its natural surroundings—a perfect blend of modern and rustic elements. My guilt over potentially tearing down such a beautiful structure began to fade as she guided me down a dirt road toward several large metal buildings.

I couldn't help but admire the way the setting sun cast a golden light on the structures, highlighting their impressive size and construction. But my thoughts quickly turned to the plans for this place and all the potential revenue it could bring. It was hard not to feel excited about the possibilities as they swirled through my mind like a whirlwind.

As I imagined the potential of the vineyard, Lana continued to tell me about how Porter Vineyards came to be. And as we walked and talked, I couldn't help but be captivated by both the property and the woman by my side. This was going to be an exciting venture, indeed. How wonderful it would be if she would share the excitement of the vision I had for her vineyard.

5

LANA

I led Jaden on a grand tour of the property. The rows upon rows of vines stretched out before us, giving me a sense of pride as the leaves moved in the warm breeze. In between sips of wine and talks about harvest season, our conversation turned flirtatious and playful. As we walked, our hands brushed against each other's, sending electric currents through my body. By the time we reached the house, it was nearly suppertime, but all I could think about was the passionate kiss we shared earlier and the hinting touches that left me wanting more. My heart raced with excitement as I realized how fast things were progressing between us, but I couldn't deny that I had never felt more alive in my life. With each step we took toward the house, I knew I didn't want this spark between us to fizzle out.

When I opened the front door to the house, the delicious scent of the roast I had prepared in the crock pot this morning enveloped my senses. As we entered the house, I turned to Jadan. "I hope you like pot roast."

"It smells amazing," he replied with a smile, confirming that he liked pot roast.

I headed to the kitchen with Jadan close behind. I could feel his eyes on me and, without thinking, moved my hips in a flirtatious manner. I swung open the kitchen door, but before I checked on the roast, I walked toward the small wine fridge and pulled out a bottle of Porter Chardonnay.

"Can you please do the honors of opening the wine?" I asked as I handed him the bottle of wine. "The wine opener is in the drawer next to you."

Jaden's fingers wrapped around the cool glass bottle as he pulled me closer with his other hand. Our eyes met, electricity crackling between us before our lips collided in a fiery, passionate kiss. In that moment, it felt like the Fourth of July had come early, and my whole body was buzzing with excitement. As our lips moved in sync, sparks of desire shot through me like fireworks, igniting a fierce attraction that only grew stronger with each passing second. The sound of Jadan setting down the wine bottle echoed before he pressed his body closer to mine, intensifying our desire for each other. Without warning, he lifted me from the floor and set me on the counter. I was so consumed with the moment, completely blind to the fact that any of the guys could walk in on us. I didn't care. All I knew was that I wanted him. Maybe it was the wine, or the fact that I hadn't been with a man for a long time.

"You're so damn beautiful," Jaden whispered. "Ever since I laid eyes on you, all I could think about was pressing my lips to yours."

"Me too," I breathed.

Before we could take things further, the back door creaked open and James entered. I quickly moved my body off the counter and walked to the other side of the kitchen, pretending like nothing had happened.

"Hey, James. We were just about ready to eat. Do you want to stay for dinner?" As much as I wanted to spend the evening alone with Jaden, I couldn't confirm James' suspicion about Jaden and me.

"Smells good," James sighed as he stepped over to where I was standing. "I'll set the table."

This wasn't the way I wanted to evening to go, but James stopping what might have happened between me and Jaden made me realize things were moving too fast.

After an awkward and tense introduction, I watched as Jaden carefully poured the rich white wine into our glasses. As he poured, I carefully lifted the lid of the crock pot and pulled out the fragrant roast, placing it on a platter to be served. We all took our seats at the dinner table, with James sitting next to me on my right and Jaden on my left. The tension between them was palpable as they both sat rigidly in their chairs, their eyes locked in an unspoken battle.

Before I could even take a bite of food, James spoke up, his voice dripping with disdain. "So, tell me, Jaden, what exactly is your intention with Lana?"

I could feel my annoyance rising at James' rude question. "James, please don't be so impolite," I interjected.

Jaden simply smiled, unfazed by James' hostility. "Lana and I have become very close business partners," he explained calmly. "I plan on stocking my nightclub with Porter wine."

The tension between Jaden and James only intensified as we ate our meal. Every glance, every word exchanged felt like daggers being thrown across the table. It was clear that neither of them saw me as just a friend —they were both vying for my attention and affection. But I refused to be treated like someone's possession or prize. I belonged to myself and no one else had any right to lay claim to me.

James excusing himself couldn't have come at a better time. As Jaden and I cleared the table, I couldn't help but feel responsible for the way James had treated him. "I'm sorry about James. He shouldn't have grilled you the way he did. My private life is none of his business."

"Does that mean I have nothing to worry about?" Jayen asked jokingly.

"That is exactly what that means. James is my employee and nothing more. I've made him well aware of where I stand with him."

Jaden took the plates from my hand and placed them on the counter. Before I could protest, he pulled my body close to his and lowered his head until his lips were inches from mine. "That makes me very happy. I would hate not being able to do this again."

He pressed his lips to mine, the sweet smell of wine on his breath as he explored my mouth with his tongue. Cleaning up the dinner plates didn't seem important any longer as we began to explore each other.

"Is there somewhere we can go that is more private," Jaden whispered as he kissed and tugged the rim of my earlobe.

"Yes," I breathed. "My bedroom is upstairs."

———

It was the big event, with so much to do, and the only thing I could think about was how good it felt to wake up with Jaden beside me. Last night was remarkable, and a night I would never forget. Was it possible to fall for a guy I had only known for a week? It was once said that there was a guy out there for every woman—a true soulmate. I was thinking Jaden was that guy.

Smiling to myself, I finished placing the vases on the cocktail tables that were covered with black table covers. The wine tasting room looked amazing. James was in charge of the music collection and I prayed his choice would be subtle and not the hard rock music he had been listening to the other day.

The tension between James and Jaden was still visible. The best option was to keep them away from each other as much as possible. Thankfully, Jaden offered to pick up the roses for the vases. Even though James didn't like it, I also put him in charge of directing our guests on where to park. In the past, he was always behind the bar, opening the wine bottles and serving. Not today. I left that task to one of the other guys.

Getting ready to check on James, I heard soft music coming over the speakers. It was an instrumental melody with horns and violins. The melancholy song was bittersweet, reminding me of the last time my father and I were in this room together. Before I totally lost myself, the wooden door opened with Jaden on the other side. He not only held the small pail of long stem roses for the event, he was also holding a beautiful bouquet of red roses mixed in with Gypsophila.

Jaden walked up to me, placing the pail on the floor. "These are for you."

"You really didn't have to do that," I said as I took the roses from his hand. "They're beautiful."

Jaden gently placed his hand on my cheek and looked at me intently.

With our eyes locked on each other, he leaned in and placed his lips on mine. The kiss was soft and drew me in. His touch swept me away to another place. I didn't want it to end.

"Get your hands off her," James shouted from across the room. "I knew I should have punched you when I had the chance."

My eyes popped open, and I pulled away from Jaden, feeling like a teenager who had been caught sneaking in after curfew. James walked toward us with determination in his steps. I knew what was going to happen, and I had to stop it before it started.

"Back off, James. You have no right to my personal life." I warned, as I placed my hand on his chest, preventing him from taking another step.

James had no problem getting past me as he picked me up by the waist and moved me out of the way so he could move in on Jaden. No amount of yelling or threatening to fire him worked. I was helpless, and before I could interject, James' fist flew, landing square on Jaden's jaw, knocking him sideways. Without a doubt, James was definitely fired.

6

JADEN

The last thing I wanted to do was to make a bad impression on Lana, but James had it coming. No way in hell was I going to stand there as his personal punching bag. If Lana hadn't stopped us, things could have ended badly for him.

Lana was upset at the situation, especially today. This was an important day for her, and the last thing she needed was an incident. As two of her employees hauled James off the property, we watched what little dignity he had left vanish as he made his last threats toward me. "You're a dead man, Edwards."

I held Lana close, trying desperately to calm her down. "Everything will be fine. James' words are only threats, nothing more."

"Did you hear what he said? He's crazy and belongs in a straitjacket," she replied in a shaky tone.

"I can handle James." I held Lana at arm's length and gave her a reassuring smile. "This is your day. Let's not let James or anyone else ruin it."

Concern was written all over her face and the only way I knew of to erase it was to lower my head and kiss her soft lips. Her body melted into mine and I could feel her relax. As much as I wanted to continue this, the wine tasting event was less than two hours away and I still needed to take care of a few things. Regrettably, so did Lana.

After a few more moments in each other's arms, we finished getting everything ready for the wine tasting. When we left the building, James was nowhere in sight. Hopefully, he accepted that he had been beaten and left.

When we got to the house, I was shocked to see Ben sitting on the porch. *Damn! He wasn't supposed to be here.* Everything was going as planned, and I couldn't risk him ruining everything I had worked so hard to achieve. "Ben, what are you doing here?"

I watched him stand up and walk toward us. "Jaden, aren't you going to introduce me?"

I wasn't sure what his game was, but I played along. "Lana, this is Ben Tate, the manager of my nightclub." No way could I let her know he was the VP at Dynasty Development.

"It's nice to meet you. Are you here for the wine tasting?" she asked innocently.

"Why, yes. Jaden has told me so much about it. I thought I would come and check it out myself," Ben replied convincingly, lying his ass off, playing along with the charade.

We headed inside the house, one at a time, with me in the rear. Lana was in front and turned toward us. "If you two will excuse me, I need to get ready for the event. Please make yourselves at home."

When Lana was out of view, I laid into Ben. "What the hell, Ben? Do you want to ruin everything?" I snapped.

"I wanted to make sure we kept our promise to the board. They are only going to make good on the Deadwood Project if you can deliver the signed deed by the end of the month."

I knew there was a timeline hanging over me, and him being here wasn't making it any better. "Let me take care of getting Lana to sign the vineyard over. You need to go back to Sioux Falls."

"And miss this event? No way."

———

The wine tasting was in full swing, and Lana looked beautiful. All who attended were seemingly having a wonderful time. As Lana continued to introduce me to the partakers, I couldn't help but feel guilty that this would all disappear for her. I began questioning whether or not I was doing the right thing. She had put forth so much effort for this event and, actually, in making Porter Vineyards a success.

As the evening went on, all I wanted was to sneak away with Lana. So, the first chance I got, I took hold of her hand and whisked her away. Making our way through the crowd, I led her to the back entrance.

"I've wanted to do this ever since I saw you coming down the stairs." I whispered as I placed my hand on her cheek and captured her lips.

Guiding her away from the bustling event building, I led Lana into the cool and dimly lit cellar. The musty scent of old oak barrels filled the air as we made our way toward the back of the room. Pressed against my side, Lana walked with purpose and confidence, leading us to a secluded area between two rows of barrels. She fit perfectly in my arms as we continued where we had left off earlier. I relished in the feeling of her body pressed against mine, exploring every inch of her essence with my hands. Her dress clung to her curves in all the right places, highlighting the beauty of her womanhood. Lifting one of her legs, she granted me even more access to pleasure her in ways that only she could guide me toward.

With each kiss I placed along her collarbone, she let out a soft sigh, her breath hitching in her throat. "I'm falling for you, Jaden," she whispered, her voice thick with longing. "I don't want what we have together to end."

A surge of desire shot through me as I heard her words. "I feel the same way," I replied, my fingers tracing patterns along her skin, enticing her further.

Feeling emboldened, I wrapped myself around her, our bodies fitting together like puzzle pieces. As we moved together, our movements synchronized and fluid, I couldn't help but wonder if this was all just a game of seduction to gain control over the ultimate prize: the vineyard.

Due to my growing feelings for her, the thought of winning the vineyard was no long a top priority in my mind.

Pushing back my true emotions, I explored every inch of her body, drawing out pleasure from within her. But even as we lost ourselves in the heat of the moment, a small voice in my head reminded me that this was all just a means to an end. And yet, as she moaned and gasped, I couldn't deny the strong pull toward her that went beyond any material desire. Now more than ever, I wanted her—for keeps.

7

LANA

The past three weeks had been a rollercoaster of emotions. Jaden and I had grown closer after the incident with James at the tasting event, but that also made me realize how vulnerable I was. With James gone, Jaden had been my rock, and I didn't know what I would have done without him. But at the same time, I couldn't help but feel guilty for accepting his help around the vineyard. At first, I couldn't accept his kindness, but he reassured me that his nightclub could run itself under Ben's capable management. And during the interviewing process for new employees, having Jaden by my side made it far less daunting. He had a keen eye for picking out who would fit in well at the vineyard and who wouldn't. I thought that hiring James was the best decision I had ever made, but now I saw how awful I was at reading people. His charm clouded my judgement, and I overlooked his true character flaws. Now I hoped I could move on from this and find someone who truly deserved to work at Porter Vineyards.

As the last interview came to an end with a successful hire, it was only fitting to treat ourselves to a picnic. As I prepared sandwiches for our picnic, Jaden's voice drifted to me from the living room, his conversation with Ben piquing my curiosity. I didn't intend to eavesdrop, but when Jaden mentioned my name, I couldn't stop myself from listening.

"Lana is smart, but she's also stubborn. It's going to take some convincing to get her to sign the deed to Porter Vineyards over to Dynasty," Jaden said, his words carrying through the air.

The longer I listened, the more every word hit me like a punch to the gut. Every moment spent with Jaden, every sweet word and gesture, was all part of a deceitful plan to acquire Porter Vineyards. The last three weeks had been a cruel façade, and I felt foolish for falling for it. Betrayal and anger boiled inside me as I realized the depth of Jaden's lies. It was clear that our relationship meant nothing to him; it was just a means to an end.

When the call ended, I slowly backed away from the kitchen door, my heart pounding in my chest. I braced myself as Jaden entered the kitchen, knowing that he would see the raw emotion etched on my face.

"I think it's best you leave," I managed, my voice quivering with emotion.

He hung his head in defeat, knowing he had been caught before meeting my gaze. "Please, let me explain," he pleaded. "What you heard... it's not what it seems."

"It seems pretty clear to me." I choked. "After all, I am a smart woman." My hand shook as I reached for my cell. "Now get out of here before I call the police."

Without another word, Jaden turned and left the kitchen. The sound of the front door closing echoed through the empty house as I collapsed to my knees, tears streaming down my face. The weight of betrayal and heartbreak crushed me like a ton of bricks.

———

The days all seemed to blend together since I found out the truth and demanded that Jaden leave. Every morning, I woke with a heavy weight in my chest as I remembered the commitment to stock his nightclub with Porter wines that I had foolishly made. But I was determined not to succumb to my feelings for him. Instead, I buried myself in work and focused on training Manny, the new man hired to take James' place.

As I made my way toward the front door, a knock sounded against it. My heart skipped a beat as I opened the door to find Ben standing on the other side. Seeing him here was a complete surprise, and the only explanation for his presence was that Jaden had sent him to do his dirty work.

"Whatever you want, you can tell Jaden he can find another woman to manipulate," I spat out as I tried to brush past him.

"Lana, I'm not here because of what Jaden did to you," Ben interjected, causing me to pause and give him a chance to explain.

"Then why are you here?" I asked, still feeling cautious and defensive.

"I wanted to tell you that when Jaden returned to Sioux Falls, he went straight to the board at Dynasty Development with an alternative plan for the Deadwood Project. Porter Vineyards is no longer part of the deal. Jaden secured another location owned by the Bureau of Land Management," Ben began. "And just so you know, Jaden never intended to hurt you. In fact, if anything, he had fallen deeply in love with you."

"Well, you can tell him I loved him too, but what he did hurt me." A bittersweet pause followed, and I couldn't help but remember everything we had shared before it all fell apart. "How is he doing?"

"How about you ask him yourself?" Ben's voice snapped me back to reality.

Before I could respond, the sound of a car door closing echoed behind me. When I turned around, Jaden was standing in front of a gleaming white Escalade, slowly making his way toward me. My heart sank to my stomach at the sight of him—tall, handsome, and full of regret. I wanted to back away from him, but my feet were rooted to the ground. The closer he got, the more I realized just how much I missed him.

"I've missed you so much," Jaden admitted with raw emotion in his voice. "I wish I could take back everything I did to you. I never meant to hurt you."

My heart clenched at his words and I felt tears prick at the corners of my eyes. *Why did he have to come back now? Why couldn't he have realized this sooner?*

"Why? Why did you lie to me? Why couldn't you tell me the truth?" I asked calmly, trying not to let my emotions get the best of me.

"I did lie. I should have told you about wanting your land from the start. But that all changed." His eyes bore into mine with sincerity. "I fell in love with you, Lana, and I couldn't follow through with it. That was what I was trying to tell you during our last conversation. You didn't hear the rest of it—when I told Ben to start looking for another location for the Deadwood Project."

"You did?" The shock was evident in my voice.

"He did," Ben chimed in from behind me, reminding me that he was still there. "I told him he was crazy, but I couldn't blame him for falling for you. After meeting you at the wine tasting," Ben paused, shaking his head back and forth. "Let's just say, I knew he was doomed." The corners of Ben's mouth twitched into a small smile, showing his approval for Jaden's change of heart.

With a few strides, Jaden closed the gap between us and gently placed his hand on my cheek. The warmth of his touch sent a shiver down my spine, and I couldn't help but lean into it. His eyes searched mine, pleading for forgiveness.

"Can you forgive me and let me make it up to you?" he asked softly.

My heart ached at the sight of him, torn between the love I still had for him and the pain he had caused. But at that moment, all I wanted was to be close to him again.

"On one condition," I replied, placing my hand over his.

"Anything," Jaden promised eagerly.

"Promise me that you will never lie to me again." I held my breath, hoping for a sincere response.

"I promise. No more lies," he vowed, determination etched on his face.

And then, without hesitation, Jaden lowered his head and pressed his lips against mine. At that moment, everything else faded away as we reconnected with each other. It didn't matter that Ben was still standing behind me, watching. All that mattered was Jaden's soft kisses, each one feeling like a balm to my wounded heart. And I was going to savor every single one of them.

The end

Subscribe to A.L. Long's newsletter and get the inside scoop on new releases and upcoming events. https://bit.ly/3jo8VZo.

ABOUT THE AUTHOR

Award-winning Author of the Independent Press Award and NYC Big Book Award, A.L. Long is also the National Indie Excellence Award recipient.

Some would call me a little naughty, but I see myself writing spicy thoughts. Being a romance writer is something that I never imagined I would be doing. There is nothing more rewarding than to put your thoughts down in words and share them. I began writing in 2013 and have enjoyed every minute. When I first started writing, I wasn't sure what I would write. It didn't take me long to realize that romance would be my niche. I believe that every life deserves a little bit of romance; a little spice doesn't hurt either. When I am not writing, I enjoy the company of good friends and relaxing with a delicious glass of red wine.

Visit me at www.allongbooks.com for all of my new releases and book signing events.

Keep up with all A.L. Long's latest releases:

A CHANCE ENCOUNTER

TAM DERUDDER JACKSON

1

SLOTS

With a sigh I thought, *Why am I in a casino?*

I didn't gamble.

Which begged the question: what was I doing dressed to the nines and standing in the middle of The Lodge at Deadwood? As I glanced around the large open space, I struggled with where to focus first. From along the walls, giant free-standing slot machines lit up the center and called to passing patrons with their bells and whistles. Their colorful graphics beckoned with everything from a buff Tarzan-looking character whose green eyes lasered in on anyone strolling by to curling magenta-colored dragons breathing their hot machine message toward the players sitting in the plush leather chairs in front of them.

On the opposite side of the room, massive big-screen TVs covered the walls, each showing a different sporting event—from baseball to horse racing to soccer. A row of comfy-looking leather couches and chairs faced the screens, separated from the rest of the casino by a dark wooden half-wall. A long brass pipe was mounted along the top of the wall, adding a touch of opulence to the partition between the sports bettors and the Blackjack tables that ran down the middle of the room.

Wendy Wilson, my friend who'd met me in the casino to show me the ropes, led me to a side room off the main one where slot machines ringed the space, each of them vying for gamblers' attention with their multi-colored lights and over-the-top cartoon graphics of everything from gold mines to exaggerated gem stones to cartoon characters like Yosemite Sam from the old Bugs Bunny shows. With purpose, she walked me to what she said was a nickel machine.

"Meaning?" I asked with a raised brow.

"You put nickels in and hope more nickels come back to you."

In confusion, I stared at the machine. Nowhere on it could I see where to put in or retrieve any coins.

"Metaphorically speaking, Sadie, darling." With a little grin, she pulled a five dollar bill from her purse and fed it into the cash slot on the machine. "You're betting nickels, but none of the machines work on coins anymore. Here's where you'll see your credits."

She pointed at a line that showed a hundred credits, one for each nickel in a fiver. "On this machine, you need to line up three diamonds in a row or three nines or a bonus in order for it to pay." Running her finger along a line on the big screen in front of us, she indicated where the figures needed to be. "You set your bet here." She pointed to a button on the flat surface of the machine. "And you spin here." Her fingers hovered over a bright white button opposite the bet. "I'll show you."

Setting her bet at a dollar, she pushed the spin button. The images spun and dropped into a mishmash of unmatched pictures.

"Bummer. Let's try again."

Again, she bet twenty credits—one dollar—and pushed the spin button. And lost.

"I can see how this game could eat a lot of money in short order," I mused as I stood beside her and watched the images fall into place with no payout.

When she bet again, she doubled down and bet forty credits. This time, she matched two pictures and a wild card and won back two dollars and sixty cents.

"Or not." Her eyes twinkled when she gazed up at me from her seat in front of the machine.

"What happens if you win and want to keep the money?"

"You press the cash-out button here." She pointed to a button and pushed it. "My cash-out is three-sixty." Pointing to another place on the screen, I saw where her "winnings" were listed. "The machine will spit out a ticket here." Right then the slot beside the currency slot lit up and a ticket printed out. "You can take this to one of the cash-out machines you'll find near the back of the casino, or you can take it to the cashier at the front." With a grin, she added, "See? Easy peasy."

"Easy peasy way to burn through a bunch of cash." I grimaced.

"That's why I told you to come with a set budget of what you can afford to lose." She slid the cash-out ticket into her wallet. "The house usually wins." Her eyes sparkled. "But sometimes, you get lucky."

I wandered over to a machine with one of the dragons on it. Something about a mythical creature hoarding treasure appealed to me. Perhaps it would give up some treasure to a novice player who honestly didn't have a clue about what she was doing. This one was a penny machine, but the minimum bet was fifty cents. I figured I couldn't go wrong with that until I glanced up at all the lines.

"Um," I began.

"No, this is good. You have more chances to win. Slide your money in," Wendy encouraged.

I dug a five out of my clutch and fed it into the machine.

"You can follow my lead or you can read the instructions." She indicated a corner of the machine I hadn't noticed. "Either way, start with a small bet and see what happens."

After placing three separate fifty cent bets and losing them all, I shot my friend a this-is-supposed-to-be-fun? side-eye.

She laughed her infectious alto laugh. "The machine is warming up. Bet a dollar this time."

With a shake of my head, I set the bet at a dollar and pushed the button. In the old nineties movies like *Honeymoon in Vegas* and *Bugsy* I'd watched on YouTube, the slots had long handles the gambler pulled after loading the machine with coins to place the bet. Pushing a button seemed a bit anticlimactic and not something over which I had control. Somehow, I'd thought I'd be pulling those levers, timing the pulls, and having some sort of say over how the icons in front of me spun into place.

Then three pink diamond icons and a funny cloud-looking wildcard icon rolled together on the screen. The LED lights stopped flashing randomly to chase each other around the sides and top of the machine while a bell chimed as my little dollar bet morphed into a fifty-five dollar payout. I stared dumbfounded at the machine while my friend jumped up and down and squealed like a wild woman.

"You won! Sadie! You won!"

"Now what do I do?" I asked in confusion.

"You can cash out at eleven times your bet or keep playing."

"What do you recommend?"

Her grin was irresistible. "You can keep playing on house money, which is always the goal. I'd cash out and play up, take ten dollars of your winnings, and find a nickel machine that appeals to you."

Doing as my friend suggested, I slid my cash-out ticket into my clutch, extracted a ten dollar bill from my budgeted gambling money, and looked around for another dragon machine that played nickels. An older lady with a ferocious scowl on her face stood up from her chair in front of a nickel dragon in the corner, and I zeroed in on it. Wendy gifted me a quizzical raised brow, but I had a feeling about the dragons.

The leather chair in front of the machine reeked of stale cigarettes, so I pushed it to the side and slid my money into the slot. Feeling brave, I bet two dollars and promptly lost them.

"What's your strategy, girlfriend?" Wendy asked when she saw how many nickels I'd lost right out of the gate.

I tucked my chin. "Strategy? There's a strategy to pushing a button?"

Planting her hands on her hips, she clarified, "No, your betting strategy."

"Oh. Well, the previous player didn't appear to have any luck, but that's how I started on the penny machine, too. So I thought I'd give this one some incentive to pay with the first bet."

Crossing her arms over her generous chest, my friend's mouth flat-tened into half a grin and she nodded to the machine. I took that to mean "carry on," so I bet another two dollars and came up empty. Feeling an uncharacteristic sense of courage, I bet three dollars and pushed the button. Breathlessly, I watched the icons fall into place, four emeralds, and jumped when the machine started chiming, its LED lights chasing each other in a multi-colored dance.

Wendy started screaming and grabbed my arm, jumping up and down and dancing. Only when several nearby gamblers sidled over to see what the fuss was about did I look at the pay line to discover my seven dollars in bets had paid $1,200.

"Omigosh! Omigosh! Wendy! Do you see this?" I gushed.

"I do indeed, babe." She lifted her hands and we high-fived. "Now you have real house money to play with."

I cashed out the machine, sliding the ticket into my clutch with the first one, and slipped my arm through my friend's, the corner of my mouth quirking up. "Now I see why this is fun."

With a "Harrumph!" the scowling older lady brushed my other arm as she pushed past me to return to the machine that had made me over a thousand dollars richer on a single push of a button. Wendy and I exchanged a wide-eyed look and managed to save our giggles until we were back in the main room.

"Let's grab a drink to celebrate your awesome start to the weekend," she suggested.

"Sure. I'll buy." I smirked, and giggles overcame us again.

After ordering vodka lemonades, we wandered over to the big screens. Wendy confessed she loved to bet on the horses. She checked the spreads, studied the information on the horses and riders that the attendant gave her, placed her bets, and settled into a plush leather seat facing the big screen where a race was about to start. Sliding into the seat next to hers, I sipped my drink and tried to find some enthusiasm for the ponies. But not even my friend's emotional roller coaster as we watched several races —a couple in which her horses placed and a couple they flat-out lost— could keep my attention on the TVs for long.

Knowing she'd bet on more races, I said, "If it's all the same to you, I'm going to look around at what else there is to do here."

The bell signaling the start of yet another race chimed, and my friend waved a languid hand in my direction, her eyes glued to the screen in front of us. "I'll catch you later."

I wandered into the saloon at the back of the casino where more TVs took up another wall. From the looks of things, the bettors sitting in front of the big screens were gambling on soccer and rugby maybe. Not being a big sports fan, it was a little unclear to me what games were actually playing. The lack of crowd noise that normally accompanied a game intensified my inability to follow the action. One thing was certain: the people watching the games were more about their bets than true fans of the teams.

I sipped my drink, enjoying the cool liquid sliding down my throat, and wandered on to another room that sort of wrapped around from the saloon back to the casino. Slot machines filled this area, too. From the looks of things, the casino at The Lodge mostly catered to people who liked a lot of bells and whistles with their gaming.

My meanderings led me back to the lounge area where I spied Wendy placing another bet. A glance up the TVs informed me yet another race was about to start. Vaguely, I wondered where in the world so many horse races were going on at once. I toyed with the idea of rejoining her, but I truly had no interest in the ponies.

As I strolled around the end of the partition, I scanned the Blackjack tables. Most of them were full. At every seat of the table nearest me sat a player, all of whom looked to be pros or something from the intense way they played their cards. The dealer maintained a stoic professionalism that only reinforced my idea about the game at that table. The adjacent table gave off the same vibe, and with no open seats, I had no temptation to join players who no doubt played far more often and for much higher stakes than my friends and I played for fun on the occasional Saturday night..

The third table in the line only had three or four players, but right as I stepped closer to them, a pair of couples who were laughing and teasing each other strolled up and grabbed the last seats.

With a sigh, I kept moving, scanning the remaining two tables for an open space.

My stomach did a cartwheel when the most handsome man I'd ever seen glanced up from his cards and locked eyes with me. A slight nod drew my attention to the open seat next to him.

And my luck changed again.

2

BLACKJACK

WITH ALL THE GRACE I COULD MUSTER, I ARRANGED MYSELF on the tall chair next to the gorgeous stranger. His broad shoulders filled out every square inch of his charcoal-gray sport coat. Since he leaned slightly forward toward the table, I couldn't quite discern the color or pattern of the shirt he wore beneath it. Of course, I might have been a bit preoccupied with the size and strength of his neck and my sudden urge to lick it.

Where did that come from?

He shifted, and a musky, woodsy scent drifted over me, giving me my answer. The man smelled positively delicious.

The dealer interrupted my wayward thoughts. "Miss? Do you have chips, or are you buying them?"

"I need to buy some."

"This table bets five to five hundred dollars."

I scanned the table, noting the piles of chips in front of the other players. Giving myself an inward shake of my head at seating myself at a serious table, I reached into my clutch, pulled out two of the five one-hundred-dollar bills I'd brought with me, and pushed them across the table.

Without expression, the dealer, a slender young woman of Asian descent, extracted a small stack of chips of varying denominations from five to twenty dollars and slid it across the table to me. The wolfish grin on the face of a rather rotund fella sitting opposite me said he thought I was an easy mark for the house. I shot him a blank stare and arranged my chips how I liked them.

The dealer called for our bets, and since this was my first hand, I played conservative, betting only a ten dollar chip. From the way the cards flew off the deck as the dealer flipped them face up in front of each of us, the woman was a true professional. A ten of spades landed in front of me, and I sort of wished I'd bet more. The great thing about playing Blackjack is that I was only betting against the house, so how the other players played didn't matter. Still, I noticed the dealer stuck the hot guy sitting next to me with a six of diamonds.

The second card landing in front of me was a six of clubs.

"Oof!" I exclaimed under my breath.

A five of hearts landed in front of the gorgeous guy beside me. From the corner of my eye, I caught a ghost of a grin tweak his full lips.

A few players ahead of me went bust, one held at seventeen, and then it was my turn. Feeling brave—or more probably reckless—I tapped the table. A six of hearts landed in front of me, and I groaned. Hot guy tapped the table, and a three of clubs landed on top of his cards. He tapped the table again, and a six of spades joined it. The dealer was showing a nine of hearts, so no doubt I was seated next to a winner. When the dealer went bust, she scooped up the bets of the rest of us who'd busted too and paid out a pile of chips to the handsome man who seemed to inch his chair slightly closer to mine as he reached out to gather his winnings.

The game ebbed and flowed, but the hot stranger played like a pro, his stack of chips steadily growing. Throughout our play, the big fella kept trying to catch my eye. Didn't take a genius to figure out what that was about. My little stack was down about two thirds when the big fella pulled out a wad of cash and asked the dealer for more chips. Right then, the older lady in the pink track suit who'd elbowed me away from 'her' machine after I won on it showed up at his side.

"That's enough for tonight, Gerald," she said, her tone impatient.

When she caught sight of me and my paltry pile of chips, her narrow-eyed sneer conveyed a world of disdain and more than a little smugness.

Clearly, she thought I'd lost all my winnings and was happy about it. Then she noticed where "Gerald's" attention strayed—and the wad of cash he was trying to hand the dealer—and clamped her hand on his arm.

"That's tomorrow's money," she hissed, but everyone at the table heard her.

"It's my money, Martha," he grumbled.

During their drama, my phone vibrated in my clutch. With play stopped while Gerald, Martha, and the dealer sorted out whether Gerald was going to continue the game, I checked my texts.

> Wendy: Met someone. Headed downtown to the bars. Want to join us?

> Me: I think I'll stick with Blackjack for a while. Send the signal if you need to.

> Wendy: Same to you.

"Everything okay?" a deep voice beside me asked.

I glanced up from my phone into a pair of green eyes that glittered like jewels, and I couldn't stop the "oh my" smile that stretched my lips.

"Aside from my play, everything is fine." I laughed.

"I could give you some pointers. Over a drink, if you'd like."

God, he had the most incredible smile, perfect even teeth, a deep dimple on one side of his face, and crinkles around his eyes that said that smile came out to play regularly.

I stared back down at my dwindling stack of chips and over at his rather impressive one then back into his emerald eyes. "Seems I could use a few pointers."

3

RAISING THE STAKES

I STRUGGLED TO CONCENTRATE ON THE DÉCOR OF THE BAR AT
the back of the casino, vaguely noting the Old West ambience with dark
polished wood and etched mirrors. The hot stranger's palm lightly resting
on the small of my back sent tiny tremors through me. I didn't dare
glance down at myself, but I hoped my dress hid my response to his
touch. He guided me to a secluded table in a corner of the room. Instead
of taking the chair across from mine, he pulled the one beside me a touch
closer. When I lifted a brow, he gifted me with a slight upturn of the
corner of his mouth, just enough to reveal that dimple that had drawn my
attention at the Blackjack table. That dimple set loose a battalion of
butterflies in my belly, and I worked to draw in a breath.

"What are you drinking?"

I'd been so preoccupied with the man beside me I missed the waitress
approaching our table.

Staying with the evening's theme, I said, "I'll have a vodka lemonade."

"And you, sir?"

I didn't miss the way the woman's expression warmed for my
companion. Though I couldn't blame her, didn't she see he already had a
date?

"Two fingers of Jameson, neat." His focus on me never wavered, which gave me a small bit of satisfaction when the waitress moved off after a few awkward seconds.

This close, his intense green eyes were mesmerizing. "What's your name?" The low timbre of his voice sent ripples of awareness through me, forcing me to clamp my thighs together.

"Sadie." While I'd worked to suppress the shivers his attention and his voice sent over my skin, my breathy response to his question gave me away.

His knowing smile confirmed it. "Sadie. Pretty name. Is it short for something?"

I shook my head. "My mom read it in some romance novel once."

He gave a sage nod. "It is a romantic name."

That dimple threatened to reveal itself again, reminding me I had a question for him. "What's your name?"

"Cash."

I laughed. "Of course it is."

Narrowing his eyes a fraction, he asked, "Why do you say that?"

"I saw those stacks of chips you cashed in before we left the table—and the two big ones you left for the dealer." I fiddled with the clasp on my clutch. "It seems you have an appropriate name—or a prescient one."

Relaxing against the back of his chair, he gave me a small smile. "Prescient. I like that." He slid his arm across the back of my chair. "Are you much of a gambler, sexy Sadie?"

Though I'd heard my name with that descriptor before, somehow it sounded more like a compliment on his lips than a smarmy come-on. The low register of his voice left me so warm, I could swear I glowed.

"I'm in town with a friend. She was teaching me how to gamble before she found something better to do."

The timely arrival of our drinks checked my word vomit. Seriously, what was I thinking to tell this man I was essentially alone for the evening?

"Here you go." The waitress set our drinks on little napkins on the table. "Is there anything else I can get you?" She directed her question to Cash, and there was absolutely nothing subtle about the way she lifted her chest as she asked it.

He barely spared her a glance. "Nah. We're good."

With a toss of her blond-streaked auburn ponytail, she turned on her heel and all but stomped away.

Seemingly oblivious to the waitress's little tantrum, Cash picked up his drink, sipped, and asked, "How long are you in town?"

With my index finger, I chased the condensation on my glass. "For the weekend. My friend was promoted at work, so we're celebrating."

He shot me a look over the rim of his glass. "By ditching you?"

I cleared my throat. "More like I ditched her."

His brows went up, but he remained quiet.

"While she watched the ponies, I wandered over to the Blackjack tables." Half-turning in my chair, I flashed him a grin and took a sip from my drink.

"Ah," he said with a nod that told me he knew what I wasn't saying. Briefly, his eyes dipped to my cleavage and back to my face. "Do you like to dance?"

"That was random."

Gifting me with that crooked grin that showed off his dimple, he said, "There's live music on Main Street this weekend. We could head down to the concert." He ghosted his fingertips over the bare skin along my shoulder blades, and try as I might, I couldn't suppress the shiver his touch called from me, a shiver that echoed in the tightening of my belly and a throbbing at the apex of my thighs.

"You don't want to keep beating the house at the Blackjack table?"

He continued to smooth his fingertips over my sensitive skin. "I'm more in the mood to play a game with higher stakes."

I might have gulped half of my drink at his obvious come-on. His smile dared me to back away from that high-stakes game even as he ghosted patterns over my bare skin with his fingertips.

When he leaned close and whispered, "Tell me you're not interested, and I'll back off," I caught a whiff of his sandalwood and citrus cologne, and I almost swooned into him.

Then I heard myself saying, "I like to dance."

4
DANCING QUEEN

THE SUN HOVERED ABOVE THE HORIZON AS THOUGH IT DIDN'T want to miss the party starting in the middle of town.

Since parking during Wild Bill Days was close to impossible in town, we'd taken the trolley from The Lodge to the main street. The narrow seats in the trolley forced us to sit with our sides plastered to each other. With a knowing smirk, Cash slipped his arm over my shoulders, pulling me even tighter to him as he murmured, "Relax. We're just taking a little ride." But the kiss he whispered over the shell of my ear implied something else entirely.

After we stepped from the trolley at the opposite end of Main from where the concert was going on, Cash casually took my hand. We wandered toward the stage where the warmup band had already started playing their set. Strategically placed big screens allowed patrons far from the stage to see the performers up close and personal. We strolled past casinos spewing people onto the sidewalks, occasionally stepping onto the cobbled street to move around groups of people buying drinks from pop-up stands outside the bars.

All the while, my focus remained on where we touched. His hand all but swallowed mine. Occasionally, he rubbed his thumb over the skin on the back of my hand, and all I could think about was what that thumb would feel like if it rubbed some other part of me.

On our way to the front of the stage, we passed several roped off areas in the middle of the street where people had set up their lawn chairs and coolers to watch the show. The space directly in front of the stage was reserved for dancing. I noticed that a makeshift dance floor of plywood covered the cobblestones and allowed people to glide their feet. The stage set up from sidewalk to sidewalk closed off the end of the street. When we came to a pop-up bar that sold mixed drinks rather than the keg beer people were drinking out of event cups, Cash stopped.

"Would you like something to drink?"

Having drunk my second vodka lemonade rather fast, I decided it was best to slow down for a minute, keep my thoughts under control. Of course, my body was flirting with open rebellion as he rubbed his thumb over my skin again.

"Maybe later," I hedged.

With a nod, he continued to lead me toward the dancing area. The band played a moderate tempo song, and Cash drew me into his arms for a two-step. The man stood north of six feet, so even in my heels, my head only came to his shoulder. Yet somehow, we fit together perfectly as he danced me around the space, his movements surprisingly light for such a big man. When I at last allowed myself to relax and enjoy the experience, he tugged me closer, my chest brushing the lapels of his sports jacket. Being that close to his body without actually touching that body was oddly arousing. The smirk on his mouth said he knew that too.

Ducking his head, he set his lips near my ear. "Are you having a good time?"

I nodded. "Yes" came out in a breathy whisper.

I could sense his smile against my ear, which told me the man knew exactly how he affected me. Why someone I'd only met a couple of hours before could have such a profound effect on me was one mystery I decided to wait to explore.

The band segued into the next song without missing a beat, and Cash smoothly led me in a swing dance that included several opportunities for him to wrap an arm around me, dip me, and twirl me until I was dizzy and laughing.

"You're a good dancer," he said as he spun me out of the pretzel move.

"You're easy to follow," I replied as he spun me back in close.

His smile turned wicked, and I squeaked when he dipped me deep and pulled me back up, his strong arms wrapping around my hips as I landed against his chest. Slowly, he let me slide down his front until my feet touched the ground again. Someone nearby let out a wolf whistle at our antics. Cash's deep laughter rumbled in his chest to vibrate into mine. My breath caught as wild sensations of desire rippled through me.

Right as I thought we'd take a break, the band rolled into another up-tempo tune, and my partner played right along with them. Cash's vast repertoire of swing dance moves made him the most exciting and challenging dance partner I'd ever had. Apparently, card playing wasn't his only talent. In a few moves, he managed to maneuver us into a corner near the front of the stage where we didn't have to compete for space with many other couples. That's when he started showing off. When he lifted me and spun me around as though we were auditioning for *Dancing With the Stars* or something, I was glad for the clingy knit of my dress.

Slightly winded from dancing three dances in a row, I said, "I think I'm ready for that drink now."

Gifting me with a grin that showcased the sexy dimple in his cheek, he slipped his arm around my waist and said, "What the lady wants, the lady gets."

He led me over to one of the pop-up bars on the sidewalk beside the dancing area where we waited in line as several other couples took advantage of the lead singer's little speech about the next song on the band's set list.

"Are you having fun?" Cash asked.

"Honestly, I thought my evening was going to be short and I'd probably end it broke."

His brow went up with his unspoken question.

"Learning how to gamble, remember?"

Chuckling, he said, "You *could* use a few extra pointers for Blackjack."

Tapping a finger to my lips, I said, "Pointers you said you were going to give me. Instead, here we are listening to music and dancing."

"Ah," he dragged out in his rumbly deep voice. "So we're both taking a risk."

Before I could ask him what he meant, it was our turn to order.

5

DOUBLE DOWN

On the sidewalk outside of Saloon #10, we sipped our drinks and watched people dance in front of the stage. From the looks of things, Cash wasn't the only good dancer in the crowd. On occasion, I'd been known to ask guys who could dance to take a turn with me, that is if they didn't have a date. Though I appreciated some of the other men's skills, tonight I had zero interest in dancing with anyone but Cash.

Forcing myself to be honest, my lack of interest in other good dancers couldn't solely be ascribed to his expert skill. Cash's clean, masculine scent with that hint of sandalwood and citrus drew me close to him. His deep rumbly voice vibrated in my chest when he'd held me to him while we danced. The more I experienced that sensation, the more addicted to it I became. The way desire deepened the intense green of his eyes when he gazed at me was an added aphrodisiac that invited the butterflies in my stomach to two-step to their own excited rhythm.

As we stood together, him enjoying a whiskey neat and me sipping a vodka soda, tingles radiated over my skin beneath my dress where his hand rested on the small of my back. From the corner of my eye, I caught a secret grin tugging the corner of his full lips. Even though I'd tried to exert an aura of cool nonchalance, he'd figured out how he affected me.

He'd noticed that touching me turned me on. Yet he didn't push, merely waited for me to make my own decision.

Talk about a turn-on.

Ever since I sat next to him at that Blackjack table in The Lodge, Cash had been seducing me. Only now as I clocked that little smirk on his mouth as he lightly rubbed circles over the base of my spine did I finally catch on. And I liked it.

"Having fun?" he asked, his grin morphing into a dazzling smile.

"So much fun. Where did you learn to dance like that?"

"My mom was a dance teacher."

"Yeah? No wonder you're so good."

He laughed. "She didn't teach me a single step." At my incredulous stare, he said, "A dance event was part of freshman orientation when I started college. There were lots of cute girls in my cohort, and I figured out pretty fast that they went for the guys who can dance. So I took a class."

It was my turn to laugh. "Bet that went over super well with your mom, you taking a class in college to learn something she could have taught you in her kitchen." I sipped from my vodka soda, which wasn't nearly as tasty as the vodka lemonades in the casino, but it was as close to my signature drink as the pop-up bar could offer.

"One of my cousins had a Thanksgiving wedding, and I surprised my mom with my mad new skills. She got a kick out of the way it all fell out." His eyes twinkled as he took a drink of his whiskey. "Plus, she got to dance with a willing partner instead of a surly teenage boy."

Grinning at him over the rim of my cup, I said, "I can't imagine you as surly."

He chuckled. "In my twenties, I got over myself."

My brow lifted. "Out of curiosity, how old are you?"

"Thirty-two." His hand on my lower back stilled. "How old did you think I was?"

Tilting my head, I pretended to think about it. "Mmm, based on the way you wear your jacket, your confidence at the Blackjack table, and the way you seem content in your own skin, I would have guessed early thirties."

He relaxed, his warm hand going back to drawing those delicious circles over my dress. "Out of curiosity, how old are you, or is that a rude question to ask a lady?"

I took another sip of my drink. "Thirty. How old did you think I was?"

"Twenty-seven or twenty-eight." He grinned.

Wrinkling my nose, I said, "How very diplomatic of you."

Cash snorted a laugh. "You already know how gorgeous you are. I don't need to flatter you."

With an exaggerated batting of my lashes, I leaned a little closer to him. "I kinda like the flattery though."

He smirked and tossed back what was left of the whiskey in his cup.

"For the record, I think you're gorgeous, too."

"You finished with that?" He indicated my drink that was now mostly ice.

"Yes."

He slid my cup inside his empty one and tossed both into a nearby trash can. When he returned to me, he entwined his fingers with mine and tugged me back toward the roped off area in front of the stage. The band played a perfect two-step song, and Cash twirled me into his arms. His exceptional control allowed him to hold me tight to his chest while he danced us around the edge of the dance floor.

The warmup band played a cover of George Strait's "Amarillo by Morning" and I discovered something else Cash was good at. With his mouth beside my ear, his baritone voice filled my head as he sang along with the band. Good thing he had his arm wrapped tight around my waist because his incredible singing had me swooning. The fact that I didn't melt all over him like hot fudge over a strawberry should probably be included in the greatest mysteries of the world.

By the time the song ended, Cash had maneuvered us into a corner that while definitely not private was at least inconspicuous. As though from a great distance, I vaguely registered the crowd cheering something the lead singer said. With his lips pressed to the shell of my ear, Cash hummed the chorus to the song again, and I couldn't stop the shiver of awareness that rippled through me. When he nibbled his way down my neck and back up to plant a lingering kiss on that super-sensitive spot behind my ear, I couldn't stop the moan that escaped my throat.

We still touched from chests to thighs. He shifted slightly, and my awareness zeroed in on the hard bulge that grazed against my center. That subtle shift left a tingling heaviness low in my belly, an answer to the siren pull of his hard body pressed to mine.

The words and the baritone rumble of his delivery heated me from the inside out. "You up for trying a new game?"

6

COIN TOSS

As the roadies swarmed the stage to switch from the warmup band to the headliner, Cash linked his fingers with mine and led me back over near the pop-up bar. Instead of joining the line waiting for drinks, he pulled me into a quiet alcove notched into the old-timey architecture of one of the buildings lining the street.

Resting one hand on the building above my shoulder while he played the fingers of his other hand through mine, he cocooned me in our own private space. "Exactly how desperately do you want to see this next act?" he asked.

I shrugged. "He's more my mom's generation. She loved him back in the day."

The corner of his mouth tipped up. "Not desperate then."

"Not really. No."

"I've loved dancing with you."

"I sense a 'but' coming." I'd been having such a great time, and I thought we were connecting. That 'but' said I might have misread the situation.

"But it's kinda crowded here. And the dance floor is kinda treacherous. I was thinking we could catch the trolley back to The Lodge, perhaps continue our conversation there."

Catching my lower lip in my teeth, I demurred. "Umm—"

His gaze snagged on my mouth. "How 'bout this?" He slipped his hand into the pocket of his jeans and produced a quarter. "Heads, we stay for a while and listen to the headliner." His eyes darkened as he stared into mine. "Tails, we head back to the hotel for a private conversation."

"Who's calling it?"

"Doesn't matter." He smirked.

My heart fluttered in my chest. "All right. Flip your coin."

The coin gleamed in the light of the street lamp overhead and landed in his palm. With a smack, he covered the back of his other hand then tilted his head to the side as he slowly peeled his palm off the back of his hand, leaving the quarter behind. His slow smile revealed the wicked pleasure he took in the outcome of his game.

"Tails it is."

Desire warred with restraint, something he must have picked up on.

"We can change the game to best two out of three if you want to be sure."

Plucking the coin from his hand, I dropped it into my cleavage. "We agreed to the outcome of the toss," I said, smiling at the way his eyes rounded at my antics.

"That's my lucky quarter," he warned.

"Apparently, it is."

Tipping his head back, he let out a joyful laugh then he snagged my hand and started strolling us up the street in the direction of the trolley stop. As we passed one of the jumbotrons the organizers had cleverly mounted from some construction company's frontend loader, the country music artist from the 90s, Aaron Tippin, opened his show with "For You, I will." It was one of my mom's favorite songs. As he sang about not normally walking the city streets but walking them for someone he cared about, Cash's fingers tightened on mine, fluttering my heart.

On the short trolley ride back to The Lodge, we were quiet, our joined hands resting on top of his thick thigh. Using the pretense of watching the passing scenery, we stole glances at each other, meeting each other's secret smiles with our own.

When we alighted in front of the lobby, neither of us gave in to pretense. With his hand on the small of my back, he ushered me to the elevator, bypassing the casino and the bar. While he stared straight ahead as the elevator rose to his floor, I couldn't help but to covertly study his handsome profile with his sculpted cheeks and straight nose. The light callouses on his hands denoted a man who worked with his hands, but his clean-shaven face and casual style said maybe not. Whatever his work was, I had no doubt he worked out. The hard body he held against me as we danced proved it. My nipples puckered at the thought of feeling that hard body up close and personal.

He stopped in front of a door and keyed it open. Swinging the door wide, he said, "After you."

As I stepped into the suite, my eyes zeroed in on the king bed that took up most of the room. Beyond it, twilight filtered through the sheers covering the glass door that led to a small balcony, a warm glow that bathed the room in soft light.

Cash stepped over to the minibar and pulled out two glasses, setting them on top of it. He dropped some ice cubes into one and turned to me. "Vodka?"

"Yes, please."

He splashed a finger of alcohol into the glass and topped it up with soda and a lemon twist. If I hadn't known better, I would have sworn he'd planned to invite me to his room, even though we'd only met a few hours before in the casino. After pouring himself a whiskey, he lifted his glass to mine.

"To chance encounters."

I clinked my glass with his. "To chance encounters."

Over the rims of our glasses, we smiled at each other and sipped.

"Would you like to sit?" he asked, indicating a love seat near the glass doors to the balcony.

I nodded and seated myself, setting my purse on the low coffee table in front of the sofa. Relaxing into the cushions, I took another taste of my drink, noting that he hadn't overdone the alcohol in it. A smile tugged the corner of my mouth.

"What are you thinking about?"

"Whatever your plans are for the rest of the evening, you want me mostly sober for them."

Sliding his arm across the back of the seat, he moved closer to me. "I like my dates to be in control." His gaze strayed to where he wound a strand of my hair through his fingers. "Women who are in control are sexy."

"As opposed to women who are too sloppy drunk to give consent?" I tested him.

"Exactly." After a small sip from his drink, he added, "I like my dates to remember who they were with."

"Huh," I snorted. "In the casino, I took you for confident, not arrogant."

His brow went up. "Nothing arrogant about wanting my date to know who she's with."

"Okay," I said. "Who are you, Mr. Cash?"

7

A SURE BET

Gently, Cash tugged my drink from my hand and set it beside his on the coffee table. His eyes never leaving mine, he lightly smoothed his palm from my knee to my hip. I answered that touch with a tightening at the apex of my thighs. Involuntarily, I clamped my knees together. A grin ghosted over his mouth.

"I like knowing I get to you, too," he said in that low voice that reverberated in my chest.

"Are you a professional gambler, or are you lucky?" My hand found its way to his bicep, and I marveled at the solid-rock feel of muscle beneath the sleeve of his blazer.

"I took a gamble at that Blackjack table, and now I'm the luckiest man on the planet."

Being deliberately obtuse, I said, "So not a professional gambler."

He indulged my nosiness, even as his thumb rubbed up and down over my dress where the top of my thigh met my hip. "In a manner of speaking, I guess I am a professional gambler."

I blinked, and he smiled.

"I work in financial planning, which involves a fair amount of speculation."

"Oh." Though I would have liked to have impressed him with something funny or profound, that maddening thumb had all my attention as it roamed closer to my center.

His eyes dipped to my mouth, and a shiver of anticipation stole over me. "What about you, sexy Sadie? Are you working your way into becoming a professional gambler? Is that why you chose Deadwood for your celebratory getaway?"

That he remembered everything I'd said to him over the course of the evening was almost as much of a turn-on as his hand on my thigh and the desire darkening his green eyes.

"I'm not a gambler. I write code for a software company." I swallowed hard as he leaned closer to catch my words that came out in a breathy whisper. "As a rule, I don't pick up men at Blackjack tables."

"Until tonight."

I blinked at the slow, sexy smile exposing the dimple in his cheek.

"It's a sure bet I want to kiss you right now."

Without my permission, my tongue slipped out to glide along my lower lip.

The sexiness of his smile intensified. "I think it's a sure bet you'd like to kiss me too," he said.

Lord help me, I wanted to do more than kiss the ridiculously hot man inching closer to me on the sofa. My eyes strayed to his beautifully defined lips, and I nodded.

"Words, Sadie. I need to hear the words."

"Yes, Cash. Yes, I want to kiss you."

The scent of whiskey on his breath and something deeper, something deliciously masculine filled my nostrils as he leaned in to kiss me. My eyes fluttered shut as his full lips brushed over mine. I slid my hand to the back of his head, tangling my fingers in the silky strands of his dark hair, and heard his moan of pleasure.

He increased the pressure of his lips on mine, inviting me to open for him. Digging his fingers into my hip, he turned me so my chest was flush with his, the contact giving my ever-tightening nipples some relief. With a sigh, I opened for him. Our tongues came together in a wild and wonderful dance as though they'd waited forever for exactly this partner. The whimpers sounding in my ears emanated from my own throat as he held me even closer to his hard body.

I sensed his smile against my skin as I squirmed in an attempt at a more intimate touch. He nibbled and tugged at my lips, teasing me until I held his face between my hands and kissed him back with an intensity that even surprised me. Then he was the one groaning deep in his throat, a sound that ratcheted my desire to an uncharacteristic point of desperation.

Tearing his mouth from mine, he panted in air, his eyes black pools of need. "Sadie, sweetheart, that mouth of yours could drive a man right out of his head." He smoothed back a lock of my hair that had come undone from my up-do. "I'm on the edge of the point of no return, so now is the time for you to tell me if I'm reading you right." Nodding toward the massive bed behind me, he said, "More than anything, I want you in that bed—with me, beneath me, on top of me. But only if you want that too."

Earlier in the evening when I left my room to meet my friend in the casino, I had no idea I'd meet a handsome stranger who'd make me want to take a big gamble. But sitting on the love seat in his suite, what I wanted more than anything else was Cash's body next to mine. Answering his unspoken question, I kicked off my heels and stood up. Then I reached behind my neck and released the clasp anchoring the halter of my dress.

8

GAMBLERS' PARADISE

THOUGH HIS POSTURE ON THE SOFA APPEARED RELAXED AS I let the straps of my dress drop, his green eyes darkened almost to black. When the fall of my dress exposed my breasts, he swallowed hard. His response emboldened me, and I ran my hands down my body, stopping where the knit fabric of my dress bunched at my hips.

"Sadie." The raspy whisper of his voice was a caress over my heated skin.

"I want to."

My answer to his implied question galvanized him into action. In one smooth move, he stood and shucked off his blazer, carelessly tossing it over the arm of the love seat. His eyes remained on mine as he gripped the back of the sofa with one hand, balancing as he toed off his cowboy boots. With an impressive economy of movement, he unbuttoned his shirt as he stepped toward me.

When he reached for me, I shivered in hot desire as my bare breasts pressed to his naked chest. Wrapping my arms around his neck, I murmured against his lips, "Where were we?"

A chuckle gusted from him before he sealed his lips to mine and devoured me. The fire of his kiss licked through my veins, sizzling my blood into a conflagration that burned low in my belly. I couldn't help but to move, to revel in the friction of my nipples rubbing against the muscled planes of his pecs, the light dusting of hair tickling and arousing me in equal measure.

Right as the kiss teetered on the edge of setting flame to both of us, once again, Cash tore his mouth from mine. "Fuck, Sadie. You kiss like a wild thing." A feral smile crossed his lips. "I have a feeling that before this night is over, you're going to burn me alive. And I'm going to die a very happy man."

Before I could respond to his pronouncement, he stepped away from me. Cool air flowed over my exposed body, and I crossed my arms over myself to hold onto some of the heat his warm skin left behind.

"Uh, uh, uh. Drop the dress," he commanded.

I bit my lip against the pleasure washing over me at his demand. Slowly, I pushed my dress over my hips and down my thighs until gravity took over at my knees, and the fabric pooled on the floor at my feet. Blatantly, his eyes roamed down my body, snagging on the lace thong that was the only garment left covering me. With one calloused fingertip, he traced a fiery trail over my skin from my collarbone, across the swells of my breasts, over one puckered nipple, and down the center of my abdomen to circle my navel in a tease that tugged a whimper from the back of my throat.

"Get on the bed."

I pulled the top sheet and comforter aside and settled on my back in the middle of the mattress. Cash dropped his shirt on the coffee table, pushed his jeans and boxers down his legs, and stepped out of them. His movements allowed me to tour his body with my eyes, and my breath caught. The sculpted muscles of his shoulders, chest, arms, and abs told a story of a man who took excellent care of his body. The cut of his jeans hid the power of his thighs now on full display in their naked glory. My eyes snagged on his long thick phallus that jumped against his navel at my inspection.

"Like what you see?" Though his words teased, there was a serious underlying question in his tone.

"So much," I breathed.

His gentle smile did nothing to distract from the desire heating his eyes. "Me too." He climbed onto the bed. "You are the most beautiful woman I've ever seen." Slipping his fingers beneath the elastic of my thong, he said, "But I want to see all of you."

Taking the hint, I lifted my hips, and he slid the scrap of lace down my legs. Sitting back on his heels, he tilted his head and eyed me. My first instinct was to cover myself from his intense scrutiny, then he whispered, "I don't know where to start with you."

"Hmm?"

His tongue toured his lower lip. "Every inch of you looks delectable."

Starting with my foot, he nibbled on my ankle bone and up the inside of my calf until he reached the tender skin on the back of my knee. A tiny "Oh" escaped my lips, and he laughed darkly against my skin. Then he grazed his teeth along my soft inner thigh, and I jammed my knuckles into my mouth to keep from crying out. This man's attentions to my legs alone were enough to get me off.

He stared hard at my pussy. "Look at you, all pink and glistening. I have to taste."

When he parted my folds with his hot tongue, my hips came off the bed. A censorious rumble accompanied his forearm landing across my hips, holding me where he wanted me. Teasing my clit with the tip of his tongue, he drew a long moan from me that someone walking in the hallway could have overheard. The sound must have been what he wanted because he slipped one thick finger inside me, expertly pumping until my head lolled from side to side on the pillows, my hands pulling his hair as my body rippled in anticipation of my climax. My cries echoed off the walls with my release as he curled his finger just right and sent me into the stratosphere.

"Cash! Ohmigod, Cash!" I screamed.

I couldn't help how I bucked and thrashed as he licked and kissed my most intimate self.

A groan rumbled from him as he continued to lick and kiss me, gentler now, letting me come down easy.

I flopped back on the pillows then tipped my head up when I sensed his smile against my throbbing flesh. Glancing up at me from beneath his brows, he teased me with his dancing eyes.

"You are sexy indeed, Sadie. The hottest woman I've ever met."

Climbing over me, he dangled an arm off the side of the bed to snag his jeans. A few seconds later, I heard the crinkle of a foil packet as he rolled back over to my side.

"Yep, foreplay with you is one hell of a good time," he said.

I blinked, and he was back between my thighs, his warm lips kissing and nibbling a path up the middle of my belly. He nosed my skin, his long inhale loud in the sudden quiet of the room.

"You smell so pretty, like flowers and sunshine and something womanly that I can't figure out." Rubbing the tip of his nose along my side, he said, "But it's my new favorite perfume."

His words gave me confidence, and I ran my hands over the sculpted muscles of his shoulders as my knee came up to graze the side of his ribs, opening myself more to him. My movement drew a moan from him as he kissed his way to my breast. When he covered my nipple with his mouth and sucked hard, I smacked my hand on the back of his head and held him right there. His teeth and tongue teasing me sent arrows of pleasure straight to my center. Then he ran the pad of his finger over the other nipple, the vanguard before he pinched and tugged at it in rhythm with his oral attentions to me.

Cash's touch told me all about how much he was loving what he was doing to me. I couldn't help but to writhe and moan beneath him because I was loving it too. The way the man played me, it was as though he knew me, but more likely, he was just that good at giving a woman pleasure.

Kissing his way over my chest, along the side of my neck and across my jaw, he reached his destination. The second our lips met, I went up in flames. Wrapping my arms around his broad shoulders and my legs around his trim waist, I clung to him as the conflagration otherwise known as Cash's kisses burned me to a cinder, a pulsing fire of want. All thought flew from my head as I rubbed my wet center along his thick length until he tore his mouth from mine.

Resting his forehead on mine, he panted in air. "We're going there, babe. But I need to suit up first."

He pushed up on his knees and took himself in his hand, pumping and squeezing his cock and giving me a good long look at what he had for me.

"Cash," I whimpered.

"Yes?" A wicked smile stretched his lips as he took his time tearing open the packet and smoothing the condom over himself. "Is there something you need?"

The side of my fist came down hard on the mattress as I shifted, raising my hips in a silent demand. "You damn well know there is."

His laughter was pure evil as he clasped my wrists in his hands and raised my arms over my head. "You gave me permission to play when you answered my question earlier by dropping your top and showing me your gorgeous tits. So just lie back and let me play."

As though he didn't trust me—which I admit was a good call—he held my wrists with one hand while he positioned himself at my entrance. Pushing the head of his cock between my folds, he closed his eyes and held himself still for a long beat. When he opened his eyes, green fire blazed into mine as he thrust deep into me, seating himself to the hilt inside my needy channel.

"Cash," I screamed as my inner muscles clamped down hard on his glorious length.

Though my experience was decidedly limited, I'd never been with anyone who filled me as perfectly full as this gambling stranger with the dimpled grin and wicked green eyes. Holding me down by my wrists, he started thrusting. Though my hands were immobile, my hips were free to move, and I met him thrust for thrust until I couldn't stay with his increasingly faster rhythm.

"Now, Sadie. You have to come now!"

He dropped a wrist to press the pad of his thumb against my clit, and that one move rocketed me into space. With a grunt, he followed me, his body going rigid, the veins in his neck standing out in stark relief against his tanned skin. I'd never seen anything more gorgeous than this man's climax ripping through him.

Afterward, he collapsed on top of me, his weight forcing me to sip air, but it didn't matter. The delicious sensation of his sweat dampened skin slicking along mine, his heavy chest flattening my breasts with his every breath, his cock still twitching inside me as the aftershocks rolled through me was pure bliss. Closing my eyes, I decided I could stay right in this spot for the rest of my life.

Instead, Cash rolled onto his back, taking me with him to sprawl across his torso. "Fuck, Sadie. That was—"

"Incredible."

"The best I've ever had." Tipping his head up, he gazed deep into my eyes. "I don't know if that was the best hand I've ever played or the most foolish gamble I've ever taken."

"Do you have to decide right this minute?"

A laugh barked out of him. "You're right. I'll have to sleep on it." Desire darkened his eyes again. "Later."

9
CASH OUT

I AWOKE TO THE SOUND OF SOMEONE BRUSHING HIS TEETH IN the bathroom. Bright sunlight poured through the sheers covering the glass doors to the balcony, alerting me the day had started without me. It took me a minute to extricate myself from the tangle of sheets and blankets created by a night spent messing up the bed more than sleeping in it. I stood and stretched, taking stock of the delicious soreness of my body. Apparently, *someone* had had the idea several rounds of out-of-this-world sex was necessary to help him figure out what kind of bet he'd made when he'd invited me for that initial drink.

Or something.

Picking up my purse, I reached inside and extricated my diamond wedding ring from its concealed compartment. After sliding it back onto my finger, I quietly padded into the bathroom where Cash, fresh from the shower, a towel draped low around his hips, his hair still damp, rinsed toothpaste from his mouth.

"Good morning, Mrs. Bennet. Did you sleep well?" Though the words came out in a matter-of-fact tone, he ruined the question with a smirk.

Reaching past him, I snagged my toothbrush from my toiletries bag. "What little sleep you allowed me, Mr. Bennet."

That smirk morphed into a wholly unapologetic smile. "Admit it. You loved every second of it."

"Maybe," I demurred.

He tweaked my nipple and soothed the sting by wrapping me tight in his arms. "Every second," he reiterated before he smacked a hard kiss on my mouth.

Letting me go, he leaned against the vanity and crossed his arms over his chest, watching me as I brushed my teeth. In the artificial light, his wedding band gleamed on his finger. After I spit toothpaste into the sink and rinsed my mouth, I caught his expression and remembered I didn't have a stitch on.

"Are you very sore?" he asked, hope in his voice.

"I'm a little sore. Yes."

Grasping my hips, he pulled me to him. "If I kissed your pussy better, do you think you'd be up for another round?"

"Babe! What's got into you?" I tried to sound aghast, but my core started throbbing as I thought about what he wanted.

"Sadie was so exciting." He tightened his grip. "You were wild last night, Stella-girl."

"It was the dancing. You know that always does it for me. Is that why you stopped playing cards when you were killing it at that Blackjack table? Because you wanted to take me downtown to dance?"

"It was the dress. I haven't seen that one in your closet at home," Chance said, his fingers digging into my skin, letting me know this conversation would be short.

"I bought it for this trip when you said you wanted me to surprise you with the role I played."

"Best one-night stand I've ever had."

I smirked. "Is that right? What if you run into Sadie again on another trip?"

A slow grin spread over my husband's perfectly sculpted mouth. "I'm counting on running into Sadie again. Like maybe in five minutes."

Taking his towel with me as I dropped to my knees, I peeked up at him through my lashes. "Or right now."

A groan met my teasing words followed by Chance hissing air through his teeth as I wrapped my lips around his length. By the time "Sadie" had finally finished with him, we'd missed breakfast in the restaurant.

———

As Chance loaded our suitcases into the trunk of the BMW, I slipped my sunglasses on and watched my friend Wendy Wilson and her pro football player boyfriend Nick Douglass step out of the lobby of The Lodge.

"How was your weekend, Stella? Did you play any more slots?" Her eyes glittered with mischief.

"I switched to Blackjack. But I only gave the house two hundred dollars, which probably ended up in Chance's pocket." I grinned back. "Did you actually go to the concert last night? I looked for you but didn't see you there."

She slipped her hand into the crook of Nick's elbow. "We might have gotten distracted."

"Huh. Guess that means the ponies didn't pay?"

"Oh, they paid. But someone offered me something more fun to do than gamble." She peeked up at her guy who smiled into her eyes.

Reaching his hand to Nick, Chance said, "I'll see you before fall camp starts, make sure everything is in place with your contract."

"Thanks, man. And thanks for the weekend." Nick cleared his throat, a hint of color riding high on his cheeks. "We've enjoyed it."

Wendy shot me a secret wink. "Yes we have. We'll see you guys back in Denver?"

"We're looking forward to joining the team for family weekend before fall camp starts," Chance said. "If you think of anything you need, we'll talk then."

"Thanks again, man. I hit the jackpot when I landed you as an agent. Appreciate everything." Nick and Chance shook hands again.

I slid into the passenger seat while Chance jogged around the front of the car to the driver's side. "So, how *did* you do at the Blackjack table?" I asked.

"I covered the weekend for the four of us plus a little extra for a side trip to Jackson Hole." He winked.

Reaching across the console, I cupped his face in my hand. "I doubt there are many sports agents out there who treat their clients to week-ends in Deadwood. No wonder your guys are so loyal to you."

Covering my hand with his, he smiled. "That, and I'm good at negotiating fat contracts for them." He turned the engine over and put the car in gear. "I might have been distracted and forgot to ask." He winked. "How did you do at the slots?"

"I won enough to cover some nice dinners on the drive home."

"Your suitcase seemed heavier when I loaded it into the trunk just now. Tell me, babe. Am I going to meet someone new who rocks my world when we hit Jackson?" The naughty expression in his eyes sent tiny tremors of anticipation through me.

Shooting him a coy look over the top of my sunglasses, I sassed, "Guess you'll have to wait and see."

"Oh, Stella. Marrying you was the best gamble I ever took." His rich laughter filled the car.

As we pulled out of Deadwood, he slipped his hand over the console. The squeeze he gave the top of my thigh promised all sorts of delights to come before the end of our summer vacation.

ABOUT THE AUTHOR

Tam DeRudder Jackson is the author of the paranormal romance Talisman Series, the contemporary rock star romance Balefire Series, and the contemporary sports romance Game Time Series. Her favorite "room" in her house is her patio where she dreams up stories of romance and risk. When she's not writing her latest romance, you can find her driving around in her convertible or carving turns on the slopes of the local ski hill. The mom of two grown sons, Tam likes to travel, attend rock concerts, watch football and soccer, and go to antique car shows with her husband. She lives in the mountains of northwest Wyoming where she spends most of her free time trying to read all the books. Her TBR piles are threatening to take over her office, and she's fine with that.

Subscribe to her newsletter at https://www.tamderudderjackson.com.

FINDING OUR WAY IN DEADWOOD

STEPHANIE WEBB DILLON

1

Clay

Staying at Hank's was getting old fast. I loved my brother, but I miss my wife. Jillian and I had a big misunderstanding around two months ago when an old girlfriend showed up in town looking for me. She tried to claim that I was the father of her child. The one she had on her hip at the time. Jillian took one look at Connie with the kid and lost her shit. I tried to tell her that it wasn't possible. First, I would never cheat on her. Second, I had not seen Connie in over eight years. Jillian and I had been married for the better part of the last seven years. We met at a town hall dance, and I fell head over heels for her. She kicked me out of the house and now I only saw her at work. Thankfully she had not asked for a divorce yet. I was hoping to win her back before that happened.

Jillian and I started Wheeler's Deadwood Tours, six years ago. We lived in Historic Deadwood, South Dakota and there was so much history and beauty to show off that we decided that giving tours would be a fun way to make a living. We didn't expect it to take off as fast as it did. We had six employees, four of them gave tours along with us. That way we could provide more tours throughout the week. There were conventions, bike rallies and all manner of things that brought people to our town. Since we both owned the business, we couldn't avoid each other completely. Jillian had managed to avoid me as much as she could though. I sat up in the bed and swung my legs off the side, running my hands through my hair I went in search of coffee.

"Morning Clay, you plan on trying to talk to Jilly today?" Hank asked as he looked at me over the paper. "Seems you should be able to prove the kid isn't yours with a paternity test. Although I have to admit, he looks like you."

I flipped him off and poured myself a cup before heading to the shower. That's the hell of it. The kid did look like a Wheeler, but I knew for a fact he wasn't mine because I have not had sex with anyone but Jillian since I laid eyes on her. I kept coming back to the thought that maybe Blake had met up with her. For cousins, we looked like we could be twins. Our hair was a few shades different, and I was about an inch taller, but the similarities were uncanny. It wouldn't be the first time someone had mixed us up. Blake worked for us for six months almost a year ago. I'd have to give him a call. He was always following the rodeo; he had an accident that left him unable to ride while he recuperated so we gave him a job while he was down on his luck. As soon as he was healed up, he was gone again. The kid was about six months old so the timing would work. I'd have to have him come for a visit.

I got dressed after my shower and decided to go out for breakfast. I wasn't in the mood for Hank's ribbing today. I wanted my wife back. She had taken Connie in and was helping her with the kid. I couldn't believe she thought he was mine. I thought we had more trust than that. It really hurt that she thought so little of my ability to be faithful. I know that when we first started dating, she was very insecure. I had been a bit of a playboy for years but that ended the moment we had our first dance. I started pursuing her with a vengeance and she finally gave in to a date. We were inseparable and when I popped the question she said 'yes' and we were married three months later. Jillian wanted kids so badly and we had not been able to conceive yet, so I think it hit her especially hard to think I may have knocked up another woman. I was just going to have to prove it wasn't me. I wanted them out of our house so I could come back home.

"I'm heading out, see you later." I said as I put on my hat and left. Hank just grunted at me. I knew he had a lot to do around the ranch, his brother-in-law had hired a foreman now because he had fallen and injured his spine several years ago. He couldn't get around as well as he used to and needed the help to run the place. It took him several months before he gave in to accepting more help. The ranch belonged to his late wife's family. Miranda's twin brothers ran the ranch along with him and they got along really well.

Driving along the main road I pulled into a spot in front of the Main Street Diner. Mrs. Mae was an amazing cook, so I ate here quite a bit. I missed my wife's cooking, but this was the next best thing. I walked in and sat down at the counter taking my hat off to lay it beside me. Mrs. Mae came out of the kitchen smiling at me.

"Goodness, Mr. Clay are you ever going to make up with Mrs. Jillian?" she asked me as she poured my coffee. "I don't know why she would think that baby is yours. Even if he looks like a Wheeler, everyone in town knows how sweet you are on her."

"Apparently everyone but Jilly." I grumbled to myself as I looked at the chalkboard menu. "I'll have the breakfast casserole this morning please ma'am."

"I'll have it out in a minute." she said as she frowned at the door and went back into the kitchen. I looked behind me to see Connie come in with little Teddy. She looked startled when she saw me. I was so tired of all this. I wanted my wife back. I got up and walked over to her.

"I don't know what your game is, but he is not my kid. I haven't been with anyone but my wife since the day I saw her." I said to Connie quietly. She paled as she looked from me to Teddy.

"Can we talk about this when I don't have my son attached to my hip?" she asked as she went to sit in a booth with him. "I know what I remember, and it was you. I wasn't that drunk."

"I want a paternity test. You have been avoiding me for weeks. I am not going to lose my wife over something I didn't do. I'll admit that he looks like one of us, but he isn't mine." I turned and went back to the counter to eat my breakfast, not that I was hungry anymore. A few minutes later Jillian came in. She looked at me with hurt in her eyes and it gutted me, but I was hurt too. I have never been unfaithful to her and the fact that she could believe for a minute that I had been hurt.

I watched her walk past me and slide into the booth with Connie and the boy. She smiled at him, and he seemed to adore her. I was going to set up an appointment for a test this week, and if I had to, I would have a judge order her to bring him. I finished my food, paid my bill and left. I had a tour that started in twenty minutes, and I didn't want to be late. We had a full schedule this week. I headed over to our office to wait for the group to gather for the tour.

2

Jillian

It felt like a knife in my heart every time I looked at Clay. I never thought he would cheat on me, but Teddy looks just like him. I remember when Connie walked in with him. I had just finished a tour and was scheduling another one when she walked into our office and looked around until she spotted Clay. She walked right up to him and tried to hand the baby to him. Clay just looked stunned. I thought at first, she was looking for one of his cousins or his brother because the kid had Wheeler all over him. The pale green eyes, dirty blonde hair, the curls and the full lower lip. When he recognized the woman and called her by name, I thought I was going to pass out right there. I told him to pack his shit and get out of the house. Connie had gotten a room at Motel six and I knew she really couldn't afford to keep that up, so I brought them home with me. No kid should be living in a hotel like that. We had three bedrooms so that allowed them to each have their own room for now.

I feel like I have been in a fog since the day she showed up. She seems really nice, and she has been trying to find a job. Theodore is adorable and a good baby. She has been helping around the house and doing some of our billing to earn money. I want to hate her, but she is just so nice. She isn't trying to make the moves on my husband, she just wants to take care of her son. I can respect that. Clay still swears that he isn't the father and that he had not seen Connie in over eight years. I wanted to believe him but why would she lie when a simple blood test would tell us that it wasn't true.

"Jillian, are you listening to me?" Connie said and I realized she had been talking while I was in my head. She looked concerned.

"I'm sorry, I wasn't. What were you saying?" I asked her as I handed a piece of toast to Teddy.

"Clay wants a paternity test. I am more than happy to do that, but I don't have insurance right now and I am barely covering diapers and formula." she said frowning at her coffee. I wanted to feel sorry for her but right now I was busy feeling sorry for myself. I wanted that to be our child and I wanted my husband. He was my best friend and I just felt so disconnected from everything right now.

"Clay will pay for all of that. I also think I may have found you a job. They are looking for someone to manage Miss Kitty's Mercantile. I mentioned that you had some management experience from before and that you were looking. They don't stay open late, and the pay is good as well as the benefits. I could watch Teddy this afternoon so that you could go talk to Ms. Lowell about the job." I told her as I started eating my breakfast. I had ordered a double serving of the casserole, knowing it would be enough for the two of us. I split it up and we ate while she gave Teddy a bottle.

"Thank you, I'll definitely check into that. I also need to find a place of my own when I start working a normal job. We can't continue to stay with you. You have been too generous as it is." Connie was holding Teddy's bottle while he lay in his car seat beside her. She really seemed like a great mom, and she was doing her best. We got a lot of looks because it was a small town, and nothing stayed secret here for long. I was a respected member of the community and people were angry on my behalf. Poor Clay had been getting a lot of crap lately. He really was a great guy and would give you the shirt off of his back. He just didn't seem to know what to do with this situation. He had made no attempts to get to know Teddy or be around him. It didn't make sense to me. Clay had always been good with kids; we wanted a couple of our own. I really wanted to believe that Teddy wasn't his but looking at the resemblance made that very difficult.

"We need to get going I have a lot of paperwork to get through today so that I can do a few tours tomorrow." I said as I threw some money on the table. We headed toward the office in time to see Clay taking off in one of the carriages for a tour. We had invested in a horse and carriage for some of the tours. People were willing to pay a little extra and loved them. It was also a great way to see everything. We kept the horses at the ranch in the evenings when we didn't have tours scheduled. It was a good arrangement. I had avoided Hank and the rest of his family since we separated. I knew they were angry with me, but I couldn't help feeling betrayed. I watched Clay as he drove the carriage off. He was so handsome. God, I missed him in my bed and in my life so much. We went inside and I sat behind the counter to do some work. Connie took Teddy into the office in the back to nap while she worked on payroll for us. She had been a big help, but I didn't have enough work to keep her on full-time.

The front door swung open, and I saw Hank come in with his cane. He had a scowl on his face when he looked at me.

"Hank, what brings you here this morning?" I asked trying to be pleasant.

"This has gone on long enough. You know good and well that kid isn't Clay's, he worships the ground you walk on. He hasn't so much as looked at another woman since the two of you got together. He told me he is finally scheduling a paternity test. I hope that will be enough for you. He should make you grovel before he takes you back." Hank grunted.

"That still doesn't tell me why you are here. Clay is on a tour; he won't be back for a few hours." I said calmly as he looked around the room.

"I'm looking for help at the office back at the ranch. We need someone full-time since Mrs. Barnes quit. You said she was good with numbers." He grunted out. I was stunned, the last thing I expected was for Hank to offer help.

Connie came out of the office and her eyes widened when she saw

Hank. He was a good-looking man, even though he was still doing physical therapy and used a cane to help him get around. Hank had lost his wife a few years back and had not been interested in dating. He looked at her with interest and I couldn't help but grin. This could be a good thing.

"I didn't mean to interrupt; I heard voices and was seeing if you needed any help." Connie said as she stared at Hank. He was an imposing figure. Tall, bald with tattoos, dimples with his scruff and built with muscles for days. He had always been a fun-loving flirt when Miranda was alive but when she died, she took a big part of him with her.

"I heard you were looking for permanent work. I may be able to help with that." He told her as his eyes ate her up. Connie glanced over at me and then back at Hank.

"I may have a job at the Mercantile." She told him as she glanced back at the office where Teddy napped.

"Does it offer room and board as well as allow you to keep your son with you?" he countered. Her mouth opened and closed as she registered what he had said.

"But, why?" she asked, confused. "I mean I thought you would hate me. He scratched his chin as he looked at me and back at her.

"Look, the kid is obviously a Wheeler. I just know he isn't Clay's. I have an idea about that, but I want to wait until the paternity test has been done. Meanwhile, I need a bookkeeper and my daughter Sadie can help watch Teddy. She also needs a woman around the house. If you are interested, have Jillian bring you by and we can discuss this further."

Hank turned and left. Connie took a deep breath and sat down in the nearest chair.

"Oh wow, that was unexpected." I said to her, still smiling. She looked at me and bit her lip looking back at the room where her baby slept.

"I don't think I can turn that down Jillian. If he is offering all of that it would certainly help me get on my feet and save money." She whispered. "I just don't understand why he would want me there."

"I know that Sadie has struggled since her mom passed. She is twelve years old and there are things that a girl needs a mom for that Hank would have a hard time explaining. She is a good kid, and she has been babysitting for the last two years so it would be a really great arrangement." I told her. We went back to work and the afternoon flew by. I heard the horses walking up the street in front of our door. Looking up I saw Clay staring at me for a minute before he did his spiel and helped the passengers down from the wagon.

3

Clay

Everyone was ready to go head off and find some dinner. The tour had gone well, and we had a few couples that wanted to add some of the more personalized tours to their agenda. I sent them in to see Jillian to get put on the schedule. I was pretty sure I saw my brother driving away from here as I pulled up.

"Hey Jilly, was that Hank that I just saw leaving?" I asked my wife. She nodded at me as she finished scheduling the couple talking to her. I went behind the desk to check our schedule for the rest of the afternoon. Our last tour started at two, but it wasn't as long as the first one. I leaned against the wall and waited for the tourists to leave.

Jillian waved at the couple and turned to me. She was so beautiful with her long dark hair, dark eyes and those long legs. I missed her so much.

"I called and scheduled the paternity tests for eight tomorrow morning. I want this put to rest so that you know without a doubt that I never cheated on you." I said as I walked out to greet the next round of tourists. I was still really hurt and angry that she immediately took Connie's side and didn't even consider that she was lying or that it was a case of mistaken identity. That was going to take some groveling on her part for me to forgive. I would eventually though because I still loved her and want her back more than anything else.

The tour went by quickly and I made my way back to the ranch to Hank's place. I wanted to know why he had been there. He knew I would be out running tours. I walked into the kitchen and saw Sadie doing her homework. She looked up and smiled when she saw me.

"Hey Sadie girl, how's school?" I asked as I ruffled her curly hair. She laughed and shook her head.

"It's okay Uncle Clay. How's Aunt Jillian?" Sadie asked me. She loved Jillian and was very confused as to why I was staying with them right now.

"She seems fine, where's your Papa?" I asked her, looking for Hank.

"I'm right here." Hank walked into the kitchen and grabbed some burgers out of the fridge. "I'm going to grill burgers for dinner. How about you throw us a salad together and put some fries in the oven."

"Sure, I can do that." I decided to wait until I got the fries in the oven to follow him outside. He was closing the lid on the grill as I walked up and handed him a beer.

"Thanks. So, I offered Connie a job today." Hank said as he tipped his beer and waited for me to comment. "Before you say anything, I know that her kid isn't yours. I'm pretty sure he is Blake's, but that boy is never going to settle down and she needs help."

"Did she take it?" I asked, thinking about the implications of this turn of events.

"She is going to think about it and Jillian can bring her by if she wants to discuss it further." He said as he flipped the burgers. I popped my head inside to tell Sadie to check on the fries. "Of course this means you need to make up with your wife."

"I never wanted to separate to begin with. We are doing the tests tomorrow. I want this done." I told him as I sat at the table and picked my beer back up.

"You know it will take a couple of days to get the results back on the test." Hank said, looking at me. "You should make her grovel a little for believing that you could do that."

"Yeah, I probably will for a few days. I just can't wrap my head around why she would still be so insecure." I finished my beer and tossed the can in the trash. "We were trying to have a baby ourselves."

"Well maybe you can try again soon. It's probably just hormones." Hank said as he pulled the burgers off the grill. Sadie came outside with some plates and cups. I went to get salad and fries. We liked to eat on the porch when the weather was mild. I saw the Rawlings twins putting up their horses and heading to their house.

"So, things are going good here?" I tried to change the subject. Hank put his burger down and looked around the property. I knew he missed Miranda something awful.

"Things are going great; beef prices are up, and we have some new horses coming in for Ford to train. Adding racing horses has turned out to be a lucrative investment and it's been paying off. I just need to get through physical therapy so that I can get back to work." Hank said as Sadie smiled at him. "She made me realize I was being selfish and stupid refusing to take the help I've been offered."

"Good girl, someone needed to give your papa a swift kick in the pants." I winked at my niece, and she giggled. Hank flipped me off but was smiling so I would take that.

Sadie hopped up and cleared the table then asked permission to go study in the stables. Hank nodded and we watched her walk over with her books under arms. Hank sighed and shook his head.

"She is just like her mama. She would rather be with the horses than people." Hank said with a sad smile. "I really miss her Clay. God, I miss Miranda, but I know that she is gone and I'm still here, so I need to move on. For my sake as well as Sadie's."

"It's good to hear you say that, Hank. We all loved Miranda, but she would want you to be happy." I said as I finished my beer. "I'm going to go watch some tv for a bit before bed."

I headed back to the living room and flipped on the news. The town was gearing up for a bike rally soon which would mean our tours would be in demand the second part of the week. We were booked solid for the next month, business was great.

4

I had set my alarm for six but found I just couldn't sleep. I was driving Connie and Teddy to the clinic for the paternity test this morning. I was praying for good news. Standing in the kitchen drinking a cup of coffee, I waited for Connie to finish feeding the baby so we could go. We were heading for work right after. She was seriously considering taking the job at the ranch. I didn't blame her. It would be a good fit for her.

"Ok Jillian, we're ready." Connie said as she threw the diaper bag over her shoulder and picked up little Theodore. He really was adorable. I was just really bitter about the whole situation. I rinsed out my cup and got my purse. I was hoping it wouldn't take too long to get the results back. I knew Clay and it was hard to believe he would cheat on me. I looked at the baby and frowned. If only the baby didn't look just like my husband.

The drive to the clinic didn't take long. We parked in front, and I stayed in the car. As Connie walked in, Clay walked out. He came over to my side of the car.

"I already left my blood sample. I'm going to go open up and get ready for our first tour of the day. Doctor said results should be back within twenty-four hours." I looked up at his hurt face and felt sick to my stomach. I was already about ninety-five percent sure how this was going to go, and he had every right to be angry with me. "Jilly, when the results come in, we are going to have a long talk about your lack of faith in me and what that means for our marriage."

I watched him walk away then put my head down on the steering wheel. A few minutes later Connie and Teddy came back out. I had been thinking about how Clay reacted when Connie made the accusation and how he was adamant the whole time that he had never touched her. He had not waivered one time on that. I had been feeling moody and off the last few months and I just realized I had not had a cycle in three months.

"You two wait here, I'll be right back. I need to run inside and get something." I said as I left the keys in the car for the air. I walked inside and walked up to the counter.

"Hey Jillian, it's not time for your annual or anything what's up?" Becky asked curiously.

"I need a pregnancy test. Can I go ahead and do that while I'm here?" I asked her, feeling anxious all of sudden. She smiled and called the doctor to ask if he had time to see me for a quick visit.

"Jillian, I have about twenty minutes before my next patient. Come on back." Dr. Parker said. I followed him into the room and crossed my arms. "What can I do for you?"

"I'm late and I'd like a pregnancy test." I told him firmly. He looked up at me.

"I thought you and Clay had been separated for the last month or so?" he asked gently. "I mean how late are we talking?"

"I haven't had a period in a couple of months and my emotions have been all over the place." I told him blushing.

"Ok, go leave a urine sample in the bathroom and then come back in here. It will just take about five minutes." He said as he sat down. I walked into the bathroom in the hall and did the test. After washing my hands, I went back to the exam room and sat down on the exam table. I couldn't believe I had missed not having a cycle in a few months. I was never regular but not usually this off either. A few minutes later Dr. Parker came in smiling at me.

"Well, you are going to have a baby. Lay back on the table and pull up your shirt. We are going to check for the heartbeat." Dr. Parker said calmly. He picked up a bottle of the gel and put some on my stomach and then waved the wand around to listen. I suddenly heard the sound of my baby's heartbeat and tears poured from my eyes. "I'm going to prescribe you some prenatal vitamins and I want you to schedule an appointment for a month from now. If you want to come in before that with Clay so he can hear the heartbeat, any of the nurses can do that for you."

"Yes Doc. Thank you." I told him as he wiped off my stomach and helped me up. "I need to go; Connie and the baby are in the car."

"You know very well, that's not Clay's son. Lucky for you, he is a good man and will be so thrilled about your news he will forgive you." Dr. Parker said frowning at me. They had been friends in high school. "I won't say anything, but you better tell him soon."

"I will, have a good day." I said as I left. Walking out to the car, Connie looked worried. I climbed in and pulled out headed for the office. I saw Clay heading out with the horse and carriage. He had one tour with them today and then he would take them back to the ranch for the weekend. The ranch wasn't too far from town so on the days we had the horse and buggy scheduled he would ride it to work. I started to get out of the car when Connie cleared her throat.

"Jillian, since we don't have much scheduled today could you take me to the ranch to see Mr. Wheeler about the job he offered yesterday?" Connie was fidgeting glancing back at Teddy. "I think it's best that I'm not at your house anymore. I'm sure your husband wants to come home and I'm sure you are tired of having me there."

"Connie, you have been very helpful. I just hate that you are saying you slept with my husband. I hate the very idea that he could have been unfaithful to me. The thing is I can't think of a single night that he hasn't come home. So yes, after the last tour, I'll take you to the ranch."

"Thank you. I'm so sorry that I came in and wrecked your life." Connie looked so sad that I actually felt bad for her. "I'll take Teddy to the office and finish the filing project I started the other day."

I watched her go into the back office and close the door. I put my head down on my desk for a few minutes. I needed to decide when to tell Clay about our baby. The phone started ringing and I got busy with scheduling for a while. When my tourists showed up, I saw Clay coming back with the horse and carriage. I met him outside while he watered the horses and helped people off the carriage and the new ones on. He helped me up and I felt the same zing I always felt when he touched me. I looked at his handsome face.

"Clay, can we talk tonight?" I asked him softly. He looked at me for a few minutes and gave me a curt nod. I watched him walk away and tried to collect myself to start my tour. I was off for the weekend; we had several bus tours scheduled but we had employees that ran those. I was looking forward to some relaxation and baby planning.

The tour went by quickly, I could do this in my sleep. When everyone had left, I tied up the reins to the post out front. I knew Clay would come out and drive the carriage back to the ranch. I walked into the office and saw him sitting behind the desk looking over the schedule. He looked up when I walked over and smiled automatically before frowning. I felt that in my heart. I did that to him. I had to make this right somehow.

"Jilly." He started to say something when Connie came out of the back office with Teddy and his diaper bag. When he saw them, he shut down. "I'll be by the house later."

"I'm taking Connie and Teddy to the ranch so she can interview with Hank." I told him as I collected my purse from the desk drawer. "If you want to follow me home after, we can talk privately."

With one more scowl in Connie's direction he left. I sighed and leaned against the counter. My head was spinning a little. As soon as I felt better, we headed to Rawlings Ranch.

"Wow, this place is huge?" Connie gasped as she took in the size of their spread. It was a beautiful place, and it was very big. I had spent a lot of time here riding with Clay since his brother lived here and helped run the place.

"Plenty of room for little Teddy to run around and play." I commented as we pulled up to the main house. Hank came out of the house and walked over to open the door for Connie. She plucked Teddy out of the car seat and followed him inside. I got out and was going to head to the barn when I felt myself about to faint.

5

Clay

It was like watching slow motion. One minute Jillian was heading towards the barn and the next I watched her pass out on the ground. I tried to get to her as quickly as I could. Scooping her up, I carried her into the house and took her upstairs to the room I had been sleeping in. I dampened a washcloth to run over her face. She didn't seem overheated or anything. She started waking up; her eyes softened when she saw me.

"Baby, Jilly, are you okay." I was freaking out. "Why don't I take you to the emergency room and we can get you checked out."

She grabbed my hand and shook her head. Biting her lip, she looked into my eyes and started bawling. Oh hell, I did not do well with her tears. I pulled her into my arms and held her tight. God this felt good. I missed holding her. She started to quiet down and wiped her eyes.

"Baby, what's wrong?" I lifted her chin, so she was looking at me. We had not been this close in over a month and my body was reacting to hers the way it always did. She straddled my lap and kissed me. I was surprised and didn't even think before I pulled her tighter and started to devour her mouth. She tasted so good, and it had been so long. She threaded her fingers through my hair and moaned. She reached down to undo my pants and I reached under her dress to rip off her thong. After she had me out, she rose up and impaled herself on my cock. She was so wet and all we had done was kiss. We groaned together as she rode me, it was like we were combustible together. No matter that we were fighting, the sex was till off the charts good. I leaned back a little and watched as she slipped one hand between us to rub her clit. When she started coming around my cock I came with her. I wasn't ready for the moment to be over, so I pulled her down on my chest and held her while our breathing evened out.

"I need to move so I can clean up." She said with a little giggle. I reached over for the cloth that I had been using to wipe her brow and cleaned us both, then tossed it toward the bathroom and pulled her back into my arms.

"Can we just lay here like this for a while? I miss holding you in my arms." I asked her, afraid she was going to bolt. The distance between us lately made my heart hurt. She was my best friend and my lover. I wanted her back. I ran my fingers through her long dark hair. "What did you want to talk about?"

"I need to sit up and look at you for this." She whispered nervously. I helped her to sit up and scooted against the headboard. She took my hand in hers and looked in my eyes. "First, I should tell you that I am deeply sorry for not believing you about Teddy. I think deep down I didn't believe he was yours but seeing the resemblance just kicked me in the teeth. Here we were trying to get pregnant and in walks this woman with a little clone of you. I was so jealous I couldn't think straight."

"Yeah, that hurt baby. I have not looked at another woman since you came into my life." I told her, looking her in the eyes. She nodded with a tear rolling down her face.

"I have been feeling off the last couple of months and when Connie came out of the clinic I decided to go in and talk to Dr. Parker." She looked up at me and a smile broke across her beautiful face. "We are going to have a baby, I'm eleven weeks pregnant."

"You're going to have my baby?" I whispered in awe. I reached over and put my hand on her stomach. "We made a baby together Jilly bean."

I looked at my wife and decided I was moving home tonight. I wasn't asking. I grabbed her face and pulled her in for a kiss.

"Connie is supposed to move here with Teddy. Will you come home?" She looked up at me and I could see the apprehension on her face that I would refuse. Part of me thought she deserved to be nervous, but she was pregnant, and her hormones must be all over the place. I couldn't bring myself to hurt her.

"Yes baby, I'll come home. Let me throw my clothes in my duffle." I got off the bed and tossed my clothes in my duffle bag. We stripped the bed and remade it with fresh sheets. I figured he would probably put Connie in this room. After gathering my things, we went downstairs together. Teddy was playing in front of the television with Sadie while Connie and Hank talked at the table.

Connie got up and smiled at Hank, she was blushing. This could be interesting. She walked over to where Sadie and Teddy were while we talked to Hank for a minute.

"So did you finally pull your head out of your ass and realize this man is all yours?" Hank teased Jilly. She punched him in the arm. "It's about time, I was getting tired of seeing his ugly mug every morning."

"Whatever, you know I got all the good looks and the hair." I threw back at him. He started to say something when we heard Connie gasp. We all turned to see her holding a picture in her hand. Her face was pale as a ghost, and she kept looking from the picture to me and back. I walked over and took the picture from her hand. Looking down it was a photo of Blake and myself after he won his first rodeo. I looked back at her and raised my eyebrow.

"You thought I was Blake." I made it a statement not a question. "Didn't you know his name?"

"I was a little drunk and I remembered his name was Wheeler and he said he worked at Wheeler Tours. When I walked in that day, I assumed it was you and when she called you Clay…. I mean it sounds similar and the two of you could pass for twins." She looked like she might pass out. Hank took her arm and urged her to sit down on the couch. "I'm so sorry and so embarrassed."

"I'm not going to say it's okay, because it's not. I will say that I can see how you would have mixed us up. Blake was home recuperating from a rodeo injury and worked for us to supplement his income. So, he didn't lie to you, but he is also not the settling down kind. I do think you should tell him. Even if the two of you don't want to be together, he deserves to know he is a father." I pulled Jilly into my lap as we talked. Sadie had taken Teddy to the kitchen to fix him a bottle.

"Oh God Jillian, I'm so sorry. You must hate me." she said with tears rolling down her face. Hank rubbed her back gently. She was clearly mortified. "I had just found my fiancé` in bed with another woman and decided to come back home to start over. I was drinking and all in my feelings when I met him. He was charming and sexy. I needed to feel desired, and he did that. I woke up the next morning and he was gone. I decided that it was just a night of fun and went on with my life but then a few weeks later I started to get sick from the smell of coffee and other foods. I found out I was pregnant and freaked. I wasn't going to say anything because it has just been a one-night stand, but I lost my job and had to move out of my apartment."

"Okay, take a deep breath. You have a home and a job now. You also have a sitter to help out. Let's see if Sadie minds watching Teddy while we follow Clay and Jillian home to get your things?" Hank said as he headed to the kitchen to find his daughter.

"Thank you for taking me in and giving me a job. I knew it was temporary and it was incredibly generous of you, especially given the circumstances." Connie said as Hank came back into the room with his keys.

"Okay, it's getting late, let's get this show on the road." Hank said as we all headed out the door.

I followed Jillian home and when we pulled up to our house, I was never so glad to be home. I walked over to her car to open her door and she smiled as I took her hand. We went inside and I tossed my bag in the corner. Hank pulled up with Connie a few minutes later and they packed up her stuff quickly.

"I'll call Blake tomorrow and tell him that he needs to come home for a visit." Hank said as he led Connie outside. "We need to get that done."

"Sounds good, we will talk tomorrow." I said as I locked up behind them. I turned to see my wife standing behind me. "Have you eaten anything today?"

She shook her head. I picked up the phone and called in a pizza order then went to find her something to snack on while we waited for it.

"You are growing my baby inside you. You have to eat." I told her as I put a plate of cheese, crackers and some carrots with ranch in front of her. "This will help settle your tummy while we wait for the pizza to arrive."

6

Jillian

I was an idiot. Clay Wheeler was a good man, and I didn't deserve him. He has been a wonderful husband since we got married and I have to believe the crazy pregnancy hormones are to blame for my stupid insecurities. I would have to figure out how to make it up to him. I know he is still hurt and I'm sure he is angry at me, but he is still taking care of me. He is still putting my health first. I reached over and grabbed his hand, and he looked up at me. I tugged on it to bring him closer and then wrapped my arms around his waist. He put his arms around me, and I started sobbing.

"Baby, what's wrong, are you hurting anywhere?" Clay asked, worried. I shook my head, but I couldn't stop. It was like a dam broke and all my emotions were spilling out.

"I'm so, so sorry. I know you didn't cheat on me, and I know you wouldn't do that." I said between sobs as I prayed, he could forgive me. "Please forgive me, I love you so much and I don't want to lose you."

Clay led me to the couch and sat down pulling me into his lap. He rubbed my back until I calmed down. He started to say something when the doorbell rang. Gently he put me on the couch and went to get the door. After paying for the pizza, he locked the door and took it to the kitchen. Fixing two plates he took them back to the living room and placed them on the coffee table.

"Jilly, you need to eat and then we can finish this conversation. Just know that I'm not going anywhere." Clay picked up a slice and held it out to me. "Eat."

I really didn't want to, but I was hungry, and I knew I needed to eat for the baby. I started to eat and before I realized it, I had finished three slices. I picked up our plates and put them in the sink. I knew Clay would never abandon our child; I just didn't know if he still wanted me. I felt wetness on my hands and realized I was crying again. *Damn hormones!!* I wiped my eyes and turned around to see my husband standing behind me with his arms open. I threw myself against his solid chest. He murmured nonsense in my ear until I calmed down. Taking my hand, he led me to our bedroom and started to undress me.

"I thought we were going to talk?" I said staring at him as he removed his shirt. I had always loved his chest. He took care of his body and worked hard.

"We are, but I thought we could take a bubble bath. Maybe not as hot as you usually like it but that way we can talk and relax." He knelt down and helped me remove the rest of my clothes. I watched as he removed his jeans and underwear then walked into our bathroom to start the bath. I followed behind him and sat on the lid of the toilet to wait for the bath to be ready. I had missed our bathtime conversations. He took my hand and helped me into the tub and then climbed in behind me. I leaned back against him and sighed.

"This is so nice." I murmured to myself. Clay picked up a washcloth and poured some body wash on it then started to wash my back. I leaned my head forward for him. As he washed my body he started talking.

"Jilly, I'm not going to lie to you. We don't do that. You hurt me badly believing that I could be capable of sleeping with another woman. I have loved you since I first laid eyes on you, and it has just grown more every day. The day we said our vows was the happiest of my life. I can't imagine not growing old with you. I wouldn't want anyone but you to have my babies and if that had meant that we had to adopt then that's what we would have done. I'm not the type to hold a grudge and I understand now that you were a bit emotional and hormonal. We are going to chalk this up to pregnancy hormones and move forward." He said as he kissed my neck and then washed my front. He slid the cloth down my belly and cleaned me then suddenly his fingers were on my clit, and he was rubbing circles while kissing my neck. His other arm was wrapped around my waist holding me against his rock-hard erection. Suddenly I was coming all over his hand. He held me as I came down and then got out of the tub to get a towel for me. We dried off and crawled into bed. I curled into his side.

"I'm very sorry and I will never doubt you again. I love you so much and I just made us miserable over the past couple of months. I can't believe she really thought you were Blake." I looked at my husband and felt my body try to stir again but I was just too tired. "I want you again but I'm so tired."

"It's okay baby, we have the rest of our lives. You need rest. Just go to sleep and let me hold you." He pulled me closer and kissed the top of my head as I started to fall asleep.

The next morning, we woke up to the sound of our phone ringing. I reached over to answer it.

"Jillian, it's Dr. Parker. I have the results." The doctor said and I looked at Clay watching me.

"That's alright, I don't need them. I know it's not Clay's baby." I watched my husband's face light up as I said it.

"You're right but he is related. Let me talk to Clay." I handed him the phone and went to the bathroom. I didn't need to be there for this conversation because we were sure that Blake was the father. When I came back in, I heard the tail end of their conversation.

"Yeah, I know, we figured it was Blake last night after Connie saw a picture of us together and about passed out on the spot. Hank is going to track him down and tell him he needs to come home for a family emergency," he listened a few more minutes and then hung up. "Come back to bed baby."

I started back to bed when my stomach growled. He laughed and got up. I grinned sheepishly.

"Well, I guess we are going to feed you first." He slipped on a pair of grey sweats and headed to the kitchen. I threw on the T-shirt he wore yesterday and some panties. Heading to the kitchen I went to make a pot of coffee and he frowned. "You're not supposed to drink coffee while you're pregnant."

"I'm allowed a cup a day and if you don't move, I'll stab you." I growled. He chuckled, held his hands up and backed away from the coffee maker. It was a joke with us about not getting between me and my coffee. The fact that I had to cut down to one cup was going to be a challenge. "I need my cup. I only get the one."

He leaned over and kissed me then pulled out my creamer and put it on the counter for me. I smiled and poured some in my cup and then fixed my coffee. "Sit down and drink your anti-murder juice while I fix us some pancakes."

I laughed at him and sipped on my coffee while checking our business emails. We had a few requests for tours and a message from Blake saying he would be in town next week. I put my phone down as Clay put a plate of pancakes on the table along with some syrup. We had some microwavable sausage links and as soon as I smelled them, I ran to the bathroom to be sick. I heard the door open and then close again before Clay came into the bathroom and wet a washcloth to press on my neck then he wiped my face. I sat back on my butt and groaned.

"Well, there is your morning sickness. Let's try some pancakes, I got rid of the other." He said as he helped me up. "We will pick up some crackers and ginger ale at the store."

Clay wrapped his arm around my waist, and we went back to the table. I decided to forget the syrup and stick to a plain pancake to start. After a few bites my stomach started to settle. He got my prenatal vitamins out of my purse and put them beside me to take. I gave him a little smile as I took it and tried to finish the one pancake.

"I think I may lay back down for just a bit." I told him as I got up and put my dishes in the sink. "I feel exhausted."

"You have been under a lot of stress and also didn't know you were pregnant. It's probably a good idea to nap when you can." He walked me back into our bedroom and tucked me in. "I'll run to the store and get supplies as well as your crackers and ginger ale. Maybe it will help to have some before you get out of bed in the morning. We also should stick to some bland foods to start. We will pay attention to anything that makes you feel nauseous, so we don't fix it again until after the baby comes."

I started to nod off again, I guess I was more tired than I realized. He kissed my head and turned off the light.

7

Clay

This week had been crazy so far. Thankfully we had good staff in place to help out at work and we had the weekends off. I drove into town to get some groceries for the house. My brain was going a mile a minute. Jilly and I went from barely speaking to back together expecting a baby. I was over the moon. Walking up and down the aisles I made sure to get everything on the list we had made up and also to get a few boxes of crackers as well as a case of ginger ale. I turned the corner and almost ran into Ford Rawlings.

"Hey Clay, how are things going with the missus?" Ford asked as he filled his cart with drinks. "I heard she passed out yesterday at the ranch. Is she okay?"

"She's fine. She was just exhausted and had not eaten." Ford smirked at me. "What's that look for?"

"My sister was like that when she was pregnant with Sadie, be sure she eats several smaller meals throughout the day. It helps keep up her energy and controls the nausea." Ford laughed at me as I looked shocked. "I won't say anything. It's your news to tell. Congratulations."

"Thanks man, I'll see you around soon. Tell Jake I said 'hello'." I went to the frozen section and picked up a pint of vanilla bean for Jillian. She liked chocolate chip ice cream, but I wanted something blander for now. I had picked up some fruit and veggies to cook along with some fish and chicken. I needed to make sure she was eating good. After checking out I stopped by to see Mrs. Mae and let her know we had made up.

Walking in the diner I saw Mae behind the counter, and she smiled and waved me over.

"Hey boy, you must have made up with Jillian. I haven't seen that smile on your face in months." She grinned at me and gave me a hug.

"Yes ma'am, we cleared the air and she apologized. We are back together." I stepped back and smiled at the older woman. She had been here for years and was a gem. Everyone loved her. "Can I get a couple of bowls of your chicken noodle soup to go and some of that fresh bread?"

"You bet; I'll have it right out." She bustled back behind the counter to the kitchen to get my order together. I looked around at the tourists and some of the regulars. I knew the difference from the scowls on the faces of the regulars. We needed to make sure everyone knew that I was innocent, and we were back together. I'm thinking a date night soon would be good. Mae came out with my bag and handed it over, I put a twenty on the counter because I knew she would try to not charge me.

"Thank you, we will be in soon for breakfast." I told her as I left and headed home.

I walked into the house and set the soup on the counter and went to bring in the rest of the groceries. After getting them put up, I checked on Jillian. She was curled up in a ball in our bed covered up. I walked over and kissed her on the cheek. She stretched and smiled at me. I missed seeing that smile directed at me.

"Time to get up and eat lunch baby. I want you to sit up slowly." I told her as I gently helped her up. "Now let's get you up. I got us some of Mrs. Mae's homemade chicken noodle soup and her baked bread."

"Yum, that sounds good. I hope I can keep it down." She said licking her lips.

"You can start nibbling on the bread first and then slowly eat the soup." I suggested as I pulled out the chair for her. I poured our soup into two bowls and sliced some of the bread on a plate. I also fixed her some ginger ale. We ate in silence for a few minutes wanting to see if she would be able to keep her food down. So far so good. "I grabbed a notebook so we could write down the foods that make you queasy."

I had placed it on the kitchen counter. I had already put sausage on the list. She ate about half the bowl and a slice of the bread and sat back in her seat.

"I'm full, that was good. I'll try to eat more later. Maybe we could make some French toast with the bread in the morning." Jillian suggested as she rubbed her tummy. She wouldn't be showing for at least another couple of months, but we knew the baby was there. My girl was glowing with excitement.

"Why don't we cuddle on the couch and watch a movie?" I suggested as I led her over and sat down. She sat beside me and curled into my body pulling a blanket from the back of the couch over us. I wrapped my arm around her and turned on the tv to find something for us to watch. We had not spent any quality time together in over a month and I missed my wife. We were home bodies, usually hanging around the house on our days off. I just wanted her all to myself.

"I know this sounds corny, but can we watch Easter Parade?" Jilly asked me as she bat her eyes at me. We had missed spending Easter together this year due to our fight and watching that movie was a tradition. I smiled and turned it on for her.

"Sure, we can baby." I cuddled her close as we watched the old movie.

8

Jillian

I felt so comfy and happy. It has been so long since we had been together like this, and I had really missed it. I was feeling better but being this close to my man was getting me hot. Clay had this ruggedly handsome face with these full pouty kissable lips, his chest was all cut from hard work and working out when he can. He was such a beautiful man I was always turned on when we were together. That's one of the things that made our marriage so special. Every time we made love it was exciting. I reached under the blanket and slid my panties off and dropped them on his chest. I heard a swift intake of breath before he growled and pulled me up to kiss me. I straddled his lap and reached to undo his pants and he lifted us up a little so he could pull himself out of them.

"Hold on to the back of the couch." Clay said as he slid down between my legs bringing his mouth to my center. Grabbing my ass, he held on as he dipped his tongue inside me, licking up and down my slit ensuring I was wet and ready for him. He continued his ministrations, alternately working my clit as well. I was so close when he thrust two fingers inside of me and pumped them while sucking my clit hard. I splintered all over him. He grabbed my waist raising up and speared me with his cock. We both let out a moan at the sensation of him filling me up. Giving me a second to adjust to his size, he then helped me ride him to completion. When we were both able to breathe again, I laid my head on his shoulder.

"Baby, I need to get something to clean us up." He said as he ran his fingers through my hair. I just shook my head. I felt whole again, and I didn't want him to move yet.

"I want to feel you inside me a little longer." I said clinging to him. He rubbed my back and kissed my forehead. "I love you so much Clayton Wheeler."

"I love you too Jillian Wheeler." He said as he picked me up while still inside me. I felt myself clinch and he moaned. "You will make me drop you. We are going to take a shower and then find some dinner. Hang on." He proceeded to carry me all the way to our bathroom and then gently lifted me off of him and put me down while he reached in and started the shower. "I can't wait to see your belly grow round with our child."

"It won't turn you off to see me get fat?" I asked him, a little worried.

"You will not be fat you will be very pregnant. I will love you no matter what and I think you will be the sexiest pregnant lady I have ever seen." He said firmly, then smacked me on the butt and put me in the shower. I giggled and started to wash my hair while he washed his. We took turns soaping each other and that ended in a couple more orgasms. There was nothing like showering with my husband. When we finished, we dried off and I braided my hair. We went back to the kitchen to fix a snack.

The phone rang and Clay picked it up. He glanced up at me and smirked then said, "Sure we will be there." And hung up the phone.

"What was that about?" I asked him, wondering what put that look on his face.

"Blake will be home Wednesday. Hank invited us over for a family dinner." Clay chuckled as he said it. "Boy is he in for the surprise of his life." I had to laugh too because finally Blake's lifestyle had caught up to him. It would be interesting to see his reaction to Teddy. We were going to have some great laughs, hopefully he wouldn't react too badly.

"Sounds good. What do you want to eat?" I asked him. "I was

thinking of just finishing my soup and having another slice of that bread. I can cook something for you."

"Don't worry about it, baby. I have some leftover pizza in the fridge I can heat up." He tells me as he pulls out a small pot to heat my soup and a plate to heat his pizza in the microwave. I love nights like this. After we get settled at the table, he looks at me and smiles.

"What are you thinking?" I ask as he looks around the room. We have a three-bedroom house, one of the bedrooms is a guest room and the other has nothing in it. We also have a basement that he uses for a gym.

"We need to decide what kind of furniture we want for the nursery." he said with a smile as he pulled his phone out of his pocket. "I have the baby furniture site pulled up."

He hands me his phone to look at our options. I tear up looking at the baby furniture because I have looked so many times imagining what it would be like to have Clay's baby.

"Jilly, are you okay?" Clay picked me up and put me in his lap. I laid my head on his shoulder.

"Yes, just emotional. I was starting to think I would never get to do this. I know exactly what I want already." I pulled my phone over to me and opened up the link to show him the saved cart I had taken pictures of. It shows a hand carved natural wood look crib that converts to a daybed. It can be raised and lowered with age. There is a matching changing table and rocking chair.

"I love it, order it." He said as he squeezed me to him. "We can wait to shop for the bedding when we know what we are having."

"I thought so too." I smiled at him through the tears and put my hands on either side of his face to kiss him. He kissed me back and then kissed down my neck and across my collarbone. I climbed out of his lap and started walking to our room, dropping clothes on the floor as I went. Suddenly I heard him coming up behind me, he picked me up and put me on the bed then crawled between my legs to see how many times he could make me come. He kissed his way up my thighs toward my center, blowing on my mound before kissing my other thigh. My legs were trembling as he worked his way to my clit and started flicking his tongue over it. He knows my body so well. Feeling him use his tongue while he holds me down just does it for me. He pulls me closer to his mouth and devours my pussy, licking and sucking while dipping his tongue into my soaking wet channel. A few more flicks over my clit send me soaring. He gently peppers kisses over my stomach as I come down some before thrusting inside me. His hands are on either side of my shoulders as he looks me in the eye.

"I love you so much Mrs. Wheeler." He whispers softly to me before kissing my lips. Then he starts moving faster until we both go over the edge.

After cleaning us both up, he crawls back in bed beside me. He pulls me over to him and spoons me. I missed sleeping with him. I always feel so warm and safe in his arms. This is how we spend the rest of our weekend. I love having him all to myself.

9

Clay

The last few days have been wonderful. I have my wife back and I'm home. Work has been going well. We stay booked due to the heavy tourism that goes through the town. Blake is supposed to be home tonight, and we are going over to the ranch to have dinner with them. I can't wait to see his face when he finds out he is a father. I pulled up to the front of our business and got the horses settled. Walking in I saw Jilly talking to a young couple about a tour, so I went to check our schedule. We were almost done for the day, so I was going to take the horses to the ranch and pick up my truck. Jillian would meet me at home, and we would ride back out to the ranch together. I had not talked to Hank the last couple of days, since Jillian and I had been in a honeymoon phase. I wondered how he and Connie were getting along. I guess we would say this evening.

Jilly handed the couple some brochures and waited as they left. I leaned down and kissed her neck making her giggle. She smiled up and me and pulled me down for a kiss. This is one of the things I missed. We enjoy working together, seeing each other off and on throughout the day. It sucked when we were separated, and she wouldn't speak to me.

"Have you eaten lunch today baby?" I asked her, knowing she forgot to eat regularly. She blushed and held up half a sandwich and some carrot sticks, she had been working on.

"I ate half of this earlier and I was going to finish it now. I just can't eat a lot at one time." She said as she munched on a carrot. I sat down beside her. I didn't have any more carriage tours today and she wasn't doing any. We were letting the tour guides we hired take over mostly.

"You're done for the day, right?" she nodded as she took a bite of her sandwich. "It's only three-thirty, why don't you head home and take a nap before we head over for dinner."

"Sounds like a great idea. I'll finish eating this on my way home." Jilly said as she finished her sandwich and got up to get her purse. I turned out the lights and locked the shop before walking her to the car.

"I'll be home shortly, just going to drop off the horses and the carriage." I told her as I closed the door. She nodded and drove away.

Riding back to the ranch I let my mind wander a bit thinking about the baby. If it would be a boy or a girl and what they would look like. As I pulled into the barn area I got down and unhooked the horses. Taking them inside to feed them and brush them down. I heard murmuring and went to find Sadie in an empty stall with Teddy in her lap and some kittens playing.

"Hey kiddo, I see you have some kittens." I said as she looked up smiling at me. Teddy was trying to pet one as it swiped at him.

"Yeah, apparently Ginger had her kittens, and they are just starting to crawl around more. I moved them all in here. Dad and Connie were talking so I brought the little guy to see the kitties." Sadie said as she bounced Teddy on her knee. "I need to take him back inside for his nap before dinner."

I reached down and picked up the baby while she stood up and then handed him back to her.

"I'll see you later at dinner." I said as she put the baby on her hip and started back to the house.

"Later Uncle Clay." She hollered back at me. Hank was in so much trouble with her. She was all legs right now, but she looked a lot like her mother with a hint of her father and they were both good looking people. Shaking my head, I climbed in my truck to head home to freshen up for dinner and to get my girl.

Walking into our house quietly, I found her on the couch covered up with a blanket. There was a catalog on the coffee table with baby stuff in it. I sat on the end and flipped through it for a minute. I got up and went to run through the shower before waking her up to go. She needed her rest. Tonight was going to be interesting.

I got dressed and headed in the living room to wake up my girl. I turned to find her sitting cross legged on the couch flipping through a magazine. She looked up and smiled at me as I walked over to kiss her.

"Hey baby. Did you have a good nap?" I sat down beside her and pulled her into my lap. She laid her head against my chest and snuggled.

"Yes, it was nice. I didn't realize how tired I was. I haven't been sleeping since you've been at Hank's." she rubbed her head against my shoulder. "I know it was my fault, but I still missed you."

"I know baby, I missed you too. I'm glad this nonsense is behind us." I playfully nipped at her neck just to hear her giggle. "We need to head over to the ranch. It's going to be quite interesting."

Jillian climbed out of my lap and slipped her shoes back on. We headed over to Hawk's place. Pulling up I didn't see Blake's truck; he must not be here yet. Going inside we spot Connie sitting on the couch playing with Teddy and Sadie close by. Hawk is in the kitchen working on dinner. I left Jillian in the living room with the girls and the baby while I went to talk to my brother.

"Hey bro, when is Blake supposed to be here?" I asked as I cracked a beer. "You didn't give him any idea what it was about did you?"

"Hell no, and miss the look on his face when he sees his son?" Hawk barked out a laugh at that thought. We always pranked each other when we were kids but this time the joke was on Blake. "Dinner is ready, just leaving it in the oven to warm."

We walked back in the living room in time to see Blake walk in the front door. He was all smiles until he noticed Connie stand up with little Theodore on her hip. He paled and looked around the room.

"Connie, what are you doing here?" he asked as he walked over and gave Jillian a hug. "How come you didn't tell me you and Clay had a baby?"

Blake looked a little hurt as he walked over to take the baby from Connie. She just looked at him and held on to Teddy.

"Well, can I hold my baby cousin or not?" he asked looking irritated. Connie narrowed her eyes at him.

"No, but you can hold your son." She said as he took the baby from her. To his credit, he sat down with the baby in his lap.

"What do you mean my son?" Blake asked as he stared at the baby who was patting his face and smiling. "That's not possible, I haven't been here in just over a year."

"That's right and Theodore is six months old." Connie said as she crossed her arms over her chest. "I was on birth control, but it didn't work."

Hank walked up behind her and put his arm across her shoulder in support.

"Why don't we watch the baby and you two can step outside and talk." Jillian suggested as she took the baby from Blake as he watched Connie and Hawk.

10

Jillian

We watched Blake walk outside behind Connie. Hank stood at the window with his arms crossed. I watched him scratch his beard and grunt then head back into the kitchen. Sadie frowned and went to her room. I looked at Clay and raised my eyebrows at him.

"Why don't I take him, and you go check on Sadie?" Clay suggested. He sat down on the floor, and I put Teddy down beside him along with a couple of his toys. My husband looked so sweet playing with the baby. I couldn't wait to see him play with our baby. I smiled and went to find Sadie in her room lying on her bed. I went and sat down beside her.

"Hey Sadie bug, what's wrong?" I asked gently as I ran my hand down her hair. She shook her head. "You know you can talk to me about anything."

Sadie sat up and crossed her legs. She looked down and pulled her stuffed horse into her arms.

"I don't want Blake to take Connie and little Teddy away with him." She whispered as a tear ran down her face. "I know they have only been here a week, but I really like her. She is nice, easy to talk to and she makes my dad smile."

"You know, just because Blake is Teddy's father doesn't mean they are going to leave with him. Things happen and there are all kinds of families. Connie works for your dad, and she wants a home for her son. Blake isn't really in a good position to provide that right now. Let's not get ahead of ourselves, okay?"

"Ok, thanks Aunt Jilly." She leaned over and hugged me. I stood up and offered my hand to her. We walked back into the living room to find Blake and Connie back inside. Connie was setting the table and very quiet. Blake was sitting in the floor with Teddy absolutely enthralled with his son. I walked over to Connie and gave her a hug.

"Hey so how did he take it?" I asked her quietly. "He looks like he is bonding with him."

Connie looked over at her son playing with his father and then looked at Hank who was bringing the food to the table.

"He wants to be a part of his life, but he isn't ready to settle down. I told him that I'm staying here with Hank and Sadie. I won't cart my son around the country to rodeo's. If he wants to spend time with him, he can visit him here." she said firmly. "I have a good job and a great living situation here. I'm not screwing that up. I like it here."

"Good, because they need you. Blake isn't a bad guy, but he has always had a wandering nature. Hank is as steady as they come, and Sadie adores you both." I told her with a smile.

"Dinner's ready." Hank announced as he went and picked up Teddy and put him in his highchair. Slipping a bib over his head he rubbed the boy on his head and Teddy smiled up at him. I saw Blake watching the interaction. He didn't look mad, just thoughtful. Sadie came in and sat down next to Teddy's highchair. Hank was at one end and Clay at the other Connie sat down beside Hank, so I sat beside her leaving the seat next to Sadie for Blake. Dinner was fairly quiet, except for Blake talking about the last couple of rodeos and how he placed in the bull riding events. Teddy wasn't on solid foods yet, so he had an animal cracker to gum while we had dinner. He had been fed a bottle earlier but was a little wired.

"Papa, I'm done can I go out to see Buttercup before I shower and get ready for bed?" Sadie asked. I could tell she wanted to get away from the tension at the table.

"Sure pumpkin, that's fine." Hank said as she kissed her dad on the cheek and took her plate to the kitchen. I figured we should probably leave soon after dinner. We heard the door close, and Hank looked at Connie. "So, are you staying?"

"Yes, we are staying. I assume I still have a job?" Connie said quietly. We were done eating, so Connie picked up her plate and Hanks and I grabbed Clay's, Blakes and my own to take to help wash dishes. I looked at Clay and then over to Blake. He nodded at me. I walked into the kitchen to see Connie standing at the sink with her shoulders shaking.

"Why don't you let me do these and you go get Teddy bathed, fed and ready for bed. It will give you some time to collect your thoughts." I suggested. She looked up at me with tears in her eyes and hugged me.

"Thank you, it's just been a highly emotional day. I'm not in love with Blake or anything, I just want Teddy to have a father in his life." Connie explained as she wiped her eyes and took a deep breath. "I'm pretty sure Blake is planning to leave in a week."

"Ya'll will figure out an arrangement, but Connie, you have a home here." I told her as I smiled at her. "We are your family now."

"Thank you." She said as she went to get Teddy.

11

Clay

"So how long has she been here and why haven't I heard about this sooner?" Blake asked us, looking pissed. She must not have told him about mistaking me for him.

"Well seems that we still favor enough that she got us mixed up. You told her where you were working, and she came to find you for help and saw me. She assumed I was the one she had been with and proceeded to get me kicked out of my house for over a month." I told him with a scowl on my face. I was still not happy about that. Especially since neither myself nor Jillian slept much during that time.

"Damn man, Jillian believed her?" Blake was shocked and glanced toward the kitchen. "You worship the ground the woman walks on."

"Hello, I mean look at him. Jillian took one look at Teddy and then back at me and started yelling." I told him in disgust. "Thankfully she admitted before the paternity tests came back that she knew he couldn't be mine and that she was sorry. When Connie saw the picture on the mantle of us together, she about died."

Blake looked up as Connie came into the room and went to pick up

Teddy. She didn't say anything, she just plucked him out of his highchair and left the room. He shook his head and ran his hand down his face.

"I'm sorry, it really was just a one-night stand. There were no numbers exchanged or promised made. Connie and I are going to have to decide how to handle this because she made it clear she isn't leaving, and we aren't looking to have a relationship other than as coparents." Blake looked up as Jillian came into the room.

"Baby, should we share our news with them?" I asked Jillian as she sat beside me. She smiled and nodded. "So, as it happens, we are going to have one of our own in about six months."

Hank looked at us and a huge smile broke across his face. He got up and pulled Jillian into a huge hug. He knew we had been trying for years to have a baby.

"Hey now, that's my woman. Hands off, get your own." I teased as he pulled me into a huge bear hug. "Guess Sadie is going to have her choice of babysitting duties."

"I'm so happy for the two of you. You will be amazing parents. Both of you have been great with Sadie." Hank looked at Blake and his smile dimmed a bit. "Blake, how long are you planning on hanging around."

"I'm not really ready to settle down and be a father. I'd like to be a part of his life, but I can't be a daily part." Blake glanced to where Connie had taken Teddy to get him ready for bed. "We are going to see how this plays out. If she doesn't want him to know I'm his father that's fine. I'll just be a cool uncle. I will send money and try to help where I can."

Hank bristled at that. I cringed because I could feel the anger coming from my brother. He was a bit traditional. You take care of your responsibilities. The thing is, he seems smitten with Connie, so I know he doesn't want her to end up with Blake.

"I think Jillian and I are going to head home." I said as I stood up and waited for my wife. She stood up and leaned over to kiss Hank on the cheek and whispered something to him. He visibly relaxed and smiled at her.

"I'm going to go let Connie know we are leaving." Jillian said as she walked to the back of the house. Blake got up and walked out. I looked over at my brother. He looked thoughtful.

"You really like her don't you." I stated. Hank got up and jerked his head toward the back porch. I got up and followed him out. He sat on the railing.

"She picked up on the system the first day, we work well together. Sadie adores her and the kid. I really don't want to have to hire someone else." Hank said staring at the sliding doors. I glanced over and saw Connie talking to Jillian.

"You know that's not what I meant. I know you haven't known her long, but I can feel the tension when the two of you are in the same room. She watches you and you watch her as well. You also seem fond of the baby. Sadie adores both of them." I said as I watched him stare at her. "Hank, you know better than most of us that time is not guaranteed. If you think you have feelings for her and that there is a chance they might be reciprocated, you need to act on it. Start courting her and let her know that she has options."

"I haven't been on a date since Miranda. I never thought I would be able to feel like this about another woman. What if she wants nothing to do with me." Hank looked at his leg. I knew he was a bit insecure about the way walked and the fact that he was still recovering from his accident.

"Take your stubborn ass to rehab. You are a strong man in your prime. She stares at you like she wants to take a bite out of you. You are a great father, provider and when you want to be you are a fun guy to be around. Give the woman a chance to see the brother I grew up with." I told him as Jillian popped her head out the door.

"You ready baby?" Jillian asked as she glanced at Hank and back at me. "Blake went out to the bunkhouse."

"Yep, talk to you guys tomorrow." I said as I put my arm around my wife, and we left. Driving home we were pretty quiet. I was very excited about the baby, and I know Clay is as well. I must have fallen asleep on the way because suddenly I'm being carried into our house. Hey, lays me down on our bed pulls off my shoes and socks, then removes the rest of my clothing.

"Stay here, I'm just going to lock up the house." Clay headed back to the other room, and I closed my eyes.

12

Clay

I locked up the house and then went to strip down for bed. Jillian had curled up on her side with her fist tucked under her chin looking so peaceful I didn't want to wake her. I turned out the light and crawled into bed then pulled her against me. She turned into me and scooted as close as she could.

"I missed sleeping with you. You're always so warm." She mumbled against my chest. I kissed her head and she looked up at me to kiss me.

"I thought you were tired baby." I said as she started kissing my neck and my chest. She straddled my body, and I threw back the covers. Jilly bit her lip and rubbed her pussy against my hardening cock. "My baby need something?"

"I need you inside me. I want you so bad Clay." She said as she leaned down to offer me a breast. I took it in my mouth and suckled her. Sliding my hands up her back into her hair I switched to the other breast and gave it the same attention. She must have been thinking about this before I came in because she was soaked. She raised up and lined my cock up with her entrance and then sank down on me. We both groaned at how good it felt. I used her hips to help guide her up and down on my cock. Her beautiful body over me and all that long dark hair grazing my chest when she leaned down. I flipped her over and then crawled down her body to feast on her needy cunt. I licked her from back to front and sucked her clit into my mouth then backed off and flicked it with me tongue until her legs were trembling. I slid a finger inside her to play with her g-spot and then gently bit her clit. She came screaming all over my face. I flipped her on her stomach and then slammed home. She felt so damn tight while she was still having spasms. I held still to try and get control. I wanted her to come again before I finished. Put my hand around her neck and pulled her up against my body and pounded the hell out of my girl. She liked it hard and fast. I was so onboard for that. I knew when she was further along in her pregnancy, I'd probably have to go easy for a while.

"Reach down and play with your clit baby, I want to feel you come with me." I told her as I held her around the waist. She immediately started to play with her clit, rubbing circles around it fast. I felt her start to tighten up and knew she was close. I bit her neck, and she came hard. A couple more thrusts and I joined her. We were both breathing hard, and I gently eased her down onto her stomach and pulled out of her. Grabbing a few tissues, I cleaned us up a bit and then went to start the shower. I came back and picked her up, taking her to the bathroom. We washed and dried off then went to crawl into our bed. Tucking us both back in, I spooned her.

"I love you Mrs. Wheeler. Don't you ever think about leaving me again." I told her firmly. I couldn't imagine not having her in my life. She was my everything and now we had a baby on the way. I couldn't wait to be a father. I just hoped that Hank could find his happily ever after too.

The End.

ABOUT THE AUTHOR

I currently reside in Memphis, Tennessee. While I am from the area I grew up in Germany and Alabama as an Army Brat. I have been blessed to experience many different cultures. I have always had a love of reading and I liked writing stories when I was young. I have three daughters, one that grew under my heart and two that grew in it. I have been blessed with many grandchildren. I also enjoy quilting, scrapbooking, singing and hanging with friends. I have a wonderfully supportive family. My husband is my rock.

f

DREAMING OF DAHLIAS

LACY CHANTELL

1

A WHITE WEDDING OVERLOOKING A RANCH COVERED IN FRESH snow sounds like the most beautiful scene Dahlia could ever imagine. Until she's trudging through snow taller than her boots, carrying the floral centerpieces, garland, candelabras, candles, and everything else she needs for this wedding into the mansion of a cabin on Hayne's Ranch.

She drops the last box a little harder than intended, and cringes.

"Rough morning?" a man asks with a southern drawl.

Dahlia blows her wild curls out of her face and looks up from where she stands with her hands braced on her knees. Her cheeks are flush and sweat trickles down her spine from the strain of getting everything inside from her SUV to make the bride's day everything they could dream of. "You've helped with every wedding I've ever set up here until today. Of all days. Seriously?" she scoffs and sheds out of her puffy jacket. Aggressively, she pulls her hair tie out of her messy bun to grab the escaped pieces and put it up again.

"It's snowing," Hunter says casually as a smirk tilts the left side of his lip. His honey-colored eyes sparkle with amusement, which only fuels the fire in her veins.

"Really? I hadn't noticed." Dahlia waves her hands at her soaked pants and boots. "You might want to shovel a path for your guests. I'm just saying."

Hunter chuckles and she just noticed the snow shovel in his hand as he walks to the door. She arches a brow at the peculiar man. Hunter bought this ranch one year and a half ago, and after six months, he made it one of the hottest locations for weddings. He has this beautiful cabin with floor to ceiling windows overlooking the woods. Freshly polished hardwood floors that glow with life. There's a curved staircase that leads to the second-floor photographers swoon over to get pictures of the bride with her long flowing train. And Dahlia gets to decorate it all. Her fingers itch in anticipation of creating something with all the flowers she and the bride agreed upon.

Dreaming of Dahlia's was her childhood dream and one she worked her way to make a reality. She's the most sought-after florist in this part of the state. And for good reason. She loves to be challenged and make sure each wedding is unique in its own way. This makes her fifteenth wedding at Hunter's place. He has a gorgeous black barn with a concrete floor. Then there's the arch on the dock overlooking the lake that many brides lover. And lastly, he has this place.

Dahlia assumes he gets a hotel or something while the bride uses his house. It never looks lived in when she's here. That must speak for how tidy of a man he really is. She stretches her neck and pulls out the bride's file, placing it on the table to make sure not a single detail gets missed. When her music comes through her blue-tooth speaker, she's transported to a different head space and gets to work.

Hunter scoops a shovel of snow from the driveway and tosses it to the side. This would be faster if he'd go get the tractor, but this work keeps his mind and hands busy while Dahlia's inside. He pauses when he spots her twirling around the floor with the handful of white *roses?* He isn't sure. He wasn't raised by a man who brought his wife flowers and never had a reason to step foot into a florist shop. But watching her work has mesmerized him since the first day she showed up. He was shocked she showed up alone, with no one to help her. That's when they're dance sort of began. She was right to bust his balls earlier for not helping unload the SUV. With the weather change, the damage the army did to his body has been prominent, and it took him longer than he wanted to get to the cabin this morning.

The intention of moving here by himself was to avoid any kind of human interaction, but she shot those plans to hell when she showed up with her curly hair and not an ounce of makeup to hide her beautiful face. He knew by making this place a wedding venue he'd have people here, but he never planned for someone like her to be a permanent person coming around. He smirks as her mouth moves along to whatever song she is listening to. In a matter of hours, she'll have transformed his cabin into something beautiful. She amazes him with each design she comes up with.

By the time he finished shoveling the driveway, he accepts his defeat that he'll need to scrap the rest of the driveway with the tractor. It winds down a hill through the woods and his ranch sits far back off the main road so it can't be seen. Another selling factor for this place when he was hunting for something to fill the void in his life. War changed him to someone he isn't proud of and took so much from him—he didn't feel like he could go home and look his friends and family in the eyes. They'd only see the shadows and scars on his haunted body. The smile that doesn't reach his eyes, no matter how hard he tries.

He sighs as he uses his left hand to lift his leg behind to knee to climb up on the tractor. He looks over the place that is his. A home he's made safe for himself and he can let his demons out without the fear of hurting someone he loves.

As he drives by the cabin and grates the snow he shoveled for good measure, a pang of sadness hits his chest when Dahlia comes into view and the cabin looks like something out of a magazine. She'll finish soon and leave, only coming back to pick up the decorations later tonight.

He glances at the sky, squinting at the clouds. There's more snow coming in. He feels it in his bones.

2

Dreaming of Dahlia's is right on Main Street of a small town called Deadwood in South Dakota. The door rings as Dahlia steps into her shop, her pounding headache reminding her that coffee is not an ample substitute for water. The shop is closed this late on a Saturday, but she has office things to take care of until time to go back to Hunter's and get her decorations. Most clients do very well about cleaning up after themselves, but once in a while she'll get a lazy family that thinks they're too good for that and leave it all to Dahlia.

She grabs a leftover sandwich and a soda from the fridge, but pauses before closing the door and exchanges the soda for water. At her computer she clicks through various invoices, billing receipts to compile for taxes coming up soon, and checks inventory to decide what to order on next week's truck.

She lives, breathes, and dreams of this place. Literally, she has woken herself up to answer the phone with an irate customer in her dream. As rewarding as this place is, it's still working with the public and that comes with its only file of drama.

"Knock, knock," a sing-song voice says as they step in the front door. Dahlia doesn't bother looking up from the computer. She'd recognize her best friend's voice anywhere.

"Hey," she says in a monotone, her brows bunched at the computer while her glasses sit atop her head.

"You know, if you actually wore the glasses, you wouldn't have headaches or that permanent wrinkle." Carly smiles as she pushes herself up on the counter and lets her legs dangle. She and Dahlia have been best friends since high school, and it shows in their banter. When Dahlia wanted to open this place, she knew the perfect person who was the yin to her yang that could run it with her.

Dahlia grumbles something under her breath and pulls her glasses down to her nose. "We're closed. Why are you here? Go out, have some fun."

Carly snorts. "You're one to talk. When was the last time you went out and enjoyed yourself? We're still in our youth, baby! Let's go. Live!"

"I'd hardly call thirty-one, *youth*."

"Seriously, what are you doing here? Go home. The shop will survive without you for one evening."

Dahlia locks her computer and stretches her hands above her head. "I can't. I have to go pick the stuff up from Hayne's place."

"You mean Hunter?" Carly leans in closer and bats her lashes.

"Would you stop? He owns the venue. It's not like there is anything more going on there." Carly hops down to follow Dahlia to the backroom.

"But there could be. You're the only person the mysterious man has talked to since he showed up. He barely comes into town and when he does, it's quick in and out without so much as a coffee. Who doesn't drink coffee while running errands? *Mysterious*," Carly says while wiggling her fingers. "Like, where did he come from? Why did he move out here alone? Who did he kill that he's on the run from?"

Dahlia stops and shakes her head. "Carly, I swear, your imagination is one scary place. Maybe he enjoys being left *alone* and working in peace. Not everyone needs relationships."

"Yup, he's perfect for you. Two people who hate people and try to socialize as little as possible. You could have your own bedrooms and only have sex when it's penciled into your schedule." She raises her voice to a nasal tone. *"Nine o'clock? Can't. Booked. How about lunch and a quickie?"*

"Carly!" Dahlia exclaims, her eyes wide and mouth open. Although the separate bedrooms don't sound like that bad of an arrangement. "Go home," she drags out as she pulls Carly to the front door. "I'll see you, Monday."

"I'm only saying these things out of love! Your vagina needs me! It's screaming for help!" she shouts from the sidewalk, and Dahlia's face turns crimson.

"I love her, I swear I do. But sometimes," Dahlia says to the empty shop. She grabs her keys and checks the time. Her phone chimes and she pats herself down. Each boob, back pockets and then glances around her person when her phone isn't there. It chimes again, and she walks to the desk to, grabbing it from under a pile of invoices.

A text from Hunter pops up.

> Snow's coming. You should wait till tomorrow to come back. Wouldn't want you getting stuck.

Dahlia scoffs and looks at her four-wheel-drive SUV. She'll be just fine and it's cute that he thinks she needs him saving her.

Her low battery alert sounds again, and she locks her phone and she slips it into her back pocket. She'll just charge it on her way to the Hayne's Ranch.

Her stomach gargles as she climbs into her car. "Seriously, we just ate —" She glances at the clock on her dash and groans. "Six hours ago..."

Food first. Then pack up from the wedding.

The loneliness of realizing Carly is right creeps up her spine as she drives. Her dating life is pathetic. Why is it so hard to find someone who brings substance to her already happy life? She doesn't want to change anything about herself and loves her life just the way it is. There's comfort in the chaos, which means she probably needs therapy. But where's the man who can handle her crazy schedule and smile inside the vortex of her life beside her? Does that man even exist?

Dahlia is so far stuck in her head, she hasn't turned the radio on. Mindlessly, she uses her turn signals, stops at red lights—hopefully—and before she realizes it, she's turning into Hunter's driveway.

"Damn it," she whines and throws her head back into the seat. "I forgot food!"

The snow is already falling in heavy sheets of huge flurries. Any tracks left by the wedding party are long gone. Dahlia pushes the button for four-wheel drive and sighs. "I'll just grab something at home tonight. I've waited this long."

3

"HE FUCKING JINXED ME!" DAHLIA TRUDGES UP THE STEPS TO the cabin. Her toes froze halfway up the hill after her SUV slid into a ditch that she couldn't get out of. After slamming on the steering wheel, cursing the universe and digging around her catch-all of a purse, she found a smashed granola bar she licked from the wrapper. Hanging her head in shame, she got out to go ask the one person out in this forsaken blizzard for help.

The hill seemed much shorter and less steep in a vehicle. Her thighs burn and her breaths labored. This is why it would be a good idea to use that gym membership she pays for monthly.

"Hunter!" she shouts through chattering teeth and a shaking body. There aren't any lights left on in the cabin. Peering through the tall windows, she sees her decoration are piled neatly on the floor, already taken down. "Asshole, why do you have to be so nice and right about everything?"

Dahlia pounds on the door again, but no answer. The snow is up to her ankles as she walks around to the back door. She jiggles the handle.

Locked.

Wrapping her jacket tighter around her, she whines in defeat, "I am really starting to dislike this man." Pulling her phone from her pocket, she prepares to do the one thing she hates.

Calling for help.

She taps her phone screen to unlock it, but it doesn't respond. She taps it harder and shakes it violently. "No! Damn it."

She forgot to plug it in when she got in the car because she thought of food. Which she also forgot because her raging hormones had her in la-la land, day dreaming about Hunter and how he could be the end to her drought.

A dog barks behind her and she jumps around, barely able to make out the white furry animal through the snow.

"Hello there. What are you doing out here?" She crouches and holds her hand out, hoping to coax the canine closer. "You should be hunkered down somewhere, out of the snow."

It cocks its head to the side as if to say *no shit. Why are you out here?*

Suddenly, it turns its head and barks into the woods. Dahlia reaches out to grab it, but she comes up short and the dog runs away.

"Wait! Come here, puppy! I'm trying to help you!" Dahlia trudges through the snow to save the furry white animal. The dog stops just inside the tree line and barks back at her again.

"Where are you going?" Dahlia pants, the cold air hurting as she inhales.

A blood curling woman's scream breaks through the snowstorm and the hair stands on her arms. Dahlia freezes and spins, trying to find where she heard the person in trouble.

The dog growls and walks up beside her.

"It's okay," she whispers. "Let's just go back."

She steps away from the tree and the dog brushes against her leg, pushing her further from the cabin. Dahlia shivers and blows her breath on her hands.

This time, the scream is closer, and it sounds right in front of her. She loses all since of logical thinking and turns to run in the direction the dog was going. It yips and barks, as if encouraging her to go faster. Every cell in Dahlia's body pushes her harder and to run with everything she has. Like death is right on her heels and is she falters, if she slows then she's a goner.

Somewhere in these woods a woman is running from something and she's screaming like her life depends on it. A gun shot rings out, and she falls to the snow covered grown and scrambles behind a tree.

What the fuck? The woman's screams go silent and Dahlia presses her back into the tree, darting her head side to side, waiting to see a gun aimed at her. *Did someone just get shot in these woods? She has to get out of here.*

The dog barks incessantly, prancing on its feet.

"Shhh," Dahlia scolds, but it doesn't deter it. She pushes to her feet and glances around the side of the tree, careful to stay hidden. Holding her breath, she peers through the snow and gathers herself. She has to get back to her car. Then she can charge her phone, call Hunter, and get out of this freaking snow blizzard. After several minutes, she doesn't see anything. The dog whines and Dahlia decides it can take care of itself.

She presses her back into the tree and takes several deep breaths. Counting to three, she spins away from the tree to run as hard as her legs can go.

Raising her eyes from the ground, she screams, but can't stop her momentum before she's barreling into a figure obscured by the flurries. Their hands clamp around her biceps and hold her upright.

"Let go of me!" She tries to break free, but the hands hold firm. The dog barks and whines from behind her. She squeezes her eyes closed. At least this way she won't see the killing blow. Maybe she could play opossum? Pass out and fake a heart attack? If her heart doesn't slow down, she won't have to fake it. She holds her breath and waits.

This is it. She's going to die in this snow because she chased after a dog who clearly didn't need her help. This man might as well have been in a white van with free puppies spray painted on the side. Hunter will come home and see her car in the ditch and that will be all that's left of her.

"What the hell are you doing out here?" the man's voice cuts through her spiral. "Zip!" he shouts, and the barking stops.

His dog. It literally lured her to her death.

"Dahlia?" Her eyes spring open at the sound of her name. Familiar honey eyes stare down at her framed by black edges in her vision. Before she can respond, she blinks and everything is black. Then...she's weightless.

4

DAHLIA LIES ON THE BED ON THE FAR SIDE OF THE ROOM. Hunter's cabin is small with an open floor concept. The only place you'd get any privacy is the bathroom. He sits in his chair beside his wood-burning stove and runs a tired hand over his face. Zip sits at his feet and raises his head every time Dahlia makes a sound in her sleep.

He can't believe she actually passed out on him. He barely acted quick enough to catch her and carry her inside. His leg aches and he massages his thigh, feeling the rough scars through his jeans.

Why didn't she listen when he said to wait until tomorrow? Or at least text him back she was coming regardless, and he'd been at the main house. At least that explains where Zip went and why he couldn't find him earlier.

She hums and rolls to her stomach, inhaling deeply. He stills, waiting for her to pop up and freak out. Zip jumps to his feet and trots across the room to the edge of the bed.

"Zip," Hunter whisper shouts, but the dog ignores him and jumps into the bed.

Dahlia squeals and jumps up, her eyes wide and cheeks flushed as she frantically looks around. Sensing her anxiety, Zip pushes her against her chest and whines, licking at her hands to calm her. Her curly hair stands in all directions and her blue doll-sized eyes lock onto Hunter, who hasn't moved.

"Are you going to kill me?" she says with a steady calm, like she's already assessed every way this could go and it's not good.

"Am I going to kill—? Why are earth would you think that?"

"I heard the screams. There was a woman, then a gunshot. Someone died out there," she points at the door. "Which means someone killed her." She carefully slips out of the bed onto her socked feet and spots her boots setting by the door. "I won't say anything, just let me go. Please. You know me. We're friends." Her voice is low and quiet. She walks on her toes, like she's worried she'll scare him—or more likely scared he'll grab the rifle by his chair and use it.

"Dahlia," he says, with his palms up. "How long have you lived in South Dakota?"

She's almost to the door. She'll grab her boots and then take her chances running for it. "All my life," she admits.

"And you've never heard a mountain lion before?"

Dahlia doesn't know what that has to do with committing murder. Hunter still hasn't moved from his seat and she grabs her boots and retches the door open—or tries. The knob doesn't turn and she yanks on the wooden barrier, but it's no use.

"Please, please," she sputters and backs into the kitchen table big enough for four people. Hunter pushes to his feet and winces as he steps toward her. "Just let me leave. Nobody has to know."

"I'm not going to hurt you, little flower. And I'm not a killer. What you heard was a mountain lion scream. I didn't even know you were out there. I was looking for Zip, who probably saved your life as a matter of fact. The only woman in those woods in danger was you." He internally scolds himself for using his secret nickname for her out loud. And in this situation of all times.

She sides steps until the table is positioned between them and reaches for the butcher knife laying on the counter.

Did he just call me, little flower? Dahlia's stomach somersaults and she wets her bottom lip. Why did it sound so intimate and why is it doing so many different things to her body? He could be a killer, unless he's telling the truth. Picturing him feeling her up is the last thing she should be doing, but, *little flower,* has her mind racing.

Hunter's eyes remained locked on her as he braces himself on the chair. "If you come at me with that, I'll have you disarmed in three seconds and pinned to the ground."

He drops his chin and the brim of his cowboy hat hides his darkening eyes.

"Put it down, Dahlia," he demands. "Unless you want to be underneath me."

Her breath catches and her fingertips graze over the sharpened metal. That threat shouldn't heat her skin and cause her to squeeze her thighs together.

This is Hunter she's having a stand-off with. She knows him, has worked with him for a year. But what does she really know about him? Her eyes wonder to the dog with its ears perked from the bed. It whines softly and tilts its head to the size, the large white ears and snout trained on her.

"A mountain lion?" she asks.

"Yes."

"You're not a murderer or killer?"

Hunter can't meet her gaze and he sighs. He stalks around the table and she's not sure what her next move is. He bypasses the knife and lays his hand atop hers instead. One deep breath and her breasts would graze his chest. "You're safe."

Her lips part as she searches his honey iris' for any sign of deception. She pulls her hand from under his and prays he can't see the reaction her body is having to his touch, his closeness, and this entire situation. She leans against the counter and pushes her hair behind her ears. "What happened? Where are we?"

Hunter mimics her stance and Zip hops down from the bed and licks at Hunter's hands.

"I found you in the woods and then you passed out. This is my cabin...where I live."

She takes a moment to study the small space. A wood stove sits in the far corner with one recliner. There's a bed across from the stove with the wall as a headboard. A closed door, she assumes, leads to the bathroom and then the kitchen they're in. This is more like a hunting shack than a permanent living space. "What about the cabin? The one I decorated?"

"It was too big. To many—" he pauses, searching for the right words. "It's too exposed. I prefer this."

She arches a brow and angles her body to face him, waiting to see if he'll elaborate what that means.

"Why didn't you call me? Or at least text me back and I would have made sure I was there. Saved you from," he waves his hand around. "This."

She waves him off and her stomach grumbles loudly. Hunter chuckles and her cheeks flush.

"Take a seat, Dahlia. I'll fix something to eat."

5

When Hunter said he'd fix *something* to eat, she thought he'd meant something quick and simple. Not a four-course meal of steak, fried potatoes, corn on the cob, yeast rolls, and green beans—the canned homegrown kind.

The meat is juicy and tender. She pokes her tongue out to lick up some escaped deliciousness on her lips. She's always respected his privacy, but here, in these close quarters and with nothing else to do to distract her thoughts, she can't help but wonder and want to know everything.

"You like it?" he asks around a bite.

Dahlia nods and smiles sheepishly at the man-sized bite she just shoved in her mouth. "I forgot to eat. Well, I remembered then forgot to stop and get anything before coming here. That's probably why I passed out."

Because that sounds better than saying it was from being terrified.

"Why does that not surprise me?" He leans back in his seat and she notices his head sliding over his left leg. Dahlia smirks and takes a drink of the water he set in front of her.

"So, Mr. Lives-Out-In-The-Middle-Of-Nowhere, I think this warrants you telling me a little about yourself." Her palms sweat at the idea of seeing into his life, his past, and figuring out who exactly Hunter Haynes is.

"What does exactly? You trespassing?" He stands, grabbing her plate and takes it to the sink.

"Blame your dog. I was trying to save it from freezing to death."

Zip barks as if he knows they're talking about him.

Hunter washes the dishes and his shoulders tense with Dahlia at his back. He knows she isn't a threat, but his subconscious is on edge either way. He grips the cloth and braces on the porcelain sink bowl.

"I'll dry," she states, brushing up from behind him.

He pulls himself together enough to clear his throat and nod. Something about her. Maybe it's the fact she doesn't shy away from him and is the only person he has any sort of friendship with since he's been home. He studies her out of his periphery. He'd have to be blind to deny she's beautiful. Even then, he'd feel the passion as she spoke. He'd feel her beauty just from being around her. It goes so much deeper than the surface. Maybe that's why he wants to share parts of himself with her.

"I served two tours before I was medically discharged," he whispers, so low she almost missed it. Instead of jumping to say *I'm sorry* or something of the sort, she takes the wet plate from his hand and continues drying.

Hunter looks at her out of the corner of her eye, but there's nothing on her features. If she's uncomfortable, she doesn't show it. "My team and I drove over a land mine during patrol. My leg got crushed…they couldn't save it."

Her hands flinch slightly before she regains her composure. She fights the urge to look him up and down. How had she missed that?

"So, when you came back…you didn't have anyone to come back to?" she asks, careful to not press too far, but enough that she can make sense of willingly wanting to isolate yourself.

"Not exactly." He places the rag over the sink divider and grabs a chair, carrying it to the wood stove. Dahlia follows him and he sits in the chair, offering her the recliner.

How does he tell her he left his family a note explaining that he would call when he got settled, and he's yet to talk to them?

She draws her legs up in the seat and stares into the fire. The heaviness in the air settles around them. So, when she asked if he'd ever killed someone...the haunted look in his eyes as she tangles his fingers, and Zip's instinct to come lick his hands tells her as much.

"You don't owe me any explanation," she says, breaking up the silence.

He tilts his head and squeezes his eyes closed, petting Zip's head. "I—I haven't talked to my family. When I got back, I couldn't sleep without hearing gunfire in the distance. When my mom tried to wake me up and I nearly attacked her...I decided leaving was in everyone's best interest. I keep telling myself I'll go back, or at least call to let them know where I am—but I haven't."

Dahlia doesn't know if she should reach out to comfort him or give him his space. Out of all the rumors, the town cooked up about the mysterious bachelor who moved to town, a military veteran who couldn't adjust to life after he came home, wasn't one of them.

"And this place helps?"

He smirks and leans back from Zip. "Surprisingly. I think it's knowing that there isn't anyone around for miles. He helps too," he points at this dog as he lays at his feet. "The wedding venue was something to keep me busy and give me something to strive toward."

He drops his chin, heat rushing across the back of his neck. He hasn't told anyone the truth about how much he's suffered since coming back and trying to adapt to a *normal* life.

"You should call your family. At least your parents. I'm sure they'd love to hear from you." Dahlia keeps her voice soft as she speaks. She knows her parents would be distraught if she disappeared and never checked in.

"You're right. I've debated inviting them this spring." He grunts as he tries to move his leg. "But I don't want them to see me as a coward or if they don't come at all..." Hunter's voice trails off and she hurts for him. Something about seeing a strong bodied man be vulnerable pulls on her heartstrings.

"You should invite them, Hunter."

His eyes lock with hers. "You know you're the only person I've told this. Even my parents don't know what I went through. What if they don't understand? They look at me and they see the same kid they raised. I don't know if I can handle that."

The cabin grows silent aside from Zip snoring at Hunter's feet and the crackling on the wood in the fire.

"Thank you," Dahlia says, her eyes getting heavy as she settles into the recliner. "For not letting me get eaten."

Hunter chuckles and pushes to his feet. "Come on, little flower. You're taking the bed. I'll sleep in the chair."

There's that name again. She has to shove down the reaction it causes and snuggle deeper into the recliner.

"Nonsense. I'm not letting you sleep in the chair. It's your cabin." She pulls the quilt from behind her head and drapes it across her body.

Hunter arches a brow and strides over, scoops her up in his arms, and carries her to the bed.

"What the hell? You can't pick me up! I'm—"

"I know you aren't about to say what I think you are," Hunter purrs as he lays her gently on the bed.

Too big? She stares at him, stunned. Never in a million years did she think a man would literally whisk her off her feet.

Zip jumps excitedly and settles in next to her. "Sleep, Dahlia. That's an order."

6

HOW CAN HE EXPECT HER TO SLEEP AFTER THE DOUBLE whammy he just served? Between calling her a something as beautiful as a little flower and putting on his show of strength? Sleep is the *last* thing on her mind.

Something flashes in her eyes and she pulls the blankets back on the empty side of the bed. "Then you're sleeping with me, solider."

There's humor in her tone to mask the uncertainty of what she just suggested. She could be reading this entire situation all wrong. It's been so long since she's been *taken care of*, she could be blowing this all out of proportion.

"Little flower." Hunter's voice drops to a husky whisper. "If I get in that bed, we won't be sleeping."

Or not. Dahlia's stomach flips, and she squeezes her thighs at his promise. Her lips part and she has half a mind to beg him to prove his point. She fights the urge to crawl to him across the mattress. "Good." It comes out breathy and full of need. There's no hiding just how much she wants this…how much she *needs* this.

Hunter drops his chin and hides the tightness in his jaw. "I'm not…" he starts and has to take a deep breath. "I'm not the same—as I was before."

"Hunter," Dahlia says his name like it's the most important thing in the world. It sounds like a melody coming off her lips and he glances at her, sitting in the middle of his bed. "Tell me what to do."

His cock hardens at her request, and he clenches his hands to hide the tremor. He's dreamed of touching her, of having her. But he never felt worthy enough to have someone as competent as Dahlia. Not when he is missing a limb and has to live secluded for his own peace of mind.

"I lost it below the knee," he admits through gritted teeth. His throat nearly closes at saying it out loud. The words come out strained, and he wants to turn away from her to avoid the pity look he expects in her eyes.

"That's not an order," she states evenly. Not acknowledging his comment in the slightest.

Hunter blows out a breath and rolls the tension from his shoulders. His brown eyes settle on Dahlia's deep blue burning gaze. God, he wants her too. "You like being told what to do, little flower?"

Holy shit! Wait, does she? She's never let someone else take control before. Honestly, no guy ever knew what they were doing enough *to* take control. But Hunter...she stares at he reaches for the buttons on his shirt. He is the kind of man that will know exactly how to *take care* of her needs.

"Never met a man up to the task," she says honestly. His lips form a circle as he lets out a low whistle to the blow she just made on all men.

"You want to know what I want you to do, little flower?" He has the first four buttons of his shirt undone and dark tattoos line his chest. Dahlia's fingers itch to trace each one and explore the rest of this cowboy.

"You want to play by my rules?" he purrs, and his shirt falls to the floor.

She forgets out to speak, how to move. Fuck, she nearly forgets to breathe. He's perfection. He's toned, obviously, since he carried her inside from the snow. But it's not in an overly bulky way. It's working muscle, not *working out* muscle. The kind you get from chopping your own firewood and living the ranch life.

He tsks and places a finger under her chin, bringing her lust filled blue eyes up from his bare torso. "You want to be fully satisfied? Fucked out of your mind until you feel like you're floating on a high so delicious you'll never come down?"

Her lips part and she blinks, trying her best to reign in her screaming vagina.

"I want you to undress, slowly. Then you'll crawl over to me and lay flat on your back."

Her blood feels hot enough to burn her skin. *Holy shit*, plays in her mind on repeat. "Now," he says, deeper and pulls his hand back to place it on the bulge in his pants.

Dahlia blushes, but not from the way Hunter is making her feel. She reaches for her shirt and remembers the embarrassing excuse of a bra she put on this morning and when was the last time she shaved...well anything? It's not exactly high on her priority list this time of year.

"Come here," Hunter whispers and holds his hand out for her. She takes it and steps off the bed to stand in front of him. He lifts her hand and places it over scars on his bare chest. The erratic beat of his heart pumps under her palm. "This is what you do to me, Dahlia. Everything I see you, think of you, hear your voice. I'm a fucking mess most of the time. Trust me when I say there has never been a woman that compares to you."

His amber gaze flicks to her lips and he dips his head, lightly brushing his mouth to hers. "Put me out of my misery and take your fucking clothes off. I think we both have suffered long enough."

"Okay," she says, finally finding her ability to speak. She throws her self-conscious thoughts out the door. Could he be saying those things just for a quick fuck? Possibly. But she doesn't think he is. There's something in his tone that tells her this is as hard for him as it is for her. They're both laying themselves vulnerable and at the mercy of one another.

His eyes track every movement until she's standing in nothing but her underwear.

"Fuck," he groans and squeezes his cock. "You're stunning. Do you want me?"

"Yes," she whispers. She's already soaked between her thighs, just from looking at him.

"Good, cause I want you so bad I can't stand it. Take those off, get on the bed and spread your legs for me."

7

HUNTER PULLS DAHLIA TO THE EDGE OF THE BED AND RUNS his fingers across her soaked center. "Already so wet for me, little flower." He slides his jeans and boxers down his thighs and his cock rubs against her entrance.

"Are you going to keep talking all night?" she groans and presses herself further into the mattress.

A throaty chuckle escapes him and leans down, bracing his hands on either side of her head to hover over her body. "I love it when you get impatient," he growls and brushes his lips quickly across hers. Dahlia huffs and reaches down to grab his cock, just to prove how impatient she is.

Hunter grabs her wrist before she achieves her goal and raises it over her head. He takes her other free hand and pins them both under his.

"I told you I'd have you pinned underneath me."

"Hunter," she mewls. No man has ever worked her up this long. Normally, they treat her like her clit is a push-to-start and barely get her turned on before shoving their cock inside.

"Yes, little flower?" he whispers, sliding the tip of his cock from her ass to clit.

"Fuck me, please," she begs.

He slides his hand between them and lines up with her drenched center. "Anything for you, Dahlia."

He keeps her hands secure above her head and he slowly stretches her wide as he thrusts himself deeply inside of her. She spreads her legs wider, taking every inch of him, reveling in the feel of him filling her up.

Hunter picks up a steady rhythm and her hands fist, and his grip tightens around her wrist. "Fuck," he rasps, and Dahlia bites down on her bottom lip as she arches her back.

"I know, I feel so fucking good," she teases, and he stills. Her eyes fly open and she looks up at the man staring down at her with furrowed brows. "I was kidding. Well, not really—I hope I feel really good. It's just—"

Hunter stands, keeping himself deep in her pink pussy. He grips her thighs and pulls her into him on the edge of the bed. "Is that what you want to hear?" He slams into her, his fingers digging into the soft skin of her inner thighs so she can't move across the bed.

"What?" she cries out, her words cutting off when he does it again.

"You want me to treat this like any other fuck?" his voice raises and Zip whines where he lays at the door.

"Hunter—I was kidd—" Hunter presses his thumb down on her clit and her body fights the overwhelming sensation he's causing.

"You do feel fucking fantastic, but it's because you take me so fucking good. Like you were made just for me. This won't be like the boys who have tried to take care of you before. Because when I'm finished and you're too exhausted to stand, I'll be carrying you to the shower where I'll take you again before bringing you back, naked to this bed, and wrapping my arms around you until we both fall asleep."

How he's able to form a coherent thought, let alone a speech while her mind is buzzing with an orgasm begging to be released, is beyond her.

Hunter slams into her again and she screams in frustration at being on the cusp of the edge, but him not letting her go. He moves, starting with gentle circles around her clit. He leans down and presses his lips to her collarbone.

"Do you hear me, Dahlia? What is going on here is nothing compared to who you've been in the past. And come tomorrow morning, you won't even remember any of their names."

She smirks. "Solider, I forgot their names the moment he carried me to this bed."

His cock jumps inside of her and her pussy tightens in response.

"Good."

Hunter sucks on her nipple then stands, readjusting his stance. He lifts her legs to place each foot on each shoulder and pushes his thumb back down on her clit.

Okay, maybe she is a push-to-start because her body turns molten and her toes curl from the pressure.

He thrusts deep inside of her and grinds his hips at the perfect angle. Everything within her shatters and a sound she's never made escapes her tense body as ecstasy overcomes her.

"Holy shit!" she exclaims and Hunter leans forward, keeping her feet on his shoulders, and bringing her knees closer to her body. His hips slap against her as he chases his own release.

He forgets about the raging snow blizzard outside. The fact that he lives away from civilization because the memories are too much for him to stand. Having Dahlia here it somehow feels right. For the first time since he's been back, he feels...at peace.

His ball tightens when that thought crosses his mind and he buries his face in the crook of her neck as he comes.

Peace. He feels...grounded.

His body tenses when her arms wrap around him and she runs a hand up and down his back. He shudders and his breath comes out shaky against her skin.

Zip barks, then jumps on the bed, wedging his wet tongue and nose between their chests. Dahlia giggles as the dog's head successfully wiggles between them and licks her chin.

"Down, boy," Hunter says between chuckles and pushes him back to the floor. He traces a finger down the side of Dahlia's cheek and tucks a curl behind her ear. To think all the hell he's endured has led him to this tiny town in South Dakota, to a woman who may have just stolen his heart in a snowstorm.

"Is this the part where you carry me to the shower? I don't think I'm a noodle yet," she says with a smirk.

He drops his head and nips on her bottom lip.

"I ain't done with you yet."

8

DAHLIA SHIMMIES FROM UNDER HUNTER'S ARM. HE LETS OUT a snore as picks up a blanket from the floor and wraps it around her shoulders. Zip hops off the bed and makes a beeline to the door, whining and scratching when she doesn't open it immediately.

"And he calls me impatient," she says with a smirk. She opens the door to a foot of snow blocking her path. Zip leaps over it, landing it with nothing but his head sticking out.

He barks at the white stuff like it's just offended him, and Dahlia pulls the quilt tighter and tries to muffle her laugh.

"I love your laugh," Hunter mumbles, his voice thick with sleep. He pushes up out of the bed and swings his legs over the side. Her eyes linger a fraction of a second on his scarred thigh and missing limb. He was so nervous about taking it off in front of her last night. She ended up sliding her hands down his body and doing it herself. He she doesn't have to hide his curves, he shouldn't feel the need to hide this part of him either.

"Love?" She bites her bottom lip, and he stands, bracing himself against the wall. "Little soon for that kind of talk, don't you think?" She means it as a joke, but she can't stop the flutter in her stomach and the way her palms sweat. His morning wood is perfectly outlined in his tight boxers and even though she's sore from all the sex last night, she can't wait until more.

He smiles at her and runs his hands through his cropped hair. "Come shower with me, little flower. Then I'll fix us breakfast. From the looks of that, we aren't going anywhere, soon."

Zip bolts back in, snow sticking to his fur, and shakes at the doormat. Dahlia squeals at the snow, landing at her feet and freezing her toes.

"I'll check the fire first, *then* we'll shower." He reaches for his sock and prosthetic.

"How about you stop trying to do everything for me and I'll tend to the stove? You just get the water hot." Dahlia doesn't give him time to argue before she's grabbing the handle to open the door and add wood. She has to scrap the ashes to the bottom first and opens the air vent for air to stoke the embers.

"You know how to do all that?" Over her shoulder, Hunter leans against the doorway, naked, wearing an impressed expression.

"Shocked that a woman can take care of herself?"

He shakes his head. "No, shocked that you never heard a mountain lion scream and have lived here your entire life, though."

Her mouth falls open, and she pushes to her feet. "I was running for my life! Besides, camping never was something my parents did. When would I be in the situation to be around a mountain lion?"

His shoulders shake with laughter, and he sighs, a genuine smile spreading his lips. "You going to come shower, little flower? Put me out of my misery of imagining what's under that blanket?"

Dahlia stands and drops the blanket to the floor. Something about the way Hunter looks at her makes her feel radiant and confident. His amber eyes burn away any embarrassment she might have felt with any other man. Hunter sucks in a breath, his biceps flex as he grips the door frame.

"Like what you see?" she teases. His gaze burns to her soul, stoking a flame and heating her skin.

"Come here. Now," he orders, and she nearly puddles onto the floor.

She doesn't know where they'll end up after this night in his cabin. But for the first time in her life, she wants to explore these feelings and this man further.

. . .

"Well, that's it," Dahlia announces as she closes the hatch to her SUV. She spent three days in Hunter's cabin. After the first day, she opted to walk around in one of his T-shirts. That might have been the sexiest thing he's ever seen.

Now, she stands awkwardly in the snow wearing what he found her in. Do they act like the last few days never happened? Go back to be acquaintance's even now that she knows his secrets? Was everything that bloomed between them a delusion of the blizzard and being forced to stay in that small cabin?

She worries her bottom lip and reaches for her door handle. She's never been in this awkward in between of was this a one-night thing or does he feel like she does and wants more? All those things he said to her, the way he made her feel...how does she go back from that?

Hunter stands off to the side, staring down the long driveway. For the first time since he's moved out here, the idea of being so far from civilization—from her—is painful. When he doesn't respond, she steps toward the driver's door, but Hunter grabs her arm and pulls her back into him, pinning her to the side of her vehicle.

"What are you doing?" she asks, looking down at where his hips grind into hers.

He stares into her wide eyes. How does he form the words he wants to say? Would she call him crazy? Or run screaming? There is a knife in his gut and it's twisting at the thought of watching her drive away. But he can't keep her here. Not unless she wants to stay. And if she says no, then he doesn't think he'll be able to handle it. He's been pushing people away for so long, he this feeling of wanting to keep someone close is foreign and it scares the hell out of him.

"Hunter?" she says his name, and he blinks her back into focus. Dahlia cups his cheek and brushes her thumb across his stubble.

"I—" he clears his throat and steps back, dropping his gaze. "Be careful."

Her hand falls to her side, and she swallows the sadness, trying to claw up her throat as she opens her door.

She has never been the type afraid to say what is on her mind.

She's Dahlia Moore. She owns Dreaming of Dahlias and has built a business from the ground up. To hell with the man who thinks she is just going to leave after having the best sex and act like nothing has changed.

Nope. Not happening. Not to her. She whirls and faces the cowboy with his dog sitting at his side.

"Hunter Haynes, I know you aren't about to send me on my way with what? A *be careful?* After everything we've talked about the last two days and what we've been doing in that shack in the woods? I have half a mind—"

He gently grips her face and presses his lips to hers, cutting her off. Her tense body relaxes, and she leans back into her SUV. "You wouldn't have made it to the end of the driveway before I caught you," he says against her lips. He pulls back and Dahlia's scowl softens.

"Well, start with that next time." She huffs in annoyance.

Hunter places a knuckle under her chin and tilts her head up. "I don't think I'll ever get enough of you, little flower. This is just the start.

9

THE DOOR TO DAHLIA'S CHIMES AS IT OPENS, LETTING THE fresh spring breeze blow in. Dahlia is bent over a potted peace lily as she shoves a card pick into the soil for the funeral it's being shipped to today. A hand snakes around her ass and squeezes. She jumps and whirls with the plastic pick aimed at the person responsible, her eyes full of fury.

"Good morning to you too," Hunter jokes, and Dahlia drops her hand to her chest.

"Christ! You can't do that to me. I nearly gouged your eyes out!"

He looks at the *weapon* skeptically. "Remember what I said last time you threatened me?" He steps in closer to her, forcing her calves to hit the pot. "I'll have you pinned right here before you can even blink, little flower."

Her cheeks flush and a stray curl drops to the front of her face.

"Holy shit, that was so hot," Carly sighs and leans against the checkout counter. "Are you sure you don't have a brother? Distant cousin maybe?"

Hunter tips his hat in Carly's direction and lets Dahlia shove him back a couple of steps. "I'm almost done here, then I need to go home and shower," she tells him.

"Hot date?" Carly asks.

It's been three months since Dahlia spent those nights in his cabin. Nights full of heat and passion. She certainly wasn't looking for a relationship in Hunter Haynes, or any man. But something happened between them she'll never be able to explain and she's not sure she'd ever want to. Like two lost souls finally beating as one and everything just made sense after that.

They make sense.

"I'm meeting his parents," Dahlia blurts and drops her chin to tug on her shirt, suddenly feeling self-conscious of every part of herself. What if they don't like her? What if they don't approve or, worse…demand Hunter leave and she was wrong to encourage him to reach out to them to begin with?

"Holy shit," Carly whispers in disbelief. "You—you're meeting *his* parents? This is serious then? No more bullshit?"

Hunter can't help but chuckle at her friend with her mouth gaping open. "I'll pick you at five," he states, tucking his finger under her chin to get her attention. "They'll love you. Honestly, at this rate, possibly more than the son who abandoned them."

Her brows furrow and her lips part to defend his statement, but he kisses her and smiles before rushing back out the door.

"You're meeting his parents," Carly mutters, her eyes not fixed on any specific space, like she's still trying to piece when this all happened.

Dahlia stares out the door after Hunter.

Yes, she is. And today.

The truck roars up the driveway to the main cabin used for weddings. He continues to live in the quaint place in the woods, but he figured this would be a better image for his parents.

"You're shaking the whole truck." He squeezes Dahlia's leg. She takes a deep breath and runs her hand over her half-up-do, trying to smooth the frizz. "You look gorgeous, little flower. Way too pretty for someone like me," he scoffs. "I don't even have all my body parts. You're way out of me league."

"You know that doesn't matter to me," she states. It's been a thing he's had to work through at his own pace. That first night, he was terrified to touch her, or her touch him. Like he thought she'd be repulsed and leave. But time and time again, she's proved that she's exactly the woman he always knew she was. There isn't a kinder-hearted person in this world that compares to *his* Dahlia.

"Look at me." He cups her cheek and guides her brown eyes to meet his.

"What if this is a mistake? This is a big deal and they haven't seen you in years. I don't want to impose."

His thumb brushes across the blush. "You didn't have to wear make-up. You're stunning without it. But yes, this is a big deal. Dahlia." He clears his throat and places his cowboy hat on the dashboard. "I lost six years of my life in hell on earth. I didn't think I was capable of feeling anything except hate and fear. You're my gravity. You keep me here, grounded, and I'm happy. I want you by my side and to introduce you to my parents. For me, time doesn't factor into emotions. I spent long enough staring at clocks and counting down days. I'm throwing all reservations out the window. I'm done living scared. But I'd really love to have you holding my hand and reminding me of everything I just said when Mom and Dad show up."

She nods and places her hand over his. "Wouldn't you know it's my stubbornness you have to thank for us being together?"

He flashes her a smile and walks around to open her door. "Does that mean you'll be stubborn enough to stay?"

"What if I decide to never leave?"

His eyebrows raise and his lips part, but no sound comes out. Dahlia quickly kisses him and opens the cabin door with her key. "Come on, solider."

He blinks after the curly-haired force. He's envisioned it enough. Waking up to her every morning, more than just the weekends or after a long night. Had she been thinking about the same thing? Was that her way of saying she'd say yes if he asked? His mind spins with the numerous possibilities, but before he can form a coherent thought, tires crunch on gravel and he steps into the cabin to brace for the reunion.

10

"YOU SHOULD HAVE SEEN HIM!" HUNTER'S DAD, JARED, SLAPS his knee. His cheeks are as red as the T-shirt he's wearing as he tells the story about little Hunter trying to catch a greased pig at the county fair. "He dove! Head first! When the pig dodged, the poor kid landed face first in shit!"

Zip lifts his head at the raised tone before huffing and laying back down at Hunter's feet.

"Language," his wife, Lydia, scolds. The laughter dies and Dahlia sips from her wineglass as they sit around the coffee table in the living space. "So Dahlia. Hunter hasn't said much about you, well I guess he couldn't have given he only called a month ago." She gives her son a sorrowful look and Hunter dips his chin, playing with the whiskey glass in his hands.

"Well," Dahlia says, setting her glass down. "I own Dreaming of Dahlia's, one of the most popular florist shops around. I graduated from college with an art degree and became a master florist after that."

Lydia wears a modest high-necked dress and purses her lips at Dahlia's words.

"Mom," Hunter says, pulling the skepticism from Dahlia and toward himself. "I'm glad you're here."

That admission cracks his mother's hard exterior, and she reaches across the table, gripping her son's hands. "Of course I'd come, sweetie. We've missed you so much and Laura—well, she—"

Hunter's gaze cuts to Dahlia and he shakes his head.

"Lydia," Jared says with a warning in his tone.

Dahlia glances between the tick in Hunter's jaw and his exasperated mother. Dahlia's heart sinks and her palms begin to sweat. She only has herself to blame. She never thought to ask if there was anyone else he left when he moved away. But you know what they say about making assumptions.

"It wasn't just us you left, you know. Doesn't she deserve some kind of explanation? A phone call? Something?" Lydia asks. Jared places his hand on his wife's leg and Dahlia goes rigid. Hunter rips away from his mother and sits back in his seat, running an exhausted hand over his face.

The reunion had been seemingly sweet until now. Granted, Lydia has studied Dahlia with hard eyes since Hunter introduced his *friend*, but nothing has made him react like this. Jared was quick to pull Dahlia into a hug after his son. She's never seen a man laugh as much as he does.

Dahlia takes in the change in the room. Hunter's dad's smile drops and Lydia stares with hardened eyes and a furrowed brow at her son. Dahlia can't fight the urge to reach out and take Hunter's hand, to show she's there and he's okay.

He glances at her touch and intertwines his fingers with hers.

"Who's Laura?" Dahlia asks, taking control of the conversation. If it is an ex-girlfriend or fiancé, she reassures herself it's all in the past. His *past*. And none of it matters.

Lydia purses her lips and takes a steadying breath. "She's the woman Hunter promised he would come home to. Then he left the moment he got back."

Dahlia's chest tightens along with her fingers, and it doesn't go unnoticed. Hunter leans onto his knees, refusing to loosen his hold on his girl's hand.

"I told her I was leaving. I told her she deserved to find someone who cared about her, because I didn't. How much clearer did you want me to be? Did you really travel all the way here to bring this up?" Hunter's voice turns cold.

"Son, of course not. We're just happy you called." Jared offers a soft smile and drapes an arm around his wife's shoulders.

"You can thank Dahlia for that. She's changed my life. She's helped me so much."

His declaration makes her blush, and she drops her chin so a curtain of curls hides her features.

The room falls silent until the oven dings.

"I'll get it," Dahlia says hurriedly. The familiar sound of Hunter's limp comes into the kitchen behind her and he wraps his arms around her waist, Zip right behind him.

"I meant what I said, little flower. Don't let anything she says make you think otherwise. In her mind, I left and came back to the same person. She doesn't understand and honestly, I wouldn't be surprised if Laura has been over at family dinner every Sunday since."

Dahlia pulls the casserole out and sets it on the counter. "Remind me to never let you go back to Tennessee alone."

Hunter nuzzles her neck and she giggles. He was so worried about how she'd react to his mom bringing up his past. But just like she does with everything, she's the definition of elegance and grace. Taking everything in stride and not faltering. At least not from the outside looking in.

"Do you regret it?" she asks.

He sighs, his breath hot against her sensitive skin. "No. If nothing else, this is the closure mom needed that I've changed. I'm happy, safe, and have made something of myself here."

"And they're going to stay here for a month…" Dahlia lets her voice trail off and spins in his arms. "Also, *friend?*"

"How did you want me to introduce you? Girlfriend? Lover?" He squeezes her hips like she loves and her lips part. "Future Haynes?" There's a hint of mischief in his honey iris'.

"Hunter," Dahlia breathes out. They haven't even said the four-letter word yet. She's never let a man into her life as much as Hunter is. To be a part of her business and opening herself up. She's certainly never told a man she loves him. The level of vulnerability that brings terrifies her.

"Dahlia," he says in the same tone. He kisses her forehead and stands to his full height. "Dinner's ready!" he shouts and her mouth hangs open as he winks and turns to the table already set for four people.

Yes, because she can totally eat and act normal after that conversation.

Surprisingly, Lydia doesn't mention the woman from Hunter's past the rest of the night. Were they a tragic high school sweethearts tale? Dahlia feels pity for the love-struck teenager who clung to the promise her boyfriend would return from the war. It's the kind of stuff they make movies about, but Laura didn't get her happy ending. Dahlia took her place.

After dinner and two more bottles of wine, Hunter shows his parents to the room they'll be staying in and then leads Dahlia to the front porch swing, grabbing a blanket off the couch as he walks by.

They sway slowly, staring at the stars decorating the sky like a million Christmas lights. Zip runs around the yard, nose to the ground as he stretches his legs from the tense evening.

"Will you stay?" Hunter asks.

"I stay all the time." Dahlia rolls her eyes.

He rubs on his thigh. A tale she's learned means his uncomfortable. She'll be the person he needs right now. Not out of guilt, but because, honestly, there isn't anywhere else she wants to be.

"I'll stay," she assures him and snuggles into his side. They'll have to talk about what he said earlier.

Mrs. Dahlia Haynes.

She chews on her lip, unsure if she likes the sound of that or not.

11

"DAHLIA, CALM DOWN. YOU ALWAYS GET LIKE THIS AND IT always turns out perfect." Carly twirls a pencil between her fingers while leaning on the counter. Dahlia checks the boxes on her paper for a fourth time and sits her clipboard down with a thud behind Carly.

"Is there something *else* that's bothering you?" her best friend asks, noticing the furrow between Dahlia's brows is from more than her everyday stress of the shop. "D, it's just Summer Fling. Is it Hunter?"

Dahlia stands back and takes in the layout of her shop. Summer Fling is the yearly end of school, warmer days, and a way for the city council to get everyone out in the town to spend money. Dreaming of Dahlias is decorated to the nines with fresh cut flower arrangements, wreathes, potted plants, wind chimes, and flowerbed trinkets.

During holiday festivities like this, not an inch of space inside the shop is left unused. The amount of money Dahlia spends on inventory would send anyone into panic mode.

The same questions circulate in her mind.

What if she doesn't sell very much?

What if she's stuck with it until next spring? Which by that time new trends will have sprouted and nothing is relevant she bought this year.

Like when all the rage was air plants, and she sold out faster than she could keep track. Now there's a shelf in her space dedicated to the un-killable beasts and she might sell one a week.

It's always a gamble when owning a small business and you'd think with time it gets easier…but it doesn't.

"Dahlia?" Carly says again, gaining her attention.

"Hmm?"

"Have you talked to him?"

Dahlia shoos her friend's worried expression away with her hand and unlocks the shop door. She props it open, pulling an open banner she designed herself to the sidewalk. Four rolling carts of potted vegetable plants and perennials line the front of her shop along the windows.

The low hum of people talking and children giggling, running with balloons or bubbles is already filling the closed off street.

"I have. We're fine," Dahlia assures her friend and plasters on her smile and waves at some familiar faces outside the coffee shop.

"His parents left three weeks ago and you've hardly talked about any of it. I'm not one to pry—"

Dahlia cuts her off with a sideways glance and puckered lips.

"What? I don't. This is the first time I've brought it up."

"We're fine. He'll be here today, actually. Said he wanted to help. I told him he didn't know what he was getting himself into." Dahlia laughs and Carly swoons with the back of her hand on her forehead.

"He's a keeper."

Dahlia has avoided the Mrs. Hunter Haynes talk since his parents went back to Tennessee with promises to visit soon. They only agreed after Hunter promised he'd go back to his hometown and see everyone. Which, by Lydia's excited expression, means Lauren will be a part of that reunion.

He asked Dahlia to go with him, and that's in two weeks. A detail she's kept from everyone because she doesn't plan to go. She's needed here at her shop. She can't just up and leave for a week or…longer. How long he's staying isn't decided. But then Dahlia keeps thinking about this Laura girl pining for him down south and her blood boils at the image of her touching what is hers. What if Hunter goes back and all the healing he's done here has made him realize what he's missing? What if he wants to stay? What if seeing Lauren brings all the old emotions to the surface?

Because he is hers. And she's his. Even if she hasn't been able to say that out loud to him.

Her knuckles turn white as she grips the wreath stand. She never wanted to be this self-conscious girlfriend that doesn't secure in her relationship. Her mind has been running crazy with different scenarios and she just wants a peaceful night of sleep for once. She wants to know without a shadow of a doubt they're on their way to forever.

"There's my flower," Hunter's tenor voice purrs from behind her. Zip sits obediently by his side with his service vest on and a military camouflage bandanna around his collar. Her stomach flips at the sight of him in a fitted T-shirt and faded jeans hugging low on his hips. She shifts her gaze to his mischievous sideways smirk and honey-colored eyes that are full of adoration.

"Yes," she whispers, and his smirk turns into a look of confusion.

"Yes?" he parrots.

"Yes," she says with more confidence. "I'll go to Tennessee with you."

Because how could she tell him no when he's willing to help her on one of the busiest days of the years? He wouldn't take no for an answer even when she reminded him it meant it would be in public and until today, he'd made a point of staying away from town at all costs.

Hunter's smile crinkles around his eyes. On the sidewalk, in front of town and everyone, he grips her hips and pulls her flush against him and kisses her like he plans to die in that moment.

When he straightens, Dahlia's cheeks are flushed and her eyes hold that same desire filled gaze he loves so much. And she just agreed to go to his hometown with him.

"You've never ridden with Zip after he's had a hamburger, have you?" he jokes. "You might regret this decision after hour ten of being forced to have the windows down."

Dahlia glances from him to the white canine beside his owner with an arched eyebrow. She's pretty sure the dog is the least of her worries.

"I do have one condition," she says, sweet with innocence.

"And what's that?"

"You are meeting my parents...this weekend."

Hunter stills and stares at Dahlia. "Your parents?" It comes out strained.

"Uh-huh," she says sweetly and pulls a single daisy from a container and hands it to an approaching child.

Hunter clears his throat and shifts uneasily on his feet. "You didn't tell me you had parents."

"Do we need to have the talk about how babies are made?" she asks with a wink.

Another child steps forward and Dahlia hands him a daisy, as well. He's never been set up to *meet the parents* before. Suddenly, this is more terrifying than the day he enlisted.

12

Sweat beads across Hunter's brow, his heart racing. He rolls and fights with the sheet until his legs spring free and he swings his legs off the bed. His foot presses into the cold floor, braces his elbows on his knees and holds his head in his hands.

Dahlia sleeps peacefully at his back and he moves slowly to not disturb her. It's still several hours before morning, but after vividly reliving the loss of his leg and what all happened that day, he won't be able to fall asleep.

Zip hops off the bed as Hunter rolls the sock up his thigh for his prosthetic. The scar tissue where his leg was removed aches more than normal this morning, and he winces as he steps forward. The door quietly clicks closed behind him and he slings his rifle over his shoulder. Zip races around the ground, sniffing and following a trail Hunter can't see.

The woods are quiet at this time of night. An occasional owl hoots somewhere high in the pines and Hunter breathes in the fresh air, desperate to flush out the lingering smell of burning flesh. The nightmares feel too real some times and it'll take him hours to get his body to stop shaking. He'll be back before Dahlia wakes up, like he has been every other time this has happened. They don't occur as often, with Dahlia sleeping in his bed and getting thoroughly fucked at night.

He used to come out here to flirt with the mountain lion. A game of cat and mouse. Something about hunting, something he knows is hunting him, calms his buzzing nerves.

And meeting Dahlia's parents today has his nerves fried.

He walks and waits, listening for the lion's scream. But he's met with silence. When the sun rises and the sky changes from indigo to purple and pinks, he knows he needs to get back before Dahlia wakes up. He's thought he knew what he wanted out of his future before he left for the army.

His whole life was planned out, even what to expect when he got back. Nearly dying was not part of the plan, and that changed everything for him.

Hunter grips the oh-shit handle as Dahlia puts her SUV in park. He never asked where she came from or what her life was like before the shop, but growing up a cowgirl on a working cattle ranch was not what he pictured.

Honestly, neither of them have discussed who they were before they met. Their pasts never mattered or determined who they are now in their relationship. But now he's brimming with questions about what seven-year-old Dahlia looked like and if she rode the range on the back of a horse.

"Are you going to let go or is that handle coming inside with us?" Dahlia asks. Hunter stares through the windshield at the ranch style home. A full porch wraps around from the front to the back, and it's obvious where Dahlia gets her love of flowers. There's hardly any grass to mow because of the flowers growing and blooming everywhere.

A couple that looks to be his parents' age sit in rocking chairs on the porch and push to their feet.

"I've never done this. I don't even know what to say. *Hey, hope you like me. I'm screwing your daughter?*"

Dahlia tilts her head and glances at her parents. "Maybe leave out that second part?" Hunter groans and a smile tugs on her lips. "They're nice people. Momma might love you right to death."

Her dad raises his hand in a wave, and Dahlia grabs the door handle. Hunter reaches across and places a hand on her leg, stopping her from getting out. He knows this is a huge step for a relationship. She doesn't strike him as the type to bring guys home to meet her folks, especially since she's never mentioned them before now.

"How many guys have introduced to them?"

Dahlia searches amber eyes for a reason behind the question, but she can't make sense of it. Heat blushes across her cheeks at the truth. "None," she admits, dropping her gaze. "I've never done this either."

Hunter nods and lets go of the oh-shit handle and opens his door. "Don't move," he orders, and she stares after him. He walks around the truck and opens her door for her first, then the back door for Zip to jump down.

"Chivalry's not dead," she whispers with a smile. Hunter takes her hand in his and stands tall beside her, facing the sidewalk to where her parents watch the two of them.

"First impressions are important. And you're important to me. I want to make sure they have no doubt about that."

Dahlia beams at him. His words of affirmation heal the scars left by every fuck-boy before him.

"Are you going to stand there all doe eyed or are you going to introduce us?" her momma shouts and Dahlia rolls her eyes. She grips Hunter's hand and leads her down the stone pathway to her parent's porch.

"Hunter," Dahlia says. "These are my parents. June and Elijah. Mom, Dad, this is Hunter." Dahlia lets go of Hunter's as her mother pulls her in for a hug.

"About time you pulled yourself away from that shop. Seriously honey, you work too much."

A smirk curves across Hunter's lips. Elijah reaches his hand out and Hunter takes it in a firm handshake. His father taught him you can tell a lot about a man by his handshake.

"You served in the military?" Elijah asks.

"Yes, sir." Hunter stands tall with Zip sitting at his feet.

Dahlia's father grunts and looks Hunter up and down with scrutinizing eyes.

"Oh daddy, stop it. Be nice." Dahlia says, taking Hunter's hand back. "Daddy was in the army, too. Many, *many*, years ago."

Elijah smiles for the first time and Hunter's shoulders relax. "You make me sound old," he jokes and leans in to kiss his daughter on the cheek. "Nice to meet you, Hunter. Come on in. Your momma has made one hell-of-a dinner for you two."

Zip whines and licks his lips. Elijah glances down at the canine. "You can come in too."

Dahlia's parents walk inside, but she pulls on Hunter's hand to hold him back. "Dad's harmless. He never talked about his time in the war. I guess there are memories people never want to relive. Are you okay?"

Hunter takes a steadying breath and squeezes her hand in his. "I'm always okay when I'm with you, little flower."

His heart squeezes at the admission as he takes in the woman at his side. He could get used to this. Facing everything in life with her at his side. His train of thought stalls, and he realizes what his heart just admitted, but his mind has yet to catch up to.

Before he can say anything more, she's leading him through the front door. His stomach growls at the smell of the home cooked meal and he makes a mental note to dive deeper into what he is feeling after he wins her parents over.

13

THE DINNER WITH DAHLIA'S PARENTS COULDN'T HAVE GONE better. As promised, it was Dahlia's turn to hold up her end of the bargain and travel down to Tennessee, where Hunter grew up. She didn't know what to expect, but a house in the suburbs with wood plank fences for privacy was not it. No wonder he felt like he couldn't breathe when he came back. She is antsy and doesn't have a reason aside from her closet neighbor was at minimum one hundred acres away.

Lydia steps out of the two-story brick house that looks identical to the one next to it. Hunter barely has time to put the truck in park before his mother is reaching for his driver's handle. Her eyes land on the woman sitting beside him, and Dahlia ignores the fall in her smile to let Zip out of the backseat. The grass is so well maintained; it looks—fake. Zip sniffs hesitantly with one paw off the ground like he has the same thought.

"What a surprise. I see you brought Dahlia with you," Lydia says with an overly saccharine smile as they follow his mother into his childhood home. There's a newly built ramp leading up to the porch and Lydia steps toward it while Hunter stays on course for the porch steps.

Dahlia sighs is disbelief and Lydia stares as her son walks past her. "I'm excited to show her around," he says, not missing a beat.

Did they really build a ramp because of his leg? She fights the urge to snap at Lydia for making Hunter feel less-than, but she bites her tongue for her soldier's benefit.

Inside, the house is set up like out of a magazine. Dahlia glances at her shoes and debates if she should take them off or not. "Dad! We made it!" Hunter shouts, and Jared steps into view from the end of the hallway. Surprisingly, he bypasses Hunter and pulls Dahlia into a hug and takes her suitcase from her hand. The foyer feels tiny, with the four adults standing around.

"Hunter didn't say you were coming! I hope the drive wasn't too much for you." He turns his attention to his son with a disapproving look. "You made her ride straight through?"

Hunter's brows raise and he glances at Dahlia. "Well—I,—"

"It was fine," Dahlia says with a yawn and Zip whines at Hunter's feet.

"Hunter, we raised you better than that, son. It's late. Why don't I show you your rooms, and we can talk tomorrow? She looks exhausted," Lydia chimes in.

Dahlia doesn't know if she should be offended about looking *exhausted*, but he's right.

Hunter groans and reaches for Dahlia. "Mom, I'm not a horny teenager. We're not staying in separate rooms. If that's the case, then I'll get a hotel and we'll come over tomorrow."

Dahlia rolls her lips between her teeth to hide her smile. She hadn't even caught that his mom said *rooms*. Thankfully, he was quick to shut that down.

"That's—" Lydia tries to say. She glances at her son's prosthetic leg hidden under his jeans. "We just thought you'd want to stay downstairs, but with that bed being a twin..."

Dahlia watches Hunter for his reaction. First the ramp, and now this. Dahlia has never once second guessed if Hunter could do anything. He lives alone, for Christ's sake—well, most of the time. But she doesn't help him do anything day to day. Did they see a fucking ramp in South Dakota?

No. She has to school her features to keep from showing the annoyance growing for this southern woman.

The house goes silent and Zip pushes against Hunter's leg. Dahlia takes her bag from Jared with a sympathetic hand on his shoulder. "We'll take the room upstairs."

Hunter doesn't wait for his mother's approval or other remarks.

"We'll see you at breakfast," Jared says as he wraps a hand around his wife's waist.

Hunter leads the way up the stairs to the spiral stairs that start by the front door. They're carpeted and again, Dahlia's politeness screams to remove her shoes, but she does the same as Hunter. The only room up here is a loft style guest room with an attached bathroom. He drops his luggage on top of the chest at the foot of the bed and Dahlia sits hers beside the chest of drawers.

"You should shower," he says, his voice hollow and empty. "I'll take Zip out."

She notices the slight wince around his eye when he steps on his left leg. "Hunter, it's me. Look at me," she urges, desperate to ease some of the strain rippling across his muscles.

"Don't, little flower. I'm okay."

"I know," she says and walks over to lay her head on his chest. "I was just *suggesting*..." He glances down to see her looking up at him through her eyelashes.

He smirks. "And what is that?"

"I'll take Zip out. You get *our* shower ready and we can act like those horny teenagers you were talking about."

He sighs and kisses her forehead. "I'm fine, really."

"I never said you weren't, solider. But you drove the entire way and I know it's because you're scared of my driving. So, I'm taking Zip out as payback."

She pulls away and Zip eagerly prances to the door. "I don't think that's how punishments work."

Dahlia pushes her hair behind her ear and smiles over her shoulder. "How about I don't let you come until I say so?"

Hunter reaches for her, his eyes darkening with desire. Her stomach flips, but she jumps back before he catches her and jogs down the steps, a ridiculous grin on her face.

"Take him out back!" Hunter shouts, and Dahlia takes a turn at the bottom of the stairs in search of a back door.

When she steps out on the deck, she's able to breathe easier. It may look like all suburbs from the front, but there are wide open fields and woods at the back. She sits on the steps while Zip runs around, stirring up quail and occasionally checking that Dahlia is where he left her.

The screen door opens and Dahlia spins. Jared smiles down at her and gently closes the door behind him. "I thought you were Hunter," he admits.

"He's taking a shower. I offered to let Zip stretch his legs."

He nods and wipes his palms on his jeans.

"Lydia is one tore up mess in there. She's worried she's offended Hunter and I've had to talk her down several times to keep her from climbing those stairs."

Dahlia doesn't say anything. She can't help but suspect it's her Lydia is trying to purposefully offend. But that could be her imagination getting the best of her, too. At least that's what she keeps telling herself.

"It's hard. Our son left for the war and the person who came back... his face is the same. He sounds the same, but—" Jared leans on the porch railing and stares out at the painted sunset sky.

"He's still Hunter," she says. Running her hands up her arms to knock off the chill.

"It's like I don't know how to talk to him. And Lydia," he blows out a breath. "I told her insinuating the stairs were too much was a bad idea."

Dahlia stands and Zip quickly races across the field, tongue hanging out and panting. "He's still your son. Just don't treat him any differently than you did before."

Jared smiles at her advice.

"I'm glad he found you up there in South Dakota. Thank you for coming with him."

14

HUNTER SHIFTS IN THE BED. DAHLIA LAYS WITH HER LEG draped over his waist and her head on his chest. But it's not enough. The cars outside, the sirens in the distance, the sound of someone closing a car door nearby—it's all too much. He closes his eyes, and those sounds morph into something more. His body screams he's not safe. He's vulnerable—exposed—and he needs to be ready.

Zip crawls up his torso from the end of the bed and licks his chin. His movement makes Dahlia stir, and she blinks up sleepily to Hunter with his eyes squeezes closed and breathing rapidly.

"Hey," she whispers and pushes up to her elbow. "Hunter," she says with more authority, and his eyes spring open. Her heart breaks at the pain etched in his features. His amber eyes are full of terror. "I'm here. What can I do?"

Zip inches up farther, completely laying on Hunter's chest. "It's all so loud," he says, sweat beading on his forehead.

Dahlia brushes a hand down his arm and orders Zip to move by snapping her fingers. She swings the blankets off and pulls on a pair of jeans and a shirt. "Get up," she tells Hunter.

"Dahlia," he sighs. "There isn't anything you can do. It's me."

She grabs his jeans and a shirt and throws them at him. "Get up. That's an order."

Hunter reluctantly does as she asks. Once they're both dressed, they quietly creep down the stairs. "It's three in the morning. What are you—"

She cuts him off by placing a finger to his lips and hands him the blankets she carried from upstairs. "I'll meet you out back." When he doesn't move and just stares, she gently pushes his shoulder. "Go. I just need to grab something from the truck."

He arches a brow, and Dahlia gives him one more push before he listens. After she learned about why he moved to South Dakota, Carly mentioned stories of things one of her cousins went through when her husband came back in a similar state as Hunter. Sleeping outside seemed to help him. Dahlia knows it's a long shot, but she wanted to be as helpful as she could this weekend. She pulls the hidden bag from under the backseat and walks around the house through the side gate. She finds Hunter staring at the stars in the middle of the open field. His shoulders look relaxed, and she's hopeful he won't take this next gesture as her trying to treat him like he's broken. Not like his mom keeps doing.

"Hey solider."

He turns and holds a hand out to take hers and pulls her into his side. "Hey my little flower."

Dahlia's cheeks heat and she hopes she never grows immune to his nickname for her. "I kind of have a surprise and I really hope you don't get mad."

She doesn't wait for his response, instead she leads him to the trees, further from the house and the noises of the busy street. Surprisingly, the brick houses and fences block out a lot of it. Dahlia walks until she finds two trees that are perfect and she holds the bag out between her and Hunter.

"What is it?"

"It's a hammock. Well, a two-person hammock. I thought—" she huffs and lies it all out there. "I know your mom has been treating like you're incompetent and I'm not trying to do that. Carly has a cousin and well— none of that matters. I thought maybe sleeping out here would help, with you know…"

Hunter steps closer and tucks one of her wild curls behind her ear.

"You packed us a two-person hammock because you thought this would happen?"

She stares up at him. How does she respond to that? What response is he wanting from her? She doesn't want to make him feel less than anything. Because to her, he's everything.

"Would it help if I said that guest bed is hard as a rock and this will be way more comfortable...possibly?" She holds it up like a child who just found the coolest rock.

"Are you afraid of me, little flower?" His voice drops lower, and he grips her chin between his thumb and finger. "Do I scare you?"

"No," Dahlia says, but it comes out breathy for a whole other set of reasons.

"Don't ever hold back from telling me what you're thinking because you're worried about how I'll react. It is my job to make you feel safe and secure in this relationship and if I've done something to make you feel otherwise—"

"You haven't," she says quickly. "I saw the way you responded to your mom's assumptions. I never want to be the reason you get that distant look in your eyes. That's all." She drops the hammock bag in one hand and grips his forearm that's still holding her chin.

"Let's put up the hammock, little flower. How is it you know me better than the people who raised me?" he mumbles, almost like to himself.

"Because I listen. I'm always listening, solider."

His gaze flicks between her eyes, then down to her lips. Her breasts rise and fall with her deep breaths.

"Then I want you to listen very, very closely. Okay?" How he felt at her parents wasn't a one-off situation. His feelings for her grow stronger every day and if he just told her to never hold back what she's thinking than he shouldn't either.

She wets her lips and nods. Her body hums in anticipation at what he is going to say.

"Dahlia, I love you."

Her breath hitches in her chest. Did he just—? She knew this though...right? I mean, what they share and have together is way more than an attraction, but to hear him say it out loud makes it all real. She gets lost in the way his soft honey eyes look down at her, like he's baring his soul to her and he's utterly at her mercy. He's making himself vulnerable, something that his entire body fights against, but he's doing it to prove himself to her.

"Say something," he pleas, worry lacing his voice. His grip on her chin waivers and she steps closer to him so her chest brushes his.

"I love you, Hunter. I think I have since you helped with that first wedding. I was just too scared to listen to my heart."

He lets out a long breath and kisses her fervently. It's pure passion, acceptance, and one hundred percent commitment. He doesn't ask her to be his forever, but she's already decided in that moment that this is the beginning of their happily ever after and it's only a matter of time before he gets on board.

15

"NANCY SAYS SHE SEES HIM SNEAKING OUT EVERY NIGHT TO sleep outside in the woods. It's so sad."

Dahlia squeezes between the woman gossiping by the punch bowl. She has half a mind to spike it just to make today more interesting. Lydia insisted on hosting a party with the small-town hero back home. Apparently, that meant not just the neighbors, but an open invitation to the entire town. The rumors have been flying about who the mystery woman Hunter brought back from wherever he's been hiding and apparently Nancy is a peeping Tom since she knows about Dahlia and Hunter's routine each night.

Dahlia leans in the doorway with her cup against her lips. Hunter laughs, a genuine belly laugh, surrounded by guys he went to school with. She can't fight her smile at the sight and decides to hang back for a bit. Every once in a while he gets the wild look in his eye and that's when she steps in to give him an excuse to step away.

"Isn't this nice," Lydia chimes. "He's back to his old self. I knew if he would just come home and give it a chance, it would work."

Dahlia bites the edge of her cup to keep from spewing the truth. If his mom wants to live in this delusional land while they're here to visit, she can. The doorbell rings and Lydia scurries away to be the picture-perfect host.

Hunter looks around, and when he spots Dahlia, he winks before nodding at something one guy said.

"He looks so happy," a woman says beside her.

Dahlia hums, not looking over at the woman. She's had people coming up to her all day, complimenting how Hunter is doing and telling her childhood stories. What's one more person?

"It's sad, really," the woman continues. "He clearly belongs here. Look at him. Surrounded by friends and people who love him."

Dahlia pivots to face the newcomer. She holds a pie dish in her manicured hands. Her hair lays in perfect blond waves down to her mid-back. Bright red painted bow lips complete her look of innocence with her big doll eyes.

"I'm sorry—who are you?" Dahlia asks, already suspicious that she knows the answer.

Her lips spread into a sweet smile. "I feel sorry for the woman who drove all the way down here with him, just for him to realize this is where he belongs and regret ever leaving."

Hunter looks past his friends to check in with Dahlia again. She's been so patient with him today. He knows what his mom is doing. It's obvious. But he won't stay. He's found something in the mountains of South Dakota that Tennessee will never be able to offer him.

Dahlia is no longer standing relaxed in the doorway. Instead, she's facing Lauren and from the look on his little flower's face, whatever his ex is saying...isn't good.

"Zip," Hunter commands and his dog falls into step beside him as he pushes past his high school friends. As he gets closer, he makes out the tail end of Lauren's speech.

"...he's back now, and that means something. Don't get it twisted that you're his savior. I've known him my whole life and have something you don't."

"Hey, little flower," Hunter drawls and plants a kiss to her temple. Her body is rigid with rage, an emotion Hunter isn't used to seeing her show.

"Hunter!" Lauren coos and holds her hands out with the pie. "I brought your favorite. Peanut Butter, remember?"

Zip moves to stand between Dahlia and Hunter, licking her hands, and pulls her out of her trance.

"Lauren. What are you doing here?" Hunter asks, his hand snaking around Dahlia's waist, pulling her close.

"Oh, don't be silly!" Lydia breaks in as she steps through the back door. "I invited her. Ya'll have been friends for years and this thing between you shouldn't stop that."

Dahlia arches a brow, but the way Hunter's fingers dig into her hip keeps her from saying anything.

"This *thing*? This is crossing a line, Mom." His voice comes out strained and low. Zip's ears perk at his owner's tone and looks around for what has him on edge.

"Lydia," Jared says as he steps into the group that's forming. "Let's not make a scene, dear. Come on. Lauren, it was nice of you to come, but perhaps you should…"

"Jared!" Lydia snaps. "She's my guest, and she's staying. Hunter has to understand—"

Hunter chuckles, but there is no humor in his voice. "Don't worry, Dad. I was going to take Dahlia to show her the lake. Mom, you can keep *her* company. Come on, babe." He moves his hand from Dahlia's waist to her hand and leads her past his mom and ex-girlfriend. Dahlia sets her cup down on a table as they pass it. His mother shouts after them, and Dahlia looks over her shoulder to see Lauren with tears in her eyes. She pities the woman who is clearly stuck on someone she can never have.

"Are you—?" she starts to ask, but Hunter sits staring at the windshield. His hands shake on the steering wheel. "Come on, solider. I'll drive."

The water laps on the shore and Hunter throws another stick for Zip to jump in after. "I'm sorry, little flower."

"Don't you didn't—"

Hunter shakes his head. "No. I brought you here. I put you through *that*. I never believed Mom would—fuck!" he shouts.

Dahlia places a hand on his forearm and forces him to face her. "Do you really think I'm going to something dolled-up-southern-barbie said get to me? She may know you from way back, but I *know* you. The real you. The one standing right here. The one who told me he loved me and let me in. I have the parts of you she'll *never* be privy to. And nothing she says will ever change that."

She moves her hands up his chest and lightly grips his T-shirt.

He breathes in the smell of her shampoo and buries his face in the crook of her neck. "I thought—I was worried she had said something to make you hate me."

"The only thing that could do that is if you tell me her pie is better than mine."

Hunter chokes out a laugh and between kisses he says, "Little flower, everything about you is better. Your laugh. Your love. The way you look at me when I test your patience. Nothing compares to this."

"Why do you let me show you how much better I am?"

16

HUNTER BRACES HIMSELF ON THE OPEN TAILGATE OF HIS truck. Dahlia steps between his legs and pulls his shirt up over his head, tossing it to the ground. She grazes her fingertips down the muscles along his ribs and down the V that disappears under the belt of his jeans.

"Anyone could walk up here, little flower." His voice is low and thick.

"I don't care." She unbuckles his belt and quickly pulls it free from the loops. Hunter grabs it before she can toss it aside too.

"Good, because the entire county is about to hear you."

"Are you sure it's me they'll be hearing?" she remarks. Her stomach tightens, and she squeezes her thighs together for relief. Hunter runs his thumb across her bottom lip and pulls it down. He lifts the belt laying in his other hand and a mischievous smirk spreads on his lips.

"I'm going to put this around your neck and fuck you. Then we're going back to South Dakota and you're moving into the cabin with me. The main cabin, Dahlia."

It wasn't a question, or even an offer. It's a demand—an order—and he doesn't wait for her to say okay. He cinches the belt tightly around her throat and gives it a firm tug, bringing her closer to him.

"I want your hot mouth wrapped around my cock and for you to stare up at me so I can watch as I fuck your mouth."

She licks her lips in anticipation. The tightness of the leather around her throat as he pulls on it makes her clit ache for friction. Hunter angles his head, his nose grazing her jawline.

"Do you like that, little flower?" He pulls it tighter and a small gasp escapes her parted lips. "You look so damn sexy with that fire burning in your eyes." He grips her hand and moves it to cup his erection through his jeans. "This...this is what you do to me. I want you every damn day and feel like I will never have enough. I wake up every day starving for your touch, your kiss, the fell of your skin. I don't want you to ever doubt how I feel about you."

Dahlia moves her hand along his cock and it pushes against the restraint of his jeans. She drops to her knees, keeping eye contact as she unbuttons his pants, sliding them down his legs and to his ankles. She rests her hand above where the prosthetic connects and massages the muscle there.

Hunter groans in relief, and his hand tightens around the belt. His cock jumps with pre-cum beading at the tip.

"How does that feel?" she asks, digger deeper into the muscle.

Hunter's head falls back, and he shudders under her touch. He bites on his bottom lip and Dahlia moves one hand, wrapping it around his cock and licks across the head. Hunter thrusts his hips forward, forcing his cock to the back of her throat. He pulls the belt tight, keeping her from moving away from him.

Her cheeks hollow and she twists her hand at the base of his cock as he fucks her mouth with urgency. A need that only Dahlia can fulfill.

"Eyes open," he orders. She looks up through her eyelashes and a tear escapes down her cheek. Hunter eases, worried he's hurting her. She moves her hand to cover his on the belt and pulls it tighter up. The last thing she wants is for him to take it easy on her.

A car door closes nearby and Hunter stills, listening for the intruder. Someone is at his back and he fights the impulse to find cover and wait. Dahlia squeezes her fingers, forcing his attention to stay on her.

Don't stop, she says with her eyes and body. The last thing she wants is for him to let up because he's worried she can't handle it and she doesn't want to lose him to his memories. Not here. Not in this moment.

The thrill of knowing there are people nearby intensifies everything. Let them find her on her knees, devouring this man. The only man she'd ever let take her like this. In the back of her mind, she hopes it's Lauren coming to see if she can find Hunter. Wouldn't it be a sight for her to see Dahlia on her knees with a belt around her throat?

Hunter fists his hand in her hair, the pain of him pulling the strands turning into pleasure as he fights his training. He rocks his hips faster. Her jaws ache and she squeezes his balls as they tighten. He comes down her throat, moaning *little flower* as he does. He doesn't care about who hears because in less than twenty-four hours, this place will be in his rear-view mirror and he'll be going home with the woman he loves.

She slides his cock out of her mouth and wipes her chin with the back of her hand. As she stands, she pulls his jeans up his legs and buttons them. He loosens the belt and helps Dahlia to her feet.

Her hair is a wild mane of curls and smudges of makeup surround her eyes.

Laughter gets closer and Hunter removes the belt, tossing it into the truck bed behind him. A couple steps into view from the tree line and balk at the sight of Hunter's naked torso and Dahlia's rustled state.

Zip jumps up and lets out a warning growl at the newcomers.

"Zip," Hunter states and the dog sits, but doesn't take his eyes off the couple.

"Everything okay here?" the man asks as he studies Dahlia. The woman with him stands back, reaching for her pocket.

Dahlia gives a sheepish smile and Hunter glances up at the man, revealing who he is under his cowboy hat. The stranger's eyes widen. "Oh shit, Hunter. I thought—we'll go this way." He stumbles over the rocks and Dahlia giggles into her hand at their quick retreat.

"Shit," Hunter grumbles.

"What?" Dahlia asks, not understanding where his tone is coming from.

"That was Lauren's older brother."

Dahlia's giggles turn into full laughter as she images how that conversation will go when Lauren finds out exactly what happened on this lake shore. Or rather, what her brother assumes happened.

Hunter's scowl softens, and he laughs, pulling Dahlia against him and feverishly kissing her soft slips. "Are you ready to go home?"

Home. To his cabin. With him.

Her laughter quiets, but her cheeks ache not only from sucking on his cock, but from the smile stretching across her face.

"Yes. I am so ready to go home."

17

"No way! What did you do?" Carly asks as Dahlia gives her the play-by-play of how her time in Tennessee went and the surprise visit from Lauren.

Hunter kept to his word, even with his mom begging him to stay. They loaded the truck up that night and came drove back to South Dakota. Only this time, they took a scenic route and stopped at several nice hotels. One of which had a hot tub that they took full advantage of.

"I didn't have to do anything. Hunter and I left. Then the lake happened and well..." Dahlia runs a hand across her throat as she remembers the moment between them. "You know the rest."

"And you're living with him now?"

The act of moving into the main cabin with Hunter was easier said in Tennessee hours away from here. Who knew she has accumulated so much stuff in her thirty years and Hunter, well he has his own demons he's fighting staying in the new cabin.

"We're still working out that part." Dahlia places the finishing touches on a wedding bouquet and holds it up for inspection. If it doesn't stand on its own, then it's not done. She double checks the pin is at the back and smiles in satisfaction.

"And you love him?" Carly asks, taking the bouquet and placing it in the cooler.

Butterflies stir in Dahlia's stomach just like every time she thinks about her and Hunter's developed relationship.

"Yes," she answers honestly.

Carly swoons with the back of her hand draped across her forehead and clutches a single dahlia to her chest. "Just think, it only took you getting stuck in a ditch to put all this in motion."

"Yeah, yeah." Dahlia grabs her checklist and runs through everything for the wedding at Hunter's tomorrow. It's more work now since they have to move their belongings out of sight when the bridal party uses the entire house to get ready. She keeps telling Hunter to update his clause to only use specific rooms, but he hasn't yet.

On the other hand, she's excited to spend the weekend in the shack with him. It's cozier, simpler, out there.

"And I'll be here, running the shop. Waiting for my talk, dark, and dreamy to walk through those doors willed by fate." Carly sighs and leans her elbows on the checkout counter.

"It'll happen when you least expect it," Dahlia says with a wink.

Carly groans and chews on the end of a pencil. "You can only say that because God decided your stubborn ass wouldn't meet anyone if he didn't literally throw you two together without an escape."

Dahlia's mouth falls open and she whirls on her friend. "That's not true."

But it kind of is.

Carly gives her a bored look and then perks up.

"Speaking of fate," Carly whispers.

The door chimes, and Hunter walks with Zip by his side. The moment he spots Dahlia, his tail wags and he boops his nose to her fingertips. She kneels and scratches behind his ears.

"Hey pretty boy. What are you doing here?" she says in baby talk.

"I knew it. You're only with me for Zip," Hunter teases, and Dahlia blows the escaped curls out of her face and looks up at him. "I needed some fuel for the generator this weekend. Thought I'd stop by and see if you needed anything before closing up."

"I mean, he is the one who found me in a snowstorm." She pushes to her feet and picks her clipboard up from the floor.

"Well, it sounds like you had a very exciting time last week," Carly says while pointing the pencil in Hunter's direction. He raises a brow at Dahlia, who smirks and shrugs her shoulders. "The lake?"

"Carly!" Dahlia shouts and pinches the bridge of her nose.

Hunter grins wide and adjusts his cowboy hat.

"The belt was a great addition," her best friend winks and Dahlia hides her face behind the clipboard.

"And we're leaving. Bye!" She throws her hand up behind her and doesn't wait to see if Hunter follows or not.

Tomorrow she'll be here bright and early to load up for the wedding at Hayne's Ranch. This couple is using the barn for the ceremony and reception. Dreaming of Dahlia's will decorate not only for the ceremony but the reception tables as well. This bride left nothing out. Dahlia even has greenery to wrap around the support beams.

It might be one of her biggest jobs yet. Thankfully, Hunter has volunteered to help. Just like every time her nerves are shot, and she's worried she's going to overlook an important detail or somehow screw up.

"Dahlia." Hunter's voice comes from behind her and his chest brushes against her back. "You're in your head." He spins her around and places a knuckle under her chin.

"Tomorrow is a big client. What if—anything could go wrong?"

Hunter opens her driver door behind her, and she steps forward, closer to Hunter. "And we will tackle anything that will happen. But you still need to eat—" She opens her mouth to argue, and he places a finger over her lips. "Something more than energy bars. You need a proper meal, which is another reason I'm in town. Let's go home, fix dinner, then fall asleep *fully* satisfied."

He quickly kisses her lips, leaving her wanting for more.

She stares at him. *How did she ever do this without him?* Admitting that out loud scares the hell out of her because it means she's relying on someone besides herself to get things done. She's lost part of her control over every little detail, gave it away willingly to this cowboy who always seems to know what she needs to hear.

He steps back and opens her door all the way. "Let's go give you something else to tell Carly all about later."

She swats her hand at him and he dodges her. "I don't tell her everything!"

"Does she know a belt has multiple uses, or should I go tell her myself?"

"Hunter Haynes, get your ass in that truck before I change my mind and sleep alone tonight."

She's bluffing. They both know it. She's way past spending nights alone with a bottle of wine. And she's never been happier.

18

HUNTER PULLS HIS PHONE FROM HIS POCKET AND CHECKS THE caller ID. His mother...again. She's called three times nearly every day since he left. But today it's been every five minutes.

He isn't truly ignoring her, he just needs space after the stunt she pulled. He wants to shout and tell her this was exactly why he didn't call when he left home before. He knows she's never going to leave him alone and honestly, that isn't what he wants.

He just wants space to feel like he can breathe. The call goes to his full voicemail, courtesy of his truly, and then an unknown number pops up.

"Hello?" Hunter says, knowing it could be a client for the wedding venue.

"It's not polite to ignore your mother's phone calls," Lydia hisses and Hunter pinches the bridge of his nose.

"It's also not polite to bombard me with my ex when I come to visit and try to make my girlfriend feel unworthy," he retorts and the line goes silent.

"Hunter, there's something you need to know..." Her voice takes a serious tone, and he sighs.

"Is Dad okay?" he asks, realizing the reason she's been calling today could be about more than her wanting him to come back to Tennessee.

"Yes, he's fine. But Lauren—"

"Mom, I don't want to talk about this. We're not getting back—"

"—was in a car accident this afternoon."

The air leaves Hunter's lungs in a whoosh. Just because he doesn't love her and wants to grow old with her like they planned doesn't mean he wants anything to happen to her. She just needs to find her person.

"Is she okay?" Hunter asks, looking down the driveway for any sign of Dahlia to fill her in.

"She's stable, but—" Lydia's voice cracks and Hunter's heart races.

There's a shuffle from his mother's end of the phone.

"Son, I know you don't want to hear this, but you need to come home," Jared says, his tone leaves no room for an argument.

"Why me? I'm not with Lauren. She has family, you guys, friends. What will me being their matter? I'm not her person for this shit."

"No, you're not," Jared states. "But she wasn't alone in the car when she wrecked. She hasn't been alone since you left home. Hunter," His dad takes a steadying breath. "You have a daughter. She was also in the car."

Hunter's leg gives out, and he kneels on the ground. His mind races around the words his dad just said.

He has a daughter.

Lauren is the mother. And they were in a car accident.

Lauren is stable but...

"Is she okay?" His voice doesn't sound like his own. It sounds far away and muffled and he can't hear through the ringing in his ears.

"Hunter!" Jared shouts, and his mother wails in the background. "I need to keep it together, son. Can you do that?"

"Yes," Hunter whispers. Zip pushes against his leg and whines into the phone.

"She's in the ICU. It's touch and go right now. You *need* to come home."

He doesn't waste time arguing. He gets in his truck and throws it in reverse. A flash of another vehicle shines in his periphery and he slams on his brakes, his chest heaving and hands shaking.

Not just his hands, his body is trembling. His lips move, but no words come out. He can't see a face, can't even imagine what his daughter would look like, but an overwhelming sense of knowing his dad is telling the truth slams into his chest. It feels real.

"Hunter? What the hell is going on?" Dahlia opens his door and pats her hands down his body, trying to make sense of what he's mumbling. She grips his chin and forces his dazed eyes to look up at her. He isn't there. The vacant stare he has when he's fighting his memories has taken over.

"Zip," Dahlia says and the dog jumps to the front seat and lies on his lap. "Listen to me. Follow my voice and come back. You're in South Dakota, you're safe. I'm right here." Dahlia recites like she's done for him before.

Hunter shakes his head because she doesn't understand. He's safe, yes. But his child, his kid, is fighting for its life and he didn't even know she existed.

"I have a daughter," he manages to choke out, and Dahlia stills.

"You have a what?" she asks, not sure she heard him right. They've never had the kids talk, and she's never thought to ask.

"Dad called. Lauren was in a car accident," he mumbles, his body still shaking. "She had a kid with her...my kid. I have a fucking daughter and she's in the ICU."

"Slow down, solider. You're not making any sense. Maybe I should call Jared—"

"I have to go. I have to..."

He's never hated himself as much as he does right now. The worry and fear staring back at him in Dahlia's eyes, the abandonment that child must've felt at not having her father. What Lauren had to go through alone...all because he couldn't handle his own shit and now he's dragging everyone down with him.

"I have to go," he says softer. He can't bring himself to meet her gaze. She'll hate him for this. His PTSD baggage was one thing, but having a child with another woman—that'll be too much. He knows it will. Because who would want a broken man with a fragmented mind that's has a child? She'll be smart to run.

She will find someone better than him. Someone suited perfectly for her. Anyone but him.

"Okay, let me pack us a couple of bags and grab what we need."

He jerks his head up to Dahlia, waiting for him to acknowledge he heard her.

"We?" he asks, truly confused. "I have a fucking kid, little flower. I'm not the man you deserve."

She shakes her head. "We. We're a team. You and me. This doesn't change that...unless you don't want me to go..." She lets her voice trail off, wondering if this changes everything for him and he is having second thoughts.

"Little flower." Hunter stands from the truck and wraps his arms around her, kissing the top of her head. "I'll never stop wanting you. I want to be by your side, always. I just don't want to drag you down with my shit."

She tightens her hold and listens to the erratic beat of his heart. He's fucking terrified it pulls on her chest.

"I'm with you. No matter what."

19

IT DIDN'T TAKE MUCH TO CONVINCE HUNTER TO FLY INSTEAD of drive. He was eager to get there, and Dahlia knew that if he got behind the wheel of his truck, he'd probably be reckless. He's been quiet most of the trip, Zip sticking extremely close to him.

She wants to ask questions. The most important being, *when did this happen?* And how did Hunter not know? She replays Lydia's incessant mention of Lauren time and time again.

They knew.

Everyone fucking knew. She bets the entire part knew, and still nobody spoke up. Nobody told Hunter he was a dad. They all kept it a secret from him. And that fact pisses her off more than anything.

She doesn't know what will happen on this trip. Everything was laid out for her in a straight line, but a child...that changes everything. Like, will Hunter want to move back to Tennessee to be closer to her? That would make sense. How could she fault him for that? Will Lauren even entertain the idea of her coming to visit in South Dakota? Will he fight for rights of some kind? Will his old feelings for Lauren reignite when he looks into his daughter's eyes and sees pieces of Lauren there, too?

She puts the car in park and stares out the windshield at the hospital.

"You don't have to go in," Hunter says, the first words he's spoken since calling his parents to let them know he made it.

"Do you want me to?" she asks, not able to bring herself to look over at him. She feels everything they've built is so close to falling apart. She'll keep her mask in place for this trip. Be who and what Hunter needs her to be and in the end she'll go back home...and he'll have to decide.

"I don't even want to go." His head falls back, and he looks at the ceiling like it'll hold all the answers. "The first view of my daughter is going to be attached to tubes and wires," he says, his throat tight and tears pooling in his eyes.

"None of this is your fault," she reminds him. "You didn't know."

"But I left." He reaches for the door handle and pauses. "I can't tell you how sorry I am."

"We'll get through it. I'm right here." Even if she feels like her stomach is trying to exit her body through her mouth.

When the smell of the antiseptic hits him as they walk inside, one hand on Zip's leash and the other clinging to Dahlia's for dear life. He walks to the desk and a few nurses eye Zip, cautiously. Normally, Hunter enjoys these moments, but his mind is miles away.

"Can I help you?" the lady behind the desk asks. Dahlia glances at Hunter, who doesn't say anything.

"We're here for Lauren—" Dahlia starts, then realizes she doesn't know her last name.

"Hunter," Lydia exclaims. She rushes forward with puffy red eyes and reaches for her son. Dahlia lets go of his hand and steps back as his dad and the man that surprised them at the lake get closer.

Hunter squeezes his eyes closed. *They all knew.* "I'm not here for you or anyone else in this town," he seethes. Dahlia is shocked that he's taking this approach, but I guess a person can only be pushed so far.

Lydia pulls back and her lip quivers. "Son—"

Jared steps forward, but Hunter moves around them to grip Dahlia's hand once more. "I want to see her."

Lydia nods and wipes her hands on her pants. "Of course, Lauren is right—"

"I want to see my daughter," Hunter cuts her off and stares his mother down with cold eyes.

"Well, you'll have to talk to Lauren first, get her permission before you can go into the ICU," Lauren's brother says, watching Hunter and Zip carefully.

Hunter's grip tightens, and Lydia has the decency to drop her gaze.

"Fine. Where is she?"

Lauren's brother opens the door to room 217. "He's here," he announces, as if that is all the detail Lauren needs to know it's Hunter. Her eyes light up when he steps into the room, but her smile fades when Dahlia comes in behind him.

"I don't want her in here," she demands, and Hunter's jaw ticks.

"You're one to be making demands. You kept my daughter from me for nearly two years."

"Because I had any way to contact you?!" she screeches and the machine besides her beeps faster.

"It's fine. I'll just be outside," Dahlia offers, clearly with her in the room, Lauren isn't going to agree to anything.

He hands Zip's leash to her. "Don't go far." She turns to leave, but he grabs her hand and pulls her back around, kissing her deeply before letting go.

Lauren crosses her arms and Hunter sits in a chair by the wall, away from her bed. Her brother closes the door behind him and it's just the two of them.

Her scowl softens, and she fidgets with her fingers. "I knew you'd come. Carter said I was insane to even want you here. He just doesn't understand what we have."

"We don't have anything except a child in the ICU. I want to see her." Hunter doesn't see the point in small talk. There are far more important things than Lauren's feelings.

She wipes a stray tear from her cheek and wets her lips. "Her name's Faith. Because she gave me faith that you would come back to me. You had to. We created something so beautiful together. How could God let that happen, then rip you away from me?"

"Lauren, I'm not the same person I was in high school. You don't know the first thing about who I am now. I love Dahlia. I'm sorry I hurt you and left this on you to do alone. It was never my intention. But I know now and things are going to be different, I promise."

She sniffles and pulls at the frayed edges of the hospital blanket. "She has your last name, you know. She's beautiful. Has your eyes and perfect nose." She stares out the window as she talks. "How will things be different, Hunter? You living all the way up there and me and her will still be here. Just like it's always been."

Hunter doesn't have time to get caught up on the details right now and, honestly, he doesn't know how he is going to make this work. But he will, he has to travel back and forth...he will. Because that's the kind of dad he wants to be.

He swallows the lump in his throat to ask, "Can I see her?" The fact that he needs her permission to see his own flesh and blood makes him see red, but he'll play by the rules if it gets him into her room.

"It's bad," she chokes out, her emotions becoming too much to bear. "It wasn't my fault. I swear."

Hunter pushes to his feet and moves over to the side of her bed and pets a hand down her hair. "I bet you're a great mother," he tells her, because it's the truth. There never was a mean bone in Lauren's body, and he hates what he did to her.

Lauren presses the call button and a nurse steps into the room. "Can I help you?" she asks.

Lauren reaches up and takes Hunter's hand. "He wants to go see our daughter, please."

20

"I'll be right here. We both will," Dahlia tells Hunter. Since she's not family, she can't go into the ICU room and they won't allow Zip in either.

"Okay," he says. His chest tightens, and he tries to shift the uneasiness away. Each footstep he takes is a solo beating drum in the balance of his future. Behind him is Dahlia and everything he's found in South Dakota, and somewhere ahead of him is Faith. Is leaving one for the other what his future will look like? Will he be forced to make a choice?

"She's right in here," the nurse tells him and opens the door. A rhythmic beeping comes from the machine beside her bed and Carter turns his head, blocking Hunter's view as he steps in.

"So, she let you piece of shit in here after all?" he asks.

"I didn't know when I left and I'm here now so."

"Yeah, you sure are." Carter steps to the side and Hunter's heart lurches. Faith has a bandage wrapped around her head, hiding an IV. Her dark lashes, *his* lashes, rest against her cheeks as her chest steadily rises and falls. He counts each of her tiny fingers and memorizes the shape of her nose.

"The doctors say the next seventy-two hours are critical. We never leave her alone. It's either mom and dad, your parents or me. She hasn't woken up since the crash."

Hunter falls into the chair beside her bed and gently brushes a finger across the back of her hand.

"She's so small."

Carter chuckles. "You should have seen her the day she came home. But don't let her size fool you. She can make you do anything she wants with a look."

Hunter runs a hand over the stubble along his mouth and chin. He can't believe it. She's so beautiful.

"She's a fighter. She will come through this," Carter says with confidence.

"Of course she is," Hunter states. *Like him.*

"The doctors say talking to her can help. The claim she can hear you. I'll give you some time."

The click of the door closing is all that tells Hunter he ever left, because his eyes never leave his precious Faith.

He opens his mouth to say something, then realizes he has no idea what to say. He doesn't know what shows she likes, what foods she spit in her mother's face, or even if she has a dog.

"I have a dog," he blurts, because that's his first train of thought. "He's white like the snow and he's my best friend. I think you'd really love him. When you wake up, you'll get to meet him...and me, I guess."

His throat tightens with emotions he's never felt for another person before. "Faith," he says her name for the first time aloud and his voice cracks. "I'm your daddy. And I really want to meet you. I need you to fight and wake up so I can teach you to do all the things that will have your mommy freaking out about.

"I have so much I want to show you. I'm sorry it took me so long to find you."

Dahlia sits on a bench outside with Zip laying at her feet. Footsteps approach behind her, and she straightens, hoping to see Hunter. Instead, it's Lydia.

"I thought I'd find you out here," she says as she sits on the bench beside Dahlia.

"Hunter is with Faith. They wouldn't let Zip or non-family members back." She runs her hands over Zip's head and tries to rein in her anger about the whole situation.

"I'm glad he talked to Lauren."

Dahlia snorts.

"Well, honey, what did you expect? They have a child and they've been in love for way long than you've known him—"

Dahlia pushes to her feet and stares down at Hunter's cynical mother. "Okay. That's enough. You're delusional or crazy—or both! Hunter will never get back with Lauren. The only thing you've accomplished is keeping his daughter from him since the day he called you. *If* he moves back here, know it's for that little girl up there fighting for her life. It has nothing to do with you or this fantasy you've cooked up."

Dahlia's panting, with Zip's leash digging into her palm. Lydia's features morph from reddening color to pale. But the rage still burns under Dahlia's skin.

"You came to his home! You sat there and all you could say was, *what about Lauren?* Then we came to *your* home, and you treated Hunter like he couldn't climb a set of stairs! You put a fucking shower bench in. Newsflash, he's perfectly capable of doing anything he wants and he gets by perfectly without being treated like a child. God, it's no wonder why he left and never came back. How does it feel to know your own child wants nothing to do with you?!"

"That's enough!" Lydia shouts and stands toe-to-toe with Dahlia. "I lost my only child. I thought he was dead and never expected to see or hear from him again! You hear the horror stories of men coming back from the war, but you never think your smiling, always happy baby boy would be among them. I couldn't even hug him when he came home." Her voice cracks and Dahlia drops her head to stare at her shoes. "My baby never came back. And as a mother, I would do *anything* to get him back. I had to try. You don't know what it's been like, so don't spout her holier than that shit at me. Not until you've been through what I have. Waiting by the phone day after day for a call that he had been found dead, frozen on the side of the road, or heaven forbid taken his own life. I spent months driving through towns, searching for my son among the home-less. I never gave up."

Dahlia blinks and tears fall from her lashes. She hadn't thought about what Lydia and Jared went through when Hunter left. "He's never going to be the man you remember. He's seen too much, been through too much. The sooner you accept that, the sooner you two can work on your relationship. But it's going to take a lot to get his forgiveness for this. He's an amazing person. I hope you can see that."

"We do," Jared says and both women turn to face the doors where Jared stands, listening. "I think you've both said your peace. Hunter's looking for you," he says to Dahlia, putting an end to the conversation.

21

"I HATE LEAVING YOU HERE," HUNTER SAYS AS HE PLACES their overnight bags in the guest room of his parents' house.

"We'll be fine," she says, gesturing to Zip chewing on a bone. "You do what you need to do."

Hunter sags onto the edge of the mattress. It's not even been an hour since they left the hospital and he wants more than anything to be back there…with his daughter.

"I need you," he says into his hands, and Dahlia rubs a hand down his back.

"And you have me. I'm right here. I'm not going anywhere."

He angles his body to Dahlia into him and kisses her lips softly. "I love you, little flower. This doesn't change that."

She wishes they had more time for him to show her how much he truly does love her, if for nothing else, but to shove the conversation she had with his mother out of her mind for good.

"I love you, solider."

"I need to get back," he says. "But I'll call you. Okay?" He crouches to Zip and rubs his head. "You take care of my girl, got it? I'm trusting you."

Dahlia smiles at the pair on the floor, and Hunter winces as he straightens. For the second time in twenty-four hours, he's leaving Dahlia behind, and it makes him feel sick. She insisted that he eat something on the way to his parents. Thank goodness she's stubborn enough to not take no for an answer.

When he gets to Faith's room, he's surprised to find Lauren in a wheelchair beside the bed. "Oh, I can give you time."

She rolls back to face him. "No, you're fine. I just—when she wakes up, I don't want her to be alone."

Hunter studies his childhood best friend. She looks so tired with dark purple circles under her eyes and her skin is so pale, he's expects to see her veins. "You should go rest, Ren."

"You haven't called me that in years." Even her voice sounds childlike. "I'm sorry I didn't tell you, Hunter. I'm sorry for all of this. You were always honest with me and when it mattered, I—" She coughs so hard her body shakes and she slumps forward. Hunter rushes to her side and helps her sit back in the wheelchair.

"It doesn't matter. But Faith needs her mommy to be strong when she wakes up. C'mon, I'll take you back, then I'll sit with her."

Hunter pushes Lauren to her room and lifts her into her bed.

"You'll be a great dad," she tells him. Her eyes are so heavy she barely mumbles a thanks before she's asleep. The hospital is quiet this late at night. He lays back in her his chair, keeping his pointer finger under Faith's hand.

"I can't wait to see your beautiful eyes, baby girl," he whispers to her.

"Hunter," a voice says far away. Something touches his shoulder and he jumps up from his chair. His mom jumps back, her eyes wide. He forces his breathing to slow and rubs a hand over his face.

"Sorry, I must have fallen asleep. What time is it?"

Lydia steps closer and hesitantly runs a hand down his arm. "It's three in the morning, sweetie."

"Why are you here, then?"

He looks into his mother's eyes for the first time. They're rimmed in red...she's been crying. Hunter jerks his attention to Faith. Then the machines hooked to her. Everything looks the same as it did when he got there, so what has his mother so upset? The only other person with her was — "Is Dahlia okay? Zip? What's going on?" Hunter panics when his mom doesn't answer right away. "Mom!" he shouts, needing her to tell him why are lip is quivering and tears well in her eyes. If anything happened to Dahlia—he won't survive it.

"It's Lauren," she chokes out, and Hunter tries to make sense of what she is talking about. He was just with Lauren a couple of hours ago. She was fine. "Honey, she's gone. The doctors said an aneurysm ruptured. Nobody saw it coming. I'm so sorry."

He shakes his head in disbelief while his mother is on the verge of a breakdown.

Faith's mother is gone. She's going to wake up and the one person she's had from the beginning, that she relied on, won't be here anymore. And there isn't anything he can do to protect her from that pain.

"Hunter?" Lydia says, looking for confirmation he heard her.

"Okay," he sighs, rubbing his hands on his jeans and pulling from his training to battle one problem at a time. "Okay. I'm not leaving her alone," he says, pointing at Faith. "I'm going to be here when she wakes up. Mom," He looks up at his mother with pleading eyes. "I need Dahlia. Do whatever you have to do to get her in here. Please, for me."

She nods, realizing he loves her in a way she didn't realize. There is no denying now, in his time of need, the one person he wants, even more than his own mother, is Dahlia. "Of course. We'll watch over Zip while you two are here. Don't worry about him. If you need anything, you call. Okay?"

It isn't until his mom closes the door that he lets himself fall apart. He cries for his childhood best friend and first love. For the man he left behind in the war. For his parents whose hearts he broke when he left. And for his daughter fighting for her life, looking far too small for this bed.

"Please, please wake up," he begs to whoever is listening.

By the time Dahlia steps through the door, tears silently trail down his cheeks. "Oh, Hunter," she says and leans down to hug his shoulders. When Lydia called and said Hunter needed her and told her about what happened, she didn't hesitate to rush over here. Zip wasn't happy about staying with Jared at the house, but he listened.

"I can't believe she's gone and now…I'm the only parent this little girl has and she's going to wake up to meet a stranger."

Dahlia rests her cheek atop his head. "We'll take it one step at a time. Together."

22

HOW HUNTER GOT COMFORTABLE ENOUGH TO FALL ASLEEP IS beyond Dahlia. It's hard for her to look at the sleeping toddler in the middle of the room. Her heart is breaking for the child, Hunter, Lauren's family. She can't help her problem-solving mind already thinking through every scenario that could happen.

Hunter could choose to stay. Would he ask her to stay with him?

Will he have sole custody or have to go to court? She never dreamed these would be questions she would be asking.

Nobody has come in since she got here, aside from the nursing staff. A whimper comes from the bed and Dahlia pushes from the wall she is currently standing on.

Did she imagine it?

Faith's head turns to the side and her lips part to let out a long cry. Hunter wakes up immediately and reaches for her. Dahlia rushes for the nurse button and within seconds, a nurse steps in. She starts to ask a question when Faith cries out again.

"Can I pick her up?" Hunter asks, his voice full of uncertainty and worry.

"Yes, yes!" the nurse assures him, excitement sparkling in her eyes that her patient is awake. Hunter picks Faith up carefully, adjusting the IV cord so it doesn't get tangles up.

He soothes his daughter and Dahlia didn't think she could ever love this man more. But the way he is talking to Faith and looking at her, it unlocks a whole new form of love.

Once the nurses check her vitals, they bring food in to see if she has an appetite. Hunter doesn't let her go. Her eyes are as beautiful as he could imagine. They're honey colored and pull him in. Carter was right. Hunter would do anything she asked. She calmed the moment her eyes landed on him, like she knew him all along. Tears burn the back of his throat as he holds her while she sleeps. He won't be missing out on anything from here on out. He's missed enough already. Whenever she cries, he'll be there. For every monumental moment in life. He'll be there.

She's never going to look back and wonder where he was. He refuses to let that be her future.

"She's beautiful," Dahlia whispers as she pulls a chair up beside him. "She looks like you."

Hunter chuckles, careful to not wake her up. "Don't put that on her. She looks so much better than me."

They both smile, and he tilts his head until it leans against Dahlia's. "Thank you, little flower."

"You're very welcome, solider. I'm going to check on Zip and get some food. You still need to eat."

A soft knock comes from the door and Lydia pokes her head inside. "May I?"

"Of course," Dahlia answers, and Hunter notes the new tone she uses with his mother. "I was going to grab some food for us. Would you like anything?" she asks.

"Oh no, Jared and I already ate. I worry he's growing attached to your dog already. He's talking about us getting one." She tries to smile, but it doesn't work. For her, losing Lauren was like losing a daughter. It'll be awhile for that kind of pain lessens.

"I don't understand how this works!" Hunter grabs the strap and yanks it from the truck entirely. Dahlia stares at it like it'll bite her. She doesn't know either.

"Okay, well…let's look." She crouches and reads the less than helpful directions on the side of the car seat. She goes over them three times and it still doesn't make sense.

Hunter's parents are upstairs in Faith's room with Lauren's family. Since Hunter's last name is on the birth certificate and there is no real reason, he shouldn't have his child, they all agreed he could take her home. Well, to his parents' house for the time being. Lauren's funeral was two days ago and Faith has been asking for her mommy consistently since she's getting better. It breaks everyone's heart to hear it.

Hunter didn't go to the service. He stayed with Faith and told her stories about her mommy from younger years. He keeps waiting for Dahlia to get jealous or doubt his feelings, which is why he tells her he loves her and appreciates her every chance he gets.

Surprisingly, the only person she wants to let hold her is Hunter. So, he is installing, rather trying to install, this car seat.

"First time?" A woman with a baby on her hip and a toddler holding her hand asks as she walks by. Hunter and Dahlia stare at her, confused. "First-time parents?" she supplies.

"No—well, I—kinda?" Dahlia stutters out. Technically, the answer is yes, but it's layered with tons of complications.

"Here, take, Jill." The woman hands the infant on her hip to Dahlia without hesitation. "You'll need the practice and I'll show you how to do it."

Dahlia sweats, not the hot kind, but the holy fuck stress kind. Does it show that obvious that she needs practice and doesn't know the first thing about taking care of a kid? Not to mention they have nothing back in South Dakota for a child. Plants are easy, sun and water. But humans?

And there is still the question of will they go back to Deadwood. She has to, right? That's where her business is, her life. Everything she's built for herself.

She bounces her body because that's something every mom in the history of ever has done.

A mom? Is that what she is now?

But if Hunter stays...no she won't make him choose between her and his child. If it comes down to it, she'll make that choice for him. Out of love.

23

"THANK YOU SO MUCH, CARLY. I HONESTLY DON'T KNOW WHAT I would've done without you these past several weeks," Dahlia says into the phone as she leans on the porch banister. Hunter called Lauren's family to come to his parents' house for a family meeting. When a bridezilla called claiming her invoice showed the wrong flower, Dahlia had to step away and put out the fire that resulted from a typo on her part.

"That's what I'm here for. Even if you didn't pay me, this is what best friends are for."

Dahlia sighs and grips the banister. "I swear I'm losing my mind, C."

"How much long will you be there?"

She checks over her shoulder at the closed back door. "I don't know. I keep waiting for Hunter to bring it up. I don't want to push him, but this living in limbo is getting to me."

"Sweetie, maybe you need to talk to him. Your feelings matter too."

A lump forms in Dahlia's throat. "I can't stay here," she whispers. It's the first time she's said it out loud. "And what if that's what he wants?"

"D," Carly says, but the door opens and people shouting has Dahlia spinning around.

"I have to go. Thank you for taking care of that for me." She quickly disconnects and watches Hunter stand with stress etched in the lines between his brows. Zip sits at his side and Faith is in his arms. "Everything okay?" she asks, pointing behind him.

"I managed to piss off an entire house with one sentence," he shrugs and Faith reaches for Zip from Hunter's arms. She loves that dog so much and he…tolerates her.

"Oh," Dahlia responds, not really sure what else to say.

"Something wrong with the shop?"

Dahlia glances at her phone. "No, just a bride freaking out over a mistake I made, but it's all taken care."

"Dahlia made a mistake? I don't believe it," he teases, and she smiles and takes a deep breath.

"It happens on rare occasion."

Awkward silence stretches between them. She has to ask the hard questions, but living with the what ifs is eating her alive.

"Hunter?" she asks at the same time; he says, "Dahlia?"

They both fall quiet again.

"I told them I wanted to go home. Back to South Dakota," he finally says. "And I'll be taking Faith with me. They can try to fight me in court if they want, but I'm not backing down from this."

"You don't want to stay here?"

Hunter tilts his head. "Of course not. I want what I've built in Deadwood. I want you, which…" he pulls a box from his pocket and Dahlia's lips part. "I know everything has changed, but my love for you has only got stronger. I'm no longer just a man with a dog. My baggage has grown by ten fingers and toes, and I understand if you have changed your mind or are having second thoughts…"

"Are you—?"

"Patience," he says with a shy smile. "I would get down on one knee, but I wanted Faith here to know that if you say yes, it's to more than just me. You'll be saying yes to me, Zip, and my daughter…our daughter, if you'll marry me, Dahlia Sommers."

Her eyes shift from the ring in the open box, Hunter's amber eyes, Faith's curious expression as she reaches for the box and Zip sitting with his head tilted to the side.

"We're going home? All of us?" she asks, making sure she understood him the first time.

"I'd really love it if you'd say yes, then us all go home," Hunter says, jokingly to cover his own uncertainty.

"Yes!" she squeals. "Of course, yes!"

Cheers erupt from the other side of the door and Lydia and Jared step out as Hunter slides his simple yet beautiful diamond ring on her finger. "When did you have time to get this?"

His cheeks redden slightly and he gazes down at her. "I've had that since I met your parents and asked your dad for his blessing. You should probably pick up my phone from over there." He jerks his head toward the door and on the porch she spots his phone leaning against a brick. Her mom and dad's face on are on the screen and they're cheering through the video call.

"What?" Dahlia grabs his phone and her mom's unmistakable squeals come through the phone. He planned this. Even in the midst of this chaos.

"That was months ago!" she says in disbelief to Hunter and her parents.

"I was waiting for the right time." Lydia and Jared embrace Hunter and Dahlia in hugs. Faith laughs as Zip barks in excitement with everyone doing a mixture of laughing and crying.

Through the chaos and the noise, he finds Dahlia's blue eyes and wild curls staring at him, and it quiets his mind. She said yes. She is his. And this is the beginning of their life.

Lydia and Jared pass Dahlia around in hugs while she takes her mom off speaker to have an actual conversation.

24

"I CAN'T BELIEVE A FLORIST WANTED A SIMPLE COURTHOUSE step wedding. We had the perfect place and you would have got one heck of a discount from this popular flower shop," Hunter teases as he wraps his arms around her waist.

"And simple was perfect."

He hums and kisses her exposed collarbone. She wore a simple white dress and sandals, while Hunter wore a button down with jeans. He bought a new cowboy hat for the occasion, but aside from that, it was just their everyday look, and Dahlia couldn't have asked for anything more.

"You didn't just do it because of me? Honest?" he asks, and Dahlia spins in his arms to face him.

"I did it for me, solider. Promise. Now your parents have Faith for the night, leaving us here, all alone. Do you remember the first time your brought me here?" she asks, running her fingers down the buttons one by one, undoing them.

"You mean when I caught you trespassing and saved you from a mountain lion? You thought I was a murderer." He laughs and Dahlia joins him.

"I meant after that...after dinner, in your bed."

His moan vibrates through his chest against her hands. He grips her ass and jerks her dress up to reveal the lace lingerie underneath. "I knew then that you were something to be worshiped, little flower. And I wanted to make sure I was the only one to ever taste you, feel you, to bury my cock into from then on."

Dahlia's stomach clenches and she pushes his shirt off his shoulder, revealing his scared, muscular chest and torso. "So certain of what you want," she muses. He slowly drags the zipper down the back of her dress and shoves it to the floor around her feet.

"I want you, now, little flower." He unbuckles his pants and pushes them down his thighs. The left pant leg get tangles on his prosthetic and Dahlia runs her fingers down his thigh to where the plastic starts. She massages slowly, awarding herself a groan from her soldier. After she pushes the pants all the way down and off, she reaches for his boxers and does the same.

She reaches for his cock, but he grabs her wrist and pulls her to her feet. "You can suck later, but right now, I want to bury my cock and come in *my wife*."

"Say that again," Dahlia breathes out.

"*My wife*," he smirks and leads her to the bed. He pushes her back, her lingerie creating a road map to all the places he wants to explore.

"*My husband*," she mewls as he ghosts his finger across the lace thong. His cock jumps in anticipation to feel her warmth squeezing around him.

He pulls her thong to the side and grazes the tip of his cock from her ass to her clit, coating it in her desire that's nearly dripping from her.

"So wet for me, little flower." He slides in between her legs, and doesn't stop until his balls press against her ass. His body shudders as he demands movement and Dahlia rocks her hips, her body begging for the same.

"You're mine," he says in time with a thrust of his hips. She cries out at how he stretches her and fills her completely. He grabs her left hand and bends to press his lips to the two rings that sit there. "To our forever," he vows.

"Hunter," she moans and moves her other hand to her aching clit.

"Yes, little flower?" he kisses her abdomen, pushing her to the edge of insanity.

"Please," she begs, arching her back and pressing the back of her head into the comforter.

He straightens and grips around her thigh, pulling her closer to him. "Forever my little flower," he whispers. His fingers tighten around her legs and he slams into her, causing her to cry out and work her clit faster. He'll take it slow later. He'll make sure she is for thoroughly sated she won't be able to walk tomorrow. They'll go again and again tonight, her cries of pleasure keeping the forest awake.

Right now, he pounds into her, their skin slapping against each other. She shatters on her back, her pussy pulsing and urging his cock to fill her with his cum.

"Fuck, you're so tight around me," he moans as his balls tighten. He grips her legs and thrusts deep as his cock throbs from his release. She wraps her legs around his waist and Hunter hovers over his on his forearms, their lips brushing as they breathe.

"I love you, solider," she tells him, wanting this moment to be branded into her mind forever.

"I'll never stop," he responds and kisses her sweetly. "Ready for round two?" he asks, pulling back and hauling her to her feet.

"Show me what you got," she says with fire in her eyes.

If you told her, this is what her future would look like. A man who loves everything about her with such passion that he can't get enough, a daughter she never expected, and a florist that she can't wait to see Faith working in one day...she'd called you a crazy. Because nobody could ever love a workaholic, independent woman. But Hunter proves her wrong every day, and she loves every minute of it.

ABOUT THE AUTHOR

Lacy Chantell is a new upcoming author. She resides in Kentucky and owns a small business. She is a mom of two toddlers and lives on the family farm with her husband. She loves to read all genres, ride her horses, hiking, pretty much anything outdoors. Inspiration hits her everywhere she goes for new book ideas and she is excited to keep telling stories for others to enjoy. Romance and Fantasy are her favorite genres to write, and she loves to put her characters through hell for them to get their happy ending in the end.

Follow her on her social media accounts or join her newsletter to keep up with releases and her future works.

www.lacychantellpublishing.com

BACKROADS & BONFIRES #2

HALEY RHOADES

1

HELLO DEADWOOD

AMY

Mia slows the SUV as we descend the slope. Through the tinted lenses of my sunglasses, I spy Deadwood below. I squint in the late afternoon sun, attempting to make out the structures. The tiny town lies nestled between mountains. Its short buildings and houses, a stark contrast to the tree-covered mountains that fence it in. Similar in size to the town of Athens I grew up in, Deadwood bustles with the swarm of tourists it draws. The vehicles driving by hold plates from a wide variety of states, verifying its tourists hustling around this little burg.

"Photo op!" Mia announces, turning on her blinker at the Welcome Center.

In our two-day trek from North Missouri to Deadwood, South Dakota, I've grown accustomed to her need for cute photos with the twins at everything from a green dinosaur at a gas station to the Corn Palace. This time, part of me worries once the boys are out of their car seats, we won't be able to get them back in for the short ride to the house.

My legs are stiff from our travels over the past two days. Opting to avoid an eleven-hour drive, we broke it up for the boys. First, we drove three hours before taking a break in Omaha. Our next section of the trip was three hours, and we spent the night in Sioux Falls. On the second day of our journey, we drove just under three hours to stop in Chamberlain. Finally, we drove four hours here.

I unbuckle William at the same time, Mia pulls Harry from his car seat. Both attempt to wiggle from our arms, insisting to walk on their own. There's too much traffic to allow them to move about without holding our hands near the busy street. They are little Houdinis, often out of arm's reach before we know it.

"Should we grab the stroller?" I suggest, unsure of Mia's plans.

"Maybe," she agrees. "That way, we could walk a bit before we climb back in the car."

With skilled practice, I pull the tandem stroller from the back of the vehicle, popping it open with a flick of my free hand.

"No! No!" Harry protests, shaking his little head.

"Ride in the stroller, and we'll find a treat," Mia coaxes with the ease of mother of four-year-old twins, instead of an aunt that recently became their guardian.

"O-tay," Harry agrees, clapping with his brother.

I secure the five-point harness around both boys before we begin our short walk to the sign that reads, "Welcome, Historic Main Street, Deadwood SD."

Mia stands proudly behind with the stroller, under the sign, and I snap several photos.

"This time, everybody wave," I suggest, and they comply for the next picture.

"Your turn," Mia calls, waving me to return to the twins, but I shake my head.

"Let's explore a bit," she urges, turning the stroller towards the busy downtown area.

I take the stroller handle from her, pushing the boys. As we walk, I regret not reading up on this place on the internet. I vaguely recall watching a series set in Deadwood with my mother years ago, but I didn't pay close enough attention to keep any of the information, though.

I'll have to learn as I go.

The boys point at random things as we walk, talking to each other in a language I can't understand. Mia calls it twin-speak and finds it adorable, while it confounds me.

"Treat please," Harry prompts, tipping his head back to look upside down at Mia.

William mimics his brother's pose.

They're too adorable for their own good. Their wavy dark-brown hair and bright green eyes add to their cute factor.

"When I was a little girl, Grandma brought me here to Main Street for ice cream," Mia shares.

"Ice cream! Ice Cream! Ice Cream!" Harry chants, throwing his fists into the air, and William follows his lead.

"Okay. Okay," she attempts to calm them. "The ice cream shop is down the street. Let's play eye spy until we get there."

"I spy with my little eyes," I begin. "Something brown."

The twins call out items, pointing all over the place, attempting to guess the correct answer. Mia grins at me, pleased we successfully distracted them from their chanting, if only for a little while.

———

Hours later, I stop marveling at the town when Mia parks in front of a quaint, two-story house. It's olive green and has an adorable porch swing. The beige and muted red accents on the post spindles, window trim, and eaves complete it perfectly. It reminds me of what a grandmother's house might look like in a children's book. Knowing Mia's grandmother owned it makes perfect sense.

"We're here!" Mia cheers, and the boys clap.

This picture-perfect abode will be our home for the next four to six weeks. It's much smaller than Mia's farmhouse, and I worry about what my future holds, keeping the boys quietly entertained so Mia may finish her book on time. I pray for many sunny summer days ahead.

That reminds me. I need to look up the local weather to see how May and June compare to Missouri.

"Yo, Amy!" Mia calls for my attention.

I blink away my thoughts as I open the passenger door. Smiling, I help William from his car seat, placing him on the sidewalk and pointing him toward the porch swing. I watch closely as he hurries to beat his twin to the wooden swing.

"Win!" William shouts triumphantly, hopping onto the cushion.

"Let me on!" Harry demands, stomping his foot.

William's little legs do not reach the floor of the porch, so his brother must brave the moving swing, climbing on as it continues its motion.

With both safely swinging and entertained for the moment, I assist Mia in unloading suitcases and the cooler. We make quick work of carrying the items to the porch steps. The wall of items ensures the boys remain fenced in on the porch while we continue.

"You didn't tell me your house was the cutest house in the world," I state.

"Grandma took great pride in owning this property," Mia shares. "She met Grandpa in Deadwood. She insisted he buy a little place for them to visit each year on their anniversary."

"Ahh. That's romantic," I coo.

I love that like me, Mia was close to her family, and it saddens me she has no living family members other than the twins. I can't imagine being alone at my age. Mom's my best friend, and I talk to my brother or his wife every week. If they didn't live in Chicago with a busy Major League Baseball schedule, I'm sure we'd talk or text daily.

"They were a sweet couple," Mia adds, bringing me back from my thoughts.

"Did you come here often?" I ask.

Mia smiles fondly. "We spent a week or two here every year. Sometimes Mom planned a girls' trip for just the three of us. Luna would love knowing the boys were here now."

I place my hand on her forearm. "She's smiling down from heaven right now."

Mia fights tears at the mention of her dead sister.

"Mia, you're an amazing mother for them. The twins are happy and healthy. They enjoy spending time with you, and love hearing stories you share about Luna," I state, hoping she realizes she's a great parent to her nephews in the absence of their parents.

"Miss Amy, I need to pee!" William informs, both hands cupping his privates.

I cringe, knowing he's waited too long to tell me. I pray we unlock the house and find the bathroom in time.

"Me, too!" Harry chimes in, hopping up and down.

Mia makes quick work of entering the four-digit code into the door. The lock disengages, and we scurry inside.

"Down the hall on the left," she calls after us.

I'm thankful the boys wear elastic-waisted shorts today, so they can pull them off without the delay of a button.

"Look at us!" Harry calls over his shoulder.

The boys smile proudly as they pee simultaneously from the sides of the toilet. I understand the male species less and less with each passing week I spend with these two little guys.

What makes them want to pee together and cross streams?

The inner workings of their little male minds befuddle me almost daily.

Boys really seem to be from Mars and girls from Venus.

"Hey! Aim at the water," I scold when they wield themselves like swords, with urine splashing everywhere.

Great. Now I'll have to clean this bathroom on our first evening here.

"Excuse me," I chide. "Hands."

The boys freeze at the doorway and pivot towards the sink. Their four hands splash water over the entire vanity.

I love these messy monsters.

When the doorbell chimes, and the boys sprint from the bathroom to investigate.

Who could it be? Everyone that knows we're here is in Missouri or Illinois. Mia didn't mention knowing any residents of Deadwood. I hope it's not a neighbor coming over to say hello.

I try to listen as I dry the vanity with a nearby bath towel.

"Oliver!" Mia greets. "Boys, come meet Oliver. He takes care of the house for me."

Ahh. She mentioned knowing one person in town from her many emails, texts, and video calls regarding the Airbnb.

I guess it's time I go meet the locals.

2

THE ARRIVAL

Lucas

I search my brain for the memory of my phone conversation with Oliver last week as I give my name to the hostess at the entrance to the Outlaw Square Deck. He mentioned something about inviting the two women renting his Airbnb to join us at the free concert on the outdoor stage. I close my eyes, praying he doesn't see this as a double date. I long to catch up with my friend, not fight off the attention of a female all night.

I scan the tables near the entrance and the seats at the railing for him. Distant movement catches my eye. I spot an arm waving over the patrons and follow it down to see Oliver's wide smile greeting me. He must be standing in a chair for me to see him.

He's a goof.

"I see my friend," I state, pointing in his direction.

As I make my way through the crowd, I crane my neck, trying to see if Oliver's alone at the table. Unfortunately, with the deck filled, I can't see past the tables and standing clientele. Making my way around the last table between us, I find Oliver alone at a high-top table for four. Relief floods me. I look forward to a night with beer, music, and my friend. I arrive at the same time as a server approaches, placing four mugs of beer on the table.

"Thought you'd be ready for a cold one as soon as you showed up," Oliver explains.

Looking past me, he raises his voice. "Mia!"

I follow his line of sight, finding two dark-haired women. They cease their dancing to the 90s rock cover band at the rail and join us at our table.

"Ladies," Oliver begins, extending his hand palm up in my direction. "This is Lucas. Lucas, this is Mia that owns the Airbnb and her friend Amy."

I smile, lifting my chin in their direction. Now, in the presence of these two beautiful women, I wish I'd have listened in greater detail when Oliver told me about them.

"So, Lucas," Mia says with a coy smirk as Amy takes a swig of beer. "What do you do for the rodeo?"

I chuckle, assuming by her facial expressions she's asking for her aloof friend. "I work for a large livestock contractor and serve as livestock superintendent at many of the rodeos we provide stock for."

Mia squints, attempting to process my answer. At her side, her tall friend's interest peaks.

"So, do you ride bulls or broncs?" Mia queries.

"Neither." I shake my head. "I prefer to keep my boots firmly on the dirt at rodeos. I do mess around with the cowboys from time to time when they practice roping or barrels."

"You don't consider yourself a cowboy?" Amy challenges.

"Oh, he's a cowboy," Oliver declares. "You should take the boys to the ranch tomorrow and see him in action."

I smirk as Amy's eyes grow wide at his suggestion.

"Speaking of boys, I better text your sister to see if they're behaving," Mia tells Oliver.

Whose boys? Mia's or Amy's?

I return my gaze back to Amy, finding her back turned towards me as she watches the band play on the nearby stage. I take a moment to scan her from head to toe. Her body moves in time with the music. She wears a white tank top with denim shorts. Her long tone legs and defined muscles in her arms hint she's athletic, while her golden skin tells me she's not afraid to enjoy the sun. I long to know if her brown hair is naturally curly or if she took the time to put all the loose curls in it for a night out in Deadwood.

Oliver nudges me with his elbow, laughing as he points his beer bottle in her direction before taking a drink. Thankfully, Mia returns her attention to the group from her phone before Oliver may tease me about checking out her friend.

"So the bulls are already here?" Mia asks, and Amy turns back towards the table at her words. "I always assumed the arrived the day of the rodeo."

"Livestock are athletes, too," I explain. "In order for them to give their best performance and not be sluggish, we roll into town days before each event. They settle into their accommodations, the vets assess them multiple times a day, they play in the dirt or sand, and most importantly, they rest after their long ride."

Mia elbows Amy in the ribs. "Who knew there was so much prep for a weekend show?" Her wide eyes encourage her friend to join the conversation.

"We like to ride horses," Mia states proudly.

"Do you really ride horses or just on a beach in the Caribbean?" I ask the two of them.

"We're from farms in northern Missouri. We know how to ride horses," Amy informs snidely. "My parents' farm kept at least two horses my entire childhood. My mom and I still go on trail rides every spring and fall."

I tip my head to her.

"I haven't ridden in about five years," Mia states. "Amy keeps trying to take me, but I seem to always have an excuse. She let the boys sit on her mom's horses a time or two."

"You should really stop by and see Lucas in action. William and Harry will love seeing the calves, horses, and bulls," Oliver suggests for a second time.

234

This time, Amy raises an eyebrow.

"Just let me know if you want to stop by one day this week," I state. "Mornings or early afternoon work best, but I can make anytime work if I know ahead of time."

"Tomorrow's supposed to be nice," Mia urges.

Unwilling to fight Mia and Oliver's prompting anymore, Amy expels an audible sigh.

"How about tomorrow morning?" she says, heavy with fake enthusiasm.

"Shall we say ten?" I suggest, and she nods with a polite smile.

I like the thought of seeing Amy again in the morning. She intrigues me with her guarded demeanor and her looks. She listens even as she uses all her strength to appear nonchalant.

"How about another round?" I raise my arm to wave at a nearby server.

The band returns from intermission, and the women return to the railing, their bodies swaying to the rock music. I share a knowing glance with Oliver.

We have the best seats in the bar.

I lean toward my friend, pointing my beer bottle in their directions and speaking over the music, but not loud enough for the women to hear. "You could have told me on the phone we'd spend the evening with two hot-as-hell women. I envisioned... Well, I envisioned them to be very different."

I assumed they'd act like the buckle bunnies at the rodeos and bars afterwards, constantly flipping their hair and brushing against me. I dreaded their overt suggestive behavior and mind-numbing conversations.

"Hold your horses," Oliver chuckles. "Mia has a boyfriend back home. As for Amy..." He tilts his head from one side to the other and back. "It's hard to tell."

"I'm not actively looking," I state.

"Since when?"

I look my friend straight in the eye.

"I'm taking a break from all that drama," I respond.

Oliver's brow furrows. "Drama?"

"You won't believe me when I tell you," I say. "Women throwing themselves at me in every town grows old, so I'm taking a break."

"A break," Oliver parrots, disbelieving. "I'll believe that when I see it."

There's no use arguing with him. In time, he'll see that this visit to Deadwood is different than all the ones before.

3
COWS!

I'm not sure how I allowed Oliver and Mia to make me agree to take William and Harry to see the animals at the ranch this morning.

I pull a long breath in and out as I park the SUV near the barn as his text instructed. I don't mind visiting the area with the boys. It's meeting Lucas here that unnerves me. I don't want him to get the wrong idea and consider me one of his many female admirers.

"Cows!" Harry squeals. "Miss Amy, see the cows?"

"I see the cows," I answer as I extricate him from the car seat.

Hand in hand, Harry and I make our way to the passenger side of the vehicle.

"Hands on the door," I instruct Harry, and he assumes the practiced position of placing one palm on the front door while I help his brother out.

"So these cows," I share, pointing at the large rectangular pen. "Are called bulls and steers." I point further to our right, closer to the barn. "Those are called calves."

"Baby cows," William proclaims proudly.

I begin to answer, but a deep, male voice beats me to it.

"Yes, calves are baby cows," Lucas answers, squatting down to the twins' eye-level. "I'm Lucas. And you are... let me guess." He points as he speaks. "You are Harry, and you are William."

"Yes!" they cheer in unison.

Lucas grins up at me, proud he guessed correctly. While he talks to the boys, I'm temporarily distracted by his muscular thighs straining the seams of his jeans, and the tightness of the sleeves of his t-shirt against his tanned biceps. His black shirt clings to his strong back, and his butt...

"Hh-hm," Lucas clears his throat.

I find his striking blue eyes looking up at me, along with the excited eyes of the boys. He rises a smirk upon his face.

I chastise myself for my errant thoughts and quickly collect myself.

"What will you show us first?" I ask, extending my hands for the twins.

They opt to grab Lucas's hands instead. I stick my tongue out at him, careful the boys don't see me, pretending to be offended.

"We'll start with the calves," he announces, walking past me hand-in-hand with the boys.

I fall in line behind them, not minding the view in the slightest.

I guess cowboys really do wear Wranglers.

And Lucas wears his well.

"Hi cows," Harry calls as we approach.

"Calves," William corrects his brother.

"Hi calves," they greet in unison, letting go of Lucas's hand to place theirs on the metal gate.

"Look at the white one." Harry points.

"I like that one," William states, pointing in the opposite direction.

"Ooo, he's pooping!" Harry yells, pointing for all of us to see.

"Ooo," William chimes in.

Changing the subject, now standing next to Lucas, I say, "They remind me of the bottle calves from home. Except they're a little older."

"So you really are a farm girl," he says, moving so close I feel his heat on my shoulder.

"Yeah," I scoff. "Why would I make that up?"

He rubs the back of his neck, drawing my attention to the sexy brown scruff covering his jaw.

"You'd be surprised at the lies women…" his words trail off.

"Finish your sentence," I urge, interested in his explanation.

It's now I notice he doesn't wear his confident, cocky demeanor from last night. He seems embarrassed by his statement.

"You'd be surprised at the lies buckle bunnies tell to get me to notice them," his voices lowers to prevent the boys from hearing him.

"I'm no buckle bunny," I spit.

Why do guys come up with these nicknames for women?

My mind scrolls through the list of known groupie fan girl names.

Rodeos have the buckle bunnies.

Baseball has the cleat chasers.

Hockey has puck bunnies or puck sluts.

Football has jersey chasers.

And golf has stick chicks and putt sluts.

Lucas clears his throat.

"I wouldn't even be here right now if Mia and Oliver minded their own business."

"I… I didn't mean to imply," he stutters.

"Whatever," I clip, walking over to stand at the fence with the twins.

"Miss Amy, I touched one!" Harry shouts.

"Me, too!" William says.

"Well, let's touch some more," I cheer.

"I wanna touch the white one," Harry requests.

"If you want to touch more, follow me," Lucas directs and the boys immediately peel themselves from the railing.

I follow farther behind, keeping a close eye on the boys, while snarling at Lucas. I can't believe he ties me up in so many knots in less than an hour with him. I share details about my life when I want to keep my walls firmly in place. I feel him pull me in as I fight by bracing my arms to hold myself back.

Why does he make me feel this way? He dresses like the guys back home; he works with animals like them… He shouldn't make me feel any different than they do.

But he does.

He… he affects me in a way that I'm not accustomed to.

I lean on the fence, watching Lucas hand each boy a bucket of feed. He encourages them to dump it in the feeding trough to draw the calves closer to the fence.

Spotting the buckets long before the boys reach the fence, the calves approach swarming the troughs.

The twins erupt in a fit of giggles, and it's the most amazing sound in the world. I breaks my heart knowing what they've lost at such a young age, and I make it my goal to allow them to experience moments like this. Their joy is infectious.

Lucas assists each boy in pouring the feed in a line down each trough. William and Harry move along the fence, petting each calf they see all now within reach while they eat.

The smile I share with Lucas is genuine. "Thank you for this."

He shrugs off my compliment.

"It's part of my job to share knowledge and the experience for the next generation of rodeo fans," he says, but I don't believe him.

It's easy to see he likes children. Not all men are at ease with four-year-olds. He's a natural. We watch the calves for a long time, pointing out the ones that are alike and those that are unique. Next we move to an area near the bulls' paddock. Of course, we maintain a safe distance as we marvel at the enormous beasts. Then we view the horses. Some we allow the twins to pet while we hold them in our arms, others we point at from a distance.

Three hours pass in what seems like minutes. When I glance at the time, I apologize for keeping Lucas from work for so long and make a quick escape with the excuse the boys need to eat or they'll turn into little monsters.

We thank Lucas several times as we load into the vehicle and wave goodbye.

"Can we come back tomorrow?" Harry asks through his open window.

"Harry, honey, Lucas has work he needs to do," I excuse.

"If you come tomorrow, you can help me do some chores," Lucas promises.

I squint my eyes closed. Now there's no way the boys won't hound me nonstop to return tomorrow.

"Hey…"

I jump at the sound of Lucas standing at my window. He places his hand on my shoulder.

"Come back same time tomorrow. We'll each take a boy on an ATV and do some chores."

His smile softens my resolve.

"It'll be fun, and the boys will love it," he encourages.

"Won't your boss frown upon you playing two days with the boys," I protest.

"Uh, I am the boss," he reminds me.

I'm equal parts excited to return and dreading it. The more time we spend with Lucas this week, the harder it will be on the boys when he leaves on Sunday.

As I drive back to the cottage, I find it funny that growing up on a farm, surrounded by the same animals with farmers that work with livestock, like Lucas, that I don't consider them cowboys.

Lucas is different.

I can't believe I spent time with a real-life cowboy.

4
LEFT!

AMY

It's a beautiful summer day, even for a Monday. The twins and I take our time eating breakfast, getting dressed for the day, and making our way out for a walk. The boys jibber-jabber animatedly as I push their stroller along the trail. I worried the gravel might be too large for the stroller, but it's not bad. The rocks remind me of the cinder track I ran sprints on in high school.

At first, I'm surprised by the number of bikes on the Mickelson Trail on a weekday morning, then I remember Deadwood is a tourist town. I love that this little burg offers history and touristy stuff, along with nature to enjoy.

"Left!" a couple announce before whizzing by us on mountain bikes.

"Bikes!" the twins yell for the fifth time.

This might be a short walk if they yell that every time a bike passes us in either direction. I decide to distract them.

"I spy with my little eyes something green," I state, hoping they'll play along with me.

"Grass!" Harry guesses.

"Nooo," I answer.

"Leaves!" they yell in unison, as they so often do.

"Yes."

"My turn," Harry states.

"No, my turn," William argues.

Their voices rise as they speak words I can't make out. They're so loud, they don't hear another biker announce "left" before passing us. Yelling ceases as crying begins.

I set the brake on the back wheel before approaching the front of the stroller, bending down to their eye level.

"What happened?" I ask, looking at each boy.

They speak over the top of each other. William bawls and Harry yells louder to be heard over his brother.

"Left!" a male rider announces, slowing to pass us.

I spare him a glance, embarrassed by the twins' behavior in such a serene environment.

"Boys," I raise my voice a bit, firming my tone. "Quiet please."

Harry ceases his explanation, while it takes a bit for William to calm his tears.

"Amy, is everything okay?"

My back stiffens at his word, and my skin prickles in his presence. When I look over my shoulder, I must do a double take.

It's Lucas standing still, straddling his bike. Only he's changed since I last saw him. Gone is his medium-length, light-brown hair I yearned to run my fingers through. Now he sports a buzz cut in a deeper shade of brown.

Holy fuck!

How's it possible he became hotter over the weekend?

My pulse quickens, and my cheeks heat.

I'm having thoughts about Lucas; thoughts that mean nothing but trouble for me.

"Amy?" he repeats.

I try to hide the effect he has on me. I pray he doesn't see.

"Just brotherly love," I inform him. "One moment they're the best of friends and the next they're at war."

"Hi Lucas," Harry waves as if nothing happened.

"Hey boys," he smiles.

I melt at the magnitude of the crinkles at the corner of his blue eyes and the deep parenthesis at the sides of his mouth in the sunlight.

It's really not fair.

Women don't stand a chance in his alluring presence.

"I thought you headed out yesterday," I blurt awkwardly, needing something to say.

"They left without me," he chuckles.

"What? Why?"

"It's not like that," he explains, his hands up, palms facing me. "I put in my two-weeks' notice, stating this was my last rodeo."

"So it was planned?" I rise, standing beside the stroller.

"Yeah, I'm ready to plant myself somewhere," he states. "I need a home base."

"Huh." I'm blown away. I search my memory to see if he hinted at any of this.

Long silence stretches out between us.

"What prompted the new do?" I ask, motioning to his hair. "Are you trading rodeos for modeling?"

I swear his cheeks pink as he runs his palm over the soft stubble atop his head.

"Just trying something new. It'll grow back," he says with a shrug. "You think I look like a model?"

Crap! I insinuated that.

"C'mon, you know by the way women look at you that you are good looking."

"But you think I'm model worthy," he surmises from my previous comment.

"Mah," I feign disinterest.

He smirks, not buying me backpedaling for one second.

"So you ride more than just horses," I state, needing to change the subject and pointing at his bike. "I gotta say, I never imagined this side of you." I swirl my finger around his new look.

"There's more to me than rodeo, just like I'm sure there's more to you than a nanny."

Touché.

"I'll be staying with Oliver for the unforeseeable future, so we'll have a chance to get to know each other better," he states.

I quirk my head.

Is he angling to see more of me?

"Maybe we could ride bikes sometime," he suggests.

"I didn't bring my bike," I state, glad I have a legitimate excuse.

"I figured as much." He pauses as a large group of cyclists passes by. "There's a great rental place in town."

Man, he will not quit.

"We'll see." I shrug noncommittally.

His smirk tells me all I need to know. He's going to make sure we meet up again.

"Well, I need to get back to my ride," he says, maneuvering his bike away from us.

"Have fun. Boys say goodbye to Lucas," I encourage.

"Bye Lucas," they say.

"Bye Harry. Bye William." Lucas waves. "Bye Amy."

"Bye Lucas," I giggle with a little wave.

I watch Lucas pedal away, his calves popping with the motion, as I unlock the brakes, taking hold of the stroller handle.

I laugh as I shake my head. We've walked less than a quarter of a mile, yet so much happened.

The short walk home does nothing to erase my steamy thoughts of Lucas. I'm like Fergie in her song *London Bridge*.

Every time he comes around, my walls come tumbling down.

———

I knock on Mia's office door.

"Come in," she calls.

Not wanting to interrupt her writing momentum, hesitantly, I peek my head in.

"Can you take a break for a minute?" I ask.

Worry floods her face.

"It's screen time for the boys and I need to tell you what I saw on the trail," I explain quickly, needing to put her worries to rest.

"Let me pee and we'll meet in the kitchen," Mia offers.

I wait on pins and needles with two water bottles on the counter beside me. In this tiny house with its old doors, I can hear Mia pee and wash her hands. When she doesn't immediately emerge, I can't take it anymore.

"We bumped into Lucas on the trail," I blurt.

This prompts her to emerge. Her wide eyes and shocked face convey exactly how I feel.

"Yep. Dude had a head to toe makeover from dreamy cowboy with gotta-touch me hair to buzz cut, hot-as-hell, hunky jock. He's staying in Deadwood with our boy Oliver for, and I quote, the unforeseeable future. He claims I don't know the real him and he doesn't know the real me. Oh, and he plans on renting me a bike, so we can ride the trail together and get to know each other," I ramble, experiencing diarrhea of the mouth.

Mia looks from me to the water bottle on the counter and back.

"I think we need something stronger than water to unpack this," she states, moving towards the short cabinet over the refrigerator. "I'll get the Jack Daniels; you get the cola. The boys are glued to the iPads. We'll sit and attempt to process everything."

5
LAST RODEO

AMY

My mind cycles at the speed of light through events on the trail, at the rodeo, and at the bar. Mia quickly, pouring two fingers of Jack over ice in a glass and filling it with cola. She slides one towards me.

"Now, start at the beginning and don't leave out a thing," she instructs.

"I planned to walk a couple of miles today," I laugh. "I doubt we even made it a quarter of a mile. Bikes kept passing us, and the twins shouted 'bike' each time. It drove me nuts, so I started a game of eye spy. They guessed at the same time, then fought over who had the next turn. Harry did something to make William cry, so I stopped the stroller." I catch my breath and take a sip of my drink. "While I bent down to calm William, I saw a guy pass on a bike from the corner of my eye. It embarrassed me for total strangers to witness my failure as a nanny. Turns out the joke was on me. It wasn't a stranger; it was Lucas. But not the Lucas we knew from last week. It's a new and improved Lucas."

"I didn't think it was possible to improve his looks," Mia mumbles.

"Right? That's exactly what I thought. Trust me, he got hotter.

Imagine his sexy scruff, here, here, and here." I motion to both jaws and the top of my head. "Now instead of fisting my fingers in the hair atop his head, I want to find out if it's coarse and prickly or soft and tickle-y."

A full body shiver moves through me.

"I saw that!" Mia shouts. "Oh. My. God. You're into him! You. Like. Lucas."

My stomach drops. In my shocked reaction to finding Lucas on the trail, I let Mia in on my secret. As much as I need to, I can't put the cat back in the bag now.

"Oh no you don't! Don't do that." She points her index finger at my nose. "Don't go all Amy on me and close yourself off. We're on an extended vacation. There's nothing wrong with having a little fun while we're here."

"Mia," I whine. "I can't get involved with a guy that lives in Deadwood when I live in Missouri."

She holds up a finger. "One, have fun, don't get involved. And two, he doesn't really live in Deadwood. He's visiting like we are. Let your hair down, throw caution to the wind, and see where things go."

She makes it sound so easy. I keep my guard up for a reason. In my experience, people use me to get to my famous brother. I learned long ago to look for motives behind everyone's actions and keep them at arm's length, so I'm not disappointed when they disappoint me by mentioning Hamilton.

"You got me all distracted by your description of the new Lucas," Mia states. "What happened after Lucas stopped?"

She's right, I didn't share everything.

"He asked if he could do anything to help with the boys. Of course, they were excited to see him and stopped fighting."

"Did he stay to see you?" she asks.

I shake my head. "No. Well... I'm not sure. He claims he put in his two weeks' notice that Deadwood would be his last rodeo. He wants to find some place to live. I think he's looking to travel less."

"Does he have a job in Deadwood?" Mia asks.

I shrug. "He didn't say. He made it sound like he's staying at Oliver's and taking an extended..."

"Vacation," we say in unison and laugh.

I swirl the liquid in my glass, and Mia takes a drink. I feel her eyes on me.

"Oliver said nothing about Lucas staying with him," she thinks out loud. "If he put his two weeks in, I bet he didn't decide to stay here until... this week."

I'm thankful she didn't say "until he met you."

"I made an awkward comment about him riding more than just horses. He invited me to ride bikes with him. He even mentioned they rent bikes in the area." I look up from my glass. "I think he plans to make sure we go for a ride together."

My stomach flip flops. I'm not sure if it's excitement at the possibility or nervousness that he plans to pursue me. I take a long drink, needing to calm my thoughts.

"This working vacation just got a lot more interesting," she smirks. "Wait until the guys back home hear this."

I reach across the small table, swatting her shoulder.

"You need to keep your nose in your writing and not in my business," I remind her. "And I need to keep William and Harry entertained and out of your hair. There's no time for Lucas."

Bless her heart. Mia bites her lip and fights her excited smile. We've become great friends, almost like sisters. Living together for a year makes us close. She only wants what's best for me, and I know she means well.

Now, if only I knew what might be best for me.

I used to believe that was remaining guarded at all times. Something about Lucas makes me consider letting my guard down a little to see what happens.

6

LET'S RIDE

LUCAS

On the quick drive from Oliver's to Mia's, I run through my mental checklist one more time.

> *Bikes-check.*
> *Kiddie wagon-check.*
> *Helmets-check.*
> *Cooler-check.*
> *Sunscreen-check.*
> *Snacks-check.*

I hope I thought of everything.

I long to prove to Amy that I care enough to pay attention to the details and listen. She mentioned the boys require frequent snacks and drinks, so I planned for that. Clearly, she cares for the twins; it's easy to see why. The little guys quickly stole my heart.

I pull behind the SUV in the driveway, releasing a long breath as I put the truck in park. I love riding bikes, but today's much more than a bike ride. It's a first date of sorts with the boys as a buffer. Amy's a tough cookie, and I'll only get one chance at this. She tagged along when the boys saw the animals; today the boys tag along on our bike ride.

Exiting the cab, I pull the two bikes from the bed of my truck, the cooler, and then the wagon. I'm fastening the wagon to my bike when Amy steps onto the porch.

"Hey there," I greet, pausing to smile in her direction.

I force my eyes to not stare at her long legs in the snug, black biker shorts. Instead, I admire her blue and red top with black sleeves to match her shorts, her brown curls in a ponytail, and her sunglasses perched on top of her head.

I breathe a sigh of relief that she's athletic and knows how to dress for biking. Part of me still worried she was like the women I've met in recent years, saying anything they can to spend time with me. The fact she couldn't purchase this bike gear in Deadwood assures me she told me the truth about her hobby.

"Are we really going to do this?" she asks, hopping to sit on the tailgate of my truck.

My tongue wets my lower lip.

"I like you up there." The words escape before I can think better of it.

Amy pinches her lips between her teeth. I assume she's fighting the urge to give me one of her snarky comments to push me away.

"City girls don't know how to make themselves at home on a tailgate," I state.

"Never claimed to be a city girl," she says.

"Never thought you were," I quip.

"What did you think of me as your first impression?" she challenges.

I warn myself to tread carefully. Amy's testing me, so I opt to be honest and choose my words wisely.

"The two of you dancing at the railing definitely caught my eye," I chuckle. "Heck, I think you caught every male eye on the deck. You've got moves."

Unaffected by my comments, she keeps all emotion off her face.

"Oliver mentioned on the phone he might invite Mia and a friend to join us that night. I must admit, I looked forward to catching up with my friend and dreaded your presence." I continue tightening the bolt under the seat of my bike with a ratchet as I speak. "Clearly, Mia was pushing for you to talk to me. I assumed she had a man and was desperate for you to have one, too. But your reactions let me know you weren't interested. I was kind of glad. I didn't want a female distraction. I needed to work and set things up with Oliver to begin my next phase of life. You came across as a beautiful, guarded, but fun woman."

I glance up, finding Amy's head tilted and a hint of a smile on her face. I tear my eyes from hers and return my tools to the toolbox before hopping onto the tailgate beside her. My thigh accidentally brushes against hers with the action. Amy's eyes dart to mine, as the heat of the brief touch flows up my leg, and my heartbeat quickens.

"If you don't want female distraction, then why are you taking the boys and me on a bike ride today?" she asks coyly.

"I didn't want a distraction, so I could talk to Oliver," I inform her. "We spoke the next day, the rodeo was a success, and my job ended." I wipe my hands on my shorts. "You're different from the women I meet on the rodeo circuit. You aren't trying to use my cowboy status as a notch on your bedpost. The fact you're not trying to use me is refreshing. I'm looking to start a new part of my life, and I figure there's no harm in spending time with a new type of woman. The fact you like to cycle, grew up on a farm, and have adorable sidekicks made me want to see you again."

"And you like the way I dance," she reminds me of the night we met, bumping her shoulder against mine.

Her comment shocks her. She quickly slides away from me, her body stiffens, and her smile disappears. I watch her refortify her walls.

"Miss Amy!" Harry hollers, running through the front door. "I want to ride a bike!"

William follows with an enormous smile on his face.

How disappointed will they be when they ride in a wagon and not a bike?

"We talked about this," Amy reminds them. "Lucas and I will be on big bikes, and the two of you will ride in a trailer behind us."

They trot over to inspect the wagon hitched to my bike. Their little hands slap against the hard plastic back and the mesh enclosure in front.

"Let me in!" Harry demands. "I want to get in!"

"Me, too," William chimes in with his more vocal twin.

"Not until Miss Amy says we're ready," I tell the boys.

"First potty time, then bike ride," Amy orders.

They sprint back inside the house, eager to start today's adventure.

7
FIRST DATE

AMY

"Mimi! Mimi!" the twins yell for Mia the moment we open the front door.

So much for my suggestion we enter quietly, since their aunt continues to write.

I hurry after them. "Boys, Aunt Mia's writing. We talked bout waiting until supper to tell her," I remind them over their yells.

"Tell me what?" Mia asks, exiting the tiny office space.

William and Harry talk a million miles per second over the top of each other. Mia's wide eyes look at me.

"Freeze!" I demand with a raised voice.

The boys cease talking and moving under my practiced magic word. I smile at Mia, letting her know nothing is wrong.

"William, you go first," I prompt, and he smiles proudly.

"We saw dogs!" he shares, his arms motioning. "They jump high and swim!"

"Really?" she acts shocked by this news even though the four of us talked about attending the Dock Dogs competition yesterday and at breakfast this morning.

Harry jumps in. "They jump for toys! And swim like this!" He moves in circles, imitating the dogs paddling.

"So you had fun?" Mia inquires, with a giggle.

"Lucas bought us ice cream," Harry informs.

"And we sat on a blanket on a hill so we don't get wet," William shares.

Mia glances at her watch. "Wow! You were there for a long time." She looks at me. "Did Lucas stay with you?"

"Lucas took me on a ride on his shoulders!" Harry tells his aunt.

"Me, too!" William says.

I smile and nod to answer her question. Mia's smile widens. With my eyes closed, I shake my head. I know what she's thinking. She likes the idea of Lucas and me spending time together. She thinks he puts up with the boys just to spend time with me. She hasn't seen him with the twins. He's just a bigger version of the boys.

"Snack time!" I announce. "Go wash your hands."

The twins trot to the nearby restroom, climbing the step stool at the same time.

Mia bumps my shoulder with hers. "You should have invited Lucas back here. Once the boys nap, the two of you could have enjoyed adult time.

Adult time?

Seriously?

I know exactly what she means by 'adult time'.

I guess I had better confess. She'll find out in a couple of hours, anyway.

"He asked me to join him at the concert tonight," I blurt. "I don't know how it's possible, but he claims the town comes even more to life tonight with the first concert of Wild Bill Days. It was so crowded today, I'm not sure how they'll fit any more people on Main Street."

She holds her palms up between us, halting my rambling.

"You have a date!" she squeals.

I release a deep, audible breath.

"O-M-G! You're going on a date with Lucas!"

"I told him I'm supposed to watch the boys so you may concentrate on your writing." I turn my back to her as I pull cheese and fruit from the refrigerator.

"Stop it!" she chides. "You know you can take the night off for a date."

As I place cheese, fresh fruit, and crackers on two plates, I see Mia bouncing with excitement.

"So, where are you going? What are you doing? What will you wear?" she rapid fires questions in my direction.

With the twins' attention on their snacks, I return my attention to Mia.

"He's coming here at four," I say with a shrug. "He mentioned dinner, drinks, and the free concert on Main Street. It's all part of Wild Bill Days... that's all I know."

My nerves spiral with the realization that I have a date with Lucas tonight.

A date.

Me on a date.

I haven't been on a date in... Holy crap! I haven't been on a date since high school.

"What's causing that face?" Mia asks, swirling her finger around my head.

"What face?" I play dumb.

"Your worried, scrunched-up face," she states. "What did I say that made you nervous?"

I shake off her worries. "You need to get back to work."

"Uh-huh," she protests. "I'm taking an extended break. We're going to have a drink, chat a bit, then I'll help you get ready for your date."

I begin to argue, but she shushes me with a pinch of her fingers in mid-air.

"Last one upstairs is a rotten egg!" Mia announces, and the twins scamper away. "Grab two beers and meet me on the patio," she orders, closing the bathroom door.

Exhausted from a big day outside, the twins lie down without protest. I turn on their light-up globe projecting the galaxy onto the ceiling and the monitor before closing their door. Descending the stairs, I watch the black and white video screen, finding their eyes closed.

I sort of hoped they'd fuss a bit, so I could avoid the looming conversation with Mia. She's team Lucas and will tell me I'm silly for dragging my feet.

With two beers in hand, I walk to the backyard like I'm walking to my execution.

Under the shade tree, I join Mia in lawn chairs, quickly popping the cap off and enjoying a sip of my beer.

"It's okay to be nervous," Mia begins, placing her beer on the tree stump between us. "Tell me what's holding you back with Lucas."

Where do I begin?

I've explained away my solo nature as protecting myself from my brother's fans, but that's not the entire story.

"I haven't been on a date in…"

She interrupts me. "You've worked for me for over a year and haven't dated once. I assumed some jerk screwed you over and you were healing."

"I haven't been on a date since high school," I confess.

"That's a long time to be alone," Mia whispers.

"I… I have a friend to hook up with if I want to," I share against my better judgement.

Something about Lucas makes me want Mia's help, and to help me, she needs to know everything.

"Remember how I mentioned people trying to get to Hamilton through me?" I wait for her to nod before I continue. "It started long before he became a Major League pitcher. In high school, his baseball talent allowed him to play on the varsity team his eighth-grade year. Colleges began inviting him to their camps all over the United States. Girls pretended to be my friend to get closer to him, and guys thought dating me might bring them in favor with the colleges interested in him."

I sip my beer while tamping down the pain rekindling within me.

"You know how things are in Athens. Everyone in all the neighboring counties knew Hamilton. I had to protect myself. I did that by…"

"Putting up your walls," she finishes for me. "Amy, I understand why you did it. I understand your need to protect yourself. But here in Dead-wood, you are Amy, not Hamilton Armstrong's sister. You are whoever and whatever you choose to be. That's why I encouraged you to take the twins on so many adventures with Lucas. I thought in spending time, you might lower your walls a foot or two while having fun. You are an amazing woman, so full of life and love. It hurts to see you hold yourself back from finding someone to share your life with."

I sit quietly as she takes a swig of her beer.

"My advice, if you care to hear it, is to go on this date with Lucas. No one knows you here, and no one knows about your brother. This is your chance to go out and have some fun. I've seen you have fun, so I know you know how to." She turns to face me, sitting on the edge of her chair. "I've asked Oliver a thousand questions about Lucas, and everything I've learned tells me he's the perfect man for you to go out with while we are here and let your hair down."

"Is it really that simple?" I ask her.

Mia nods. "You'll be surrounded by more than one-hundred-thousand strangers attending Wild Bill Days, so you won't be alone on your first date. I think that's great for your first time out with a guy. There will be events going on everywhere you look, and that will give you much to talk about. You won't have to worry about the long, awkward pauses. You like spending time with him, don't you?"

I don't fight the smile that slips upon my face, and I nod. "He makes it easy."

"I knew it!" she giggles. "You'll have so much fun. Trust me. I see it in both your eyes. Come on, I'll help you choose an outfit and get ready."

"Why did I ever agree to this?" I mutter.

"Stop," she drawls. "You'll have fun. Just wait and you'll see."

8

FIRST KISS

LUCAS

After a phenomenal day with William, Harry, and Amy, watching the Dock Dogs competition on Main Street, I'm giddy with excitement to see what the night brings.

I park my truck along the street in front of the house. Before I open my door, Amy appears on the porch. I stifle a groan.

It'll be agony to keep my hands off her this evening. And I will keep my hands off of her, well, most of her.

I don't plan to charge like a battle ram and knock down all her walls on our first date. I'm not looking for a quick lay, and I guarantee she isn't either.

My heart quickens with every step I take toward the gorgeous woman waiting for me on the porch. She stands before me in a simple black tank top with silver grommets around the neckline, khaki shorts that show off her long legs, and black, strappy sandals. Her sun-kissed skin glistens in the light, and her long dark-brown curls fall to her shoulders.

I love she wore her hair down. I can't wait to feel her soft curls in my fingers and her lips pressed to mine.

Yes, this will be a long, long night in her alluring presence.

"Hey," she greets with a slight, nervous wave.

"You look captivating,"

"Lucas!" Harry screams, bulldozing his way through the screen door towards me on the sidewalk, followed by his twin shadow. "Lucas is here!"

"Hi, Lucas," William says with a wave at my feet, halting my walk towards my beautiful date.

"Hi guys." I smile, bending down, handing flowers to each of them. "Can you do me a favor and give these to Miss Amy and these to Miss Mia?"

With an excited nod, they walk back to the house to complete their task. I watch William hand the wildflowers to Amy and dart into the house with his brother.

Amy lifts the small bouquet to her nose, inhaling their sweet scent. She lifts them between us.

"Thank you for these."

I jut my chin and resume my walk in her direction.

"I was ready, but now I'll need to place these in water." She turns, opening the screen door. "Would you like to come inside?"

"I'll wait on the porch," I answer, taking a seat on the swing.

I fear if I go inside, the twins will keep the two of us much longer than I intend. I've waited two weeks to get Amy all to myself, and I don't plan to share her with them tonight.

"I'm ready," she announces, emerging once more.

I'm humbled by her breathtaking beauty and the promise of her attention this evening.

"Where will we go first?" she asks, walking towards my truck.

"I thought we could walk, if you don't mind," I suggest.

Amy's megawatt smile assures me she likes my plan.

On the half-mile walk towards Main Street, I share about my other visits to town and the one time I took part in Wild Bill Days. Block after block we find the streets and sidewalks grow busier with tourists.

As we discussed during our stroll, we stop for an appetizer and beer in one establishment. Then we people watch as we walk further down the street with our drinks in hand.

"I can't believe how many lawn chairs there are," Amy says.

"I showed you they started setting them out before noon," I remind her.

I placed our lawn chairs out and a blanket on the hill at ten-thirty this morning on my way to pick up the boys and Amy. Although I explained to her and the boys how crowded the town would be for the daytime activities, they were not prepared for it. It prompted me to share even more details with Amy for tonight, but she still seems surprised.

"At least we'll be able to hear the concert, even if we can't see it," she states as we walk past the stage.

When I reveal the lawn chairs, reserving our seats for the concert, I hope she's impressed with the effort I put in to planning for this evening and not focus on the fact I planned on her attending the concert with me before I asked her out.

The large speakers blare music as the first opening act performs. I place my hand low on Amy's back, guiding her through the crowded sidewalk. *The next act will start...* I glance at my watch. *They start in twenty minutes. With two hours and ten minutes until the main act performs, there's plenty of time to walk around, but if we plan to eat we need to decide now.*

"Ready to eat?" I prompt.

"I'm not starving, but I would eat some fries," Amy says, looking over her shoulder at me on the sidewalk behind her. "We could split a meal and nibble again after the concert," she suggests.

I love women secure enough with themselves to eat what they want. The fact Amy wants to eat carbs and three times on our date impresses me.

"Duck in here," I instruct, guiding her to an outdoor patio area between two historical buildings.

We wait behind two other couples before we're ushered to a small table in the back corner. I don't wait for a menu, knowing the staff is slammed tonight.

"Please bring us a burger, medium, American cheese with fries and two refills of Coors Light," I order for the two of us.

When the server leaves, I explain, "They'll grow busier by the minute. I ordered now because I didn't know how long it would be before they came back by."

Amy understands. "Sounds good to me. I didn't think the town could really hold this many people."

I open my mouth, but Amy stops me. "I know. I know. You told me it would be this crowded."

I chuckle, loving how easily the two of us get along.

"Don't laugh at me," she swats my shoulder.

I grab her wrist, tugging her and her chair closer to mine. My eyes lock on hers as I inch my mouth towards hers. When she doesn't protest and doesn't pull away, I press my lips gently to hers. Her eyelids flutter before growing heavy and then closing.

My lips softly massage hers as I convey my growing feelings for her in a small public display of affection. It takes all my willpower to end our kiss after a few simple pecks.

The quick kiss confirms everything I expected. Amy and I share a chemistry like none I've experienced before. It promises explosive things to come between the two of us in our goodnight kiss and beyond.

9
PERFECTION

AMY

Approaching my house, I feel as though I walk on pillowy clouds. While I enjoy my time with Lucas and the boys, I lacked faith in our evening alone. Seven hours passed in the blink of an eye. I thought a perfect date didn't exist, but Lucas delivers an amazing evening that will live in infamy in the record books.

We share food and conversation like old friends. We tease and laugh, sing and even dance. Lucas shows me a magical night amongst the history, music, and tourists in Deadwood.

I long to slow my pace, prolonging our walk back to my place.

I now know exactly how it feels to never want the night to end.

"Did you always want to work with children?" Lucas asks as we round the corner onto my street.

"I thought I wanted to be a teacher for bit, but college really wasn't for me," I share. "Mia's nanny job fell into my lap at the exact moment I needed it."

I pray he doesn't ask why, because I'm not sure how to explain it all.

"Are you close with your family?"

Okay. I guess I can't avoid this question if I hope to spend as much time as I can with Lucas before we go our separate ways.

"Mind if we sit on the swing for a bit?" he asks, while waiting for my answer.

"I grew up close to both parents. We lost my dad when I was in high school," I begin. "It was tough, but I grew closer to my mother. Mom is my best friend. And I'm pretty close with my little brother, too."

"How old is your brother?" Lucas asks, genuinely interested.

I remind myself he's asking innocent questions.

"I'm four years older than my brother," I answer.

"So, he was in middle school when your dad passed?"

I nod.

"I can't imagine losing one of my parents in middle school or high school." He plays with a strand of my hair, tickling my bare shoulder. "Do your mom and brother still live in Athens?"

"Mom still lives on our family farm," I share. "And my brother, his wife, and daughter live in Chicago at the moment."

"At the moment..." he pauses, brow furrowed. "Will they be moving soon?"

"So, you probably noticed I'm... umm... I like to keep others out." I clear my throat, my nerves heavy in my voice.

Lucas moves his fingers to rub circles on my bare shoulder in support.

"My brother's kind of famous," I state.

"Would I know him, then?"

"I don't know, but imagine that you do," I answer.

"I'm sorry I interrupted," Lucas apologizes.

"It's okay. From a young age, my brother was in the spotlight and people tried to use me to get to him," I explain. "I was hurt several times before I constructed my walls and closed myself off out of self-preservation."

He doesn't speak, yet shows me his support as his hand pauses on my shoulder, gently squeezing me in support.

"My name is Amy Armstrong," I announce.

I'm caught off guard by Lucas's laughter. "That sounds like an introduction at Alcoholics Anonymous."

I replay my statement in my head and laugh with him. He's right.

I shake my head. "It's hard for me to trust."

"Amy, I want to know you. I like you. I only asked about your family, so I'd get to know you better."

"Even though I'm four years older, I grew up in his shadow," I murmur.

"I don't see you in anyone's shadow," Lucas states, deep with conviction. "You're a beautiful, funny, caring, dynamic woman. I'm drawn to you. It's not because of your little brother; it's all you."

He pulls me up. Standing in his arms, he looks down at me with his kind blue eyes.

Tonight is the best night of my life.

Beneath a dark, velvety sky with twinkling lights and a bright moon, Lucas pulls my chest to his with one hand on my lower back and one at the back of my neck. His kiss claims my mouth as he explores, and his tongue teases, then tangles with mine.

Like a cat rubbing to mark with its pheromones, I press my body tighter to his, my hands clinging to his back. I can't get close enough as I want and need more from him.

Ka-thump.

Another one of my walls crumples at our feet. I'm slowly opening up and baring more of myself to this man. If I'm not careful, soon I'll hold nothing back, offering all of me to him.

The porch light flickers above us.

"I'm going to murder her," I growl, my lips brushing his as I speak.

I feel his chest vibrate with laughter against mine. "I thought only parents flicked the lights."

"Parents and nosey bosses, evidently," I hiss.

He kisses the corner of my mouth, soothing my ire for the moment.

"She's excited to hear about your date," he murmurs. "I'm sure Oliver will be the same way when I arrive at his place."

"When will I see you again?" I ask.

Oh my god!

Could I sound more desperate?

"I mean…"

Lucas presses his thumb against my lips, silencing me.

"I'll call you after my run in the morning," he vows. "You decide on something we can do with William and Harry tomorrow."

At my smile, he kisses me once more, finding it hard to peel himself from me and step off the porch.

Swooning like a school girl after her first kiss, I enter the house somewhat prepared for Mia's interrogation. Instead, I find the living room along with the kitchen empty and dark but for a nightlight. I climb the creaky stairs, praying the sound doesn't disturb the twins. Mia's door stands slightly ajar, but no light or sound is present.

Could she be asleep?

And… if she's asleep, who flicked the lights, interrupting our kiss?

I kick myself for reacting as I did. With this house built in the late 1800s, I notice a flicker of the lights from time to time. Lost in the most amazing kiss I've ever experienced, I should not have noticed the flickering light.

I remove my clothes, sliding between the cool sheets. My mind flows through every moment of my time with Lucas. It amazes me how easy the night seemed. While learning more about this amazing man, I slowly let my guard down, sharing parts of me with him. Not only did I survive a date, I enjoyed it.

Wait!

I didn't… he doesn't…

I didn't tell him everything about Hamilton. He doesn't know all about my brother. He left knowing my brother was famous, and that was enough for him.

I can't wait for my next date with Lucas.

10

MIGHT WRECK ME

AMY

One week later, Mia invites Oliver and Lucas to join us for a bonfire in our backyard.

"Come get 'em while they're hot, boys!" Mia calls out, extending her sticks skewering sizzling hot dogs over the crackling bonfire in our backyard. Harry and William stand on either side of her, eagerly cooking their own, their little faces glowing in the light of the flames. With the warm summer night fading, it's the perfect time for a cozy backyard bonfire.

I smile fondly as I slide a hot dog from William's stick and load it up with mustard and relish for him. He climbs onto the nearby picnic table bench, ready to taste the meal he cooked himself over the open flame. I help Harry with his plate, then fix my own.

Lucas saunters over, a plate with two hot dogs in one hand and two cold bottles of Coors Light in the other. He settles onto the picnic bench next to me, our thighs brushing as he hands me a fresh beer. I believe it's intentional when he gifts me with his crooked grin, making my heart skip a beat.

"Thanks for the beer." I clink my bottle against his.

As Lucas digs into his hot dog slathered in chili and cheese, I can't help admiring the scruff-covered, rugged lines of his profile accentuated by the firelight.

Across the table, Oliver regales the rambunctious twins with stories from Lucas's wild rodeo visits in past years. He tells of a time the two took the ATVs out and Lucas tipped over in a river. William and Harry giggle as I'm sure Oliver embellishes in his retelling.

"Lucas can't drive," Harry laughs, pointing in Lucas's direction.

"You saw me drive my bike," he reminds Harry. "And I drove over here tonight."

Harry shakes his head, still smiling wildly from the funny story.

I giggle to myself at Lucas's nonchalant reply, my knee pressing more firmly against his in shameless flirtation. Ever since our breathtaking first kiss the other night, I feel an electrifying new sense of freedom in allowing myself to engage with Lucas without restraint.

As the hot dogs give way to rounds of ooey-gooey s'mores, Lucas's arm finds its way around my shoulders, pulling me closer. He smells of wood smoke and the leathery scent of his cologne.

Eventually, in the hypnotic movement of the flames, the twins nod off against Mia's sides, chocolate still smeared around their mouths.

"Alright, alright, I think that's enough excitement for one night," she chuckles, rousing her sleepy charges. "Say goodnight, guys."

I shift to stand.

"I can tuck them in," Mia offers. "Stay and enjoy the fire."

I want to argue, but her eyes and slight nudge of her head encourage me to remain with Lucas. I resume my seat, placing a few inches between us on the bench. Lucas props his feet on the bricks surrounding the flames. I don't miss the smirk on his lips as he raises his beer bottle to his mouth.

———

With the boys safely tucked into bed and sound asleep, the four of us enjoy the warmth of the fire pit, sipping on beers, and stargazing as an occasional firefly blinks in the darkness of the yard.

Well after eleven o'clock, Mia finally lets out a jaw-cracking yawn, fanning herself.

"I don't know about y'all, but this girl's about to turn into a pumpkin. I need rest if I plan to spit out new chapters tomorrow."

Mia bids us goodnight and heads inside, leaving the three of us. I glance at Lucas. His eyes share his mutual lust. I extend my hand between us, and he quickly entwines his fingers with mine.

"That's my cue," Oliver states, rising. "You two kids have fun and remember protection."

I choke on my sip of beer, coughing and sputtering.

"Easy there, tiger," Lucas says, releasing my hand to pat my back.

When my reaction to Oliver's comment ends, I find Lucas and I alone in the low light of a now much smaller fire. Nervousness floods over me. My body longs to cuddle tight to the man beside me and explore each other. However, my brain warns me to protect my heart. I know very little about him. He doesn't live here, and I'll be heading back to Missouri soon.

Lucas wraps his muscular arm around my back, tugging me to his side. My head rests on his shoulder as I gaze into the fire.

"The bonfire was a great idea." His low, husky voice stirs even more turmoil within me. "The boys seemed to love it."

"Back home we gather around the fire every month, but not in the winter," I share. "We don't always have hotdogs and s'mores, but friends always join us."

"Guy friends?" he queries, and I laugh.

"Neighbors join us," I answer. "Mia has guy friends that visit frequently. They started out helping with renovating her house, and now they come over to hang out with her."

"I'm sure they come to be with you, too." His fingers fiddle with the tips of my ponytail as he speaks.

"What I'm about to tell you is not common knowledge," I state, spinning to face him. "Since they're coming to visit for the weekend, you'll probably figure it out on your own, anyway." I worry my lip, searching for the best way to put it into words. "Mia's in a relationship with more than one guy."

His eyes widen a bit. "Are they aware of each other?"

I nod. "The four of them have a weird relationship that works for them. I gave up trying to figure it all out long ago. They make her happy, and the guys don't fight over her. Well, Dutton and Lee fight occasionally, but that's just because they are brothers."

"Brothers?" Lucas scoffs. "Three men, two brothers... share Mia?"

Smiling, I nod again. "It's hard to judge them when you see how happy they all are." I shrug. "You'll soon see."

"I don't dare judge. I couldn't... I'm not a man willing to share," he states, then takes a swig of his beer. "So Mia's three boyfriends are the guys that come over often?" he asks.

He genuinely seems interested in the fact that I claim I don't have a boyfriend. It says a lot about his character that he won't poach another man's girlfriend. I'm like Lucas in the fact that I prefer monogamy.

I'm surprised when he pulls me fully onto his lap, my thighs straddling his. He buries his face in the crook of my neck and inhales the scent of my hair before nipping the sensitive skin beneath my ear. A gasp escapes at his lips' intimate exploration of my neck and collarbone. Between my legs, I feel his erection swell. I affect him as he affects me. I feel like a flame about to be splashed with an accelerant.

Too fast.

We're moving much too fast.

"Wait," I whisper breathily.

Lucas pauses, his lips still to the flesh of my neck. His hot breath prickles my skin.

"I..." I falter.

"Slow," he states. "We'll move slow."

I pull back to gaze into his blue eyes.

"Slow, but I need to kiss you," he confesses.

I nod slightly. My belly flutters with the desire in his tone. The passion between us burns violently. I have no doubt I'd find myself in his bed tonight if I didn't set limits.

I close my eyes for a moment. Thoughts of Lucas's naked body over mine swarm my mind.

"Amy," he murmurs.

"Slow," I restate, wetting my lip.

"I can do slow," he vows, his hands sliding up and down my back.

I want him to kiss me again. I need his lips on mine. I long for the connection and euphoria I experienced in our first kiss. Having felt it once, I'm now greedy for more.

Lucas leans towards me, pausing a hairsbreadth from my mouth. He's seeking my permission, letting me to control our speed. I waste no time slamming my mouth to his. His hands cup the back of my head, tilting me for better access at the same time as his tongue glides along the crease of my lips. I give him the entry he seeks, parting for him. Our tongues tangle and our teeth collide, causing Lucas to growl.

I feel as if I'm floating away. The magic of our kiss overwhelms me. My fingertips clutch his shoulders. I'm pleased to find our first kiss wasn't a fluke. The connection between us is much too much to contain.

I want more. I need all of him. I long to feel this magic magnify the orgasms he'd award me. I stop myself from grinding against his cock, igniting a passion we can't come back from.

I pull my mouth from his, staring into his wild eyes, aware of my heavy breaths. Lucas's hands slide down my back, resting at my hips. His nostrils flare with his ragged breaths.

I slip from his lap, setting on the bench at his side. We place our heels on the bricks in front of us, and Lucas cuddles me tight to his side as we stare at the remaining red embers of the bonfire.

That was close.

I need to tread carefully. I fear this man might wreck me.

"This is nice," Lucas says in a gruff voice. "For five years, I've moved city to city, working 24/7, jumping any time my cell phone pinged, giving everything to my job. Most of my alone time was spent in my apartment slash office in the front of the livestock trailer or in a cheap hotel room. I didn't realize how much fun I could have sitting around a bonfire in the backyard with close friends. I'm beginning to realize how different the life I led and the life I want truly are."

"You really have no idea what your next job might be?" I inquire, unable to fathom quitting a job without another lined up.

"My employer paid for everything, so my paychecks built up in the bank," he shares. "Food, lodging, work clothes, hell, even my beers were work expenses because we talked business. Other than buying an occasional present for my parents, I really didn't spend much. So, I figure I'm owed a couple weeks of downtime before I hunt for my next job."

"Any idea where you might move next?" I ask, then realize he might interpret it as me getting too attached too quick. "Warm weather, cold weather, coastal, land-locked... Do you have a state or two in mind?"

I want him to know I'm not asking him to move to Missouri.

"I have absolutely no idea," he chuckles. "My degree's in livestock management and my work experience... Well, you know about my job. So, I'll probably look in that area."

"That doesn't really narrow down the location, does it?" I laugh.

"I'm enjoying free time, visiting with Oliver, and..."

His unspoken words weigh heavy in the air between us. I imagine them to be, "and spending time with you."

As the bonfire smolders and the inky blackness swallows us whole, I allow myself to fully embrace the peace and promise of Lucas's warm, steadying embrace. The future will carry us off into the great unknown, but tonight, here under this canopy of twinkling lights, looming mountains, and towering pines, is all that matters.

11

T. E. F. N

Amy

Where did the time go?

My weeks with Lucas passed too quickly.

Suitcases on my bed, the lyrics to John Denver's *Leaving on a Jet Plane* flow through my mind. Mia and I plan to load the vehicle tonight and leave bright and early in the morning. She finished her book two weeks early, and she can't wait to get back to Athens and her men. While I'm eager to return home to see Mom, I find I'm dragging my feet.

This is a novel feeling for me. I allowed myself to let down my guard in this historic tourist town. The part of me I keep hidden leapt free like an exuberant child. No one knows my brother here, no one knows I'm the big sister to a famous, World Series pitcher, and no one tries to use me to get to him.

I will miss Deadwood.

And I will miss...

Lucas.

I sit on the edge of my bed, letting my thoughts sink in.

———

After bathing the twins and tucking into bed, I knock softly on Mia's bedroom door.

"Mia? You have a minute?"

"Come in!" Mia calls out.

She's sitting cross-legged on her bed, her laptop and various note-books spread out around her.

I enter hesitantly and perch on the edge of the mattress.

"I... I want to talk to you about something before we leave tomorrow."

Mia picks up on my uncharacteristically nervous tone. "What's going on? Is everything okay?"

Twisting my hands in my lap, I share, "It's about Lucas."

Understanding washes over Mia's face.

"Ahh. You aren't ready for goodbye, are you?"

My cheeks flush as I nod.

"I know it's fast, but... I'm really going to miss him, Mia. He's wonderful with the boys, and I've come to care deeply for him these weeks we've shared in Deadwood."

Mia sets aside her writing materials, giving me her full attention. "Have you told him how you feel?"

"No!" I say quickly, then look down. "No... I don't even know if he thinks of me as anything more than the nanny he spent time with on vacation. And besides, we'll be leaving at dawn, heading all the way back to Missouri. It would just be... terribly difficult, unrealistic even, to continue anything serious from so far away."

My voice catches in my throat as I admit, "But I think... I think I might love him, Mia. And the idea of never seeing Lucas again... It feels like my heart is breaking."

Mia reaches over and gives my hand a comforting squeeze.

"Oh Amy... I knew your feelings developed fast and deep. I hoped the two of you spoke about your feelings and life after Deadwood. Why didn't you say anything sooner?"

"I don't know. I suppose I was scared," I admit quietly. "Letting Lucas in has been so wonderfully unexpected after keeping my walls up for so long. I was afraid to risk ruining that by confessing my true feelings or suggesting we stay in touch."

Gently, Mia says, "Well, it seems to me you now have a choice to make, Amy. You can remain silent, leave Deadwood behind, and always wonder 'what if'... Or you can find the courage to put yourself out there, confess your feelings to Lucas, and see if he feels the same way. At least then you won't have any regrets."

My eyes shimmer with unshed tears as I weigh Mia's words. Deep down, I know my friend is right. This may well be my last chance with Lucas.

Can I really make myself that vulnerable?

"You deserve to be happy, Amy," Mia states firmly. "And from what I've witnessed between you two, I think there's a real chance Lucas could make you happy if you'll let him."

Lucas

At dusk, on Oliver's patio, I take a long pull from my beer bottle, staring pensively out at the dusty Deadwood street.

"I don't know what to do. Amy and the family she works for are leaving town at first light," I inform my friend of a fact he already knows as the host for Mia's Airbnb.

Oliver leans back in his lawn chair.

"You got it bad for that pretty little nanny, don't you?"

"Like a damn fool," I admit with a rueful chuckle and run a hand over my hair. "I can't explain it. I've never felt this way about a woman before. Normally they're the ones getting all doe-eyed and clingy with me after a night."

"But Amy ain't like those buckle bunnies you're used to foolin' around with," Oliver says knowingly.

I shake my head adamantly. "No sir, she's different. Real with a kind soul. Watching her with those kids... I can't get her outta my head."

"So what's the issue? Just tell her you want her to stick around!"

"You think it's that simple?" I argue, taking another swig of beer. "She's got her whole life back in Missouri. She's close to her family and folks that depend on her there. I'd be a goddamn idiot even considering asking a woman like that to uproot herself for me?"

Oliver considers this for a moment. "Well, way I see it, you need to ask her to stay or you need to ask if you can go with her. You won't ever know if you don't try. You quit the rodeo to find a new purpose. Maybe this gal's part of that?"

I worry my lip, thinking about the way Amy's brown eyes twinkle when she laughs, or how she tucks a stray lock of dark-chestnut hair behind her ear when she's pensive. These little mannerisms are seared into my memory.

"I'm not sure if she feels the same way. I mean, she likes me, and we have chemistry, but I'm not sure she feels as deeply as I do," I admit gruffly. "Hell, for all I know, she's using me as a distraction to keep her occupied in Deadwood. Damn my big dumb heart for getting all tangled up in her without even knowing if she wants me the same way."

Oliver raises an eyebrow. "Are you tellin' me the same Lucas Ramirez who used to wrestle 2,000 pound bulls is too chicken to ask Amy how she feels? Where's that daredevil courage you're known for?"

I shoot my friend a look, as some of my bravado returns to my eyes.

He's right.

I've always been a risk-taker, grabbing life by the horns no matter how dangerous.

Why should this be any different?

Setting my beer aside, I resolutely push myself to my feet.

"You know what?" I smirk at Oliver. "I'm gonna go for it. I'll shower, then I'm driving over to Amy's place and telling her exactly how I feel, consequences be damned. If she doesn't want me, at least I can say I gave her a chance to make me the happiest son of a bitch on the planet."

Oliver claps me on the shoulder proudly.

"That's the spirit! Get on over there before you lose your nerve, boy!"

With a determined nod, I spin on my boot heel and head inside. My heart pounds, but my mind is made up. By this time tomorrow, I'll either have Amy by my side... or be licking my wounds over losing the first woman he ever truly loved.

Amy

I'm four chapters into my newest dystopian romance book when I'm interrupted by a sudden, insistent knocking at the front door. My breath catches in my throat as I glance at the clock.

Who could that be at this late hour?

I close the Kindle app on my cellphone, leaving it on my bed and hurry to answer the door. I'm shocked to find Lucas standing on the porch, hands shoved in his pockets. He's a sight to behold in his snug, white t-shirt and well-worn jeans with the casual confidence I find so disarmingly attractive.

"Lucas!" Surprise coats my voice. "Why... What are you doing here?"

He awards me with that crooked grin that never fails to make my heart flutter.

"Good evening, Amy. Sorry to just drop in unexpected like this. I... uh... I need to speak to you. It's important. You got a minute?"

I glance back inside, finding Mia hovering nearby. She smiles, waving at him, and then she disappears through the kitchen.

"Of course, come in." I sweep my arm wide.

Lucas steps past me into the cozy living room. As I close the door behind him, I can't help but drink in his familiar western scent of leather, fresh air, and just a hint of wood smoke. It's incredibly comforting... and I realize with a pang how much I will miss it.

"So..." I sit, facing him while trying to keep my expression casual despite my heart hammering in my chest. "What's on your mind?"

Lucas seems to struggle to find the words, running a hand over his brown, cropped hair.

"Amy, I... well, I hate to make things any more complicated for you than they already are. But I got a feeling I just... I can't let you go without telling you how I feel."

My cheeks flush, my stomach does nervous backflips, and my breath catches.

Could this be...?

"Weeks with you have been... amazing," Lucas states, holding my wide gaze. "In all my years on the rodeo circuit, I never met a woman quite like you. You're strong and kind with a warm soul. I love watching how good you are with Harry and William..." He trails off and shakes his head, almost in disbelief. "You got under my skin, Amy. I've never felt this way about anyone before."

I'm stunned.

Did he really just speak the words I've longed to hear, or did I imagine it?

My heart feels as if it will burst as everything I've been secretly hoping finally comes tumbling out of Lucas's mouth.

He feels the same way!

"The truth is..." Lucas looks down briefly, then meets my eyes again with ardent sincerity. "I think I'm in love with you, darling Amy. And I know the timing is all kinds of wrong, but... I don't want to lose this. Lose you."

My breath catches as he steps closer, taking my hands gently in his calloused ones.

"I'm serious as a heart attack, Amy. If you'll have me... I want to move with you to Missouri. Try to make this thing between us work for the long haul."

I search his ruggedly handsome face, scarcely daring to believe this is really happening. The last of my carefully constructed walls crumble in the face of Lucas's heartfelt admission.

"You'd just... uproot your whole life?" I manage to ask, feeling dizzy with hopefulness. "For me?"

Lucas lifts one hand tenderly, brushing a stray lock of hair from my cheek.

"I already turned my life upside down by leaving the rodeo," he murmurs huskily. "This just makes all that worth it. You're worth it to me."

I feel myself lean into his touch, hardly able to breathe.

"Lucas... I... I love you, too," I confess at last. The words feel free and right. "I can't believe I fell in love so fast and deep."

His face splits into a breathtaking smile that crinkles those gorgeous blue eyes. Cupping my face in his powerful hands, Lucas pulls me into a long, smoldering kiss that leaves me weak in the knees and clinging to him for support.

When we finally part, while our foreheads rest together, Lucas murmurs, "I can't wait to make a life together, just you and me, and Mia, and those little rug rats. I can't wait to start fresh with you in Athens, Missouri."

I smile like a lunatic and nod, my heart so full of hope and love that I think it might burst. Against all odds, I found my future with the most unexpected man in the most unexpected place.

I'm thankful Mia fell far behind on her writing, I'm thankful Georgina had this Airbnb, and I'm thankful that the rodeo visited while we were in Deadwood. It took all of them to bring Lucas into my life.

Seems I'll leave Deadwood with more than just my suitcase.

T. E. F. N. = The End For Now

Amy and Lucas's complete story is in the works. Follow my newsletter with the QR code below for information on a new series *Backroads & Bonfires* by Haley Rhoades, releasing in Late 2024.

ABOUT THE AUTHOR

Haley Rhoades's writing is another bucket-list item coming to fruition, just like meeting Stephen Tyler and Ozzie Smith, and skydiving. As she continues to write contemporary romance, she also writes closed-door romance and young adult books under the name Brooklyn Bailey, as well as children's books under the name Gretchen Stephens.

Haley's under five-foot, fun-size stature houses a full-size attitude. Her uber-competitiveness in all things entertains, frustrates, and challenges family and friends.

Haley's guilty pleasures are Lifetime and Hallmark movies. Her other loves include all things peanut butter, *Star Wars*, mathematics, and travel. Past day jobs vary tremendously from a radio station DJ, to an elementary special-education para-professional, to a YMCA sports director, to a retail store accounting department, and finally a high school mathematics teacher.

Haley resides with her husband and fur-baby in the Des Moines area. A new grandma known as "Gigi", she spend many evenings on video calls with her grandson Murphy or traveling to spend time with her latest obsession. This Missouri-born girl enjoys the diversity the Midwest offers.

http://www.haleyrhoades.com/

FEARLESS PROTECTOR

VIA MARI

1

MASON

I TAKE THE ELEVATOR DOWNSTAIRS TO KENNY'S CASINO AND spot the others huddled in a corner of the bar talking to Kenny. Cole turns around and slaps me on the shoulder. "Good to see you. It's been a minute." He lowers his voice. "I heard they have you taking care of the Italian family members while they're visiting in Vegas."

Jay, one of the security team leaders, holds up a pitcher of beer and a glass. I give him a nod and reach over the top of the others to grab my drink as I answer Cole, making sure we're not overheard. "It's been a good assignment. Low-key enough right now, but after everything that's gone on in Vegas, we can't be too careful. They have extra soldiers and enforcers covering the family right now so that we can attend the wedding, but after next week, it'll be all hands on deck again."

Garrett, the soon-to-be-groom, walks toward us from the back and gets a round of slaps on the back and a fair amount of ribbing from the guys. "We send Cole to Deadwood, South Dakota with one mission, and he ends up putting down roots with a wife, kids, and all. We send Garrett to give him a hand, expecting him back in a week, and now he's getting married too." Matt, one of the other leaders of the team, looks around dramatically. "Clearly something's in the beer around these parts."

I chug back my beer, happy to have a few days off and be with the group who took me in as part of the elite bodyguard team for the Larussios. A job that not only takes a certain skill set, but also takes knowing someone who has the ears of the boss to get into one of the positions. A job I enjoy and wouldn't trade for the world, including any female, although these guys look happy enough with the women they adore.

Damian and Dereck talk quietly amongst themselves and look up when the pitcher of beer is passed around, each refilling their glass. They too are happy to be on a well needed vacation from the regular grind of protecting the Larussios and their extended family.

Sheldon and Nick join the group a few minutes later. Sheldon extends a hand, and I shake hands with him. "Good to see you. It's been a while. We heard you got assigned to the Italian side of the family out in Vegas. How's that working out for you?"

I grin. Word gets around our elite little crew. "There's nothing not to like about it at all. I haven't had any issues. I just do my job and keep to myself. They're incredibly generous and have been more than decent to me. I like the area, with the exception of the heat, so it's been a good fit. Plus, it's not bad being close to the Larussios enforcers, Tommy, and his boys either. It's come in handy for me and the guys protecting the rest of the family a few times.

Cole takes a pull of his beer. "No doubt. Tommy helped us clear up things here in Deadwood last year when the Chicago family had a hit put out on Kenny." I find my way to a seat at the bar just as the empty pitcher makes its way to me. I grin at my thirsty friends. "Next round is on me," I tell them, waiting for the barkeep with the long dark ponytail to turn around, but not minding the view of that ass in those skintight jeans while I wait.

Sheldon and Nick slide onto the stools beside me with their beers while Matt tells us the story of his tour of the Deadwood Cemetery where Wild Bill Hickok and Calamity Jane are buried and then his hike through the trails earlier this morning.

Cole points to a beige and brown detailed trail map on the wall. "There's definitely a lot to see in Deadwood. Trails, ski hills, historic landmarks. You name it, we've got it. Kenny, Lacy, PJ, and I use to play in some of those areas as kids. When we got older, we went out to the trails to park after dark with our boyfriends and girlfriends."

The bartender finally turns around, and her violet blue eyes and pixie-like features take my breath away. Beautiful doesn't quite describe what God created when he made her.

I hold up the empty pitcher with a grin. "Another of the same, please?"

She takes it from my hand, and my fingers brush with her softness before she abruptly pulls it away and puts it under the tap.

Garrett comes to stand beside me. "I'm glad you could make it, Mason."

I shake his hand. "Me too. Tommy and some of the other Larussio boys are coming in on the next plane. They were handing off the details to the backup crew and then planned on taking off. They should be here in a couple hours."

He laughs. "I hope we have enough beer. Man, those boys know how to party on their off time."

I take a drink of my beer. "That they do. I can't believe you're tying the knot tomorrow. From the single life to the married club with two little words. Congratulations, man."

Garret laughs. "I'll say I do to Lacy all day long, every day of my life. Just you wait, my friend. Someday the right woman is going to come along and sweep you off your feet. Then we'll see who's laughing. I'll remind you of this conversation at your own wedding one day."

I narrow my eyes at my friend. "Not in this lifetime, man. I'm not looking for a wife, just a good time and a whole lot of it."

The sexy little bartender places the pitcher of beer down on the counter, and it sloshes all over my hand and brand-new watch. Her eyebrows raise, and she doesn't even open her mouth to apologize. Instead, her violet blue smoke-filled eyes glare at me as though I've just spilled beer on her instead of the other way around. But there's a hint of a guilty smile under those soft looking pink lips that she can't hide from me. Still, she tries. "I'm sorry."

"You don't look sorry in the least, now do you, little miss?"

Those eyes flash. "The name is PJ, not little miss."

2

PJ

THOSE HAZEL GREEN EYES SEE ALL TOO MUCH AND KNOW exactly what I did and that it was no accident at all. Serves the fun-loving playboy right. I've seen my share of the waltz through town kind of guys who like to have a little fun and then pretend you don't exist when they see you at the diner the very next morning.

At least they looked sheepish about it, even a little guilty as they walked out the door without saying a word. But this douche bag? He seems proud of having fun with a woman and then just leaving her in the dust while he travels back to the city. He may not have said it like that, but that's probably what he meant.

Asshat... A fine-looking asshat, no doubt, with that tussled sand colored hair and that black t-shirt that fits over those muscles in just the right way. But still...

The music on stage announces the start of the show. The guys grab their drinks and head to the tabled seats reserved for Garrett's bachelor party while Marla comes on stage to entertain the boisterous and growing crowd.

She's gone all-out tonight, her long blonde hair brushed to a high gloss, pink lips that match her high heeled shoes, and her little white pasties and panties to match. Now that Lacy's no longer working here,

Marla gets the lion's share of the tips. I have no doubt she'll be raking in the money tonight because these friends of Cole and Garrett's make damn good bank working for one of the most ruthless crime families around the globe.

I've heard all about those boys who walk a fine line between right and wrong from Krissy and Lacy. I don't know how those two got so lucky to have landed the good ones among the bunch, but they did. Cole and Garrett are solid. They love Krissy and Lacy with all their hearts, but their friends and coworkers are a rowdy bunch at best. At least from what I can see.

A night of listening to them live it up, the wedding and a dance to get through tomorrow, and then they'll all pack into that private jet they flew in on and go back to the desert and their Mafia crowd where they belong. Only for Lacy and her wedding to Garrett will I put up with this alpha macho shit. I glance at my watch just as my replacement walks through the door. I pour myself a beer and take a drink as she walks behind the bar.

Her kind old eyes raise in surprise. "Bad night, or just starting the bachelorette party before you get to the actual party?"

I grin. "Something like that. Thanks for covering for me tonight. I would ask Lacy if she weren't the bride, and Kenny is over there with Cole and the guys. We appreciate being able to hang out with our friends tonight. It was very nice of you to step in."

Lettie glances over at the reserved table. "Oh, be still my heart. If I weren't married and twenty years younger, those young men would be in trouble." I drink some more beer and watch the asshat they called Mason who keeps checking his phone, like he can't wait to get out of this small town and get back home. Lettie clears her throat. "Maybe you can hook up with one of them and let off a little steam, my dear. You don't want to turn into an old maid, who never had one bit of fun to look back on."

I roll my eyes at the well-intentioned matchmaker in town. "I've had enough love 'em and leave 'em to last me a lifetime. No thank you. Besides, I don't need a man to have fun. I plan to let off a bunch of steam with the ladies tonight; no assholes needed, thank you very much."

Lettie smiles, but it doesn't reach her eyes. I toss my apron onto the back of the counter and head out for the night without saying goodbye. I slide into the plush leather seat of my brand-new SUV. I don't need a man to take care of me or to show me how to have a little fun. I can do that all by myself. I turn onto the main highway and head toward the outside of town where the party should be in full swing.

I may have missed having dinner with the ladies, but I don't plan on missing any more of Lacy's special night. The band is going strong, and the sound of music reaches the parking lot as I head to the entrance. A strong lead guitar and drum set makes it almost impossible to hear anything other than the band as I walk in.

I make my way through the crowded bar until I see the ladies at a table closer to the band than my hearing will like. I stop by the bar and opt for pointing to the domestic on tap instead of yelling at the barkeep, who can probably barely hear a thing until this particular song is through.

He gives me a nod and pours the amber liquid into the tall glass. "Thank you," I mouth, sliding some bills his way, and heading toward the ladies before he has time to make change. "PJ, you made it," Lacy says, pushing the pitchers of margarita and a tray of half-empty shot glasses toward the center of the table to make room. The sight makes me glad I opted to stop for a light beer on my way in. A couple of those little drinks and I'd have a headache from hell tomorrow.

"I'm glad you could make it," I tell Eileen, who smiles broadly. "Kenny and I had Lettie cover for us at the bar tonight. Hopefully the crowd won't give her too much trouble, but she's handled that group before with no issue. Everyone listens to what Lettie has to say in town."

Eileen laughs. "They sure do, or they will regret the day they didn't. At least Kenny's there if anything comes up," she says.

I watch Krissy laugh at Patti and Jules while those two tip back their second shot since I got to the table. "Those ladies are going to be in bad shape tomorrow. Glad Krissy could come. She looks like she's having a great time," I tell Eileen.

She nods. "Maddie's watching the kids tonight at our house. I'll go home here in a while and give her a hand putting them down. Kenny and I thought it would be nice for Cole and Krissy to have a little time to let loose."

I grin. "She's certainly doing that!"

Eileen sips her wine. "That she is. I'd be doing the same thing if I had two littles in the span of two years and pregnant with a third. I don't know how she keeps up to them and all the stuff she does around their place, helping board the horses and everything."

I take another drink, and Lacy leans into me. "Jules, Patti, and me are going to try some whiskey shots. Eileen's going to behave herself tonight and go home early."

The band ends with a drum finale. "Don't go anywhere, folks. We'll be back after a short break."

Lacy hands me a shot. "You promised to let loose and have fun tonight. All work and no play..." she singsongs, holding the shot intended for me up in the air. Patti and Jules raise their glasses, and Krissy raises her water glass, giving me a grin. Clearly you have to be pregnant or nursing to get out of this part of the night.

Lacy rolls her eyes at my hesitancy. "I'm only getting married once, and I'm going to enjoy every single moment and experience all the things, even an enormous fricking headache on my wedding day, probably."

"Fine..." I tip my glass. "Let's get this party started then."

"Bottoms up," Jules and Patti say from across the table simultaneously, bursting into laughter. "Jinx!"

We all hold our glasses up and toss back the shot of aged Deadwood whiskey. I gasp as it goes down, almost choking on the strength. "That is smooth..." Lacy says, holding out another shot and laughing at me the entire time.

It's hard not to have fun when she is around, and contrary to popular belief, I don't want to be by myself for the rest of my life, or not have fun. I do want to have fun; I deserve to have a little fun even. I reach for another shot. "Let's show them how it's done in Deadwood, because I use to be able to do this without any problems at all."

The band comes back on, and Lacy pulls us onto the dance floor. I try to resist. "I can't line dance sober much less after those shots." She laughs, half dragging me to the floor before linking her arms in mine as the line of surprisingly in sync women begin to dance, and I try hard to follow along.

3
MASON

THE PITCHERS OF BEER ARE MAKING THEIR WAY AROUND THE table, and everyone is having a good time, but someone has to keep their cognitive skills enhanced. I volunteered for that tonight. A couple beers early in the night was enough for me. A few Coca Colas later, and I'm watching the rest of the group living it up. And wondering where that cute little barkeeper with the fiery violet blue eyes went.

Jay gestures to Garrett and a couple of the guys who are in a heated battle of pool at the tables in the back. "Garrett's running the table tonight. Cole doesn't lose often at pool."

I watch Garrett sink one ball and then another. "Garrett's going easy on the drinks tonight. He doesn't plan on having a headache from hell tomorrow like our other friends, you included."

Jay laughs. "It's not often we go out as a group. Someone has to be watching the family."

"It was nice of the Larussios to help out with the coverage and to fly everyone out for the occasion."

Jay nods. "The Larussios and Chase Prestian are the best to work for. I wouldn't trust Chase and Katarina with just anyone while I'm gone, but Tommy has quite a few men on the payroll, enough to send some of them to cover us and himself while the rest of us are out here."

Cole takes a shot and misses by a mile. He pulls his phone from his pocket and steps away. A few minutes later he walks over. "Hey, Maddie called. She's over at Kenny and Eileen's watching Darcy and little Cole. He has an earache. Can you give me a ride to Eagle's Swallow; it's on the edge of town. Krissy isn't answering her phone."

I grab my jacket and toss some money on the table. We get a little razzing by the guys for not being able to keep up to them with drinks before we leave, but it's all in good fun. Cole shrugs into his coat as he walks across the parking lot, before jumping into the passenger seat. "Thanks for the ride. One too many to be behind the wheel. The temperature's supposed to drop tonight."

A quick glance at the dash climate control confirms exactly that, reminding me of another icy road and accident years ago. "Yeah, I don't like that 32-degree temp mark. A little on the iffy side for me if it starts raining."

Cole looks into the back seat. "You brought the bags Garrett needed? I was going to ask if you brought the extra supplies or if they would come in another trip. A little extra firepower and ammo never hurts when you're dealing with unexpected events."

"I took the private jet, so it was easier to carry it along." I crank the heater on the rented SUV. "It's definitely getting a little chilly. I think the desert sun thins out your blood after a while."

Cole closes the door and reaches for the seat belt as I pull out of the parking lot as he tries Krissy again. "They keep the music so loud she probably didn't hear her cell. We'll have to run him up to urgent care tonight. Poor guy gets those recurrent ear infections. They'll probably have to put tubes in until he outgrows them."

"Poor little fella. Good thing he has you two to care for him. What's the bartender's story? PJ? If looks could kill I would have been dead on the floor tonight."

He laughs. "You do not even want to go there, my friend. That woman will cut your heart out and feed it to the wolves. No man outside of this town has a shot in hell with PJ after some dumb fuck from the city broke her heart years ago. The sad thing is she's such good friends with the guys in town that no one sees her like that."

I don't understand that reasoning. "If I ever thought about settling down, not that I would, it would have to be with someone I could have as a friend too. To share everything with. I mean, isn't trust what holds two people together through thick and thin; isn't that what friends do? I don't see how you're married to someone without being their friend."

Cole nods. "You're not wrong. That's what Krissy and I have. It wasn't an easy road to begin with; the trust thing, I mean. We had our bumps in the beginning. I pulled her out of a rough situation. She had to find herself before she was ready to be with me or anyone else. But she did, and we'll be together for a lifetime. But, PJ, that's a whole other situation. She holds a grudge, longer than most people I know. She is a fiery spirit!"

I laugh. "Yeah, I could see something flashing in those eyes. That woman is fine as hell too. I tried to talk to her, and she dumped beer on me like I wasn't worth the time of day."

Cole rolls his eyes and grins.

"No, she literally dumped beer on me for absolutely no reason."

Cole laughs. "You get what you get with Priscilla Jean. All I can say is out of towners, beware." He pulls into the parking lot of a rustic log cabin type establishment and parks next to a gray minivan. "That's Krissy's van. I'll go get her. She and I can head over to Kenny and Eileen's house and then to urgent care. Their daughter, Maddie, is watching them there tonight."

I follow him into the rustic bar where the live band is giving it their all in an effort to show everyone a good time. Cole jabs my elbow and gestures to the dance floor. "That's something I never thought I'd see again. They got PJ to dance."

My eyes follow his to the women dancing in a line and in sync with the music and each other. I'd recognize the ass on the end anywhere, but now her long, wavy hair is bouncing with every move she makes, free from the ponytail that she wore at the bar.

The ladies turn, in time to the music. As if feeling the heat of my gaze, PJ's bright glossy eyes connect with mine, her soft features framed by all that hair. Her face is flushed from laughing and dancing hard, but there's something else in that look she gives me that I find hard to ignore.

The two of us make our way toward the ladies on the floor. "It looks like PJ is learning to have a little fun again. It's nice to see. It's been way too long."

Krissy spots Cole and walks quickly across the dance floor to him, her eyes full of worry with the others close behind. "What's wrong? Why are you guys here?" she asks, a little out of breath from dancing.

Cole explains the situation, and she pulls out her phone with wide eyes. "I'm so sorry. I never even heard the phone ring. Thanks for bringing Cole out," she says to me. "I'll get my things."

Cole looks around as we follow Krissy back to their table. I take in all the empty shot glasses and some full ones too. "Where are Lacy and Patti; I thought you were all here together?" Cole asks.

Jules slips dramatically into a chair and grabs a full shot, tossing it back. "Lacy and Patti went over to meet a few friends at the Eagle's Nest. It's their grand opening tonight. They'll be back before 11 pm. Then we are all going to have a few more drinks, a last hoorah dance, and head home at midnight."

Cole nods. "The owners are good friends of Lacy's. I heard they were opening another bar but didn't realize it was tonight." He looks at me. "Krissy was DD and supposed to take the ladies home. She'll drive us out to get little Cole and then over to the urgent care. Can you make sure these two get home safe?" He gestures to PJ and Jules as they both reach for a beer.

I smirk and lower my voice so only he can hear. "Sure, babysitting a couple of drunken women? No problem. But you will owe me, my friend."

He grins. "Consider it an IOU. Garrett probably already knows where Lacy and Patti are, but I'll give him a text and make sure he's aware. He quit drinking hours ago and can pick them up and take them home."

I watch as he places his hand protectively on Krissy's lower back, as they head out to get their little guy. PJ's gaze trailing over my body heats my skin. I turn to find her looking at me with curiosity and a half-inebriated haze as Cole and Krissy head out the door. "So have you ladies had enough fun yet?" I ask, because by the look of things, they're going to be hurting in the morning if they don't rein it in pretty soon. And it's far from midnight.

I get a set of wide eyes from Jules. "Not on your life, mister. Do you know how often it is that PJ lets loose, even a little?" She puts her forefinger and her thumb together to show me exactly what a little is. "Well, it has been a hot minute. There's no way we're leaving now. Not when Mr. tall and good looking has been singing to her all night long. No, we're definitely staying," she says, picking up two more shots and handing one to PJ who throws it back with a melodious little laugh that travels straight to my dick.

PJ pins me with a look. "We're definitely staying. We're having way too much fun to go home now. If small town fun isn't your thing, don't stay on our count. We can find our way back to town. Plenty of friends who will drive us home. Not some stranger from out of town who we barely know and don't want to get to know anyway."

My eyes narrow, watching that sassy little mouth move. I resist the urge to tip her over my lap and paddle that little ass, letting my gaze trail past her face instead. There is no possible way to miss that cleavage and those peach-sized breasts now that she's divested herself of that ugly green apron she had on back at Kenny's bar.

PJ feels the heat of my gaze, and her nipples harden right in front of my eyes. The little miss can deny it all she wants, but whether I'm from out of town or not, she feels the attraction too. I know it, and she knows I know it.

"Come on, Jules. We don't need men to dance with to have a good time." She gives me a little huff, grabs Jules' hand, and tugs her back to the dance floor, leaving me to watch the two young women who have had way more than their fill of alcohol but managing to stay in sync with the music just the same.

A waitress stops by the table. I load up all the empties and put them on the tray for her and slide a couple fifties on top for good measure. Who knows what she's had to put up with from the drunk little she-devil tonight.

I glance back at the dance floor, and my jaw locks tight as the long-haired crooner on stage with the steel guitar makes a show of singing to PJ. Jules is swept away by a cowboy with an urge to dance, suddenly leaving PJ standing in the middle of the dance floor, all alone, while couples swirl around her.

My feet move before my brain has a chance to check in. I close the distance between us and twirl her around to face me, snake my arm around her waist, and take her by the hand. "Jules got swept away by a cowboy. I didn't think you'd mind a quick dance."

Her face flushes as she sizes up the situation and inhales a deep breath. "I didn't even realize she was gone. Oh my stars. I must be three sheets to the wind if I'm dancing with you," she says.

It's hard not to laugh. "If that's what it takes to get a dance with the prettiest girl in the room, fine." I spin her around and then pull her back to me.

She looks up at me, still completely flushed, and those violet eyes flash. "You may be able to dance, but I'm not some girl you can sweet talk out of her panties and then toss away the next day without even a thank you, ma'am. I know how this works. You'll be back on that big jet you flew in on before you know it, and I'll have my panties safe in hand."

I whisper in her ear, "Darling, I do want those panties. But you're not in any condition to consent to giving them to me right now."

4

PJ

THAT MAN WHISPERING DIRTY TALK INTO MY EAR CAUSES MY stomach to flutter with unsettled need. Maybe I should listen to my friends and let completely loose. Hell, if nothing else, there is no denying that this man turns me right the hell on with those snug fitting jeans and powerful arms. And what better way to get over being jilted than to be the one to leave after a round of hot sex? At the moment, that sounds pretty damn good to me.

I contemplate that as he spins me around, but once my mind is set, there's not much to think about. A slow song comes on, and he takes my hand to guide me from the floor, but I'm far from done with him. "How are your slow moves? As good as you dance?"

Mason raises his eyebrows. His hand snakes around my waist, and he draws me into the hardness of his body with one swift move. "My slow moves would have your panties in my pocket in no time at all, Priscilla Jean."

His words and the way he says my given name, while his thumb rubs those little circles near the sensitive flesh of my nape cause my nipples to harden and center to clench. Good lord, this man is hot. I wait until the song is almost over, wrap my hands around his neck, and pull his face down so that I can whisper in his ear as the song ends. "Show me your moves, city boy. Follow me, and you can make good on your promises."

I walk toward our table, grab my jacket, and head for the door and toward the trail that I know like the back of my hand. All the while, my heart is racing with the thought of what I'm about to do. It's been so very long since I've been this turned on. So long since I even thought about wanting a man like this.

His boots crunch the dried winter sticks under the light layer of snow as he follows me over the trail.

I inhale the crisp wind of winter's edge in the air, surprised at how breathless I am when I reach the secluded little arbor that overlooks the bluff.

Mason's hand on my shoulder spins me around. Those eyes penetrate me like they do. "It's cold out here, sweetheart. I don't want to be responsible for you getting sick."

I don't answer because if I do, I might never be able to do this again if I don't take the step tonight. Not one time has someone ignited a desire this strong and most definitely not since my heart got crushed. I shouldn't be doing this, I know it, but still, I take the chance. "I thought you were going to take my panties?"

Mason is quiet for a minute longer than it should take, and already my chest squeezes tight knowing what's coming next. "Oh, sweetheart. The thought of taking your panties off that sweet little ass is definitely on my mind, but you've had way too much to drink to make that decision. Besides, I promised Cole that I would get both you and Jules home tonight. I'll have to take a raincheck on that offer. When your head is clear, sweetheart."

My chest beats hard with embarrassment, and tears threaten at the back of my eyes. I will them to stay right where they are and not to fill my eyes, because getting turned down is bad enough, but crying? Damn it all, why the hell did I let myself drink so much or think that I could do this with a complete stranger, no matter the attraction?

I turn away from him and look down the hill toward the bar. The wind bites into my skin, sobering me a little but not near enough to make this colossal mistake go away. "I'm sorry for coming onto you like that. I seriously do not know what's gotten into me. I never act this way. Ask anyone. I'm not that type of girl. I'm really sorry."

He strokes a hand down my hair and puts his hand on my shoulder. "Stop, PJ."

I inhale a deep breath. "It's just that I'm usually a very low-key, keep to myself kinda gal. I don't usually flirt; I don't drink. Well, at least, not like this since my younger days, and I certainly do not dance or tease men about giving them my panties. Tomorrow's look in the mirror is not going to be pretty. For some reason it's important that you know that about me even though you'll probably be half way across the country."

Mason's arm wraps around me, and he turns me to face him again. "Look at me."

Those hazel eyes connect with mine. I'm not so drunk that I don't know what comes next. I feel the connection, almost in slow motion. Whether from the drink or just the attraction, I know what's coming. I want it more than I've wanted anything in a very long time.

His lips lower and capture mine in a kiss that takes my breath away. When he finally breaks our kiss, he strokes a finger down my cheek. "You have nothing to be ashamed of; attraction is the most natural thing in the world. When you look in the mirror tomorrow, all you're going to see is a beautiful woman who was having a great time and had the attention of every red-blooded male in the bar tonight."

"Except you."

"Not true, sweetheart. If you hadn't had so much to drink, you'd have found yourself waking up in my bed tomorrow morning. Know that." He kisses me again and pushes my hair from my face. "I think you owe me a souvenir of the night, beautiful."

I inhale, feeling immensely better about the situation and me as a human. "What do you want?" I ask, my eyes narrowed as he contemplates his question.

He smirks. "Your panties. Take them off and give them to me."

My mouth gapes. "You can't be serious."

He shrugs. "Maybe, but I am. I can't think of a more perfect souvenir."

I shiver as the wind blows right through my light jacket, and my face stings from the wind. "The moisture in the air is turning to ice. We need to get back."

"Your choice. You take them off now and give them to me, or I get to take them off later on."

My stomach dances with butterflies, and I feel like a girl about to embark on my first date, but it's not really a date. In fact, it's nothing of the sort. "I think I'll hang on to my panties for now, kind sir."

He smirks and takes my hand as we walk down the trail toward Eagle's Swallow. The light snow is starting to feel a bit more wet but looks glossy on the ground. I gesture to the ground. "It's getting icy."

His jaw tightens as he guides me into the bar with a hand to the small of my back. He looks around, and neither of us see Jules anywhere. He gestures to the dance floor. "She was dancing with a big, beefy tall guy in a black hat just before we left the bar."

Even in my condition, her leaving the bar without texting me and being with that guy means trouble. "She was with Bobby Ray. Jules had way more to drink than I did and was probably just dancing with him to be nice or keep the peace."

Mason's hazel eyes go hard, penetrating me with their intensity. "Tell me what you mean by that, PJ."

I swallow hard, my blurry mind already swirling with a thousand scenarios of where they could be or what could be happening to Jules. "He's been hanging out with buddies of Jake Eldridge. Cole, Garrett, and your bodyguard friends may have sent Jake packing out of town a while back, but his friends haven't forgotten that Lacy is the one who got him run out of town or that we are friends with her. Mason, we really need to find Jules."

His jaw locks tightly as he leaves my side, moving in and out of the tables before stopping to talk to the waitress who was taking care of us tonight. It doesn't take long before Mason's walking quickly back to me and takes my arm. "Where would he have taken her? His place or hers? She said they left together a short while ago. Let's go."

My chest tightens and intuitively, deep in my soul, I know something is wrong. "Wait, coffee. I'll be more help to you with a strong black coffee." I walk to the counter of the bar with Mason at my heels. Jared, the barkeeper I've known all my life, gives me a long glance. "You okay?"

"No, Jules left with Bobby Ray. We're going to find her. Can I get two large coffees to go, really fast, please?"

Jared nods and turns to the coffee pot on the back counter, then pours two large while I toss some bills on the counter. Mason takes a long, hard look at the county map that's under the glass of the bar until Jared walks over with our coffees. "Bobby Ray wouldn't hurt Jules," Jared says.

I narrow my eyes at the well-meaning but naïve bartender who is friends with everyone in town as I take the cups. I don't answer him because there's no time to get into an argument about it with him. "Thanks for the coffee." I catch up to Mason who clearly has no patience for what Jared does or does not think and follow him out to his SUV.

Mason opens the door. I hand him his coffee before climbing in with mine, while he closes the door and walks around to the other side. He places the cup in the holder next to mine and cranks the heat before rubbing his hands together as he settles in. "It's getting colder; you see the moisture swirling in the air. "Where does Jules live?"

I take another drink of coffee, never feeling as helpless as I do right now as he pulls out and heads to the main road. The one night I decide to let loose a little and get absolutely loaded something like this happens, leaving us to depend on someone I barely know. A stranger who doesn't know his way around town or anything. "PJ, I asked you where does Jules live?"

I look at him. "Sorry, I'm just worried. Jules lives all the way back in town."

He looks both ways down the long, dark road. "Where does Bobby Ray live?"

"He lives farther out this way somewhere. It's been a hot minute since I've been out this way. I vaguely remember driving by his place before, but I'm pretty sure I can get us there. Take a left, and it's about three or four miles before you turn off toward his house."

Mason peels out and then veers down the long stretch of highway. "Call Garrett." The dashboard lights up as the connection between the car and his phone links. "Garrett here, I was just going to call you, Mason. Do you have PJ and Jules?"

Mason's hand clenches on the steering wheel. "I have PJ. Jules left the bar with a man named Bobby Ray. PJ told me he's friends with Jake Eldridge. We're heading out to his house now. I was calling you to make sure you had Lacy and Patti."

"We have the ladies, but only thanks to Tommy's men and the fact that we haven't let up on her security since Jake Eldridge left town. There were too many red flags that kept popping up and too many of his old buddies still running around this town for me to be comfortable loosening up her security."

"Good thing you didn't, Garrett. Damn, I hate like hell this is happening on the night before your wedding. How'd it play out; anyone hurt?" he asks, watching the road ahead intently as we drive.

"Jake Eldridge had some of his friends try to pick the ladies up at the new bar they were at, but thankfully Tommy's guys intervened before they could snatch Lacy. I'm just glad they were here so we could enjoy the night. Him and his boys took the guys who tried to snatch the ladies with them when they left."

"They're going to be in for a long ass night answering to Tommy and his boys. I'm sure the Larussios are going to want to know what the hell they were doing back in this town because I'd put a good wager on them being sent by the Chicago boys."

"Exactly," Garret says. "I'll let Tommy know we need Bobby Ray and Jules' location asap. In the meantime, I can have some of the guys head out your way and come myself."

Mason clears his throat as the wheel of the SUV pulls to the right, and he corrects course. "No, the temperature's dropping out this way. The roads are getting slick, real slick. I don't like the combination of temps and moisture on the roads. We'll find Jules, handle Bobby Ray, and get back to town. PJ doesn't know the address, but she knows the area. We'll find her. You just take care of Lacy and Patti."

I continue surveying the area, watching for something familiar, anything that will tell me we're getting close to Bobby Ray's place. But there's absolutely nothing but desolate trees that have lost their leaves in a swirl of white, while visibility gets harder and harder. I wait until after he's disconnected his call. "We're never going to find them."

He points up ahead. "I think we just did. The farther away we get the worse the weather is. They've been driving in this sludge. You see the tracks up ahead?"

I turn my eyes to the front of us and take in the tire marks ahead. The sludge and accumulating ice pulls the vehicle again. Mason does something with the gears and keeps control of the wheel, bringing it back in line. "Not all SUVs are created equal," he says. "This one could use a little more weight in the back, but in all fairness, not many vehicles are good on the ice. It's going to turn into an ice-skating rink soon."

I point to the fork in the road. "There. They went right." I have never been so thankful for bad weather as I am tonight, realizing there's no way I would have remembered which way to go to Bobby Ray's place without the tracks.

Mason takes a right and slows, following the trail but cutting the lights. "I'm not sure how far ahead they are, but we're going to take it nice and easy and err on the side of caution to make sure we don't spook him."

My heart is still racing with what I heard on the phone, but everything muddles around in my mind right now. Lacy and my other friends are safe. All I can focus on now is the fact that we need to find Jules. I drink some more coffee, hoping it starts to clear this self-induced foggy brain. "I'm so sorry for everything. If I hadn't gone outside, Bobby Ray wouldn't have had a chance to take Jules. This is all my fault."

Mason takes my hand. "It's not your fault. We didn't have a security detail on you and Jules, like we did on Lacy. That's the only reason Jules was taken, and Lacy wasn't. No one thought Jake Eldridge would come after her friends. Did Jake ever put pressure on you or her other friends when he was trying to persuade her to sell her house?"

I shake my head. "No, Jake left us all alone. We grew up together. I mean, we were never real friends, but he never bothered us when he was harassing Lacy."

Mason nods. "This is a new pattern of behavior. The timing of it with Lacy getting married to Garrett tomorrow tells me it's more of a personal vendetta than a business one. Probably a little of both, but it's just too coincidental." He slows. "Anything look familiar? Are we getting close?"

I nod, because the clearing and barren field that was bursting with corn in the summertime finally looks familiar. I can picture exactly where we are now and what it looked like then. "Right around the corner to the right. He lives in a one-story log cabin. The road takes you to the side of his house, and there's a long gravel drive that leads up to the garage on the other side.

Mason turns in and then pulls off to the side of the road. "Keep the engine running and stay put. But if I don't return in twenty minutes, I want you to get out of here. Get back to the highway as quickly as you can, and call 9-1-1. Understand?"

5
MASON

PJ's eyes spark. "I'm coming with you!"

"I need to get in their fast. I don't have time to argue with you or look after you right now, or you'll learn what a spanking for bad behavior feels like from me."

Her eyes widen in surprise, but I don't miss the little smile she tries to hide. "This shouldn't take long if things go according to plan." I lean over and open the glove compartment. I hear the inhalation of breath as I remove my weapon. "Let's hope it's just precautionary." I pocket the Glock before closing the door quietly and making my way toward the cabin.

I sneak around back, staying close to the walls of the house, skirting along the evergreen bushes heavily dusted with a sheen of ice. The first window I come to looks to be a bedroom. I glance in, keeping my weapon down but on the ready. The room is empty other than a twin-sized bed and nightstand with a lamp. The minute I get closer to the patio door, voices spill through the walls. "You're going to regret the day you ever laid eyes on me, Bobby Ray. They're going to come for you, and when they do…"

"Shut up, Jules. Just shut the hell up. I need to think, and you flapping your lips is not helping a damn thing," a man yells.

I head back the way I came, skirting around the house and toward the front, farthest away from their quarreling in the back and right up to the front door. I turn the knob lightly, not expecting it to open, but it does. I make my way into the living area cautiously, walking softly on the carpeted floors in the dark, stepping around the couches, and around the corner, heading toward the sound of their voices.

Jules sits in a high-backed wooden dining room chair with her back to me, wrapped with blue rope that looks like it belongs on a fishing boat and should have an anchor tied to its end. I sneak into the room and place the butt of my gun at the base of Bobby Ray's neck before he has time to realize I'm there or react. "Take a seat, Bobby Ray."

He doesn't comply; instead, he continues to stand in place. I keep my gun right where it is nudging him forward, in front of Jules and another chair. He exhales loudly. "Look, I don't want any trouble, man. This isn't my fight. I'm just holding her for Jake and his boys, that's all."

I laugh. "I think whether you want it or not, trouble just found you." I push him into the seat next to Jules. "Sit. Don't move, or I'll shoot. No other warning about that, got it?"

He glares at me, but he has a healthy respect for the gun in my hand, and I don't plan to give him a reason to think I won't use it. Because I will, if I have to.

I look around the room and grab a length of the blue rope that's laying in a heap on the floor next to Jules. Her eyes are focused on the gun too. She's talking so fast at first, I can barely make out a word she says. I stop her. "Slow, breath, and tell me slowly what happened, okay?"

Jules swallows hard, gives me a little nod, but looks at me with eyes that still look hazy and glazed. "One minute we were dancing, the next I was feeling ill. We went outside for some fresh air. I remember him wanting to get some smokes from his truck and then bam, everything went dark."

I tug on his ropes to make sure he's nice and secure, while refraining from slugging the guy who likes to drug women. "You're safe now, Jules." Ice starts hitting the window coming in sideways and hard, causing a pelting sound to echo through the cabin. "I'm going to go get PJ. She's waiting in my vehicle. I'll be back in a..."

PJ walks into the room, the same way I came, looking as guilty as she should. I close the distance between us in a few steps. "Did I not leave you in the vehicle and ask you to stay?"

Her eyes flash up at me. "I couldn't just sit there and do nothing when one of my friends was in trouble. I was trying to help. You could say thank you."

My eyes narrow at the sassy little miss, who at least has sobered up for the most part since leaving the bar. "You, I'll deal with later. Right now, help me get Jules untied." I find a pair of scissors in the kitchen drawer and work through the bulky rope, while PJ rubs her wrists as we get her out of the binds that were digging into her skin.

I put the scissors back where I found them in case Bobby Ray gets any ideas, because like it or not, we're all here to stay for a while. At least, until mother nature is done storming outside. I kick Bobby Ray's black boot. "What did you give Jules; the truth?"

His eyes dart around the room. He knows that none of his friends are coming to help him. It's just him and me now. "Date rape drug."

PJ throws her arms around Jules and holds her tight. I connect with Garrett while keeping an eye on the big, bearded dude who sits glaring at me as though he didn't have everything he got coming or that he's not deserving of so damn much more after what he did.

Garret answers on the first ring. "You have Jules?"

"We've got her. Bobby Ray had her tied up, but she wasn't hurt. He used the date rape drug to knock her out. Fortunately, the side effects aren't long lasting."

Nothing that a little sleep and steady hydration won't fix. The weather's gotten worse, though. There's no way we're getting out of here for a while. The roads were like an ice rink the last couple miles here, and it's way worse now. The windows on the cabin are solid sheets of ice. We're going to have to wait it out. We'll do our best to get to town first thing in the morning. Hopefully the salt trucks have been out by then. Hope to see you tomorrow, buddy."

6

PJ

MASON GETS OFF THE PHONE AND LOOKS AT THE TWO OF US.
"We'll stay here tonight. Why don't you ladies get freshened up. I'll see
what's in the refrigerator and start cooking. You need something to soak
up the rest of the alcohol and drugs that were put in your system," he
says, glaring at Bobby Ray.

He points out of the dining room and down the hall, gesturing for us
to go.

I give Jules a wink and roll my eyes skyward. "Yes, sir," I mock,
heading down the small hall to check out the rest of the house. "He's so
bossy, arrogant, and what's the word I'm looking for?" I ask Jules.

"Hot as a long day in Texas," she drawls, as we make our way down
the hall. I know Jules; she'll try to make light of it to make sure everyone
else feels okay, but I don't feel okay. The enormity of everything that
could have happened keeps swirling in my still alcohol-dazed mind.
Things could have turned out way differently for her tonight if it were not
for Mason.

Jules puts her hand on my shoulder. "Are you okay?"

I turn and give my friend a hug. "No, nothing's right. I feel horrible
about drinking so much and leaving you at the bar, like the worst friend

ever. I'm just glad nothing else happened. It didn't, right?" I ask, all of a sudden seized with a moment of fear.

Jules face turns somber, and she shakes my shoulder. "You listen to me. I am a big girl. I was drinking. I am responsible for me, not you. And it's not either of our faults that Bobby Ray hooked up with Jake Eldridge, and would do such a crappy thing to me, understand? Sherriff Cates is going to have a hell of a lot to say to him tomorrow."

She's right, we're both adults, but this feeling of guilt is not going to go away quickly. "I'm just so glad that you're okay. And, more than a little ashamed of myself for thinking so poorly of Mason at first. He really came through tonight. I mean, seriously came through for us. I don't know if we would have found you without him. I bet by now even the emergency vehicles can't make it out on the ice."

Jules, ever the matchmaker, gives me a wink. "Yes, he did. You should have seen him marching Bobby Ray over to that chair with that gun of his at the base of his neck. He was a man in charge; I'll tell you that much."

The longer we're away, the guiltier I feel about how badly I've completely and unfairly treated Mason from the very start because of baggage I've never let go of from the past. "Let's take a look at the sleeping arrangements and head back. I'll help Mason cook us something to eat."

Jules makes her eyes go wide dramatically. "You, cook, and with an out of towner? Oh, this can only mean one thing. Don't tell me you've gone and fallen for the bodyguard? We have to quit letting them come to town. These handsome devils waltz into town, and my friends get all googly eyed and lose all of their common sense."

My face heats with embarrassment. No one knows me better than Lacy and Jules, because that's exactly what this man has done. "Stop it. I'm just trying to be nice. The devil's probably hungry after all that … you know … with all that macho shit he does."

Jules laughs. "Fine, let's go be nice to the tall, dark, out of towner who has your panties in a twist." I don't tell her that he almost had them in his pocket too. My overactive hormones and attraction for the hot bodyguard is what got us into the situation in the first place, no matter what she says.

Thank goodness he was able to get the situation under control. I may not be the damsel in distress type, but there's no denying he was the hero to the rescue tonight and didn't take advantage when he could have done just that.

Jules points to the kitchen. "Go, cook with Mason. I'll get the bedroom situation sorted and see if I can find some clean sheets or wash some for the beds."

I head back to the kitchen. Clean sheets. Very, very good idea. Mason is boiling water in a pot on the stove and puts a pound of spaghetti noodles into the water. He pulls out a bowl of ground beef from the microwave above the stove and separates the little frozen bits as he puts it into a fry pan. "It's not quite dethawed, but it's close," he says, breaking the rest of it apart with the edge of the wooden spoon. "The kitchen is pretty well stocked except for fruits and vegetables. Spaghetti and garlic rolls with no salad will have to do."

Bobby Ray clears his throat. "I don't eat rabbit food. And I need to take a leak."

Mason ignores him and looks at me. "You want to finish the hamburger? I saw some canned mushrooms and some onion in the fridge. It's not exactly Mamma's sauce, but it'll work for a night like this. I'll untie him, run him to the bathroom, and then pop in some dinner rolls when I get back."

I take the spoon from his hand, and his fingers brush against mine, sending that tingling charge right to the very end of me. My cheeks heat, remembering his rebuff of my earlier advances. Well, that's not going to happen again, that's for damn sure, no matter how attracted I am to the sexy as sin devil and his snug fitting jeans.

He unties Bobby Ray and walks him to the bathroom, but he's careful about where and how he holds that gun of his. Mason isn't taking any chances with being overpowered by the heavier man who would like nothing better than to get out of the trouble he's undoubtedly going to be in come tomorrow.

I finish up the meat, mushroom, and onion mixture and pour in the sauce to heat while finding the rolls in the freezer. I have them out and the oven preheated by the time he returns with Bobby Ray in tow and ties him to the chair. "Would you mind finishing those while I run out to get my bag? I have some handcuffs in the bag that'll make things easier for the rest of the night."

I look at the meat sauce gently bubbling. "Sure, no problem at all. I've got this," I tell him. "The instructions on the rolls said to put them in the oven for a few minutes, until they're golden. I think all this mystery around cooking is just a big over-exaggerated thing. A few minutes in the oven and dinner will be ready."

He comes to stand beside me. "Time to drain the noodles, or they'll be mush."

I inhale deeply and laugh. "You didn't tell me to drain the noodles."

Mason laughs and grabs some potholders. "Well, move over, little missy, and let me show you how it's done." He adjusts the lid and tips the pot, letting the water run out. "No colander around here."

I watch as the noodles drain. "Truth be told, I'm not much of a cook. I can find my way around the kitchen when I need to, but I'm a pretty simple person; no lavish four course meals or anything for me."

Mason moves the pot back to the stove. He sure doesn't act like the asshole I thought he was, and I know that's not just my overactive and neglected for far too long libido talking. My eyebrows crinkle as I get out of his way. "I thought you were a city boy. City boys don't say Mamma or little missy. Where are you from?"

Bobby Ray moves the chair he's sitting in, and it scrapes the floor, causing both of us to look his way. He doesn't say a word, just glares at us from the position he's liable to be in all night long.

Mason grabs his coat. "I grew up on a ranch down in Texas, but my parents have both been gone for some time now. A car accident on a stormy night took them both. My aunt took me and my little sister in until we were grown in a suburb near Chicago. I guess a few phrases just hang on a little."

My chest tightens learning his parents were in an accident, and still, he risked coming after Jules in bad weather.

He touches my shoulder and pushes a wayward piece of hair from my face. "It's been a minute since I thought about that. I'll be right back." He looks at Bobby Ray. "You move an inch, and I'll leave you in that chair all damn night."

I pull my arms tight around my middle as he heads out into the weather, and the cold, damp air blows into the room, regardless of the heat generating from the stove.

Jules walks into the kitchen, looking much better than she did before. "A hot shower is all I needed. The beds are all made. A little food and something for this headache that's already starting to throb, and hopefully I won't be as hung over as I should be tomorrow morning. Note to PJ. Do not let Jules drink so much ever again." She glares at Bobby Ray. "Then maybe I can be prepared the next time some asshole tries to slip drugs into my drink. You asshole." She turns to me. "You should jump in the shower; the water should be warm again by now."

I grimace, because the sheer fear and pure adrenaline of Jules being taken may have sobered me up some, but the after effects of all that alcohol is bound to hit me like a freight train later. "I'll take one later. I don't even want to look in the mirror right now. My hair is probably a mess, makeup is nonexistent or all over my face, dark spots under my eyes from lack of sleep this week, and..."

Mason walks in through the dining room, dangling three pairs of hand cuffs. "You look beautiful to me."

7

MASON

PJ LOOKS FLUSTERED AS SHE AND JULES GET THE MEAL AND plates on the table. "I'm going to get Bobby Ray settled into one of the bedrooms for the night. These handcuffs will be a lot easier to deal with than untying and retying him."

Bobby Ray glares at me. "I was just doing a favor for a friend. Just to scare Lacy into giving Jake what he wants. That's all. I wasn't going to hurt her. I may be an asshole, but I'm not an asshole like that."

My eyes narrow. "News flash. You are that asshole. You're just lucky PJ and Jules are here, or that I don't want them to see anything that would keep them up at night." I finish untying him and keep a close eye on every move he makes with the point of my gun. I'm not about to take chances with the lives of the ladies with a man who would probably do anything not to face the consequences he has coming.

I frog march the asshole down the hall to one of the bedrooms with a twin bed, cuffing him to the wrought iron headboard. "You even try to get out of that cuff, and"—I tap his chest with the point of my gun—"I won't fucking hesitate."

I walk back down the hall and dish up a bowl of spaghetti, then grab some utensils and a bottle of water from the fridge to bring back to Bobby

Ray. The minute I leave the dining room, the ladies start whispering again. I smirk, turning to go give the man some food.

It's not like I've never been the topic of a lady's conversation, but not PJ's. The one who seems to have wiggled herself right into my mind and doesn't want to leave, no matter how many reasons I give myself for not getting involved any deeper than a kiss.

I place the food on the end table next to Bobby Ray, just close enough that I'm sure he can smell it and get good and hungry. "We have some friends who took Jake and his buddies away. They're going to be spending tonight learning the plan for Lacy and Jules. I'm going to give you a chance to tell me your side of the story before I decide what to do to you tomorrow."

His big beady eyes narrow. "I know who your friends are. I don't want any trouble with the Larussio crime family. What do you want to know?"

"What was the plan for Lacy and Jules?"

He inhales a deep breath and gives the spaghetti a sideways glance. "They were going to take Lacy, and I was going to grab Jules. They were supposed to call me when they had Lacy, and then they were going to drive here, pick her up, and take them both to Chicago."

Those Chicago boys don't quit. I'll give them that much. "The Bernatelli family?"

He glares at me. "What about them?"

I narrow my eyes at Bobby Ray. "Don't play with me. Were they behind it?"

Bobby Ray let's out a loud huff. "You're going to make me say it? Do you know what they will do to me?"

"Do you know what I will do to you, or the Larussios will do to you if you don't?"

His eyes dart around the room, taking in his position, contemplating a few minutes before he decides that battling with me or the Larussios is just not going to be in his best interest. "They thought Lacy and Jules could be used as a bargaining chip to get Cole to sell some of his land. They're still looking for a way to get their casinos into the area."

"Yeah, and their drugs, women, and guns too. Cole won't sell."

His head snaps up. "One of these days those Bernatellis are going to give you what's coming to you for sticking your nose in business that doesn't have anything to do with you."

"If I were you, I'd eat your dinner. It may be the last hot meal you get for a while."

"You said you wouldn't turn me over to the Larussios if I gave you what you wanted," he whines.

I walk to the door and open it. "Right, but I didn't say anything about not handing you over to Sheriff Cates," I tell him, closing the door and rigging up an outside lock with another of the cuffs.

8
PJ

THE MINUTE MASON AND BOBBY RAY ARE OUT OF EARSHOT, Jules nudges me. "What kind of man runs around with three pairs of handcuffs in his bag? Tell me that?"

I grin. "He's a bodyguard for some pretty bad ass people from what I heard. I'm pretty sure they come in handy on the regular."

Jules laughs, settling into the seat next to me. "Well, we only have one bad guy here." She leans in close. "What the hell is he planning to do with the other two sets? Maybe he plans to use them to capture the woman he's had his eye on since he blew into town."

I smirk, putting more than a healthy share of spaghetti noodles on my plate, carbs be damned. I don't tell her I'd gladly succumb to a little hand-cuff treatment, or that spanking he threatened earlier, but I've already been rebuffed once. That's not going to happen again, no matter the reason he didn't take me up on my offer.

My mind is sobering, and my heart just can't take the pain. I rolled the dice and came up empty. I don't plan on taking that chance again.

Mason walks back into the room and slides into the chair next to me and across from Jules. She hands him the bowl of noodles. I wait until after he finishes putting a heaping pile on his plate before passing him the sauce to go on top of it.

Our fingers brush, and my cheeks warm with embarrassment, excitement, and just plain human attraction. I avoid Mason's eyes and focus on the food in front of me, but the warmth of his gaze continues to settle on my skin while his touch stays on my mind.

Jules finishes first, starts putting things away, and running water to wash dishes in the old porcelain cabin sink. I finish just as Mason does and start clearing the rest of the dishes while he snags the last of the rolls left on the plate. "I'm going to go check on Bobby Ray one last time and then get some sleep. Don't stay up too late, ladies. It's going to be a long day tomorrow."

The kitchen is cleaner than it's probably ever been when we hear the shower start.

Jules yawns and covers her mouth. "I'm so tired. Hopefully the weather will clear. I can't believe this is happening the night before Lacy's wedding. We're supposed to be there with her on her special day. I'm going to go get some sleep. Hopefully we can get into town."

"It'll all work out. Go get some rest. I'm going to be right behind you. I want to shower quick too. I showered before I left for the party, but all the grease from the bars is lingering, like a heavy film all over my hair. I smell like French fries and who knows what we'll have time for in the morning."

Jules tiredly nods, making her way down the hall while I finish up a few things, stalling until I hear the shower turn off and the door open and close down the hall. I walk quietly toward the main bathroom, and the fresh scent of soap lingering in the air hits my nostrils. The same scent that was all over Mason's skin as he held me close on the dance floor and out on that bluff.

A wet bar of soap is sitting on a clean cloth on the ledge of the shower. I pick it up, inhaling deeply, thinking of that long, delicious kiss. But that's the last thing I should be thinking about right now. I should get in the shower, get rinsed off, and go to bed.

Tomorrow will be a better day. A special day when I see one of my best friends walk down the aisle with a man she adores. I eye the green duffle bag that Mason probably forgot when he went to bed. I wonder what's underneath the large gray towel that he's left tossed on top of that bag.

None of my nosey business...

I turn on the water and run a hand under the faucet, testing the temperature. Thank goodness he didn't use all the hot water up. That would have been just the way to top off my day from hell. Instead, it's nice and warm and feels good, even if it's not the rainwater showerhead that I have at home.

I get in and pull the dark navy marina-like shower curtain. One glance down at the mangled mess of soap that sits on the tub ledge has me reaching for the one I know damn well is Mason's and not Bobby Rays.

I inhale its freshness. I may smell like a man tomorrow, but I'll smell like a damn good one. I use the clean washcloth and lather his scent all over it, using it to wash away all the booze, grease, and smoke along with the weariness of the day.

By the time I'm ready to get out, the water is turning cool. I shiver as I open the shower curtain and a rush of cool, air hits me. I grab Mason's towel and wrap around myself, soaking in its warmth and the delicious smell of him and the familiar scent of his soap.

I eye my clothes with a grimace, not relishing the idea of wrinkly clothes tomorrow. I sneak a peek toward Mason's bag, then back at my clothes. I'm unzipping his bag before I have a chance to talk myself out of it and pulling out a black t-shirt. My undies will do, freshly put on tonight. I couldn't care less if they wrinkle; besides, his boxers will fall to the floor the moment I put them on.

I towel dry my hair, before tossing the towel over the shower rod to dry and my clothes next to it, so they won't wrinkle. I rummage through the cabinet doors below the sink, hoping against hope that there's something I can use because sleeping with wet hair in this chilly cabin would not be smart. I hold up the old dusty relic, and plug it in, smiling as it begins blowing hot air out of the big ass vent on the side.

The minute I'm done, exhaustion from a long day of work, partying, and emotional fear kicks in like a lion. I yawn my way down the hall, coming to the first bedroom door. I grin. A piece of two by two has been nailed to the outside of the door. I guess Bobby Ray is tucked in good for the night.

I glance into the next bedroom at Jules sleeping soundly. The light begins to flicker in my dull ass brain. Now I know why Jules, who is usually a night owl on steroids, was in such a hurry to turn in. To take the only other twin bedroom.

The one that is not with the tall, dark, handsome, fine specimen of a man who must be sleeping in the only bedroom with room for two.

I should dump her on the floor and take her bed, but she needs sleep more than I do with the amount of alcohol she put away tonight. At least I went home, showered, and had something substantial to eat before heading to the party. The little matchmaker.

I'm not about to go into that bedroom down the hall where a hand-some bodyguard sleeps. I've put myself out there once tonight. That took more courage or stupidity than I thought I had in me, but I'm not about to be rebuffed again. I pad back down the hall and feel my way around in the dark, until my hand runs along the arm of a sofa.

This will have to do. I go to sit on the sofa, and a hand snakes out, reaching for me, and pulls me on top of him. "What the!"

"Don't be scared. It's just me," Mason says, stroking my hair.

"What are you doing here? I thought you were in the bedroom," I whisper hiss.

"I saved it for you."

"Oh.."

"You smell like me. Have you been using my soap, Priscilla Jean?"

God, I love it when he says my name like that. "Uh huh."

He runs his hands along my back and tugs at the end of my t-shirt that's risen up and now barely covers my ass. You're wearing my shirt, aren't you, little missy?"

Oh, lord his western charm. "I didn't have anything else to wear."

He pushes my hair away from my face. "You can get up any time you want, but I'd like you to stay."

My chest tightens, and my stomach flutters. I am far from drunk now. I'm as stone cold sober as they come, maybe a little hungover with the aftereffects, but I know exactly what I'm doing. If I stay, this is going all the way, because Lord knows we both want it to end exactly that way.

And then tomorrow will come, and he won't acknowledge that I exist. He'll be halfway back to Nevada while I recharge my hatred of out of towners. But, if I know what to expect, how can I be mad? It makes more sense now than it ever did. I don't know why it took me so long to realize it. "I want to stay," I whisper in his ear.

Mason cradles my face and kisses me long and hard, pushing my hair from my face, and then trails a path of heat down the length of my spine. He draws back from the kiss but keeps his lips against mine. "I want my shirt back, Priscilla Jean."

I sit up slightly, my knees sliding to either side of his waist, while he lifts the shirt up my back, only breaking our kiss to slide it over my head. My eyes have adjusted to the dark, and I watch as he takes in every inch of my body. "More beautiful than anything I could have ever imagined."

My stomach flutters again, and this time I kiss him, because after that, he can have any damn thing he wants. He pulls the blanket that was laying over the top of the couch over us. "I want you something fierce; not easy and gentle, but in the worst of ways." He pushes his pajama bottoms down and rubs his hard length against me.

Oh, good Lord, he knows what I like. I've gone to heaven and died already. "I don't like it easy, Mason. Take me your way, but do it fast because I swear I'm going to explode."

And he does, driving right to the very end of me, again and again, pulling me down atop that long, hard rod, hitting that special spot, over and over again, until my mind fills like a million stars on a clear summer night.

9
MASON

•

I LAY FOR HOURS WITH HER ON TOP OF ME, LISTENING TO HER sleep and feeling the soft whisper of her breath against my chest as I cradle her in my arms. Never once have I shared my bed, always leaving before any awkwardness could occur. Never once have I slept even an hour with another soul. But yet, I would kill any man dead who interrupted the sleeping angel in my arms right now.

This is what it feels like when you've found the one. The one they always say will sneak up and cause you to forget everything you thought you wanted in life; the one who will steal your heart before you've barely had a chance to know what happened. This wasn't supposed to happen to me.

I stroke my dark-haired angel as she sleeps against my chest, holding her tight with the knowledge that things in my life will probably never be the same. Because I already know this is different from anything I've ever felt. My chest expands, breathing in sync with hers as the realization syncs in and a full day and night exhaustion pulls me under.

The next time I wake, hours later, the warmth of her body has been replaced with the blanket the two of us shared last night. I put it on the back of the couch and head to the bathroom.

My bag is still laying on the floor where I left it last night, and my t-shirt is folded and sitting on top of it, along with a folded piece of spiral notebook paper, the edges torn as though it's been ripped right out of its binding. I lean against the sink counter while I open the letter. Something again, I've never received from any woman in my life.

Dear Mason:

Thanks for a great time. I don't expect you to continue babysitting me today or to feel tied down to me for the weekend after what happened last night. Enjoy the wedding, and I will do the same.

Jules and I are taking Bobby Ray's truck into town to meet the ladies for hair and nails, and we'll go to the church with her and her dad later in the day.

Warm regards,

PJ

My jaw tightens with irritation. "Warm regards," I say aloud. She came onto me, flipped my world upside down, and now it's have a great life. What the hell.

I get ready for the day and head into the kitchen to make some coffee, finding it's already been made. I pour a cup and spit it into the sink and run it down the drain with water. "Damn, that's awful."

I roust Bobby Ray from a sound sleep to let him relieve himself in the bathroom. I give him some of the horrible coffee to go along with a bagel and banana that will have to tide him over after someone comes for him.

I have far better things to do than to deal with him today, including setting a little missy straight on a thing or two. I get into the rental with my bag tossed into the back seat and head toward town, veering clear of a salt truck the minute I hit the main drag. She could have at least waited until she knew for certain the roads were clear.

My jaw clenches tightly recalling the night the police came knocking on the door and the people from social services took us to a temporary home for the night until our aunt could come. The roads were bad that night too. The thought of her in a ditch up ahead somewhere spurs my speed, faster than I should be going on roads that were a few hours before covered in a sheet of ice.

I keep a close watch out, not seeing any signs of a car in the ditch, but I'm not going to rest easy until I know that they're safe. "Call Garrett."

His voice comes over the vehicles speaker, and I hear the rest of the guys in the back. "I just dropped Lacy and the others off at the salon. Tommy's men are guarding them while we eat some breakfast and figure out a plan for later. I thought Jake Eldridge got the message the last time, but him and those Chicago boys don't listen so well. It's like they have a one-track mind when it comes to honing in on the territory around here and bothering Lacy."

My hand tightens on the steering wheel as I maneuver around a patch of ice that hasn't melted. "The guy who took Jules, Bobby Ray, he's tied up in one of his side bedrooms. He said he was supposed to hold Jules for Jake and his boys, until they got Lacy.

"I may be wrong, Garrett, but I got the distinct impression that this was more personal than business related to the land they wanted last year. I would have gotten the information out of Bobby Ray, but the ladies were in the house. Maybe send Tommy or a few of his boys over there now. Everyone's gone."

Garrett clears his throat. "He's always had a thing for her; even when she told him nicely, he kept on. She thought he was trying to be a middleman between her and his dad when Eldridge Sr. wanted her land, but I think he was just using it to get her."

"You may not be wrong. This was probably his last-ditch effort to get to her before you married her. You didn't find them?"

Garret almost growls in my ear. "Wherever the fuckers are they better stay hidden because every one of our team is on the prowl searching for those assholes. Jay, Matt, Damian, Dereck, Sheldon, Nick, Cole, and Tommy's boys. Every single one of them are on the lookout. He messes with Lacy or any of the ladies again today, and that's going to be the last thing that son of a bitch ever does."

"Copy that, my friend. I'll be there shortly. I was taking my time and making sure the ladies didn't drive off the road. They should have waited for me, and I would have given them a ride into town. They must have been up early despite the shots they put away last night."

"Lacy chugged down one of her gramma's concoctions last night, with a few pieces of bread and something for a headache. She said she was a little peckish this morning, but aside from that, just fine. I'm not one to get into anyone's business, but did something happen between you and PJ last night?"

"Nothing terrible, why?"

Garrett doesn't answer right away. "She just about bit Jules' head off for bringing you up in the car when I gave them all a ride to the salon. Said that as far as she was concerned you were already on that jet plane back to Vegas."

My hand tightens on the wheel. "Did she now? It seems Priscilla Jean needs to learn some manners, and I'm just the man to teach her a few." I disconnect the call, easing my foot on the gas, already contemplating the little miss' fate.

10

PJ

LACY SQUEALS AS OUR FRIEND TURNS THE STYLING CHAIR around, and she sees her hair and makeup for the very first time while my freshly manicured nails dry. "Sally, I can't believe it's really me. You are so talented." Her bright red curls cascade past her shoulders from a pearl slide that keeps her hair in place and matches the ones on the old-styled wedding dress that start at her cleavage and end at her navel. Our dearest friend has always been beautiful with all the creamy lightly freckled skin, but she looks extra special today, just as she should.

Sally narrows her eyes at me. "You next, while Liza works on Lacy's nails. Did you even brush your hair today or just throw it up in that messy bun for me to detangle while you nurse that coffee and hangover you're trying so hard to hide?"

I laugh. "You're not far off. It's a long story, but I'm sure it will be all over town tomorrow. Jules and I stayed out at Bobby Ray's last night. He drugged her so that Jake Eldridge could get to Lacy. One of Cole and Garrett's buddies was with us and took care of Bobby Ray, but the roads were too bad to get back into town. The good thing is that we're all okay. I ended up with a shower, but the only thing available to wash the smell of the bar from my hair was a bar of soap. So don't pull too hard."

She rolls her eyes to the heavens. "Good Lord. Say no more. I heard all about what happened to Jules when I was getting bakery goods this morning. Sheriff was in getting some for his crew, and it's all everyone is talking about. Garrett called him last night. That no good Bobby Ray is going to wish he had never cozied up with those Eldridge boys and their friends from out of town. That's a fact."

I don't doubt a word she says. He has that and more coming after what he did to Jules who's quietly sipping her coffee and seemingly tuning us out. "Earth to Jules," I tell her as I get put in the hot seat and Sally goes to work on my rat's nest. "Ouch!"

Sally gives me a roll of her eyes. "You did this; now I have to undo it, so sit still." I don't tell her more than half of the fault lies with a blue-eyed devil who likes to snake his hand in my hair and wasn't gentle one little bit.

I smile, just the way I like it...

I pick up one of the soft rollers from the basket next to me and toss it gently into Jules' lap. "Hey, you okay?" I ask, gently, because no matter how fast we got there, Jules didn't know we were coming and had to be scared out of her ever-loving mind. She put on a strong face last night, and she tries that again today, but none of us our having that. We've been together through thick and thin for far too long.

Lacy sits on a rolling stool and slides over in front of her while her nails dry, and Liza starts on the next. "You listen to me, Jules. You know how I dealt with the Jake Eldridge shit last year? I confronted him. Maybe that would work for you too."

We all look up in surprise, because not one of us have heard that story. "Garrett and Cole might have sent him packing with the rest of their bodyguard group, but I had to get some closure. I called him up and let him have it with both barrels. I got it all out of my system. Maybe you should have unloaded on Bobby Ray too."

Jules gives Lacy a smile. "We only need one tiger in the bunch, babes, and that's you. Me, I will deal with it, but it will probably be by pounding out miles beneath my feet for a while. Besides, I am absolutely fine. You hear me? I will not let Bobby Ray or Jake Eldridge make your special day be anything except that, understand? I'm just glad his plan was spoiled, and Jake didn't get to you. Now, tell us how excited you are to be walking down that aisle and don't leave out one little detail."

It doesn't take much prodding for the conversation to shift back to Lacy and the love of her life. By the time she's finished giving us all the details about the surprise she has in store for Garrett, Sally has me looking like a fairy tale princess ready to take on the world and is ready to do the same for Jules.

The bell over the door rings as Krissy walks in and smiles at the group, but it's a half ass smile at best. The green hued pallor of her skin, the one I've seen for at least three weeks straight, is more than a little obvious today, and she didn't drink a drop last night.

I give her my best empathetic look. "More morning sickness?"

Krissy nods. "Oh my gosh, yes. I never had anything this bad with Darcy or little Cole. I swear this little one is turning everything I put in my stomach upside down. I think he or she is gonna be a hell raiser like their daddy."

I laugh. "Right, because we all know that you were a little angel back in the day."

She gives me a set of wide eyes. "Don't you do that, Priscilla Jean. Cole's told me all about what you got up to growing up. And I don't think he left one thing out."

I grin. "He has a big mouth."

"Yeah, he told me what you did to Mason yesterday too. Told me you dumped beer on him for no apparent reason. And that Mason was asking all kinds of questions about you on the way to Eagle's Swallow."

I roll my eyes as everyone turns to me. "It's nothing, with a capital N."

"Liar, liar," Jules singsongs. "That chemistry was off the frickin' charts last night. I thought those two were going to combust."

My chest tightens, because this is exactly what I don't want to hear about for the next six months every time I turn around. "We had a good time, but we're not a good match. I'm looking for a tall, dark, and handsome man who has got both feet in town, not flying back to the desert and taking care of a bunch of mobsters."

Lacy looks at me with those serious eyes. "Those mobsters saved Kenny's casino and my gramma's house. And give Cole and Garrett jobs. If it weren't for them standing up to that Chicago bunch and folks like

Jake Eldridge and his daddy, I don't know what this town would have turned into."

I sigh. "Fine … so they're good mobsters, but still. Once the wedding is over, he'll be on his way, and I don't intend to be the one left hankering over the likes of him. So I left him a note this morning saying as much." I swipe my hands together. "Done, over, finite."

Krissy smirks but then looks a little ill. Sally gestures to the chair next to Jules. "Take one of those and put your feet up until I'm done. They're way more comfortable than the others. Jules won't take near as long as PJ did. I thought we were gonna have to cut all those knots and tangles out; I swear it."

I roll my eyes at the good-natured lady with a heart of gold, whose sense of humor is far from funny. "Ha-ha."

She looks out the window and smiles brightly. She turns to me. "Looks like we're in for a little show, lady, because I don't think the tall, dark bodyguard took too kindly to being brushed off by our little Priscilla Jean."

I turn to the window, and my mouth gapes as Mason stalks toward the hair and nail salon in those snug fitting jeans, a t-shirt, and a light jacket.

11

MASON

I PARK THE SUV AND HEAD TOWARD THE LITTLE SHOP ON Main Street, with one thing on my mind, striding across the sidewalk to get to the glass door that stands between me and my dark-haired beauty. All eyes are on me as I walk in, but I only have eyes for one.

Those violet blue eyes look at me with open surprise as I close the distance between us and take her hand. "Ladies, if you'll excuse us, PJ and I have some things to clear up."

Her mouth gapes, and she sucks in a breath. "We've said all there is to say, Mason."

I put a hand on the small of her back and guide her right into the back of the shop and into a room lined with rows of color, curling rods, and the like and close the door. "I woke up and you were gone. I didn't much care for the note."

PJ pulls her hand from mine, putting some distance between us and goes to stand against the wall of the storage room. "What do you want me to say? I said it all in the note. We had fun. That's it. Now you can go back to your life."

I take a purposeful step toward her.

She takes a step back...

I eliminate the distance, placing my hands on either side of her against the wall. "Tell me you didn't feel what I felt. That you're immune to the attraction that we share. Tell me that last night was just a roll in the hay to you, and I will leave and never come back. But don't you dare lie to me, Priscilla Jean. That was me underneath you last night when you weren't thinking of every reason that we shouldn't be."

Her lip trembles. "Like I was telling the ladies. We owe you a lot for last night, but this thing"—she gestures a finger between the two of us—"me and you. This thing we have? A long-distance relationship will never work. You have your job, and I have my life here. Like I said, it was a fun night, but I don't want to draw out the obvious conclusion."

I touch her lip, tracing my finger across its softness, and watching every myriad of emotion pass through those violet blues. "You thought you would dump me before I dumped you?"

She inhales as her chest heaves with emotion. "Something like that."

I lean down and push a lock of hair from her face so that I can whisper in her ear. "I don't intend on being dumped or dumping anyone today, little missy. This thing we have between us, it's only going to end one way, because I don't plan on leaving you or this town."

Her gasp is an exhaled breath against my ear. I cradle her face in my hands, connecting with those wide eyes so she can see for herself that my words are sincere. I think for once in her life, Priscilla Jean is at a loss for words. She just stares up at me as though in a dream.

I stroke a finger down the creaminess of her smooth and silky skin. "You are mine, PJ. I'm not letting some baggage in the past or a job location get in the way of that, for either of us."

Her eyes moisten. "You would give up Vegas, the big night life, the desert, and all the people you take care of out there, for me?"

"I would, and I did."

She narrows her eyes at me like she does. "When did you decide to do that?"

I smile because now the sassy miss who's managed to worm her way into my heart is getting her spunk back. "Last night while I watched you sleeping in my arms."

"Before I got up and left you that Dear John note?"

I stroke a finger down the side of her cheek. "I know why you did it. Cole told me what happened in the past, but I'm not that guy, PJ. This feeling is as new to me as it is to you. But I'm not going to break your heart if you take a chance on me."

She dabs the corner of her eyes with a dainty finger that's been painted with white tips and glitter and nods. "I'll take a chance on you, Mason. I'm sorry I left you this morning. If it means anything, it was one of the hardest things I ever had to do. I was just trying to protect my heart from all the hurt that would follow if you left me."

I fold her into my arms. "From now on, protecting you, all of you, is my job, understand? I just want to feel my arms wrapped around you and for you to know that you're protected, safe, and all mine."

A persistent knock on the door pulls us from our moment. "Hey, lovebirds. Time to get to the church and get dressed!"

Mason laughs. "Is Jules forever going to be interrupting at the most inopportune times," he whispers.

"I'm pretty sure she took that single room last night to leave me no choice but to sleep with you."

He grins. "Then your friend is forgiven. Now let's all get ourselves to the church on time so Lacy and Garrett can say I do. I've got something important to take care of first, but then I'll meet you there. Wait for me, okay?"

12

PJ

I climb into the back of Krissy's van with Patti and Jules still bubbling with excitement. Lacy turns around from her seat up front, and her face is positively glowing. "I'm actually doing this. I am going to get married in the same church my grandparents married in and my momma and daddy too. It may have been reconstructed over the years, but the heart and soul of its presence in Deadwood never changes. It's part of what makes the history so special."

My arms wrap around myself as we drive, contemplating all that has happened with Mason in such a short time before we park next to the entrance in the back of the church. When we reach the back rooms reserved for us today, the dresses are all hanging on a rack. The lady volunteers hover around, making sure we look our best and don't forget one single detail.

When Lacy turns around, it's almost impossible to keep the tears at bay, but we all try as hard as possible. I hug her lightly so as not to wrinkle her or get one bit of this makeup on that beautiful long white dress. "You look absolutely beautiful. Garrett is one lucky man."

Lacy beams with happiness. I squeeze her hand while Jules and Patti say a few things before we have to leave. I glance at the clock. "Come on;

it's almost time to do this thing. The music will start soon, and the guys should be arriving any minute."

We make our way to the area we're supposed to meet at, and Lacy's father is escorted in by a couple of our friends who went to pick him up for the occasion. Lacy hugs her dad and dabs at her eyes. "I can't cry, dad, but I'm so glad you're here," she chokes.

The rest of us leave them to have their special moment and make our way to the area right off the entrance where we'll couple with the guys and make our way up to the pulpit and watch with the rest of the town as Lacy's dad escorts her down the aisle.

A loud gunshot breaks the serenity of the moment, and then another, and another, each permeating the air and causing my chest to tighten with the greatest fear I've ever known.

The entire group turns toward the exit, and all I can think about is Mason, Garrett, and Cole. Neither of the three are in the church. Mason's words ring over and over in my mind. *I have something important to take care of first; wait for me, okay?*

A mind-gripping fear settles over me.

Before my brain can keep my feet from moving, I've lifted my dress and am running out the front door of the church and down the stairs. Jake Eldridge lays in a pool of blood while men I've never seen begin lifting him. Mason is lying on the ground with his eyes closed. *No, no, no. It can't be possible.* "Mason!" Tears spill down my face so fast I don't even try to swipe them away. My heart breaks in two right then and there.

He moves and turns toward me, just as I reach the bottom step. Mason's eyes connect with mine from the ground. I don't need to say a thing; he's been in sync with me from the very first time we met. "Come here."

I tear over to his side, dropping to the ground and giving not one care in the world to the condition of my dress. "Mason, tell me you're okay; baby, tell me you're okay."

He grins and pulls me into his arms, kissing my lips so hard I can barely breathe. "I'm more than okay. Didn't I tell you to wait for me? That does not mean putting yourself at risk, when I'm out here protecting you, okay," he says, wiping the tears and smudge from under my eye.

I nod and then nod again. "I love you, Mason. If I didn't know it the first time you kissed me, or last night, or today when you came for me, I know it now. You are more than worth taking a chance on. I love you so much."

He picks himself up off the ground with me in tow and pockets his gun as the sheriff arrives with sirens blazing and pulls to a stop. Garrett has his arm around Lacy, and Cole has his arms wrapped protectively around Krissy, while the other bodyguards deal with the police.

Mason whispers in my ear, "I love you too, Priscilla Jean. I probably have since the very first time you dumped that beer on me, and that little show of fireworks flashed through your eyes."

He gestures toward the men on the ground next to Jake Eldridge who the sheriff is putting in cuffs.

"Is he dead?"

He's not, but him, his dad and some others still want the territory in this town and will go to great lengths to get it. That's why Tommy and his boys took the others away before the sheriff arrived, and why I have a job in Deadwood."

I hug him tight. "Our protectors."

Garrett clears his throat. "Let's get this wedding started so I can say I do!"

———

I hope you enjoyed the third story in the Ruthless Guardians series and are having a great time reading all the stories in the anthology. If you're new to my series, and would like to read it from the beginning, download the expanded first one, Fierce Protector, Cole and Krissy's story free.

ABOUT THE AUTHOR

Contemporary romantic suspense author Via Mari likes to keep her readers on the edge, fanning themselves as the action unfolds and the heat rises. Her books, featuring the most handsome, intense males, exemplify extreme romance, with powerful men who will stop at nothing to protect the women they love.

Via was raised in both the United States and United Kingdom. Since childhood, she has enjoyed reading books that carry you away. In fact, you can still find her in the early hours of the morning, curled up in an overstuffed chair by a crackling wood fire, reading a page-turning novel, especially during the harsh winters of the Midwestern United States.

When not writing, Via spends her days with her husband. She enjoys gardening, shopping at the local farmers market, and walking in town or around a big city. And she loves traveling to research her next novel.

She also loves interacting with her readers, so feel free to connect with her on the following social media sites! If you want to stay updated on the latest releases and claim a copy of an exclusive story, **sign up for her newsletter.**

BLUE DOG BLACK DRAGON

JULIEN BRADLEY

1

APRIL

Born on the same day, April, Mae, and June were elevated to small town celebrity status when their mother's decided to name the three little darlings after the months of spring. Upon entering preschool, the girls became fast friends, and remained as such through high school. Even graduation hadn't separated the trio when they chose to attend the same college.

Deadwood, a historic town nestled in the northern Black Hills, became their first true love. Enamored with the town's allure, unruly atmosphere, and adventure, the three women attended Wild Bill Days rodeo during their freshman year and were instantly captivated. Determined to spend as much time there as possible, they'd all found seasonal employment during the summer break throughout their college years. After graduation, the three friends had made a pact that no matter where their jobs, family, or life took them, they would always come back to Deadwood for a 'girl's' weekend annually. For the three women, Deadwood held a certain aura of enchantment and mystique. It was a place where they never aged, they always had fun, and could be their true selves. Wild Bill Days had been the traditional get together weekend, until the George Mickelson bike trail opened in 1998. Built on the historic Chicago, Burlington, Quincy Railroad Line from Deadwood to

Edgemont, it traversed some of the most beautiful scenery and back-country in South Dakota. So, when family and obligations became too demanding in early summer, it became their next go-to weekend to enjoy one another's camaraderie, biking along the abandoned tracks on the annual 105-mile trail trek.

Among the three friends, April had remained faithful to her first love, the Black Hills of South Dakota. Early on, she'd dreamt of opening an antique store in Deadwood. A dream turned reality with financial support from her friends. For many years, she'd enjoyed moderate success during the tourist season as a mercantile owner, up until the winter of the Covid pandemic when most small businesses faltered or failed. When she wasn't working, her favorite pastime was traipsing up and down the hills and byways of the Black Hills looking for hidden treasures and learning the history of the place she called home. Bursting with abandoned mines, ghost towns, rail lines, and logging trails, the region held a plethora to explore surrounding Deadwood. Many of the towns no longer existed. Towns like Flatiron, Pluma, Kirk, and Glenwood were merely dots on a map, covered in meadows, trees and shrubs. But there was an air of mystery along the old trails that bore deeper than the mines dug into the ground. Along the mountain streams, gulches, and canyons, she often wondered what life had been like for the people brave enough to venture into this rugged hill country. She'd spend many an afternoon hiking, biking, or snowshoeing along every logging trail, abandoned train track and mining road in the region, trying to picture in her mind the triple decked train tracks she'd seen in old photos. She felt transported back in time every time she stepped off the beaten path, into the heart of the Black Hills.

In her rambling, one of her greatest finds had been the bungalow she owned on Kirk Road. Nestled against a mountain of Precambrian granite, pegmatite, and metasedimentary rocks near Whitewood Creek, it was her own piece of paradise. The babbling of the creek, her personal lullaby to sleep. And, located mere feet from the George Mickelson bike path, she rode the trail every chance she got.

It was an early spring day when April dusted off her bike seat, checked the brakes and put air in her tires, marking her first ride of the season. Climbing out of Deadwood gulch up to Lead proved to be more difficult than she expected, especially after a winter of binge-watching streaming channels and indulging in ice cream treats. Once past the trail divide, she felt the down draft coming from Terry peak, and the forecast held a strong prevalence of rain or snow. It was not uncommon. The dark threatening clouds hovering around the mountain tops were a daily occurrence year-round as steam rose out of the forest floors and grassy meadows giving an eerie, mystic façade. Despite its threatening appearance, it didn't always rain, and once the fog burned off from the gulches, the sun usually found its way through the mist, shaping up to be a lovely day.

Getting to the high line near Englewood was a grueling task and yet, April's favorite part of the trail. Her legs worked tirelessly ascending the mountain, and she distracted herself with thoughts of yesteryear and what the landscape may have looked like in the days before gold was exploited in the Black Hill's. It fascinated her how and why civil engineers chose the paths that they did, laying down the railroad bed, or what it took to drag railroad ties, build hundreds of trestles and bridges over gulches and streams. Powered by horse and steam in the early years, it took a well-coordinated team of an engineer, firemen, brake, and door-men, to run a hog, feeding wood or coal into the hungry firebox and producing enough heat and steam to power a steam engine. It was diffi-cult to picture how a single freight engine laden with rock and earth could even make the climb out of Deadwood gulch at all. Several spurs once serviced active mines and lumber camps, as well as depots of boom towns along the rail line all long since abandoned. Steep cuts clung to the edge of shear rocks with a sharp drop into a gulch on the opposite side, while other places bore open tunnels through mountain tops accommo-dating a narrow-gauge track with barely enough room for a steam engine to pass through on either side.

She took advantage of the numerous stops along the ascent enjoying the scenic overlooks of the gulch's cities of Lead and Deadwood. Still bare of foliage, the trees were unintrusive to the view as they were in the summer. April made it a point to rest at a circular picnic table made of stone with the best view of the valley floor to hydrate. Tracing her finger along the creek below, she could see the trees that lined Whitewood creek and the alternate bike route. She decided to take the Kirk trail back to Deadwood. It was a bit more rugged, but it was shorter, and there were several bridges which passed over the creek adding to the splendor of the ride.

It was early afternoon by the time she reached Rochford and the Moonshine Gluch Saloon. A small establishment for a small community, it was open year-round weather permitting. April made it a point to stop for lunch. Their sweet potato fries were to die for, and the owner and friend would make a portabella burger, a non-menu item, especially for her, when she called in advance.

With her belly full, April began the easy coasting back to Deadwood, and once again marveled at the landscape of this place she called home. The sun peaked out briefly, luminating the lush meadow lands along the creeks and streams. It was this section of the trail which crossed several private properties. Dismounting her bike to open and close the cattle gaits slowed her momentum. In the shaded areas, water leached out of the ore deposits along the face of the mountain where icicles formed. The air was crisp and fresh with the smell of new grass, cow manure, and aromatic pine. "God, I love this place," she said aloud, basking in the unseasonal weather. The blissful moment was fleeting however, as a light mist of rain wisped across April's cheeks and thunder rumbled high in the mountains.

Despite the slowdown, April reached the junction of Englewood and Kirk trail in suitable time and took the rougher trail along the creek. She wasn't that far to Deadwood, and even less to Kirk Road. If a downpour did occur, she'd simply head for home. It would have been nice just to lollygag along the trail that meandered next to Whitewood Creek. This was her carrot for a workout well done. But the weather had other plans, and the strengthening wind made time of the essence. As if to emphasize the point, an updraft blew a whirl of grit and dust, penetrating under her protective eyewear and she was forced to stop at the Wasp/Bismarck shelter up ahead.

The Wasp number two mine was a moderately successful operation, encompassing both a surface and underground workings area spanning approximately 130 acres and had only one known mineshaft. Built on the east side of the mountain dividing Whitewood and Yellow Creek, it towered above the valley floor at an elevation of around 5,600 feet. Typical of the mines in the Black Hill region, it exhibited characteristics consistent with the interior plains. Primarily a gold, silver, and tungsten mine, the size of production remained small. Over time, the Homestake Mining Company purchased it, until it was played out of anything of value and eventually abandoned. But not before its tailings and hazardous substances became a major causal factor in the degradation of flora, fish, and fauna along the creek. For decades, nothing survived in the grey sludge runoff. It wasn't until environmental legislation forced mines to cease disposal of toxic waste into the creek and clean up their practices that allowed nature to slowly rebound.

April dismounted her bike inside the familiar shelter and prepared to ride out the strange weather phenomenon. She had been caught in storms before, but there was something different about the one she was witnessing. Shielding her eyes, she looked out across the grassy flat along the creek and noticed a change in the stone marker which stood at the foot of the mountain. It was—*glowing*. Curious, she left her bike and approached the stone. A closer inspection revealed the commemorative plate embedded in the face of the rock had melted away. *That's weird*. She was about to touch it when a fluttering sound caught her attention. Hanging in a tree a few yards away, small pieces of parchment with Chinese symbols dangled from string tied to its branches. She wanted to take a closer look, but a violent wind gust whistled through her helmet as a blinding flash of lightning lit up the afternoon sky. Splinters of fragmented stone flew like dust particles as the shards whirled around her, piercing through her flesh and clothes. April dropped to her knees, protecting her mouth, eyes, and nose with her arm. It was over in a nano second. She uncovered her eyes long enough to see the boulder split wide open, revealing the geode of amethyst inside. Gazing at the colorful array of red, yellow, orange and gold, the gem glowed with intensity, projecting an image of a magnificent dragon onto the dark sky. Mesmerized, April crawled closer and reached to touch the glowing rock, absorbing its warmth. It was comforting, powerful and—beautiful. Another crackle of lightning and the dragon image disappeared, replaced by an image of a dog. The wind howled a mournful sound, boring through skull like a freight train entering a tunnel. *Did an early spring tornado find its way into the gulch? Impossible!* But, if true, April knew she had to move quickly and seek shelter. As she stood, the trumpeting sound of a train whistle heralded a pending doom, and the roar of a great beast exploded in her brain. April clasped her hands over her ears unable to drown out the sound. Around her, the sound of splintering trees, and the crashing of rock against rock shattered her eardrums. The ground quaked, sending tremors throughout her body. *Was there an avalanche? Had there been an explosion? Did she really see a dragon in the sky?* April fell to the ground, squeezing her eyes tight and curling into a ball. The last thing she remembered was sending up a prayer that whatever was coming, it would all be over soon.

2

HANK

Hank stood on the precipice of the broken tracks overlooking the creek bed, the reins of a Sorrel named Copper in his hand. Having spent a good part of his life in the city, he was a mediocre horseback rider. Still, it was the best way to access remote locations within the Black Hill mountains. Staring down at the smoldering remains of the railroad bridge, two engines, the smaller one stacked on top of the other laying in a heap. A phrase from his estranged father-in-law came to mind. "zhēnshi yītuánzāo," he muttered to the horse. The mare nodded as if to concur. Hank scratched his beard. If he had to make a judgment based on his current observation, it appeared the train had been traveling too fast for the downward gradient. Meaning, either the brake man had been sleeping on the job, or more likely, the valve to the brake was stuck disallowing for enough steam to power the brakes, a frequent problem on steam run engines. At any rate, it looked like the cow catcher must have clipped the railing at just the right angle, toppling the bridge and two engines into the creek. Hank looked to his horse, "Welp, let's hear what the hog boss has to say." He started down the creek embankment leading the horse rather than riding. He was a railroad man, not a cowboy.

It was clear nothing would be getting through to Deadwood for quite a while. Cribbing over the gap wasn't a viable option and rebuilding the bridge would take months before traffic could resume. Hank mounted his horse to cross the creek then dismounted on the other side making his way up the muddy incline toward the rest of the train.

He was astonished to see the tender of the second engine along with the freight cars coupled behind marginally derailed. One of the engineers stood in the doghouse on the deck of the tender scratching his head. Hank approached and extended a hand, "Hello, Hank McCormick, railway official with the Chicago, Burlington, Quincy. Can you tell me what happened?"

The engineer eyed him warily and scoffed. "That didn't take long." It was no secret among the engine crew, the big brass frequently rode the route between Edgemont to Deadwood. They even had hand signals alerting the rest of the crew to their presence. It had been sheer happenstance, Hank arrived in Deadwood just days before to see his daughter when word came in early this morning about the accident. The engineer breathed a sigh of resignation and accepted the outstretched hand. "Karl Whitters, hog boss for engine number 3116. Yeah, I'll tell you what happened."

According to the engineer, the bridge was already ablaze prior to the train's approach. It was an unlikely scenario considering no train had passed that way in over nine hours, alluding to arson, a serious assertion. Hank considered the Wasp number two mine spur not far away. Holding onto the thought, he urged the engineer to continue.

"I had time to slow the speed enough for the engine crew to jump to safety. A good thing too. Creeks up, someone could have drowned just as easily as being crushed by the engine. It was too late to stop the train completely before the bridge."

The engineer's quick thinking had indeed minimized casualties. But by the grace of God, the passenger cars and caboose had all remained on the tracks with the passengers who were already on their way back to Englewood. From there, they would be rerouted. As far as Hank could tell, there'd been no conceivable reason the engineer with a seasoned crew would concoct such a story. Thanking the man, Hank walked to the rear of the train, hoping to talk to the conductor. Before he reached the caboose, he heard a man exclaim, "Well looky what I found."

A lanky, young man dressed in overhauls crouched down on his haunches stared at the object. Pointing, he said, "I ain't never seen britches like that on a woman before." Hank walked his horse over for a closer look.

From a distance, it appeared as if a little girl might have dropped her ragdoll in the dirt and he nearly disregarded the whole thing. Upon closer inspection, he realized the object was a woman, half dressed and semi-conscious lying on the ground. "What the—"

"Whatcha got there Beaner, and how the hell would you know what a female's britches are supposed to look like?" The conductor said as he approached. Taking Hanks hand, he gave it a hardy shake, "Long time no see, Blue Dog."

The name made Hank smile. He'd been given the nickname after rescuing an Australian cattle pup from certain death at a stockyard in Omaha. Blue Dog, Bluey for short was such an ordinary name given to an extraordinary dog. With a merle coat and icy blue eyes, Blue Dog was the first and only animal Hank had ever owned. More than a pet, Bluey was hardworking, intelligent, loyal, and a faithful companion. Hank took the dog everywhere, and except for a surly bar keep, everyone loved that dog, so long as he was exercised daily.

Standing shoulder to shoulder the two men contemplated the situation. Neither seemed to know what to make of the matter. Beaner, the simpleton he was, had drawn his own conclusion. Looking up and waggling his eyebrows, he whispered, "Ya think she's a burlesque dancer from one of those carnival side shows, boss?"

"You're a real pain in the neck, Beaner," The conductor scoffed, "Now make yourself useful and go fetch a blanket." Beaner rose slowly to his feet and ambled in the direction of the caboose, kicking at the loose rock as he strolled.

"Moron," the conductor muttered. To Hank, "Let's get a closer look."

Baring only minor cuts, the woman appeared in good condition. Despite being underdressed, there was no evidence of hypothermia, nor did it appear as though she had been violated. Though, abuse would lend a better explanation for her improper dress and the remoteness of her location. Hank took stock in the surroundings.

Near the spur for the Wasp number two mine, up the line sat an engine waiting on the tracks with ore cars already three-quarters full. On the western slope, another spur, this one requiring a winch system pulled the cars up the steep grade servicing the cyanide mill that managed the tailings. The mine shipped out thousands of carloads of sand to be used to fill and ballast. Overall, it was quite an engineering feat. None of it lent a clue as to how she got here.

Walking back to his horse, Hank grabbed the bedroll behind his saddle. Gently he laid it over her body. The closer vantage point revealed a woman of middle age, her skin a vibrant hue despite the cool air. Her hair was dark and tangled, her cheeks rosy, her skin smooth. Her couldn't see the color of eyes, but they were adorned with long, thick lashes, and her lips red and plump. She appeared well-nourished. Her frame, slight of build, possessed well-defined legs and muscular arms as though she wasn't afraid of arduous work. In short- he found her to be—very appealing. She moaned softly. Not in pain, more like the sound a child tucked into bed would make. It was impossible to comprehend how, or why, she was here. He only knew he had to get her somewhere safe. The conductor turned to him and said, "She's not one of mine. I would have remembered a female passenger dressed like that."

Scooping her up in his arms, Hank hoisted her onto his horse with the conductor's assistance. Despite her moderate frame, it was a struggle not to jostle her awake. Saddling up behind her, he cradled the woman in front of him, her head resting on his chest. She snuggled in, like his old blue healer did when he was a puppy. Once secured, he gave Copper a gentle nudge and said, "alright girl, let's go home."

3
LI

LI STOOD OVER THE SINK ENJOYING THE MIDMORNING sunshine while she worked the rubber stopper onto the jar of her first batch of mullein tincture. She breathed a contented sigh, feeling proud of her accomplishment. She loved working in her uncle's apothecary. He and his wife each possessed a wealth of knowledge regarding traditional Chinese medicine, were patient teachers, and much easier to live with than her grandparents. She'd learned something new every day about indigenous plants and how they could be substituted for traditional plants from China. Her favorite pastime was foraging in the mountains, gulches, and streams. The Black Hills held an abundance of raw material, it's worth far greater than gold, and harvesting was much safer than mining. Breathing in the mountain air wafting in the kitchen window, she felt—happy. It was pleasant living in Deadwood, more so than her former home in Seattle.

A ward of her mother's parents, Li was nothing more than a commodity. Her grandfather began accepting suiters as early as second grade and betrothed her to a man three times her age upon completing her education. With an eight to one, male to female ratio, among Chinese Americans, thanks to the Chinese Exclusion Act of 1882, it was her only value. But it wasn't her only worry. Life had become dangerous in Chinatown.

There was a sharp rise in anti-Chinese sentiment, up and down the west coast. Chinese men were denied work and stripped of their businesses. Many were run out of town, or worse, murdered. Some were being shipped back to China. Even her grandfather's cleaning business fell under scrutiny.

But fate had been kind to her the cold February day when a delegation of commissioners arrived from China. Conducting business with the empire builder, James J. Hill, the Chinese prince was interested in all things American, particularly the educational system. During his visit, he was astonished to see Chinese girls among the students attending a public school. Because he spoke neither English, nor Cantonese, she'd been selected as a translator. Enamored by her talent, the prince requested her as an interpreter during his American tour. Insulted by the proposal, grandfather had been well compensated to restore his honor.

The Pacific Coast Riots detained her return to Seattle. Too precious a commodity to be killed in a mob attack, grandfather decided to have her live with his wife's sister until the street violence subsided. That's what brought her to Deadwood. He wasn't through making money off her yet. Little did he know that her birth father also resided in the community.

Her aunt had shared with her the disgraceful relationship between her parents. Among the whites, it was illegal. For her mother, failure to marry a Chinese man was an egregious dishonor, and a betrayal to her family. Secrecy had been maintained until Li's mother died in childbirth. Because her predominant Asian features, Li easily melded into her mother's family. Her grandfather would have rid himself of all traces of his daughter's dishonor had it not been for her father's money—his name never mentioned, except in venomous whispers.

Li heard the heavy foot fall climbing the backstairs. "That's odd," she said to the calico cat sitting in the open windowsill. "Father's home early." Giving a wide yawn, the calico stretched its legs then rolled over with disinterest. Li placed the glass jar on the counter next to the other tincture. She called to her uncle in the front of the store, "Shūshu, wǒ yào shàng lóule," and headed upstairs.

Li found the woman lying on the chaise lounge quite fascinating. She was familiar with women's western wear as well as the traditional hanfu, qipao or tang suit, to which this woman's clothing bore no resemblance.

Her uncle's store carried the finest silks from China along with American and French made textiles. Li slid a finger beneath the cuff of the woman's shirt and rubbed it between her fingers. The fabric was like nothing she'd ever felt. The ill-fitted pantaloons looked tight and restrictive around the arm and leg bands, yet the material was soft, stretchy, and liberating all the same. Her exposed skin was a dark tan, the flesh on her arms and legs taught and muscular, representing long hours in the sun. Clearly, she worked on a ranch or in the fields, defying the prominent Victorian code of conduct as well as dress. In short, she was mesmerizing.

Her father, Hank had retrieved a woolen blanket and a pillow from the cedar chest. He appeared quite flustered by the woman and her homely, yet provocative attire. "Did you find Calamity Jane's long-lost daughter?" she said in jest. The corner of her father's lips crinkled in a smile. Li sobered her tone, "Who is she father, and why have you brought her here?" Her father fussed a bit more with the pillow before he answered.

"I found her near the train wreck this morning by the Wasp number two mine."

"How did she get there?"

"Don't know. The crew claim she wasn't part of the passenger manifest, and I don't blame them. Dressed like she is, they probably thought ole Calamity Jane had rose from the grave as well."

"What are you going to do with her father?"

"I'm going to run and fetch doc Howe. Can you watch over her, Wǒ de tián lián, until I get back?"

Li blushed. She loved that her father tried to speak Cantonese, even when his term of endearment wasn't quite accurate.

"Of course, father. But you should know, Doctor Howe told uncle he was traveling to Lead this morning on business."

"Then I better get a move on," He kissed her forehead. "Make sure no one knows that she's here. It's our secret." He winked and headed back down the stairs.

Li couldn't help but smile. It amused her how her father treated her like a five-year-old while her grandfather had been ready to marry her off at the ripe age of ten. It was strange the difference in cultural perceptions. Her father had been her champion when it came to freedom of choice. It was in direct opposition to grandfather's beliefs. More than anything, Li wanted to attend a university like her uncle's sons had done and study pharmacology. Her uncle Wong said, she didn't need to attend a university for that, offering to take her with him on his trip back to China where she could study Chinese medicine from the greatest scholars. She, however, didn't want to leave America. For better or worse, it was her home, a home she was determined to keep. All she had to do now was figure out a way to make it work.

4

APRIL

APRIL JACK-KNIFED UPRIGHT FROM THE FAINTING COUCH
sending a shockwave to her brain. She rubbed at the ache. *Where am I?*
Blinking her eyes to adjust the dim lighting, she took stock in her
surroundings.

The couch she sat on was merely the tip of the authentic antiques in
the room. The modest flat had a simple layout. The living space doubled
as a dining area, living room. A wood burning fireplace occupied an
outside wall where two mahogany Edwardian salon chairs faced a hearth
made of an ore rock façade. There was a magnificent floor to ceiling book-
shelf standing on the opposite wall filled with a variety of books, scrolls
and periodicals. She'd explore that, momentarily. A roll top writing desk
graced the corner of the room with an octagon shaped window above to
let in natural light. The adjacent room was a galley style kitchen. A round
table occupied the formal dining area. At the back of the room, an
ornately painted, free-standing, folding screen divided the living from the
sleeping area. It was stunningly authentic, this window into the past. *I
need the name of their interior designer,* she mused. Taking deep breaths, April
waited for her equilibrium to return, then swung her feet to the floor.

A woolen blanket slid from her lap as April stood. Her head still
throbbed, from what, she couldn't say. At least there was no dizziness,

and her balance was good. The last thing she remembered was tucking her head between her knees and kissing her ass goodbye as the windstorm swept into the Whitewood creek valley. She rubbed her head feeling for bumps but found nothing. Smacking her dry lips, she reached for the lip balm in her zipped pocket. It was—gone. No matter, her mouth was parched, and walked to the kitchen.

The kitchen looked like something out of an early 1900's Sears and Roebuck catalog. Herbs and wildflowers hung drying from the rafters. A cast iron woodburning stove occupied a great deal of the space. There was an old-fashioned ice box on the wall next to the larder. A butcher block work area cluttered the middle of the kitchen with barely enough room to walk around. An actual hand-pump for a water spigot sat next to the sink located at the end of the wooden counter. Not a single appliance was in sight.

April worked the pump for several minutes just to get a trickle of water. The water had an offensive sulfate odor and a rusty color. She crinkled her nose and cupped her hand to drink. The taste was as bad as the smell with a high concentration of iron, and dissolved minerals. She drank it anyway, thirsty enough to drink from a horse trough.

"Wouldn't you rather use a cup?"

April nearly choked, startled by the young feminine voice. Standing in the archway separating the kitchen from the living room stood a young girl, it was hard to gage her age. She watched as she made her way gracefully toward a cupboard retrieving a delicate teacup and handing it to April. "Perhaps you would like tea instead? I find herbs help disguise the foul taste." Without waiting for a reply, she collected the teapot from the stove and began filling it with water.

April had no time for tea. She needed to get home. The hour was late and surely her neighbors would notice her absence. "Do you know how I got here?"

The young girl continued her task, "My father said he found you by the trainwreck near the Wasp mine and brought you here. He's gone to fetch the doctor."

"Trainwreck? How can there be a trainwreck without train tracks? Are you sure you heard him, right? Where am I?"

"In Deadwood. We live above my uncle's store."

April was relieved and confused. Why hadn't she been taken into urgent care, and what doctor still made house calls? She asked, "Is your dad one of the volunteer first responders working the Mickelson trail ride this weekend?"

The young girl turned to face her, "My father works for the railroad." She furloughed her brow, "What is the Mickelson bike trail?"

"The George Mickelson, you know, the trail along the old Chicago, Burlington, Quincy line."

"What's a bike trail?"

April rubbed her forehead. A different line of questioning was in order, "I own a business in Deadwood. I might know your uncle. What's his name?"

"Fee Lee Wong."

"Fee Lee—" That made no sense, "You're trying to tell me we're standing in the Wing Tsue building?"

Li smiled, "Yes, Fee Lee Wong emporium."

"But that's not possible. The Wing Tsue building was torn down Christmas Eve, 2005. And don't you mean, great uncle? Lee Wong took his family back to China years ago and never returned."

The girl's skin paled, "How do you know of my uncle's plan to travel to China?"

That's her takeaway, April exclaimed inwardly. To Li, "It's all part of Deadwood's history. Being family, how would you not know that?'

The two females stared at one another. Neither understood what the other was talking about. April tried a different approach, "My name is April," she said extending her hand. "I own the coffee and gift shop on the south end of town near Chubby Chipmunk chocolates. What part of town is this?"

The young girl looked at April as if she'd asked an obvious question. "I am Li. And you are in Chinatown of course. How does a chipmunk make chocolate?"

Again impossible. Nothing but markers and plaques existed of the original Chinatown in Deadwood, least of all the building in which they were allegedly standing. April walked to the window over the sink facing the street looking for familiar landmarks. She gasped. Where are the cars? Where was the highway? Where was the new construction on the north end of town? Her knees buckled. This couldn't be Deadwood, at least the Deadwood she knew. Holding onto the counter, she looked closer at her surroundings, suddenly realizing there was absolutely no evidence of modern convenience, technology, or electricity anywhere. She said in a half-crazed tone, "What year is this?"

Li looked at her strange, "it is the year of the dog."

"The Georgian calendar, please."

"It is 1910."

April sat on the floor. "That can't be."

She began replaying in her mind the events leading up to her current situation. She either went mad, was dreaming, or something beyond comprehension happened during the storm at the Wasp number two mine. "I need to leave," she said abruptly. Rising to her feet, she felt woozy and lightheaded. Li came quickly to her side.

"You can't leave April. The doctor hasn't seen you yet."

"Don't you see? I don't belong here."

Li's posture straightened, "I know Chinatown isn't desirable, but the doctor is white, and he will come to see a white person."

"No, no." April looked at her bike shorts, shirt, and athletic shoes. "Look at me. I don't belong here. Look at what you're wearing and look at how I'm dressed. Are you part of a reenactment?"

"You mean, like a play?"

"Yes, are you dressed in costume for a play?"

Li smoothed her dress, "Why, no. These are my everyday clothes," she said sheepishly.

"Then you understand. I don't belong here; I don't belong anywhere in this Deadwood."

"Where do you belong?" Li said looking puzzled.

That was a complex question.

"I come from a different place. A place like Deadwood, but not your Deadwood. A place where there's electricity, cars, computers, and concrete roadways. Water doesn't need to be hand pumped, you simply turn on a faucet and it flows freely. In the Deadwood I come from; Chinatown is gone. Your uncle and his family go back to China, never to return to America. I must get back there, and quickly. I don't belong here."

"I don't think I like your Deadwood. Are you a devil, or a trickster?"

April shook her head, "No, at least, I don't think so. But someone is playing a trick on me. I'm in the wrong space and time, and I need to get back to my time." She began making her way toward the door.

"Wait, you can't go out there," Li pleaded. "People will see you don't belong as you said. They will become very superstitious. They may think you're an evil spirit."

April couldn't argue that. If it was truly 1910, mystique and the supernatural still existed in the minds of guileless people. She grabbed the rain slicker hanging on a wooden knob near the door, "May I borrow this?"

Li nodded, "It's my father's."

Donning the jacket, April opened the door.

"Wait, I'm coming with you." Li scrambled to grab a shawl and tossed it around her shoulders.

April questioned the wisdom of a white woman and a young Asian girl seen together on the streets of Deadwood in 1910. Perhaps Li would be viewed as a house servant of a prominent family. Historically, a great deal of prejudice still lingered toward the Asian community. There may have been exceptions, at least according to the annals of the local historical society. Fee Lee Wong being among them. But was she willing to risk the child's safety on an assumption? Glancing down at her attire, she rolled her eyes inwardly. *Well, if Calamity Jane got away with it, I can too.* The child may prove useful in navigating back to the mine. Conceding, she said, "Alright, let's go."

It was astonishing at how sparse the rest of the town east of Main Street appeared. At least the main thoroughfare hadn't changed much. The streets were paved in cobblestone, minus the horse drawn carriages. And, instead of cars and motorcycles lining the parking stalls, horses tied to hitching posts in front of water troughs while pedestrians made their way along the boardwalks. The buildings looked stunningly new, freshly painted, with the stone façades absent of present-day moss and weathering.

They'd cut down Pine Street and began following the Whitewood creek canal eventually paralleling the train tracks. But the most shocking difference between the past and present was the robust train yard at the south end of town. April had only seen pictures and diagrams of what the train yard had looked like before it was demolished. Now, it was a beehive of activity as the depot manager shouted orders to men dressed in over-alls laboring over manually operated switch track levers, maintaining signal boxes, and inspecting freight cars. What a thrill it would be to stick around and observe a part of Deadwood history in action. Li pulled her from her musings. She whispered, "This way. If I'm seen, my father will whip my hide."

April followed, quietly considering what she could recall of the man who'd carried her to his loft. "Somehow, I don't believe your father seems the type to use corporal punishment for such a minor offense."

Li conceded, "It is true, my father is not a violent man. He doesn't even carry a gun. But you must understand, two females wandering about the train yards unescorted is unacceptable in this Deadwood. For a Chinese girl, I think it's illegal."

April posed no argument, "Then, I guess we'd better stay out of sight."

To the best of her knowledge, the two managed to circumvent the train yard unseen. Crossing the trolley line heading up the mountain to Lead, they disappeared into the trees along the railroad track. Again, April found herself behaving like a tourist, enchanted by the landscape. Marked by the crisscross of railroad tracks and signs of commerce, access to civilization seemed everywhere and yet, it all felt wild and untamed. She searched for familiar roads, natural landmarks, buildings, historical markers, anything that would give her a clue as to her loca-tion. None of it existed, not U.S. highway 85, Kirk and Yellow creek road nor the homes and resorts along the way. Even Whitewood creek ran an unfamiliar course. There was only one constant between time-lines. She said to Li, "We best stick to the Chicago, Burlington, Quincy railroad."

They'd walked several miles, a typical midweek workout for April and yet, she felt drained of energy, as if an unseen force were siphoning it away. She couldn't remember the last time she ate, or even went to the bathroom. And other than the water she had back at the flat, she felt parched and dehydrated. When she and Li reached a familiar junction, April leaned forward resting her hands on her knees, "Finally." The kirk trail spur was about a two-mile walk to the Wasp number two gold mine. April glanced at Li, then up at the sky. The sun was edging over the western side of the valley. That wasn't near concerning as the daily afternoon storm clouds banking up over the horizon. Li's eyes followed.

"We need to go back," Li said keeping her eyes peeled upward. "That's a dragon storm, it doesn't belong in the year of the dog."

April didn't know much about the characters of the Chinese calendar, except what she'd read on a place mat in a restaurant. All she knew was that she'd been born in the year of the rat, whose characteristics were uncannily well matched to hers. It prompted the question, "What happens when the dragon interferes with the dog?"

"I don't know. I've never seen it before. Perhaps my uncle knows. We should consult him about this before moving onward."

April shook her head, "There's no time. Besides, I think this dragon may have brought me from my time to you, for what purpose, I couldn't say. But now that you mention dragon, I could swear, I'd seen a black dragon in the sky, right before I came here. If this dragon brought me here, maybe it can take me home."

Li's face brightened, her voice filled with awe, "Then you are truly fortunate. You saw Li Tie Giai's black dragon. He is one of the immortals eight and a protector from evil spirits. He is depicted as a frail old man with an iron crutch. He symbolizes strength in spirit and stability despite his physical limitations."

"I don't know anything about that, all I remember are clouds in the shape of a black dragon appeared when I touched the amethyst stone."

"You mean the great talisman near the gold mine?"

"You know of it?"

"I know it well. I used to go there often to gather medicinal herbs and to meditate."

"Why did you stop?"

Li's voice became low, "An evil has poisoned everything that grows there. It is unsafe."

"Do you know of the pieces of parchment hanging on tree branches with Chinese letters?"

"Yes, they are Fulu, magic symbols and incantations for deities and spirits. They are used for exorcism and recipes for potions or charms to treat ailments. They protect from evil spirits and misfortune."

"Did you make the Fulu's?"

Li bowed her head slightly, "My uncle is a healer, or doctor as you would call him. He uses the talismans for healing alongside medication, meditation, acupuncture, astrology, or massage. I thought I could use them too."

"What are you trying to heal?"

"The water. It is extremely sick. There is an evil presence at work killing the plants, fish, and birds. The people who drink the water downstream from this place are also sick as well as the animals. Many have died. My uncle tells me I can no longer harvest the plants from this place."

"And the amethyst stone?"

"It is the energy center, the great talisman that binds it all together."

April considered this information, "I know for a fact, the cyanide used to extract the gold from the ore high on the mountain is highly toxic along with the tailings dumped into the creek. It poisons everything it encounters." She pursed her lips, "Your spells will work, but not for another seventy years. Whitewood Creek won't receive attention until the year 1983 when the federal government will order the Homestake Mining Company to clean up the toxins to protect the environment. Even then, it will take over a decade before things begin to grow and live along the creek." Rumbles of thunder echoed off the valley walls and lightning danced across the tops of the western mountains announcing the eminent storm. Panic caught in April's throat, "I must hurry."

Breaking into a full out run, April and Li raced along the spur to the base of the mountain below WASP mine number two. April was surprised how well Li was able to match her pace with the restrictive clothing and delicate footwear. The path was a minefield of rocks, fallen trees and other debris and she was grateful for her athletic shoes, while Li bound over the obstacles gracefully as a deer. They'd reached their destination to find the amethyst still glowing as it had in the previous storm. The pieces of parchment paper whipped in the wind like a tailless kite caught in a storm. April proceeded forward, surprised when her shoes sunk just below her ankle bone in water. The creek was higher too, something she hadn't noticed before. "That's strange," she said aloud, trudging across the grassy area, her tennis shoes squished as she walked closer to the stone.

Li kept her distance, calling out from drier ground, "be careful."

Fat droplets began hitting the ground, first a few, then in greater numbers. The sky was completely black now over the west mountain. Removing the rain slicker, April stepped closer to Li and tossed it to her, "Take this. I won't need this where I'm going."

Li's expression was one of concern, "What are you planning to do?"

"I'm going to place my hands on the stone and see what happens."

She was about to move away when Li touched her hand, "good luck."

There was a feeling of static electricity where Li's hand rest in Aprils. Not like the shock one received from friction when they touched an object, but a welcoming sensation, like a boost of energy. "Best you get back home. Your father will worry. Please thank him for finding me. And thank you for helping me find by way back home."

"What the hell are you doing?" an angry male voice shouted.

April and Li turned, stunned to see Li's father atop a brown horse riding toward them. A thunderous boom like and explosion rocked the valley walls as quarried tailings and ore created an avalanche on the eastern slope. Frightened, the animal suddenly reared on its hind legs throwing Li's father to the ground. Wasting no time, the horse bolted away. Li cried, "Father, are you alright?"

Li's father popped to his feet undeterred by the incident. Cursing, he'd pulled his fedora low over his eyes hiding his expression, but his body language said it all. He was a powerful man, both in physical stature and determination. To April, it felt as though he'd channeled the storm sending a bolt of lightning in her direction.

Her voice filled with dread, Li shouted, "Father, how did you find us?"

"Never mind that," Li's father said vehemently. "We have to leave this place, now."

April whispered to Li, "Goodbye," and she hurried toward the glowing geode.

"Get out of the water," the man shouted angrily, "If lightning strikes, you'll be electrocuted."

The clouds began swirling into a familiar pattern. Within seconds, the great black dragon appeared. April heard the man arguing with Li, urging her to stay put as he rushed toward her. *How will this work*, she wondered? *Will father and daughter be swept up in the dragon's wings if they get too close or be electrocuted?* Unwilling to find out, April urged, "Stay back. I know what I'm doing." She had no idea what she was doing, all she knew was that she had to get home.

A flash of lightning danced through the valley like a high-speed rail as April reached the stone. Placing her hands on either side, she watched, helpless as her two companions fearlessly stepped onto the marshy soil. In an instant, everything went dark.

5

HANK

HANK REFRAINED FROM DONNING THE WAISTCOAT DRAPED over the back of the chair, before heading out for the day. Primarily, because the warm weather didn't require it. Second, he couldn't abide the peculiar glances women gave him as he walked down the street. Embolden, they often asked, "Are you dressed in character?" The notion of a railroad man being involved in a vaudeville production was absurd. Though, Li harped on him excessively about the need to update his wardrobe. It wasn't a priority.

Taking a seat at his favorite corner table, he read the paper at his leisure, drinking his coffee. He liked the hot beverage, a far more satisfying choice than the tea his daughter insisted on drinking. He had to remind himself he hadn't been subjugated to the higher purpose of tea steeped in Li's culture. For him, he just needed something to get him going in the morning, not a ceremonious ritual. He looked at the checkout counter, the woman operating the expresso machine glanced up from her work and smiled. *It was divine providence, the yardmaster spied Li and April as they made their way toward the old gold mine.*

Since he and Li's arrival, April had shown them nothing but kindness and respect, particularly in their moments of terror and confusion, easing their way into the twenty-first century. It was horrific for April to wake up in a time to which she didn't belong. He understood that experience first-hand. And yet, whether the past or future, there was an innate fascination exploring an era one could only envision, creating an alluring call to adventure.

Glancing over at his daughter while she checked out a customer, he could see she was in her element. Service with a smile, and finding purpose in her task, Li had enjoyed the freedom she would have never experienced in their Deadwood. *What would have been her fate*, he wondered? Her extended family denied reentry into America, the foundation of the Wing Tsue building all that remained, her Chinatown no longer existed. The burst of cold coming from the air conditioning had nothing to do with the shiver running down his spine.

His two women bonded, spending their days traipsing up and town mountains and valley's searching for plants and herbs, to dry or brew, distilling tinctures and creating ointments and salves to sell at April's coffee and gift shop. His heart swelled with a certain pride watching his daughter interact with the people interested in her products. She'd found her calling and it made him appreciate the woman even more. April took the chair across from him. "I see your enjoying your morning routine."

April had been instrumental in helping him find purpose in this new world as well. His intimate knowledge of the Chicago, Burlington, Quincy railroad proved to be an invaluable resource, landing him work at the train museum where he held lectures at his leisure and served as a tour guide on the 1880 excursions. Taking his hand in hers, April said, "It's such a lovely day, what do you say we all go for a bike ride this afternoon."

Cycling. It had taken him more than a beat learning to ride a bike. April was a proficient rider, and she kicked his butt, climbing the steep mountain trail. Even Li surpassed his ability. There was no denying it was the best way of getting into remote places without long arduous hiking or riding on horseback. Nonetheless, it was a minor blow to his ego. Still, he enjoyed spending the day biking along the once vital railroad line between Edgemont and Deadwood. It was—relaxing, and contemplative. At times, his heart took on a certain melancholy, a yearning for the past and familiar. It was fleeting. This was his life now, this present, this leap into the future. Powered by a supernatural stone, a train crash, and an unexpected storm, he'd stopped wondering how or why a blue dog and a black dragon had been brought together. It must have been clandestine, a mystery only the almighty or the Eastern mystics could explain. His obligation now was the welfare of his only child, a blossoming relationship with this woman from the future and simply enjoy the moment.

Hank returned April's pro-offered gesture, "That sounds good."

ABOUT THE AUTHOR

A career nurse for over 40 years, Julien Bradley has heard many stories worthy of sharing. From patients and families to co-workers alike, these stories are inspiring, poignant, hopeful, and most importantly, relatable. A product of her midwestern roots, Julien aspires to capture the essence of the heartland in both setting and characters, leading readers on a road trip paired with a trusted driver heading toward new and familiar places with a renewed excitement.

Researching a topic is a trip down the rabbit hole for Julien, plunging feet first and not resurfacing for days. Just ask her family. Immersed in weaving fact into a work of fiction is a delicate process, one which brings boundless joy to this author. Incorporating real time events into fictional contemporary romance with a flair for family drama, she hopes to spark an interest in her readers in subjects near and dear to her heart and inform as well as entertain.

Encouraged to put pen to paper, Julien's greatest influence in becoming a writer/published author was initiated by her daughter, a published independent author in her own right. Unlike her daughter who had been writing stories since early grade school, however, Julien began her journey later in life and touches on the experiences of those with a little silver around the temples.

Julien has self-published three novels in the *Bakken* series, Beneath the Bedrock, Between Fracture Lines, and Beyond the Bust and two series companions, The Steel Town Orphan and the Ranch Hand, and the Blue Skirt Maverick and the Fly Boy. Her next WIP is entitled Muriel Way, a mother-daughter story about following one's passion, the vulnerability of aging, mending broken relationships, and finding hope and peace with our limitations. Don't worry, a bit of spicy romance will be added for good measure.

Fun Facts:

- Favorite children's story: Millions of Cats by Wanda Gag. She's read this story in each of her children's second grade classes.
- Her hobbies and life interests include hiking, biking, camping, reading, writing, gardening, and spending as much time with family as possible.
- She is an avid animal lover, among her favorites are Beagles, Australian Shepherds, and orange tabby cats.
- She found her dream job in the senior years of her career as a holistic nurse working for an

integrative health clinic for the past 10 years. She thoroughly believes in food as medicine.

- Her family's favorite vacation spot of all time, the Black Hills of South Dakota.
- Authors she reads most: William Kent Krueger, Sylvia Day, John Sanford, Nevada Barr, J.D. Robb.
- Favorite book of all time: Ordinary Grace by William Kent Krueger. Second: Freedom by John Franzen.

Website: https://www.julienbradley.com

GUNSLINGERS AND HEARTSTRINGS

CICI CORDELIA

1

Northwest Nebraska - October, 1875

Dewey Bower's breaths came in short, ragged bursts as he rode hard alongside the members of the Red River Drifters, led by Clayton Harrow. The thunder of hooves echoing against the hard-packed earth mingled with the jingle of spurs and creak of saddle leather. Dark clouds cast shadows across the wide prairie, the breeze carrying the scent of damp earth and dying sagebrush.

A feeling of dread tightened his muscles as they approached the lower valley where a scattering of small homesteads had been erected over the past year. Buffalo grazed freely on the plains, huge beasts whose hides and meat were vital to these settlers struggling to improve and farm their land as they eked out a life here.

Unfortunately, Clay and his buffalo hunters had claimed the valley and its bounty for themselves. Four months of riding with the gang had soured Dewey's initial eagerness to join Clay's Drifters. Dewey had craved adventure, but with increasing dismay and disgust, he'd observed how the riders indiscriminately took down the massive creatures, only to leave the meat to rot. Most times they took the hides, but far too often it was just for the thrill of the hunt. It sickened him.

Now the Drifters headed for the front of a rough-hewn cabin where Clay had heard the family living there killed a buffalo or two that'd roamed onto their land. As they cantered around the side of the cabin, the evidence was plain to see: a hide, stretched on a rudimentary rack, almost fully cured.

Clay brought his horse to a hard half-turn. "Follow my lead, boys," he rasped. "I'm makin' an example of this sumbitch." He dismounted and stomped toward the door.

It burst open and a man wearing tattered dungarees ran out, barefoot, clutching a rifle in big, rawboned hands. "I done tol' you—Oh, damn." He came to an abrupt stop. "Mister—Mister Harrow, sir." His Adam's apple worked as he took in the mounted men surrounding the small cabin. Slowly, he lowered the rifle and laid it on the uneven ground.

Clay set his shooting hand on his holster. "Rawling. You been poachin', I hear." He tapped his pistol. "Know what happens to poachers?"

When Rawling tried to back up toward the half open door, it swung wider and a tow-haired boy slipped out, also barefoot, and wearing nothing but a pair of dingy smalls. "Paw?" He ventured closer to the edge of the narrow porch, shivering in the chilly air.

Even from yards away, Dewey could see how the youngster's ribs stuck out. By the size of the cured hide, the buffalo his father had killed wasn't very big. Dewey'd also wager the meat had been split between neighboring families. It was the way of these settlers, to share anything they had with those less fortunate.

"Go inside, son," Rawling urged, never taking his eyes from Clay.

A figure draped in faded blue suddenly appeared in the doorway, and Dewey shifted uneasily in the saddle as a young woman grabbed the boy, her other arm supporting a belly heavy with child. "Ben, come with me." The fright evident on her face was in stark contrast to her calm demeanor.

Clay's laughter mixed with a few other chuckles as some members of his gang eyed the woman and child. "You got yourself a nice family," he commented to Rawling who had edged to his wife's side and tucked her and the boy behind him. When he attempted to push them inside the cabin, Clay drew his pistol and aimed it. "Naw, let 'em see what happens when folks steal from me."

A cold shiver raced down Dewey's spine. When had these buffalo hunters changed their purpose to terrorizing innocent, God-fearing folk, threatening them?

It wasn't right, wasn't what he'd signed on for. It gnawed at his conscience.

Like a young fool, he'd believed Clay's vow that the gang hunted the herd for meat, with the hides a bonus livelihood. When they'd left a carcass behind, Dewey assumed local plains dwellers would benefit. He'd soon learned otherwise. The Drifters didn't share, nor did they help others who needed the meat for food and the hides for warmth. Led by Clay, they'd soon become more of an outlaw gang that reveled in buffalo slaughter.

The terrified faces before him served as a harsh mirror reflecting the desperados they'd become. His stomach churned with the realization.

I can't live this way a second longer.

Dewey spurred his horse forward, kicked-up dust stinging his eyes as he positioned himself between his boss's gun and the family trembling on the porch of their cabin.

Clay's eyes narrowed dangerously. "What the hell, Bower?" he ground out. "Move aside, this ain't your business."

Dewey pulled his own gun from its holster. "These folks are defenseless, Clay." He nodded toward the hide. "Look at it. A small adult male, I'd say. Not enough to feed hungry mouths for very long."

Clay sneered, "So what? They stole from me." His frown darkened. "You gone soft?"

The air grew thick with tension, a standoff that stretched on amid a child's whimpers and his mother's attempt to quiet him.

When other cabin doors started opening, Dewey figured things could get real dangerous, real fast. "Look, boss," he reasoned, "they ain't done you wrong. Shot a buffalo, is all. Just one, as far as I can see."

He gestured with his free hand, pointing out several other settlers who had begun sidling around the corners of lean-tos and poorly constructed sheds. Men who watched with caution, with fear–and holding weapons. Knives, rifles, even a pitchfork. "More'n blood makes a family out here. You want to go against that many kinfolk?"

His words echoed through the stillness, the truth of them resounding with a few of the gang members who shifted uneasily in their saddles.

One of them muttered, "We ain't murderers."

Another agreed with a terse, "Let it go, Clay."

The biggest member, a shaggy, unkempt hunter who called himself Mountain, took up the reins as the massive stallion beneath his bulk snorted and danced. "I ain't stickin' around when they's hides t' collect." He turned toward the trail leading into the hills, galloping hooves breaking into the standoff stretching on for what felt like an eternity.

Finally Clay, with a venomous snarl, begrudgingly lowered his gun. The air seemed to breathe again, though the settlers' rifles and makeshift weapons never faltered.

Yet, amidst the fragile peace, Clay's ugly glare was a silent vow of retribution. "Let's go," he growled, swinging into the saddle and kicking his horse to spur it forward.

Silence reigned as they rode toward the hills, Mountain and his stallion a dark blot in the distance. Every strike of hooves against rough ground and pebbles sounded like a death knell to the bond these men once shared. Dewey knew he'd just severed ties with the Red River Drifters.

If the rest breaks away, Clay'll blame me.

He'd just made a dangerous enemy, though it didn't matter; he was done. It was time to move on.

2

Late May, 1876, five miles outside Cheyenne, Wyoming Territory

Frederick Hayes gazed across the wide expanse of the prairie. In his pocket was a pouch containing the balance remaining from a cattle sale he'd finalized a mere week ago. Half had gone toward a Schuttler covered wagon; the rest he'd secure in a bank, once he and his daughter reached their destination.

They'd packed carefully, following the Utter Brothers' instructions on what provisions to bring for the one-and-a-half-month wagon train journey from Cheyenne to Deadwood.

"Where the gold is," Frederick whispered to himself.

He glanced at Melanie who sat by his side in the high wagon, alight with anticipation. Pride burst in his chest. His only child, motherless from the tender age of thirteen, had grown into a spirited and intelligent young woman.

After his beloved wife, Beatrice, passed away, he'd done his best by their daughter, building a comfortable life on their modest ranch, raising beef cattle. He'd never thought to leave Cheyenne for greener pastures, always assuming Melanie would marry someday and begin a family of her own. Wyoming would one day become a state, and all they needed would be within their reach.

Then came the wagon train, bound for the gold mining country. Organized by Charlie Utter, financed by both him and his brother Steve, the train originated out of Georgetown, in Colorado Territory, and would stop in Cheyenne for a week, gaining more travelers and stocking up on extra provisions. With good news of gold in the Black Hills, the Utters assured all who listened that mining the bountiful vein would make folks rich.

Frederick was one who listened. With the sale of his cattle and land, his nest egg was quite bountiful. If gold mining didn't prove profitable, he would build a new ranch, bigger and better.

"Father." Melanie's soft voice broke into his whirling thoughts, and he turned to smile at his precious girl. In her green dress and dark cloak, a felted porkpie hat perched on her raven plaits, she made his heart swell with love.

He patted her hand as it rested on his arm. "Any regrets on leaving for the unknown?"

"Not a single regret." The wave of her hand encompassed the prairie and far away hills, her expression bright with excitement. "Just look at it. What an adventure we will have!"

Frederick smiled fondly. "I believe you have wanderlust in your veins, Melanie. Others your age might balk at attempting such a trek."

"Pssh," she retorted, her dimples appearing in a wide grin. "Never back down from a challenge. Isn't that what Mother always said?" Her mirth faded as sadness shadowed her blue eyes. "She would approve, Father. Onward, ho! 'Tis my new battle cry."

"That's my girl," he replied approvingly, her positive attitude helping to banish the last remnants of guilt he'd experienced in pulling her away from their settled lives.

The familiar landscapes of Wyoming soon gave way to the uncharted horizon. Their wagon followed fourteen others, with sixteen more behind them. Like sentinels of hope, the sturdy covered wagons rolled along over rough ground and brush, most pulled by teams of horses, several others with lumbering oxen.

Gamblers, prospectors, and other fortune-seekers manned the wagons. Spying a few 'ladies' of questionable repute sharing space with some of those gamblers, Frederick found himself unsurprised. Whatever awaited them in Deadwood Gulch, he reckoned additional female company would come in handy.

Each person on this journey carried a story and a dream—

A dream of Gold Fever.

————

That evening, the wagons converged in clusters, four or more to a group. The Utters explained this to be a safety measure, as the surrounding wilderness held its share of dangers.

Frederick had halted beside a gaudy painted wagon owned by a rather flamboyant couple who had traveled from Georgetown and knew the Utter brothers well. On the grayer side of fifty, Lester and Lil Hamilton possessed as bad a case of gold fever as anyone Frederick had met so far.

"You'll take heed, Mister Hayes. I'd bet there'll be scoundrels afoot in those golden hills," Lester avowed, his silver hair blowing in the breeze.

Beside him, the plump Lil repeated, "Scoundrels, to be sure."

Frederick politely tipped his hat to her. "Yes, ma'am. I shall be as careful as possible."

Melanie smiled at the Hamiltons. "Father taught me how to shoot. He says I'm a dead-eye." She patted a pocket in her cape.

"Land sakes, missy! You've been carrying a loaded gun in that blanket you're wearing?" Lester exclaimed, while Lil looked suitably impressed.

"Well, it wouldn't do me much good if it were not loaded," Melanie reasoned. "But no, I left it in the wagon." She rose from the nest she'd made of her cape. "I should keep it with me. In case of scoundrels."

Before Frederick could stop her, she darted toward the rear of their wagon. Fondly, he commented, "Ever the vigilant one—"

Her sudden holler of, "Unhand my bag, you lout," had him up on his feet and running.

Rounding the corner of the wagon, Frederick gasped at the sight of his daughter trying to wrestle one of their carpet bags from a straggly-haired man. Even from a distance the thief's smell proved ghastly.

"Here, now," Frederick shouted, hurrying to her side. "Let go of that!" He got hold of the man's shoulder and tugged.

Suddenly there was a pistol in Frederick's face and a growling, "I reckon I'll take the gal and her bag," in his ear, as the thief attempted to back away with Melanie still clinging to the handle.

Unarmed and fearful of antagonizing the man holding a gun near his daughter's head, Frederick could do nothing but watch and shout for help as the thief dragged Melanie off into the deepening night gloom, her cries of anger growing louder.

Suddenly, a single shot rang out, and the miscreant dropped to the ground, releasing his grip on Melanie and writhing in pain as he clutched his leg.

Stunned, Frederick ran forward and caught her up in his arms. "Dear child, are you hurt?"

"Only my pride," she retorted, leaning against his chest. "I'll not leave my gun in the wagon again. Not in this rough company."

"A smart sentiment, young lady." The gravelly voice came from behind them.

Frederick and Melanie turned to see a tall, slender man in a set of worn buckskins. A dusty flat-brimmed hat covered his shoulder-length wavy hair, and his drooping mustache bracketed a wide, unsmiling mouth. In one hand he held a deadly-looking Smith & Wesson pistol.

Shrewd eyes narrowed on first Melanie, then Frederick. "You know," he stated as he holstered his gun, "that's the first time in a hell of a lot of Sundays I've had to shoot anyone." He tapped his temple with a long, callused finger. "Bad eyesight."

Gently setting Melanie aside, Frederick came forward, his hand outstretched. "Sir, you saved my daughter's life. I am in your debt. Frederick Hayes, from Cheyenne, at your service."

The stranger shook hands. "James Hickok. From just about all over the West." He nodded toward Melanie. "Glad to see you are unharmed."

She studied him closely. "Hickok? Your name rings a bell. In fact, I have read it in the paper."

"I suppose you have. And you can call me Bill," he replied. As her eyes widened and Frederick stared in recognition, Hickok gave a lopsided smile half hidden under his thick mustache. "Or Wild Bill, if you prefer."

"Mister—er, Wild Bill—would you join our campfire and share a meal with us? My daughter made trail beans and soda biscuits. There's plenty extra," Frederick offered.

"Two of my favorite things," the famed gunslinger and retired lawman answered, removing his hat and slapping the dust from the brim. "I'd be right proud to partake, soon as I dispose of this troublemaker." He prodded the wounded thief, who groaned and cursed weakly. "One of the prospectors, likely. Utters will send him packing. No room for this kind of lowlife in their wagon train."

Once the thief had been dealt with and the Hamiltons retired for the night, Frederick led their guest to the campfire he'd set earlier in the evening. While Melanie dished up their supper, he produced three tin cups. "Coffee, if that's all right with you. Melanie probably wouldn't object if I add a splash of whiskey to it," he said, winking at his daughter.

She laughed and held out the coffee pot, using her apron to protect her hand as she poured a measure of the steaming brew into the cups. "After my little, um, adventure," she stated, nodding toward the wagon, "I might just join you fellows."

They enjoyed the simple yet filling meal and warmed their bellies with the whiskey-laced coffee. Frederick found Hickok's tales of travel and tribulations vastly entertaining, though he could recognize the danger behind such a life. The man had been shot, thrown in jail, attacked and severely wounded by a bear, and came close to dying more times than even he could count. While Frederick had little doubt Wild Bill liked to exaggerate some–the way adventurous types were wont to do–he recognized the ring of truth, and knew he'd enjoy the man's company on the long haul to Deadwood.

Melanie excused herself for the night, brushing a kiss across Frederick's cheek. Others settled in their wagons, here and there raucous chatter and the occasional bark of laughter vying with the nickering horses and lowing oxen.

Frederick reached into his vest for a cigar, offering one to Wild Bill. They smoked at leisure, the conversation circling to Frederick's desire for land.

Hickok blew out a smoke ring. "You might want to speak to the Utters," he suggested. "They know where to stake out and purchase clear land."

"Clear land?"

"Yes, cleared of tribal possession," he clarified, nodding toward the dark horizon. "Closer to the Black Hills and Deadwood Gulch, I'd say. If you still plan on mining, the Gulch area might be your best prospect. Tomorrow you can ask 'em. I'm sharing their wagon. Be glad to drive the team while you boys have a chat."

3

Mid-July, 1876, Deadwood, Dakota Territory

Melanie waited for her father to finish securing their wagon, sighing when she spied the dust coating her boots. Stomping her feet knocked off the worst of it.

Their arrival in Deadwood five days earlier had been a blend of nervous anticipation and excitement for what new adventures lay ahead. The town, buzzing with the clamor of construction and the boisterous energy typical of a gold rush, contrasted sharply with the serene atmosphere of their previous home in Cheyenne.

They'd purchased several mining implements for extracting minerals and would soon venture to the Gulch camp right outside of town. For now, they settled some of their wagon belongings in a room her father had rented in the only operating hotel, a small, one-story establishment nearby other hastily erected shanties and thick canvas tents.

She'd been grateful for the two narrow, yet surprisingly comfortable pallets set against thin opposite walls. A tin basin and water pitcher took up space on a crude table. A single window, covered with oiled canvas, lent scant light into the room. Mister Linden, the owner, promised the future addition of real glass. In the meantime, he had provided plenty of tallow candles.

Across from the hotel was a saloon owned by a gent named Billy Nuttal. Realizing his patrons also needed food, Nuttal offered items such as pickled eggs and dried buffalo backstrap alongside his whiskey. After a few meals there, Melanie had found the eggs more to her liking.

Her father soon joined her. "All buttoned down tightly," he said, retrieving his pocketwatch from his vest to note the time. "We're to meet a young fellow by the name of Bower. Mister Utter, as well as Nuttal, assured me of his qualifications as a carpenter."

"Are you thinking of hiring him to expand the cabin?" she queried. Two days ago, her father had signed for ten acres of land a few miles outside of Deadwood, mostly pasture with the added bonus of a small building. "Would he build our barn as well?"

"I believe it could be satisfactorily arranged," he replied, and crooked an arm. "Shall we, my girl?"

She clasped his elbow. "We shall, indeed."

———

Dewey leaned against the rickety wall of Nuttal's #10 Saloon as he waited for Frederick Hayes, one of the Utter Brothers' wagon train people. The man was in need of employing someone for an expansion of his newly acquired ranch. According to Nuttal, Hayes and his daughter had bought ten acres and a dilapidated cabin.

At least there'll be something to work with.

In the three months since he'd arrived in the Gulch area, he'd staked a claim, done a bit of gold panning, and found enough nuggets to rent a small room in the hotel across the street. At the time it'd been more of a shanty than a hotel, but an offer to help reinforce the lopsided building had provided Dewey with additional work as a carpenter. Word grew in Deadwood and soon he had people willing to hire him to fix what they'd started. Once the sawmill established itself, others joined the carpentry business, but there was plenty of work to go around.

Casting a glance in the direction of the open area where the wagon train had settled, Dewey spotted a stout fellow approaching, sporting a thick mustache and wool felted Homburg hat. This must be Hayes, for on his arm he guided a young woman, presumably his daughter, over the ruts in the road.

The young woman flung back her head and laughed at something her father said, causing her flat-brimmed hat to slip off and hang by its ribbons, revealing silky black hair bound in a single plait that fell over the bodice of her white shirtwaist.

Dewey straightened, a flutter of excitement—a feeling long forgotten —thrumming in his chest. The dirty, half-wild streets of Deadwood saw very few women, and those they did were of questionable nature. But even wearing the plainest of clothing, this sweet-faced miss was a breath of the freshest air.

"Mister Bower?" The gruff inquiry snared Dewey's attention. "I'm Frederick Hayes, and this is my daughter, Melanie."

Stepping away from the saloon wall, Dewey extended a firm hand-shake to Hayes. "Pleasure to meet you." His gaze shifted, settling on Melanie, intrigued by her unwavering stare, unusual for a gently reared female.

He tipped his hat with a murmured, "Miss Hayes," before refocusing on her father. "I understand you're looking to build on ranch acreage you recently purchased."

"That's correct," Hayes confirmed. "We bought ten acres with the promise of a fair price for whatever future land we might want. What we have thus far contains flat pasture. Eventually we will need a barn, but for now our horses require shade from the sun. There's a small cabin, only two rooms, and we'd like to add a few more, make it into something sturdy that can stand up to whatever this region might throw at us."

"Dakota Territory can be a demanding mistress," Dewey admitted. "But she's fair to those who understand her ways."

Miss Hayes stepped forward, her voice steady and sure. "We're prepared to meet her challenges."

Dewey had to admire her spirit. His lips curved into a warm smile. To her father he said, "Let me know when you've secured your supplies. Talk to Mister Linden about wood and nails. He might be able to get what we'll need, and at a fair price." He paused, curiosity getting the better of him. These folks had traveled with Utter's wagon train, after all. Upon seeing Deadwood and the stark realities of the mining camps, had they decided against digging for gold?

"Sir," he began frankly, "I know you came in with the Utter group. It may seem bold of me to ask, but are you still planning on mining in one of the camps?"

Hayes released a heavy sigh. "To be honest, I ponder the wisdom of subjecting my daughter to that rough life—"

"Father," Miss Hayes interjected, clearly irritated, "I am perfectly capable of dealing with 'that rough life,' as you put it. I consider myself quite plucky, in fact."

Dewey let his gaze wander over the lovely young woman, from the top of her raven hair to the tips of her dainty boots. Slender yet shapely, tall for a woman, she would still fit nicely under a man's chin. Innocence as well as intelligence shone from her wide blue eyes.

Indelicate as it might seem, he felt compelled to ask, "Can you shoot a gun, Miss?"

Her rosy lips curved in a smile. "I can, sir. With unerring accuracy." She patted her pocket. "Would you care for a demonstration?"

Now it was her father's turn to protest, "Melanie!"

A gentle laugh was her response as she took her father's arm and gave it a squeeze. "I can look after myself, you know."

"Heaven help me, I do know." Hayes turned to Dewey, who'd struggled to contain his amusement at their banter. "Bower, by any chance are you a miner?"

"I am, but it's been weeks since I visited the camps. Work in town has kept me very busy."

"Would you be willing to join us on our first panning attempt? Having someone of experience along would surely be appreciated."

"I'd be glad to serve as your guide," Dewey replied, managing—barely —to hold in his anticipation of spending more time in Melanie Hayes' company.

"Excellent!" Hayes took her elbow. "Is tomorrow too soon?"

"Not at all, sir." As Dewey watched Frederick Hayes and his daughter depart, excitement suffused him for the chance to return to mining combined with the challenge of showcasing his woodworking talents.

"I'll work hard," he promised himself. Standing taller, he vowed to make his mark in Deadwood and put his past transgressions behind him.

4

THE NEXT MORNING, MELANIE EXITED THE HOTEL, STEPPING carefully over the uneven porch planks. Repositioning her hat to stave off the bright sunlight, she breathed in deeply, then coughed out air tainted with a mixture of horse manure and dust. Still, being outside was preferable to the closed-in feeling of the room she and her father shared.

She took in the bustle of her surroundings, how men shouted, horses neighed, and hammers pounded as more structures were erected, some little more than heavy canvas supported by split logs. The town would grow quickly from its rudimentary roots. In another year, barring the gold veins drying up, Deadwood might be quite the modern spectacle.

A clink of spurs caught her attention and she smiled to see Dewey Bower striding toward her. Over his shoulder he carried the sort of canvas bag that she had seen other miners toting on their backs, similar to what she and her father had also purchased.

The morning sun had already dampened his shirt with perspiration. Muscles rippled across his chest and down his sinewy arms. He cut such a manly figure, Melanie found herself unabashedly staring.

When she finally dragged her gaze away and met his twinkling brown eyes, her entire face burned in a flush. Still, she had never been the retiring sort and was far from a tittering maiden. Her chin lifted. "Good morning, Mister Bower." Her steady tone belied the mad flutter in her heart. "You are quite punctual."

He tipped his hat to her. "Morning, Miss Hayes. Please, call me Dewey." He patted the bag. "I took the liberty of purchasing some of Nuttal's eggs. In case you and your father get hungry."

"No backstrap?" At his sudden expression of distaste, she laughed. "Ah, not so fond of buffalo, are you? Well, I join you in that sentiment. I also thought to pack a few items. And you may call me Melanie." She was enjoying this chance to chat with the handsome carpenter.

"Thank you . . . Melanie. I must say you're smart to wear trousers instead of a skirt," he commented, glancing approvingly at her attire of pants and one of her father's old work shirts. "But you might want to tuck your hair up under your hat. Where we're going, it's best to look more like a lad than a lady."

"Ah, I see." Removing her hat, she coiled her plaits over the crown of her head and arranged the wide brim to shade her face. "Better?"

"Oh, yes." His low reply sent a pleasurable shiver up her back.

Just then her father stepped off the porch and joined them. "Bower, good morning. I admire a punctual man."

"As I do." Dewey shook the hand he extended. "It's about five miles to Gulch Camp. Some of the miners walk the trail, but we can go by wagon." He gestured toward a stable further down the rutted street. "There's one I'm allowed to borrow, plus a draft horse to pull it."

"Very much appreciated," Melanie said, impressed at how he'd thought ahead.

———

They neared the south edge of the mining camp, where the churned-up mud near Deadwood Creek had hardened in the heat. Dewey brought the horse and wagon to a halt a few yards away from one of the roped off areas where miners hitched their horses and stowed wagons. At one end an awning made of ropes and canvas sat nearly empty, indicating most of the miners working today had walked in or camped here all night.

He ground-tied the horse under the awning, then collected the bags, handing one to Frederick and slinging his and Melanie's over his shoulder.

"I can carry my own," she protested, trying to take it from him.

Dewey adroitly avoided her attempt. "You'll be too busy watching your step." At her questioning look, he pointed to the ground. "Holes everywhere. Some are big enough to swallow you whole," he teased.

"Oh, my." Careful to walk with care, she didn't protest further. He kept an eye on her feet, making sure she stepped carefully. When he glanced up, he caught Frederick's approving nod.

Hoping for the best, Dewey led Melanie and her father to his creek claim site, glad to see it undisturbed. Granted, it was a small claim, but anyone could have taken it over. He hadn't meant to abandon it.

"This is my original claim," he said, setting down his and Melanie's bags. "I thought it might be best if you get a feel for mining here. Then if you want to stake a claim for your own, the office at this camp can get you settled. The straw boss is fair and honest."

Surprisingly, only a handful of men worked their sites today, but for that Dewey was relieved especially when a few miners they encountered eyed Melanie as if they'd figured that she wasn't a lad after all. In all fairness he understood their attention, for the trousers and shirt she wore enhanced her delicate femininity instead of detracting from it.

Dewey's glower in their direction, coupled with his hand on his holster, was enough of a discouragement to make them mind their own business.

For several hours they remained at the creek, Dewey demonstrating how to sift through water and silt. Gold panning was a slow, methodical chore, yet there was no denying the satisfaction of unearthing nuggets, no matter how small.

"I found something," Melanie exclaimed, prodding a chunk of what appeared to be a slimy pebble. She swished it in some clean water, examining it closely. When she held it up and sunlight hit it, Dewey saw the yellowish sparkle.

He moved to her side and peered into her palm. It was indeed a gold nugget. "Looks like you struck a vein, Miss Melanie," he commented, finding her excitement contagious.

Frederick had also crouched next to her. "Let's see that treasure of yours."

She handed it to him, watching as he turned it between his fingers. "Could it be fool's gold?" she asked. "I have read about miners finding such a thing."

Dewey shook his head decisively. "No, not here. The gold found thus far in the Black Hills has been verified and registered. It's one of the straw boss's duties."

Her success had fueled his own fever, and he eagerly resumed his position at the creek. "Ready to find more?" he asked, dipping his pan into the water.

Having retrieved her nugget from her father, Melanie tucked it into her pocket. Her smile threatened to outshine the sun. "Most assuredly!"

5

"ANOTHER HOT DAY," MELANIE COMMENTED TO HER FATHER as she used her hat to fan her face. "I am glad we didn't choose to pan gold again." She fumbled for the handkerchief she kept tucked in the watch pocket of her skirt and blotted the back of her neck.

Yesterday's mining attempts had yielded two more nuggets, both found by her father. His whoop of delight had echoed over Deadwood Creek. A quick meal of pickled eggs, paired with the soda biscuits and huckleberry jam left over from their wagon train days, had been an enjoyable affair, fueling them for another hour of panning before they'd given up and traveled back to town.

They had plans to meet with Dewey at Nuttal's and discuss the additions to the cabin as well as the new barn and stable. Knowing she would soon see him again sent so many nerves tumbling inside her, Melanie had to force herself not to clutch her stomach like a girlish ninny.

Feigning a calm front, she took her father's arm as they crossed the street and entered the saloon.

Nuttal's was—as usual—noisy and filled with the sounds of clinking tin dishes and hearty laughter. Dewey was already there, seated at Wild Bill's table and engaged in a quiet conversation with the legendary gunslinger. At her entrance, he jumped up with a wide smile and pulled out a chair, seating her carefully before greeting her father.

Wild Bill inclined his head politely. "Good to see you, Frederick, Miss Hayes. I hear you dipped your toe in Deadwood Creek and panned a few nuggets."

"We have, sir," her father affirmed. "And I see you have met young Bower. He's a solid, hardworking sort."

While Dewey flushed at such praise, Hickok regarded him thoughtfully. "I have heard good things about you, Bower. Been watching you around town. You've got a keen eye and a steady hand. Ever thought about law enforcement?"

Visibly surprised, Dewey pondered the question before meeting the older man's eyes squarely. "I can't say it hasn't crossed my mind. With all that's going on in Deadwood, a man could make a difference."

Wild Bill nodded. "How about I show you some of the ropes? Someone of your capabilities could be invaluable in keeping the peace around here."

Melanie's father turned to Dewey with obvious approval. "That's a fine offer. You'd do well to learn from one of the best."

"I agree." Dewey accepted the hand Wild Bill held out and gave it a firm shake. "Thank you, sir. I wouldn't think of refusing such a generous offer."

The retired lawman's grin softened his usually fierce demeanor. "My friends call me Bill."

6

DEWEY WIPED THE SWEAT FROM HIS BROW AS HE HAMMERED the last nail into the new addition. He stepped back to admire his handiwork, a sense of pride swelling in his chest. In barely a week—and with Frederick Hayes' help in raising the walls—he'd significantly enlarged the cramped, modest cabin.

With a bedroll and lantern waiting for him each night in the temporary, three-sided lean-to he'd erected in the clearing where the new barn would sit, Dewey hadn't needed to travel back and forth to town each night. Mister Linden had been kind enough to allow whatever time was needed in which to complete the work on the Hayes property.

Now the cabin boasted a new wing, making it into a more comfortable dwelling. Though crude on the inside, Frederick's assurance that he could finish the inner walls himself afforded Dewey the freedom to return to Deadwood and continue working for Mister Linden as well as starting an apprenticeship with Wild Bill.

As Dewey wiped the sweat from his brow, a familiar feminine voice called out, "Supper, if you're ready."

Turning, he saw Melanie emerging from the cabin. She carried a roughly woven basket, her steps light and graceful on the uneven ground.

Her father followed behind her, holding a few horse blankets to use as a place to sit.

"Evening," he greeted them, his voice echoing slightly in the open space.

Frederick clapped Dewey on the shoulder. "It's such a beautiful sunset, we thought we'd enjoy our meal outside."

Melanie set the basket down on an old stump doubling as a makeshift table. The mouthwatering fragrance of meat wafted out. "One of the miners gave us three hares in exchange for some of the quince preserves I brought from Georgetown." Her dimples flashed in the lowering light. "There's also corn cake and apple butter. I hope you're hungry."

Dewey couldn't hide his grin as his stomach rumbled. "I could eat."

Frederick spread out the blankets, one of which held tin plates and some forks. They served themselves, finding comfortable positions on the cushioned ground. The rustling of the wind through the trees provided a soothing backdrop, occasionally punctuated by the distant yip and lonely howl of a coyote.

Dewey paused mid-bite, tilting his head slightly at the coyote's call. "The wildlife seems to be speaking to each other tonight."

Melanie smiled, her pretty eyes reflecting the last rays of the setting sun. "I love to listen to them. It reminds me that we're just a small part of this world, sharing it with everything from the tiniest critters to the mightiest beasts."

Frederick gave an approving nod. "You've got the right of it, daughter."

The next few minutes passed in companionable silence as they enjoyed their meals against the backdrop of nature's best music.

With a final scrape of his fork, Frederick laid down his plate on the edge of the blanket. "Delicious as always, my girl." While Melanie blushed at the compliment, he turned his attention to Dewey. "Young man, how is the extension coming along?"

"Just finished up. Tomorrow, I'll start working on framing the barn." Dewey gestured with his fork. "Might need to rustle up a few men from town to help raise the trusses once they're built."

"You've accomplished so much in a short amount of time," Melanie commented as she collected their empty plates. She cast him a smile that lit up the world. "It's hard to believe it's the same place."

He met her gaze, warmth expanding in his chest. "Thank you, Melanie. It's been a good challenge."

As the sky further darkened, Frederick stood. "Well, I suppose we should call it a night. It's getting late."

Melanie nodded, helping to fold the blankets. "Yes, Father."

"I can't thank you enough for including me in your evening meals. It's a true kindness." Dewey addressed them both, though his eyes lingered on Melanie as he hefted the basket. "I can carry this for you," he added, gaining him another sweet smile.

And he realized the sense of camaraderie and belonging both Melanie and her father had afforded him made the harshness of life in Deadwood far less daunting.

Together they walked the short distance to the cabin, a lantern's glow spilling softly from the uncovered windows. "I heard it'll be a month or longer before any buildings around here will have actual glass," Frederick said, laying the horse blankets over the new hitching post. "Is there any oiled canvas left in town?"

"There is, sir," Dewey answered. "I'll fetch some tomorrow before I get started on the barn frame. Might not be enough for the add-on but I know how to make shutters. It'll help fill in those openings."

As they reached the cabin door, Melanie stopped and faced him. "Goodnight, Dewey," she murmured.

"Goodnight, Melanie." Dewey held out the basket. Their fingers brushed momentarily, a spark of connection in that brief touch. As she stepped across the threshold, the light from the cabin's interior outlined her silhouette.

Just before the door closed, Dewey caught Frederick's eye. The older man offered a knowing chuckle, a gleam of approval in his eyes, before he followed his daughter inside.

7

Gripping the newly installed newel post, Dewey gave it a firm shake, nodding in satisfaction at its sturdiness. Deadwood might be coming together in a hurry—out of necessity—but anything he built in this town would hold up. He'd make sure of it.

Stepping back, he surveyed the reinforced porch of the hotel. It'd taken two extra hands, local boys whose folks had been part of the Utter wagon train, but they'd been eager to learn and glad to help out for the coins Linden paid them. Dewey was grateful for the labor; it meant he could return to the Hayes ranch site a few days sooner and resume work on the barn.

And I'll get to see my darling Melanie.

He missed her something awful. Had it truly been less than a week since he'd walked in the summer moonlight with her? In one single unforgettable moment, their lips had met in a first tender kiss.

Days later he could still feel her mouth against his, sweet as ripe peaches and softer than a rose petal. She'd kissed him back, her arms linking around his neck when he'd pressed her close.

"Dewey," she'd sighed when they broke apart.

Just his name, that was all, yet the look in her eyes had told him everything he needed to know.

After several more impassioned kisses, he'd walked her back to the cabin, tucking her hand in his, guiding her carefully over the rough ground. At the half open door, he'd wished her goodnight with a tremble to his low voice, thrilled to hear the quiver of longing in her response. Retreating to the lean-to, he'd curled into his bedroll and dreamed of the day he'd ask Frederick for his daughter's hand.

Smiling at the memory, Dewey set aside his hammer. Another two days in town, and he would head back to the ranch site. With the extra wages he'd earned from the hotel reinforcement and other odd tasks, he could begin planning the sort of future Melanie deserved.

His contentment had grown with the three meetings he'd enjoyed with Wild Bill, soaking in the man's vast experience and ideals. Despite his dangerous past, Hickok had a reputation of being tough but fair when it came to upholding the law. Dewey found his mentorship fascinating and invaluable.

Craving a drink to ease his thirst, he headed across the rutted dirt street toward Nuttal's saloon.

Inside, the air was already stiflingly hot. A few men stood at the makeshift bar, sipping their whiskey from tin cups. Three of Nuttal's four rickety tables sat empty, the other occupied by a brisk game of poker. Dewey spotted Wild Bill, facing the door as was his habit, studying his cards, a thin cigar clamped between his teeth. Two of the men at his table were unknown to him, but the third was an unpleasant surprise.

"Jack McCall," Dewey muttered under his breath as he crossed the room to lean against the wall. Unobserved by the saloon's occupants, he studied the man who swayed in his seat even as he brought a half-empty bottle of whiskey to his thick lips and guzzled.

The last time Dewey'd seen McCall was in late May at the mining camp deep in Deadwood Gulch. Drunk, staggering around, picking fights, McCall had a reputation for stealing anything he could squirrel away without getting caught. He'd finally been chased off and told never to come back.

Dewey doubted anyone at the table, including Hickok, knew what level of rotten they were currently playing with. McCall would cheat for sure. The drunker he got, the meaner, not to mention dishonest as hell. Determined to inform Wild Bill, Dewey stepped forward just as McCall threw his cards to the floor and half-rose in his seat.

Even in the dim room Dewey could see the glaze of alcohol in the man's eyes.

"Bastards, all a' you," McCall snarled, leaning so heavily on the table, poker chips and empty cups slid across its scarred surface. "Cheatin' sumbitches—"

"Son, you're drunk," Wild Bill replied calmly. "Not the best time to be playin' poker, you understand." Reaching into his pocket, he withdrew a handful of coins and held them out. "Why don't you take this and get a bite to eat, soak up that whiskey? Maybe come back when you're sober, win back some of your losses."

Glaring at Wild Bill, McCall managed to fully gain his feet, ignoring the outstretched palm and its assortment of coins. "Go t' hell," he slurred, pushing back from the table and stumbling out the door.

Dewey strode over to the table. "I know that man, and he's a drunkard, a thief. As dangerous as they come."

Hickock frowned. "I figured as much. He drained two bottles of Nuttal's best, right here at the table. If he can ride without falling over, I expect he'll leave town and not come back. Troublemakers like him aren't welcome in Deadwood." Nodding toward the bar, he offered a faint smile. "How's about you and I get a few of Nuttal's pickled eggs and some of that tree bark he calls backstrap? I'm buyin'."

"Well, as long as you're buying, sir," Dewey replied with a chuckle, taking a seat at the table.

8

Hayes Ranch Site, Outside Deadwood

Melanie folded laundry she'd pulled off the makeshift clothesline her father had erected from a length of rope attached to one outer wall of the cabin and an abandoned fence post.

"Father, we should go to town today," she commented, smoothing the wrinkles from his favorite shirt.

"And why is that, darling?" His question was innocent enough, but she caught the mischievous twinkle in his eye. "Perhaps you might want to meet with a particular young man?"

She slapped both palms to her flushed cheeks, emitting a groan tinged with laughter. "You know me too well."

"That I do." He paused, meeting her gaze with silent understanding. "Dewey is a fine man. A hard worker and dedicated. I couldn't ask for a better fellow to be courting my only daughter."

"Father, we haven't—that is, we only—oh, let's just ride into town and see what's what!" Flustered and reluctant to reveal more of her feelings, she hurriedly stacked their clean clothes on the slab of wood currently being utilized as a table, before adding, "Aren't you curious about what's been built this past week?"

"Of course I am, since Deadwood is growing like weeds in a garden. I believe I'd like to have a visit with Wild Bill, too." Her father reached for his hat, hanging on a nail near the door. He placed it on his head and gave her unruly braids a brief glance. "Better wear a bonnet, child. The sun is fierce today."

Behind the cabin, her father and Dewey had put up a temporary shade awning for the horses, enclosing it with enough wire and odd pieces of wooden planks to create a corral. A makeshift gate worked as an entrance and exit. Until the barn was built, it would have to do. So far, their well-mannered beasts had not tested the boundary by trying to push against it or jump over it. Two troughs filled with water and grain crowded one side of the awning.

The horses nickered softly as Melanie approached, nuzzling her for the sugar cubes she had in her apron pocket. "Greedy, aren't you," she cooed, sharing the cubes between the handsome pair. Taking their leads, she guided them beyond the fencing to the wagon and helped her father hook them to the neck yoke.

He boosted her onto the seat and took his place next to her, snapping the reins lightly as she removed her apron and smoothed her skirt. Then gave her a wink. "Let's go see your young man."

———

"Thanks, Mister Linden," Dewey said, accepting the wage pouch from his employer. "You're a fair man to work for."

Linden slapped him on the back. "And you're a hardworking son of a gun, for sure. I ain't never seen anyone who could get things built so fast and so well." He led the way out to the porch of the hotel, squinting into the afternoon sun. "You headed back to the Hayes place?'

"Yessir." Dewey dropped his hat on his head. "But if you need me for anything else, I'm happy to take it on."

"Good to know." With a final handshake, Linden retreated, leaving Dewey on the hotel porch with a heavy coin pouch and anticipation lighting him up from inside.

After subtracting basic necessities from his total wages, he had a substantial nest egg started, courtesy of not only Linden but Nuttal, the Utter brothers, and now Frederick Hayes as well. Half the town had already benefited from his carpentry know-how. He'd heard talk of other businesses coming to Deadwood, in addition to the sawmill. The steady work plus the additional law apprenticeship he'd received from Hickok would lay the foundation of a solid profession.

Anxious to see Melanie and speak to her father, Dewey turned toward the smithy. He'd reinforced and expanded the shanty himself, until it provided enough shade and water troughs for six or so horses. Now the business was run by a former miner who'd arrived in town with a bag of gold nuggets and big plans. Dewey had been happy to forego payment for his labor in order to secure a permanent trough spot for his horse, especially as summer's heat could be unbearable.

As he re-tucked his shirt into his trousers, he glanced toward Nuttal's, and thought he'd stop by for a visit with Wild Bill, who usually played poker in the afternoons. Dewey paused to let a horse and rider pass before stepping into the rutted street—

And two things happened, almost at once.

He spotted Jack McCall advancing toward the saloon, his hat tilted precariously on his head and fingers hovering over his gun. A potent mix of determination and menace emanated from him, each stride charged with the unmistakable threat of an upcoming showdown.

At the same time, Melanie and her father strolled along from the other direction, mere yards from the saloon entrance, oblivious to any possible trouble.

The entire town buzzed with stories of Wild Bill's afternoon poker games at Nuttal's saloon, his table always surrounded by eager spectators. As the door swung open, McCall's hand moved away from his holster and gripped his gun.

"Oh, no," Dewey rasped. "No, no, no."

Time seemed to grind down to tiny seconds as he sprinted forward just as Frederick stretched out a palm to push at the door. Melanie laughed in that bright way she had about her, the sound soft and sweet.

Frederick's booted foot stepped over the threshold, followed by Melanie's dainty laced up shoe—

Dewey's legs couldn't move fast enough as he flew across the street. *Please, please, God.* "Melanie!"

She paused, turning her head to glance his way. Her face lit up with a dimpled smile, her lips parted in a greeting, then her eyes grew wide, noting his frantic pace.

Just as he reached them, a shot rang out, loud and sharp and deadly.

Dewey flung himself at them, shoving both Melanie and Frederick to the hard-packed floor at the entrance of the saloon, covering them with his body.

———

The sound of men yelling turned the air blue with curses. Melanie's ears rang from the piercing punch of a gunshot in the crowded room. She groaned, bruised from the hard fall to the dirt floor.

Her father stirred, muttering, "What—what's going on?"

"Keep down," Dewey ground out.

She blinked, focusing on his perspiring face a mere inch from hers. "Who?" She licked her dry lips and tried again. "Who was shot?"

"I don't know." He rose, pushing away from her, then tugging her up. Her father quickly scrambled to his feet and drew her into his embrace.

"Both of you stay here," Dewey ordered, as he strode further into the dimly lit saloon.

Melanie swayed on her feet from the rush of nerves coursing through her. "I want to see what happened," she protested.

"No you don't, child." Her father tightened his arms. "Whoever shot his gun probably killed somebody. He might still be nearby."

"Ah, damn it, he's dead," a gruff voice shouted. "Git that sumbitch!"

"He ran out the back," someone else hollered, punctuated by thumping boots and jingling spurs.

Dewey appeared suddenly, urging her toward the door. "Been a killing," he announced tersely. "No place for you, Melanie—"

"Who?" She craned her neck to see around his shoulder and caught a glimpse of a man slumped over a table, a pool of blood mingling with cards and chips, darkening a curly, light brown mane of hair. His hat had tipped over on the floor.

A familiar-looking hat.

"No. Not Wild Bill," she whispered hoarsely, feeling her throat close up with grief as Dewey guided her outside into the afternoon sun. Her shoes dug into the dirt, forcing him to halt. "Why would anyone do this?"

"I don't know, sweetheart, but he won't get away with it." Dewey sighed roughly. "It was Jack McCall who shot Hickok. He escaped out the back. Men went after him and they'll catch him."

Heartbroken, Melanie stiffened her spine against the need to curl up and sob aloud at the loss of such a good man. Tears rolled down her cheeks. "He needs to pay for what he's done."

———

One Week Later, Hayes Ranch Site, Deadwood

Dewey threw down the copy of the *Black Hills Pioneer*, its cheap ink already smudged. "Acquitted, by God. I can't understand the stupidity of men, that they'd believe a criminal over actual facts."

Frederick picked up the single sheet newspaper and scanned its contents. "Says here McCall killed Mister Hickok in retribution for the murder of his brother." He adjusted his spectacles and quoted, "*'Should it ever be our misfortune to kill a man . . . we would simply ask that our trial may take place in some of the mining camps of these hills.'*"

"I doubt McCall ever had a brother. And we can only hope the truth comes out. He killed Wild Bill for no other reason than in some sort of mad rage." Dewey shook his head sadly. He'd heard through the town grapevine that McCall had bolted from Deadwood immediately after the sham of a trial held at McDaniel's Theater. With such a murderer on the run, one could only reckon he'd commit another crime, something that would ultimately bring him down.

Melanie carried the coffeepot from the stove, refilling their cups, then took the only remaining chair at the table. Weariness darkened her pretty blue eyes, attesting to more than one sleepless night. In the week since Wild Bill's murder, they had all grieved. Dewey moved to her side and placed a bolstering hand on her shoulder, relieved when she graced him with a small smile.

Over her head he met her father's gaze. In a short span of time, Frederick Hayes had become a father figure, and Dewey held the man in high respect. His original plan, of asking for Melanie's hand in marriage, had been derailed by Hickok's death. It hadn't seemed right to pursue happiness in the face of such tragedy.

But if he had learned nothing else, he'd discovered the fragility of life. Of how a person might think they'd have many years to marry, produce children, build a future.

He parted his lips to speak, but the older man only smiled and nodded. Somehow without words he conveyed his approval of Dewey's suit. It meant a great deal.

"I'll just take a bit of a stroll over to the stable, check on the horses," Frederick said. As he passed Melanie, he dropped a kiss on her head.

He offered a wink to Dewey before heading to the door.

Heart near to bursting, Dewey bent to take his beloved's hand, kneeling there on the rough floor next to her chair. Bringing her slender fingers to his mouth, he kissed them, one by one.

As her beautiful eyes widened in surprise, he murmured, "My love, marry me . . ."

EPILOGUE

Mount Moriah Cemetery, Deadwood, Dakota Territory
   Aug. 3, 1879

A breeze flowed through the air, offering respite from the otherwise stifling summer morning. Frederick Hayes removed his hat and held it to his chest as he gazed at the wooden grave marker.

Wild Bill, J. B. Hickock killed by the assassin Jack McCall in Deadwood, August 2, 1876. Pard, we will meet again in the happy hunting ground to part no more . . .

Beside him, Melanie pulled a handkerchief from her pocket and blotted her forehead. "Such a hot day, isn't it? But I would not miss paying our respects." She pressed her cheek against his arm. "He was a good man. May he find eternal rest here."

"Amen," Frederick murmured, clasping his daughter close.

Thinking back to that awful day, three years ago, could still send a shiver through his frame. If not for Dewey's swift actions, he and Melanie might have walked right into the path of McCall's bullet. The bastard had shot only once, but no one present at Nuttal's that day could have known his full intent. Perhaps he'd plotted to shoot everyone, not just Hickok.

In the end the man had been tried a second time, then hung for his crime. Justice had been served. But it did not keep Wild Bill's friends from mourning him.

The clomping sound of tiny boots roused him from his musings, and Frederick smiled down on the raven-haired tot who threw himself against his legs with an excited, "Grampa!"

"There's my boy." Frederick swept an arm under his grandson's rump and hefted him up. Eyes the color of the sky held the sort of mischief only a rowdy young'un could get himself up to. But for now, he laid his curly head on Frederick's shoulder and yawned.

Dewey joined them at the gravesite, doffing his hat for a moment, eyes closed as he offered a silent prayer of his own. With a brief touch of two fingers to the rough-carved wood, he paid his final respects before turning to Melanie and kissing her lips gently.

"I spoke with Calamity." He gestured in the direction of the famous sharpshooter, standing with her head bent, callused hands clasped behind her back. "She's claiming the right to be buried next to Hickok, if possible."

"If that's what she wants, then her wishes should be honored," Melanie replied. "She cared very much for him."

For a few additional minutes they stood together in the quiet cemetery, while William James Bower—named in honor of their departed friend—dozed on Frederick's shoulder and Dewey held his wife gently, one hand on her burgeoning belly.

There'd be another grandchild to dote on, come the fall, one more blessing. Frederick reckoned they'd had their share of those, starting on the fateful day he and Melanie chose to join Utter's wagon train. And look where it took them. A new life in a rough-and-tumble place. He couldn't imagine living anywhere else, especially now that Dewey and Melanie's ranch adjoined his.

They departed the cemetery, Dewey carrying their slumbering son. Frederick clasped his daughter's arm, guiding her carefully over the uneven ground. At her sigh, he murmured, "Are you weary, my girl?"

"A little. I shall be quite relieved the day I hold this babe in my arms," she replied with a soft laugh, "instead of my poor old tummy."

As they reached their wagon, she turned to give him a hug. Into his ear she whispered, "If it's a girl, Dewey wants to name her Beatrice, after Mother." She drew back to peer into his face. "Is that all right with you?"

"Oh, child." Overcome, Frederick embraced his precious daughter. "Most assuredly."

ABOUT THE AUTHOR

Cheryl Yeko and Char Chaffin are award-winning romance authors known for their heartwarming and captivating stories. In addition to writing together under the pen name CiCi Cordelia, Yeko and Chaffin also publish individually under their own names. Their talent for crafting complex and relatable characters and their ability to craft engaging and emotional plots have made them fan favorites in the romance genre.

Their books have won or finaled in many writing contests, including Heart of Excellence Readers Choice Award, Heart of the West Great Beginnings Contest, The Beverley, InD'Tale Magazine's RONE Award, the International Digital Awards (IDA) Contest, and more. As a writing team, they bring a solid know-how for accomplishing the foundation of what makes a great romance read: a strong story, a passionate romance, fascinating characters, and a happy-ever-after ending.

Learn more about us at: CiCiWriter.com/

A THOUSAND MILES FROM BOYHOOD

BETTY BRANDT PASSICK

A THOUSAND MILES FROM
BOYHOOD

IN MID-JUNE 1876, I FOUND MYSELF SEATED IN THE JOCKEY BOX
of a prairie schooner in Charlie Utter's wagon train outside the city of
Cheyenne in the Wyoming Territory, watching the sun rise and the
morning haze disperse, awaiting Charlie's signal to depart for the gold-
fields of South Dakota.

I found age thirty-nine a peculiar time of my life. Like Lazarus of old, I
had begun to experience the miracle of being brought back from a grave
somewhat of my own making. I had sought to build a reputation as a
gambler and showman—and made a good living; now, as though grave
wrappings dropping from my eyes, I had begun to understand what my
mother Polly Hickok had said was true. What I needed to be about in the
few days I'd been given by God Almighty was building character, not a
reputation.

A vision of my new bride, Agnes Thatcher Lake, came to mind...a
vintage, dark-eyed, sultry French woman, whom I had married a month
earlier, waving goodbye from the boardwalk of the Rollins House, deli-
cately dabbing at the corners of her eyes, teasing me one final time to
reexamine my decision to leave her.

"For what?" she had pleaded the previous evening. "...to spend
endless hours panning for gold in the hope of discovering a flake that glit-

ters in the sun in a stream flowing from the igneous rocks of the Black Hills. What about me—am I not the treasure you hoped to find in life?"

I realized at that very moment I hadn't been completely honest with her...not about my diminished gun skills or failing eyesight, nor the fact I had itchy feet to travel to the Dakota Territory to seek the fortune I hoped would sustain me the rest of my days.

We had honeymooned for a month in Cheyenne, finding the city the scene of one high circus atmosphere of barkeeps, gamblers, merchants, buffalo hunters, prostitutes. Gay music discoursed from gambling and saloon building fronts. Vice and riot were in full and unlimited control of the city's four thousand citizens made up of itinerants, and the occasional Indian. Daily, five-card stud poker games beckoned to me wherein I demonstrated my gaming prowess to Agnes—and indeed, won my share of purses, however within days, she declared: "James Butler Hickok, when you gamble you become a drunken, swaggering *homme.*" Then she smiled and kissed me hard on the lips.

Once more, a sense of gratitude washed over me that I hadn't run into any the likes of Davis Tutt, a former friend and soldier, who a decade ago challenged me to a duel, which turned deadly for him. Since, I became renowned as a "gunslinger" and frequently found myself in toxic situations, whenever some drunken drifter longed to put a notch in his gun. The frontier had produced men afflicted with moonstruck madness.

Truth be told, all of Cheyenne seduced Agnes and me, even the opera house, Atlas Theater, Cheyenne Club, Inter-Ocean Hotel, and retail businesses. Then suddenly, for reasons yet unexplainable, she became bored with the whole. One recent morning she opined: "Cheyenne's surrounded by nothin' but sparse thin grasses turned into sun-bleached hay...and *odeurs* of shit, drunkenness, and airin' the paunch... This is a God-forsaken, God-forgotten place. How I long for Ohio."

If I was honest, the city had been somewhat a disappointment to me, as well, in that a gunslinger and cardsharp by profession, I missed finding a stiff on the floor of a tavern, and quick-draw duel fought in the street. Days earlier, my mind evoked the original plan of traveling to the gold-fields of South Dakota, a plan interrupted by a chance meeting with Agnes Lake.

Agnes, upon learning of my desire to travel by wagon train to the

Dakota Territory, had been surprisingly quick to affirm my resolve: *"Oui,* James, you must *commencé* your business... I shall remain with *de cirque,* though you must take into consideration my travel requirements *across* l'Amérique... I promise to keep you informed of my location, of course, so you will know at all times how to reach out to me."

I had responded simply, "Pet, I shall miss you dearly and promise to send for you in time." In my heart of hearts, I feared I might never see her lovely face again.

———

Our torrid love affair—at least, on my part—began with a campaign of letters five years before. I met the widow and proprietor of Lake's Hippo-Olympiad circus when a full-bosomed, beautiful, woman of mature age burst through the doorway of the marshal's office in Abilene, Kansas— the office to which I had recently been appointed—to inquire about paying the performance fee, or at least, what I understood her to say.

"Bonjour! ....*la commission de performance,"* she announced in one supple breath.

The French-speaking woman was of fine breeding, I could tell, well beyond any of my previous exchanges with Illinois Evangelicals—LaSalle County, the place of my birth and childhood—Kansas Cherokees, or pidgin-speaking slaves of the South, whom I'd overheard while scouting for General George A. Custer's 7th Cavalry during the Civil War.

I gestured for the madame to sit in my chair behind my official desk to complete the paperwork. She hastily reviewed and signed the document, withdrew the fee from her large cloth handbag and carefully counted out the bills onto the desktop, before launching into a full dissertation on the glorious life of the circus, sounding much like a barker calling out the next performance.

Everything she knew about the circus she'd learned from her previous husband, employed as a clown performing at a "Big Top" near her home in Alsace, France. Mr. Lake had died two years ago, slain by a non-paying fella who'd stolen into a tent to see a performance. Mr. Lake had been killed by the man he was trying to evict.

My ears perked up at hearing her sad story... She too was familiar with the complications that can happen in life, particularly in the lawless west, circumstances about which I was well acquainted.

How her eyes twinkled and danced as she described her mastery in the art of tight-rope walking and training lions. I couldn't take my eyes off of her.

'Twas then it occurred to me, on the face of it, she was utterly obtuse to my reputation as a marksman and lawman—an oversight about which I was eager to enlighten her

Agnes concluded by noting her departure from Abilene would occur in one week's time, which provoked me to inquire about an address, should additional correspondence be required for repeat shows. Cincinnati, Ohio was the place the circus called home.

Again, I held myself back from blurting out the fact that friends and enemies alike called me "Wild Bill," a reputation I'd earned for taming lawless frontier towns like Abilene, but restrained myself lest she consider me addle-headed...reasoning, such embellishment to an Alsaceian woman was best done through perfumed notes, *eau de cologne*—the most popular perfume imported money could buy, at least according to an honorable gentleman I once met at a poker game, but could no longer recall exactly where or who had provided the vital insight.

Within the week I posted my first letter to Agnes. She recognized my overture for what it was, although five years would pass before we met again—in Cheyenne. She was in town to visit friends. We married within the month by a Methodist minister at the home of a saloon keeper.

For our wedding Day, I shed my coonskin shirt and pants for clothes selected by Agnes: Prince Albert frock coat, bosomed shirt, pants held up by braces, neck wear, calfskin boots, and black sombrero. Agnes wore a long black dress garnished with a flourish of sequins across the bodice and stylish feathered hat from her travel closet. Our Christian vows included the standard promises; an exchange of rings would have to wait until they could be ordered from a jeweler out East. The design Agnes had in mind was dual intertwined ringbands to remind us of our meeting related to her circus.

Curiously, the minister doubted my sincerity in the union and wrote thusly on the license, as though to provide documentation for some future review... I had, however, lied about my age, stating I was 46, not 39. Agnes was eleven years my senior.

Our wedding night revealed Agnes an exotic animal, far exceeding all the other women I'd known, white or Indian. By nature, a seductress; by trade, a contortionist and high-wire traipse artist. Most capably she utilized whips, ropes, rings, and rigging, every circus tool at her disposal to demonstrate man as an object of her insatiable desire, night and day. She understood well the art of delighting me in her capture. The jangling of the circus calliope playing in the background only added to my delight and pleasure.

I found it hard to reconcile that before Agnes I had believed myself to be a happy, content man, my life a tapestry of exploration, imagination, and fearless machismo woven across the vast frontier. In her presence, I became as meek and gentle as a lamb, happy to be her showman and actor wherever her circus should take us.

———

Shortly after daybreak, the tall, lanky Charlie Utter finally stood at the lead wagon and fired his shotgun across its bow, signaling the launch of the thirty or so schooners, carrying a hundred souls bound for the great trail to the Black Hills. He was the utmost helmsmen, a pioneer who had the courage and ambition to overcome the obstacles that always develop when one tries to do something worthwhile, especially when it's new and different.

Charlie indicated my turn to join the layout. I had agreed to drive the wagon with food and supplies for the trail crew, my wonder horse Black Nell tied behind, packed like a mule with supplies. The scene before me was dream-like in the lifting morning prairie fog, a train of white-canvas-topped boats on wheels, pulled by teams of horses, mules, and oxen, gently lurching forward from the rocky outcroppings that defined the landscape north of Cheyenne.

Moments earlier, I had paid a young chap three cents, the cost of a stamp, to hand deliver a perfumed note to Agnes. I wrote simply: "Pet, we will have a home yet, and our lives will be so blissful—Love, James."

Now, the reins of the team of mules in my hands, the wagon's mechanics growling beneath me, I felt my chest swell recalling my first job at the tender age of eighteen as stagecoach driver in Kansas and Nebraska, where I'd honed my abilities as a gunslinger. Bandits along the trail stealthily prepared to relieve the gold carriers hired by the stage company to transport, along with the contents of the fat wallets of passengers. I became skilled with my .44-caliber Colt Dragoon revolver to where I could hit an oyster can at 100 yards.

Two frontier companions, Buffalo Bill Cody and Texas Jack, had joined the wagon train in Cheyenne, according to Charlie. The hard-riding, fast-shooting duo exemplified excellent horsemanship and accurate marks-manship. I had stayed with Cody's family in Leavenworth, Kansas, one autumn and winter at the Big House so I'd known him a long time. A couple years ago he invited me to join his troupe, and we performed in Rochester, New York. As a kid I had bragged to my sisters that someday I would do things Kit Carson never dreamed of doing, then there I was— me and Black Nell, famous like Carson. Rochester was where I also discovered my revulsion for theatre and left the troupe to return west.

Calamity Jane linked with the wagon train at Cheyenne, too. The buckskin-clad, gun-slinging, foul-mouthed cowgirl with an affinity for alcohol had become legendary. Initially, I knew her as a remarkably good shot and a fearless rider for a girl… Nowadays, I wanted nothing to do with her.

From my years of experience, I knew each day on the trail would begin at sunrise, and soon after a breakfast of hoecakes and bacon we'd have our first encounter with Plains Indians, though the Fort Laramie Treaty of 1868 with the Sioux and Cheyenne tribes had created a large reservation for the tribes, which included the Black Hills. Still, squirmishes broke out —most recently the Battle of Prairie Dog Creek in central Wyoming in June.

Mid-day we'd take a short break for a meal; camp would happen every evening as the sun was setting. After a meal of hardtack, tubers, and rabbit stew came the music of banjos and "black boxes"—fiddles, and enough apple jack to spawn copious stories of frontier adventures from farmers, missionaries, teachers, and abandons alike. I always found the tales of Missionaries indelicate regarding their conversion attempts of the Natives, who seemed curious about the power of "the white man's book of heaven." In the end, the preachers and their families ended up just as dead as hundreds of other civilians encountering the territories of hostile Native tribes. The white man sought to steal their land; missionaries, their culture. I garnered the ways of the Indian much as I had the perils of the African slave.

The 'ladies', in general, I feared would find the dangerous trail to Deadwood challenging—if not deadly, even though I accepted their work demanded a periodic trek to new towns. There, they survived as dance hall girls, sweethearts, and lonely doves. Calamity Jane, born Martha Jane Canary, had followed in her mother's footsteps, forced into the occupation when at fifteen years of age both parents died, and she, being the eldest of six children, became the sole provider for the family.

On our first evening around the campfire, Buffalo Bill Cody and Texas Jack provided an Indian war battle reenactment, along with Black Nell and me, wherein I was *killed* during the battle. Calamity Jane, an excellent equestrian, performed a few shooting, riding, and roping stunts. Cody promised more attractions to come: a bison hunt and train robbery.

Calamity Jane waited for me after the show. Still a young woman at twenty-five, it was hard to tell there was a woman beneath all that buckskin.

"Wild Bill, yer lookn' devilishly handsome," she said.

"Miss Martha Jane—you did some real fancy ridin' again out there tonight."

"Thank-ya, Wild Bill... wit'cha been up to...been a while since I seen ya."

"I recently married a woman named Agnes Thatcher Lake—heard of her?"

"Can't say I have... Yer lady wit'cha on da trail?"

"We said our Christian vows a month ago in Cheyenne...likely, she's returned to Cincinnati by now...owner of a circus, she travels a lot."

"I was thinkin' we could hook up, get a drink in Deadwood some night."

Martha Jane's advances were about as vague as a bull moose preparing to mount a cow in heat.

I looked for an opportunity to excuse myself when I saw Charlie Utter in the distance. I tipped my hat, and with the other hand motioned my intention to depart in his direction.

"Been waitin' on a chance to speak to Charlie about his experience prospecting in the Colorado goldfields... I'm thinking he must not-a hit a gold vein, after all, he's leading this wagon train."

Outwardly she seemed to understand being sidelined...her good looks had vanished like chaff in a dry wind years ago; her buckskin attire, equally unattractive. Nonetheless, I valued her attempt to compete in a man's world.

Week one on the trail proved uneventful except for broken wagon wheels, and a few new cases of chicken pox and diarrhea—when the first white crosses began to mark the trail's edge.

A considerable number of travelers, unsuccessful from the California gold rush, with insufficient funds to purchase provisions for another three-week, three-hundred-mile journey, found their supplies dwindling; then, when fresh water became harder to find, fights began to break out— along with guns, knives, axes, and shovels. Fortunately, I was on hand to help quell argies. I carried a pair of Colt 1851 Navy model cap-and-ball revolvers, and my reputation as a gunslinger spread throughout the camp.

One evening, mid-way to Deadwood, breezes rippling across the prairie grassland that brought fragrant aromas of sage and lupine, I told a story from my early twenties of an attempt to shoot a mother bear with two cubs at her side; the ball ricocheted off the bear's skull, which only annoyed it, and a fierce brawl ensued, during which time I managed to slit the bear's gullet with my knife, but not before being nearly crushed to death. My chest, shoulder, and arm were severely injured, and I was bedridden for months. I showed the scars on my body to any who cared to see.

On another evening, Charlie Utter, a handsome, mustached man five years my junior, who liked to surround himself with the ladies. introduced me to Madam Mustache, Dirty Em, and a few of their working girls. I took him aside and whispered, "You know I'm a married man." I had followed the advice of my hero Kit Carson, whom I met during a trip to Santa Fe, New Mexico Territory. We spent an evening together, when Kit warned me about t*the perils of fraternizing with the ladies of the town.*

"The girls have to eat, too, you know," Charlie joked, grabbing the madam at the waist and pulling her close to his taut body, followed by a hearty roar.

Daily I added to my notes to Agnes and mailed them as often as we neared a town with Pony Express. One of the crew rode into town for supplies and to drop off letters—Fort Laramie was the first stop. In my most recent note, drenched in *eau de cologne of dirt*, not imported, but readily accessible on the trail, I had confessed the joy she had brought me during our month together when, seated in the tub large enough for two, she poured pitchers of water and massaged soap into my long flowing hair. Two weeks on the trail and I pined for a leisurely bath and the touch of her scintillating fingers that reached the deepest recesses of my mind and body. Our time together had been short...too short.

Near Newcastle, fifty miles from Deadwood, during another evening seated around a petite campfire—wood also had become a scarce commodity—the sound of locusts filling the night air, I heard myself confess to Charlie and a few others that I thought I would be killed in Deadwood.

The rest of the journey, I wondered: *Had my words been a premonition?*

Reaching South Dakota, the trail turned into rugged terrain and dangerous curves, and the wagon violently pitched side to side, threatening to dislodge me from the seat—a few travelers in fact ended up with broken ribs and limbs. The animals suffered greatly too...mid-afternoon one day a mule pulling my wagon unexpectedly dropped from the heat. Charlie and others pulled the beast off-side, hitched another in its place, and the train continued.

In mid-July we arrived in drought-stricken Deadwood. The boom town, long and skinny, lay at the bottom of a gulch. In 1874 discovery of gold caused the area's population to surge from a handful of miners to tens of thousands of Anglo settlers, regardless of the fact the Black Hills region had been designated Sioux land and off-limits to whites.

A thousand men in the streets greeted us, vigorously clapping and yelling as one by one wagons processed down the dusty, narrow main street. Originally I assumed their reception was due to the arrival of mail and other supplies from Cheyenne. Only then did I realize the hearty reception was due to the fresh delivery of prostitutes.

My foremost glance of the town revealed most every branch of business: a mercantile with food stuffs and sufficient inventory necessary to pan for gold. The Gem Theater, a theater-hotel-brothel combination, nearing completion, offering food, bed—feathers, hair and Pulu mattresses, hot baths…and girls, lots of them, based on the lineup standing along a second story balcony, with signage proclaiming song, dance, and pantomime occurring nightly. Banking houses offered to buy gold dust and bullion.

I made note of the Nuttall & Mann's Saloon, which advertised "A fine assortment of Wines, Liquors and Cigars," where I planned to devote afternoons gambling to earn money needed for food and lodging—and to prevent my arrest for vagrancy.

First, I proceeded to the post office located within a mercantile and inquired about letters from Agnes, where I assumed they'd piled up like a logjam in Deadwood Creek.

Indeed, Agnes' letters, short but sweet, were filled with words of affection and long phrases of love and passion, even quotes from a French poet of antiquity. The circus had moved on to the southern-most states. In every note she wrote, "I miss you beyond what I ever thought possible," and signed them, "Love you James, Agnes."

———

I arose early the next morning to purchase panning gear at the mercantile then walked to the stable to retrieve Black Nell housed at a stable. My stallion transported me the three miles to the banks of Deadwood Creek. The slightest fragrance of yellow sweet clover filled the air, unbeknownst to prospectors plastered along both sides of the creek for as far as I could see. I was struck by the unfathomable unlikelihood of gold being found in such an uninspiring stream, in a gulch full of lifeless trees.

My eyes caught sight of a petite prospector—young man or boy, I couldn't tell which, standing nearby at the edge of the stream, pantlegs pulled knee-high, feverishly dipping a wide shallow pan in the current, the pan the size of the wide-brimmed hat made of beaver fur on his head.

A few moments later he peered up at me from beneath the hat, exposing his face, when he spoke.

"You watchin' me, hopin' to steal my gold?"

He was a boy of maybe twelve or thirteen years of age.

"Nah—fact is I've spent years as a lawman in Hays City and Abilene, Kansas, upholding justice, much like the marshal here in Deadwood, I suspect. I'm studying you, hoping to get the hang of how it's done... panning for gold, that is. How's it happen you look professional at your young age."

"Spends a lotta time in streams in these parts, ev'r since the gold rush of '74... What brings 'ya to Deadwood? and I means no disrespect, sir, but my pa says you's the kind a fella who appears a well-kept man."

"I arrived yesterday on Charlie Utter's wagon train, all the way from Cheyenne in the Wyoming Territory. I don't expect you to understand, can't say I do myself, but a month ago I married a beautiful woman—it's every man's dream to marry the likes of Agnes Lake—then I up and left her to come in search of seeking my fortune in gold. Folks across the frontier know me as Wild Bill Hickok."

A few men near the boy ceased their panning and stared at me, as though trying to put a face with a name.

The boy dropped his pan and walked toward me with one hand extended.

"I heard of 'ya! Ples'ure to meet yer acquaint'ance, Mr. Hickok."

We briefly shook hands, the boy seemed to blush at the very thought of our chance meeting.

"My name is Johnny E. Perrett. Welcome to Deadwood...it's officially part of the Great Sioux Reservation. Indians got all of Western South Dakota—gold and all, according to the government. But nobody pays that treaty no mind...we's still out here trying to find the gold that God put here for ever' body, and we's sure findin' a lot of gold in this creek. Won't be long and miners will-a claimed all of the land in Deadwood Gulch. Ya come at a good time!"

The boy returned to the creek bed while I looked for space along the bank to remain near to the boy, fearing a tussle would occur if I should be perceived to invade another's territory. I found a thickly weedy area to sit and organize the items from my bag, miscellaneous items from the mercantile plus a few sheets of note paper. The note to Agnes, begun late last night after a long bath in the hotel, spilled out onto my lap. I re-read my final words: "Agnes Darling—my Pet, should we never meet again, while firing my last shot, I will gently breathe the name of my wife, Agnes."

I recalled my confession to Charlie Utter during the last days on the trail... *Did I really believe I was going to be killed in Deadwood?*

The boy interrupted any further thoughts of dying.

"You say you got a fine woman back in Cheyenne? I gots me a girl, too...her name is Mollie B, and I wouldn't leave her side for no gold; I hopes to marry her one day, course that depends on findin' a big nugget so's I can sells it to buy her a ring. Shoot!...I still ain't man e'nof to ev'n grow a beard."

"You'll get there soon enough," I said, brushing a finger across my straw-colored mustache that encircled my upper lip and ended just above at the chin line.

"This the first ya panned for gold, Mr. Hickok? Let me tell ya, if'n you do find anythin', no matter how small, I suggest ya put it in a safe place right away. Squatters and thieves, when they learn ya found gold, will follow you and try to steal it. There are days I suspect I'm being tracked by mean culprits hoping to find where I live and learn where my gold's hiddn'...my campsite's been burgled more than once. More likely, they's liable to try to kill ya and take it from ya rite on the spot. Pa and I staked a claim near the gulches of Iron Creek and Potato Creek, mostly I divide my time between Deadwood Creek and Potato Creek."

"How long you lived in the Black Hills?"

"My pa come from Wales, that's pretty much all I know about my kinfolk. My ma died when I was born...wish I'd had the chance to know her...bet she was sweet as honey. Tell me, what's yer ma like."

"Pamelia Hickok—folks call her Polly...reached age seventy a year or so ago. She's likely waitin' on a letter from me as we speak, longing to know my current residence, I suspect. I was born in Troy Grove, Illinois, one of six kids. I'm a middle child. She's a good mother, a God-fearing woman. Not a day goes by her words of wisdom don't swirl in my head, words like: "God made people to bring joy and goodness into the world, to spend their whole lives being a blessing to others," a conviction she's preached heartily to me since I was a young boy."

"She must be real proud of ya, Sir...bein' you's a lawman and all, I mean."

"I think about her a lot and all the wise things she said as I've gotten older. She always spoke the truth as she saw it...nothing wrong with that...and she was good me, I mean there wasn't anything she wouldn't have done for her children. Kinda sorry now I didn't stick around longer with her on the farm; she coulda used my help, but I had to get on with making a life for myself. I've seen a lotta good days—bad ones, too. Life is harder than one imagines at seventeen."

The boy had become absorbed with relocating to a recently vacated spot a few feet downriver.

I hurriedly moved my items to remain close by, trying to recall exactly when first I believed it was a "sin" to kill another human being. Surely, the idea originated from my mother, as she was the only person in my family to attend church meetings, whenever a traveling Presbyterian minister came to the area. When an angry mob hanged African American men in the town square, the tenor of her voice changed: "Thou shalt not kill!"—she said, and for effect, deepened her voice to sound as though the words she had uttered were spoken by Moses himself on the very day God handed down the 10 Commandments. Her beliefs dictated her behavior and character. Even before the hanging, she had involved the family's small farm as a stop on the Underground Railroad. In time, I joined General James Lane's Free State anti-slavery forces in Kansas.

Redepositing my items on the shore, I contemplated: *How strange, a thousand miles from boyhood that my mother's words still occupied so many of my thoughts.*

I glanced at the boy now innocently splashing in the shallows.

"I was about your age when my father died...grew up fishing on the banks of the Little Vermillion in Illinois...left my mother, siblings, and our small farm on the prairie to seek my fortune around age seventeen."

"Uh-huh, bet yer pa is proud of ya, too?" Johnny said, unexpectedly intrigued by something at the bottom of his pan.

"I don't really know, I guess so—I mean, what has a kid at seventeen done to make a father proud?"

"My pa is proud of me, and I ain't done notin' special—it's a rule every pa lives by," he said, his three-foot frame now fully erect, his cobolt blue eyes staring intently into mine, man-to-man.

I nodded. "You're right, of course."

The boy resumed a bent-over stance over the creek, both hands clasping the pan, staring into the stream.

My mind diverted to my initial meeting with David McCanles when I was twenty-four and worked as a depot stable-hand for the Pony Express Rock Creek Station in Nebraska. A few men always accompanied McCanles who was part of a Confederate gang, or so I was told, whenever he stopped by the station. Early on, he gave me the name "Duck Bill" and began taunting me, calling me a hermaphrodite. A year later, I got hired to guide a detachment of Union cavalry through southern Nebraska and stopped by the station, McCanles and his gang were engaged in a dispute with the manager over the property. McCanles spied my six-foot frame and resumed taunting, finally threatened to take me outside to give me a lashing. As he approached, I pulled out my .36-caliber Colt Navy revolver and shot him in the chest. Two others from his gang lunged at me, and when the melee was over three men lay dead at my feet. The bullet from my gun had killed McCanles; the origin of the other bullets remained uncertain. I wasn't charged with murder, members of the calvary testified the killing had been in self-defense. A few years later, *Harper's New Monthly* reported on the "McCanles Massacre." The writer claimed he had interviewed me, said I'd personally killed 10 men and gave me title "Wild Bill." After that, my life went in a new direction, when my reputation became "gunslinger," yet I'd never been in a gun fight before.

A familiar formidable anxiety welled up within me. How I dreaded the day I'd reach heaven's gate, and when asked by God to account for my sins—nay, more so, I feared Polly Hickok should precede me in death and I'd first have to answer to her—"Why, when presented with the chance to evade murder, had I failed to heed God's mandate: Thou shalt not kill?"

The noon sun bore down on us like bacon in a hot cast iron pan on an open fire.

The boy abruptly dropped his pan and sat along the stream, preparing to put on his shoes.

"Well, that's it for me t'day," gettin' real warm in the sun...back on the morrow—ya gonna be here?"

"I reckon I will see you then." I said, nodding.

I watched as he picked up his gear, shoved it in a sackcloth and walked off, waving to me one final time as he neared the bend of the creek and disappeared from sight.

Various prospectors looked as if likewise ready to break for the noon meal, though not a speck of shade offering relief from the sun was to be found anywhere.

I decided to finish my note to Agnes. Seating myself as comfortably as possible on a large reddish rock, I added a notation that Charlie Utter, the trail master, had insisted the "Thatcher" family to which he was familiar was of German descent, not French, and a distant relation of his father's. What did Agnes think of Utter's claim? "Are you in fact—German?" I penned. I inquired if she had changed her surname on circus advertisements to state: "Proprietor: Mrs. Agnes Lake Hickok." Lastly, I wondered if I had ever explained how I got the name "Wild Bill." Bill had been my father's name, and after my father's death, I went by either J. B. Hickok or Bill Hickok, the later stuck for some reason.

Next, I wrote a note to my mother: "Mother, I report that I have arrived safely in Deadwood in the Dakota Territory, and am at this moment resting quietly beside the gentle waters of Deadwood Creek, where I've assembled my newly acquired gold-panning equipment, a process I shall initiate momentarily. This morning I met a boy, Johnny Perrett, who has promised to teach me everything he knows about panning. Further, I should inform you approximately two months ago, I married the beautiful Agnes Thatcher Lake, of the Lake's Hippo-Olympiad circus fame and fortune. Her circus is currently touring in the southeast. She's a lovely, mature woman, and I am certain at your meeting you two shall get along very well."

I checked my timepiece. By early afternoon each day I planned to return to town for several hands of poker. And, resolute to follow master Johnny Perrett's words of "keeping a sharp eye out for thieves," I deemed never to be without my .44-caliber Smith & Wesson No. 3 American revolvers, or knife strapped to my waist, should I encounter the malice of a roaming bear.

Thus, my daily schedule was set for the foreseeable future: panning for gold in the morning, followed by an afternoon of poker. Then, an evening meal surrounded by friends, old and new.

It was uncertain exactly the day and hour I would return home to my beloved Agnes.

———

The only time I had been to a croaker for my failing eyesight was in Kansas in 1872 when I served as marshal. Based on my ability to read a chart with letters in different sizes and fonts from ten feet away, he pronounced a similar deficiency inflicted on hundreds of people on the frontier, he said, "likely caused by bacteria and poor hygiene," the kinds of issues difficult to eradicate if traveling one day to the next as a gambler on horseback.

Last night, during a conversation in my hotel room with Charlie Utter, he informed me of a physician who might have knowledge to help with my eye problem. The hotel manager said the guy had arrived within two days time from Custer and had taken up space on the first floor, though his signage hadn't thus far gone up outside his office.

Preparing to depart, Charlie added: "I passed Calamity Jane on the stairway on my way up to your room, Hickok... What do you imagine she's doing on the second floor?"

I considered his inquiry figurative and gave no response.

The following morning I summoned a hotel boy to deliver a note to the croaker asking to see him at his earliest convenience. His reply stated I should stop by around nine.

"Come into my office...sit on the table, apologize for my tardiness. I was out late into the night," the croaker said, throwing on a white jacket as he spoke. "Parents found their fourteen-year-old boy hanged in the hay-shed behind the house. They, of course, are bereft at having lost their son," he added, while laying out examination tools on a fresh towel on a dresser lined with an assortment of bottles of ointments, liquors, and pills.

"A young boy hanged hisself?" I stammered in disbelief.

"I realize most Black-Hiller, tender-feet like you believe that Dame Fortune is gonna open her cornucopia and rain down showers of gold on one and all—but truth is, these are hard times. The cost of supplies goes sky high when hundreds of people arrive each day trying to compete...

kids often get the brunt of it, and who they gonna tell if they're *starving?*"

"But the kid had a whole lifetime ahead of him… some bad days, but a lot more good days."

He nodded in agreement. "Rest assured, most deaths in these parts are not suicides—robberies or swindles upon travelers are reported with much greater frequency, often leaving victims dead or beaten badly… which ultimately leads to death. Seems like finding gold would be the main concern, the real problem becomes keeping it. Infectious diseases are taking a toll; small pox has broken out in the town, new cases reported every day. A lot of tuberculosis…and of course, the common afflictions from strong drink."

At the very moment the croaker stopped talking, I found him planted directly in front of me. "Your note stated you're having trouble with your eyesight. Tell me about your symptoms."

I explained my fading vision, which had affected my shooting skills. My eyes were light sensitive, constantly irritated and itched.

He swiveled on his heels to return to the dresser and reached for a crude instrument I'd not seen before.

"This device is of my own creation, call it an ophthalmoscope…allows me to look inside the eye and see the details of the retina."

He placed it a few inches from one of my eyes, then the other, then back and forth again revisiting each eye, making notations in a notebook.

"You have what's commonly known as ophthalmia. Only thing you can do is improve hygiene and a healthy diet, along with drops to alleviate the itching…but your vision is not likely to improve. You may find it beneficial to wear dark glasses and stay out of the sun.

"Dark glasses don't do me no good the moment I'm trying to see who's shootin' at me," I quipped.

"I realize it's not practical in certain occupations, Mr. Hickok," handing me a bottle of eye drops while scribbling his fee on a small piece of paper imprinted with his name, "$3.00 for the examination and $1.00 for the drops."

On my way out of the room, I thanked him and slipped four bills into his hand.

Departing the hotel, I caught a glimpse of Calamity Jane rambling along main street in her suit of buckskin. I waited for her to walk with me to the stable to retrieve Black Nell. She said she'd been up all night and was on her way home.

Reaching the stable we parted ways. I said, "Take care Martha Jane… get your rest." She smiled civilly, too dog-tired to speak another word, I presumed, and went on her way.

Black Nell once more effortlessly carried me to Deadwood Creek. How I loved the black beauty, which under different ownership, particularly a person of grand wealth, could have been one of the finest show horses in the country.

I found the boy twenty feet upstream from his location the day before. He spied me as I gingerly wound the reigns of the stallion around what once been a thriving thicket.

Relinquishing my bag near the boy's gear, I removed my boots, rolled up my pantlegs a turn, and walked with pan in hand in his direction.

"Good morning, Mr. Hickok! I sees ya come ready to pan for them nuggets today… I hear two thousand dollars in gold's taken from Dead-wood streams a few days ago—Ya ready to get rich?"

"Counting on you to show me the right way to go about this."

For the first time I took note of his stunted skeleton beneath an over-sized shirt and pants.

"Ya, hungry?… Boys are always hungry. Brought you some dried apples and beans I picked up at the mercantile yesterday."

"Thanks, Mr. Hickok! Our only food somedays is what rabbits and birds I kin trap and catch and the sod corn we grate into flour. Sometimes pa trades with the Indians for things they needs, tho mostly they's lookin' for guns and 'munition. They give us furs we trade in town for coffee, flour, bacon, and the like."

The boy opened the small bag of dried apples and ate a few slices with relish.

Finishing, he said: "I'm willin' to teach ya what I know, not much to pannin', really…mostly takes stick-to-a-tiveness," his words had a ring of desperate positivity, as he prepared to demonstrate.

"Ya jes dip the pan into stream an make circul'r movements under the water, as the pan tilts and swirls, the gold goes to the bott'm…a tech-nique ya'll learn over time."

"What about those guys?" I said, pointing to three men working in tandem a half dozen yards away. They had set up a long wooden crib a few feet above the stream, one shoveling earth into the crib; another wielding a pickaxe to loosen fresh dirt in a patch of ground; a third man dipping water from the stream in a pail and pouring the water along the surface. "Don't I need to purchase more equipment than a pan?"

"Anoth'r way of goin' 'bout it... my way is simp'ler, gets the same results, septn' I don't have to share my findins' with no one but me and pa."

"Tell me about where you live...your pa got a nice log cabin, a few acres, a mule, and crops growing in the field?"

"We live simple, pa says...no need for the all the fancy nic'ties of life, thems for other folks. We getn' along jes fine the way we is."

I dipped my pan in the stream and began to swirl the water, periodically stopping to stare in search of anything reflecting in the morning sun.

The boy momentarily observed my technique before he resumed working his own site.

"Yer getn' the hang of it, Mr. Hickok," he said, "...probably work a bit fastr' tho."

"This kinda reminds me of all the hours I put in learning to shoot a gun as a boy...," I continued, "served me well when I became a stage-coach driver. I honed my skill even more when I scouted for General Custer infiltrating enemy lines and reporting my findings, for which I won various accolades. My quick draw and deadly aim saved my life and others more than a time or two."

"Ya have led a intres'tin life, it seems...ever been in a gun fight?"

"I was twenty-eight when I killed a man in a duel. The place was the Springfield, Missouri, town square in 1865. The trouble started during a poker game at a hotel involving a former friend and Confederate soldier, David Tutt."

"Ya shot yer friend?"

"We *were* friends, or so I thought, but it turned out he held personal grudges unbeknown to me. Tutt effactually cleaned me out during the card game...first my money then he grabbed my watch, a fine gold hunt-ing-cased Waltham, as collateral and walked out the front door."

"Did-ya get mad and go after him to get yer watch back?"

"Outside the front door I found Tutt standing a distance away, and he challenged me to a duel."

The boy ceased his panning and stared at me in disbelief, "Tha's scary, real scary... ."

"Tutt's shot strayed while mine found its mark... I vowed never again to find myself in shootout."

I ceased panning, my mind now absorbed with the hundreds of times I had struggled to find words to explain such killing...*the conundrum leading up to two grown men, inched to within twenty-five yards of one another, suddenly drawing their pistols, and taking aim. Polly Hickok had been right. I could have chosen better.*

I searched the boy's face for what he might be thinking...*perhaps a critique of my character.*

"Ya gotta put yer back into it," he said, exaggerating his movements.

We both doubled over with laughter as he persisted to wildly sway and contort his physique, demonstrating panning for gold.

He surprised me when he pulled a small bag from his pocket and withdrew a plug of tobacco, placed it inside one cheek, then offered the bag to me. I declined.

"Don't ya chew, Mr. Hickok...thot jes 'bout ev'ry man chews, and woman."

"I have my vices, for sure...consumption of tobacco's not one of them. Don't hang with loose women either."

The boy shrugged his shoulders and replaced the bag in a pocket.

I resumed panning. I had taken many roads in my life, had sundry adventures... Already I knew I didn't care to spend more days in this stream panning for gold; I continued, but only for the sake of the boy whose sustained gaze scrutinized my every effort.

My thoughts were elsewhere... *Neither were there any words to sufficiently explain the death of my deputy five years ago during a shootout with saloon owner Phil Coe. Catching a glimpse of someone moving towards me, I responded with two shots. The person was Deputy Williams. After that, I was relieved of my marshal duties, and so began the downfall of my career as a lawman. Since, the accidental death haunted my every waking moment.*

I stood and scanned the bleak, lifeless scenery around me that seemed a reflection of my life. Gone too was the sparkle of life I had embraced as a boy.

"I'm calling it a day," I said. "See you tomorrow...hope you find that big gold nugget, and if you do come by the hotel and tell me all about it."

"Ya stay safe, Mr. Hickok...wish ya good luck gamblin' today...hope yer poker hands 'er full-a lucky cards."

"Don't look for me tomorrow, Johnny... I'm gonna sleep in for a change," I added.

———

Two additional gambling houses, watering houses for Deadwood's twenty-five thousand thirsty men, went up almost overnight on either side of lower Main Street, known as the "Bad Lands" of Deadwood, each certain to keep their doors open day and night.

I preferred the elaborately accoutered Nuttall & Mann's Saloon for a single stool whose backdrop was a wall lined with the pictures of budded, blossomed, and blushed ladies, from which I had clear visibility of those entering the barroom through the front and back entry points.

Arriving through the back door, I passed by the reception room, parlor, and office to reach the large room with an ornate bar as its center-piece and huge back-bar mirror, complete with long rows of booze in cut-glass decanters, and glasses, and goblets suited to the various liquors from bourbon to imported Lacryma Christi.

By noon drifters and prospectors half-filled the smokey room, some who'd come for whoring and wagering—nearly all for whiskey-drinking. I myself had taken to heavy drinking after failure of my old west show and the loss of some much-needed income, and for a short time drunkenness sent me on a ruinous path, a path from which I'd been fortunate to recover. I only imbibed on occasions of dire need ever since.

On this day, now into my third week in Deadwood, walking to a reserved table I surveyed the lineup of fools eager to give up their life's earnings, be it a bag of gold dust, placer mining claim, or cold, hard cash in a game of five-card stud poker—poker being king of the games.

Missouri River steamboat captain William Massie and "Colorado Charlie"

Rich, a card dealer I'd met in Cheyenne, already occupied seats at the table. I had come across them in the early days of my arrival in town. They invited me to join their poker game, agreeing to my stipulation that I be permitted to sit in the same seat each time we played. Since, we three along with one other, a hairy-looking man from the hills who refused to divulge his name, had played myriad hands with one of the saloon's greasy dog-eared decks.

I noticed an admirably well-dressed fella in dark suit and tie standing at the opposite end of the bar. Upon closer observation, he was the owner of a uniquely crooked nose, *perhaps broken over losses in a card game brawl*, I surmised. The man inched closer to our table with every hand dealt, as though awaiting the courage to join the game. Ultimately, he staggered over and landed adjacent to me.

"Gentlemen, may I join in a hand or two of poker?...name's Jack McCall," he said, flashing a boozy smile.

I motioned with my hand for him to sit in the open seat. Instead, he held firm in his stance and began to insist—then demanded that he be permitted to occupy my stool.

After a long minute had passed, and seeing he was not easily deterred in his request, I raised my tall, sinewy, wide-shouldered frame from the stool to politely address him, eyeball to eyeball.

"A gambler by profession, and not one who only occasionally engages in the game, you can understand I prefer to see who walks through the door, and the seat I occupy allows for such observation...as on occasion, there have been those who turn into poor losers, and the combination of cards, libations, and guns—along with a growing indebtedness—often produces tenuous situations."

I returned to my seat and directed a formidable look at Rich to indicate he should proceed with the deal.

McCall remained motionless seconds longer before stammering to the open seat to my right and dropping onto the vacant stool, nearly falling onto the floor. Recovering, he withdrew a wallet from a pocket inside his jacket and dropped a few bills onto the table. Rich responded by pushing a small pile of poker chips across the tabletop in front of him.

Each player threw in an ante, and Rich dealt two cards to each player, one face-down, visible only to the player to whom it was dealt, the other face-up, visible to all players.

Clockwise from the dealer's left—McCall, me, Massie, and Hairy—announced his betting position. Hairy quickly folded. McCall called and raised the bet to five. Each remaining player matched the bet.

Rich dealt another face-up card and another betting round followed, then dealt another card after that betting round, and finally, one more card to each player to have a total of five, four face-up and one face-down. The final betting phase ensued after which the showdown began.

One by one each player revealed his hidden face-down card and showed the full strength of the hand he'd been dealt. My hand had the highest value—a pair of tens. I grabbed the pot and stacked the fresh chips to my right.

The dealing position moved to McCall. He loosened his tie, ordered another bourbon from Sam Young, the bartender, and reshuffled the deck.

A small crowd began to form as each player put in the ante for the new hand. Hairy won the second hand. McCall motioned for Sam to freshen his bourbon and dropped more bills in front of Rich. Sam delivered a fresh drink. McCall slammed down the contents in a single gulp.

I dealt the third hand—and won the pot a second time, as well as the next hand dealt by Massie. My piles of chips now quite ample, I flashed a momentary confident smile across the table at my peers.

Thereafter, McCall beckoned Sam's return at the start of each new hand.

After losing several more hands, McCall arose from his stool, jerked out his six-shooter and shot out an overhead light, barely missing the crystal chandelier.

Panic-stricken patrons ducked under tables for cover.

I focused my attention on McCall's eyes, one hand on my revolver, looking for the minutest indication he planned to redirect that gun in my direction.

"You're a rotten scoundrel and a dirty cheat, Hickok," he bellowed. "I'll be back tomorrow, and this time *you're* gonna pay BIG!"

Guardedly, I watched him storm out of the saloon.

Sam reappeared. "Can I get you gentlemen anything?" Almost in unison, Massie, Rich, and I asked for a beer.

Another man from the hill country, part of the crowd who'd been watching our game, warily slid into McCall's seat. By the coon tail hanging from the back of his hat, I figured his main occupation was trapper. He leaned a Remington Rolling Block rifle against the wall behind him, and adjusted the Colt Cavalry revolver at his waist, sliding it towards his back as far as possible.

"Got a name?" I said, admiring the revolver.

"Friends call me Beaver Dan—the Sioux call me *Mika*, beaver…. I can hand over my guns to the bartender, if you prefer."

"Not necessary, my friend… Sioux gave me the name *Matoskah*, white bear."

Sam delivered the beers. Rich reshuffled the cards, and we played on without further disturbance until time for the evening meal.

"Take care of the chips will you, Sam," I said, preparing to depart.

Sam arrived with a tray, and I tossed a chip in his direction as a tip.

Rich, Massie, and I strolled next door to the dining room of the Gem Theater and ordered the special: Filet of Buffalo aux Champignons with Sweet Potatoes and Tapioca pudding for dessert, washed down with a bottle of Claret. We remained for the burlesque show, and invited Dirty Em and Madam Mustachio, the two seasoned veterans who'd worked in many of the California and Nevada mining camps, to join our table after the show for some brandy. Madam Mustachio said she preferred employing high-end ladies who were talented singers, dancers, and balladists.

"Seems like just about every female in the town is employed in your business, Madam Mustachio," I said.

"Nearly, around ninety percent I'd guess…that's a lot of female companionship," she said with a flirtatious smile, her dark eyes twinkling irresistibly in the milieu.

"Calamity Jane ever ask for work here?" I added, breaking the spell.

"As I understand it, she inhabits a shanty at the far edge of town… preferring to work for Dora DuFran who runs a string of cathouses. I hear Martha Jane dresses up like a proper lady."

We thanked the ladies for their companionship, and on my way up to my room, I ordered a hot bath at the front desk. "A hot bath for one," I clarified.

Having informed young Johnny yesterday that he would not find me at the creek on the morrow, I relished the thought of breakfast in bed the subsequent morning.

———

On the afternoon of Wednesday, August 2nd, I—Sam Young—was behind the bar at Nuttall & Mann's Saloon and later gave my eye-witness account to Deadwood's Marshal Con Stapleton of the events that transpired on that fateful day. I came to know Wild Bill Hickok during the years we both called Hays City, Kansas, home. Later, I settled near Fort Laramie, Wyoming, and in 1875 worked as a teamster for the Newton-Jenney Expedition sent to map the Black Hills. In early 1876, in my mid-twenties, I took a job as bartender at the saloon in Deadwood.

I recall Wild Bill's uneasy mood as he entered the saloon after the rowdy incident with Jack McCall the previous afternoon. I thought to myself, a renowned gambler, Hickok had surely been in similar situations before. People can go crazy when they lose at gambling, especially if they've lost everything they own, though their reaction regularly depends on how much whiskey they've consumed; then it became more likely they'd threaten to kill the fella who just emptied their pockets. I reckoned Wild Bill had probably been threatened a thousand times and nothing usually came of it. The majority of gold-diggers in Deadwood just went home, slept off the drunkenness, and the next day went back to working in the mine. A lot of how well men react also depends on whether they have a family to go home to... Jack McCall didn't have a family, at least none that he claimed.

Wild Bill, who enjoyed the ambiance of saloons—along with the risks and rewards of gambling, the alcohol, and dressing well—stood cautiously at the entrance to the bar, half inside and half outside, scanning the place for any sign of McCall. He looked at me, and I indicated it was safe to come inside, the place was nearly empty. Wild Bill, yet ill at ease, stepped to the card table only to realize Charlie Rich occupied Hickok's favorite stool. I couldn't hear their conversation very well, but seemingly Wild Bill repeatedly asked Rich to move to another seat. Rich, who could be given to bouts of stubbornness, based on my experience— he often refused to pay his bar bill at the end of the night after a few too many pints. In the end, Rich refused to budge from the stool, and Wild Bill gave in and took the open seat so the game could begin.

The first hand had hardly been dealt when McCall stumbled through the front door. He was drunk as a skunk and soon fell onto a table, overturning it along with some stools. I noticed he carried a holstered gun. As McCall picked himself off the floor, I glanced at Wild Bill seated with his back to the front door. The faces of the three men seated opposite him reflected alarm of gigantic proportions. Wild Bill, by then aware of an incident occurring behind him, attempted to turn on his stool and stand but was prevented from doing so, as a moment later McCall was upon him, drew his single-action .45-caliber revolver, pointed it at the back of Wild Bill's head, and pulled the trigger. The legend fell from his stool onto the floor in a heap—dead.

I raced to restrain McCall, along with the help of others. I could tell he was so drunk that I was pretty sure he'd not remember he killed a man a day or two afterwards.

One patron stated his intention to retrieve the marshal, and within a few minutes he and his deputy arrived and hauled McCall off to jail.

I asked one of the ladies to find the coroner to notify him of the murder and to please come and remove the body. During the wait, I picked up Wild Bill's cards from the floor. The deadman's card hand was all aces and eights.

"Why was Wild Bill Hickok murdered?" Marshal Stapleton asked. Was it merely over losses incurred in a poker game, or perhaps the motive was fear among the camp's corrupt element that Hickok was about to be appointed marshal? I didn't know anything more than a good, honorable man lay dead. I informed the marshal I'd seen enough killing in this stinkhole of a place called Deadwood... And all I could think about was leaving, but at this very moment I don't know where I'd like to live next.

———

My name's Charlie Utter, and it was I who published in *The Black Hills Weekly Pioneer* the funeral for J. B. "Wild Bill" Hickok at my camp outside of Deadwood, today, Thursday, August 3, 1876, at 3 o'clock P. M. I am pleased to see so many from the town in attendance.

At this time, I will deliver the eulogy I have prepared for my recently departed, long-time friend, Wild Bill: Friends and acquaintances, it is with deep sadness that we have come today to mourn the untimely loss of a former Civil War soldier and scout, gunslinger, gambler, showman, actor, and renowned lawman. Wild Bill Hickok's considerable notoriety largely comes from his efforts in bringing law and order to the Frontier West and his display of fairness and courage.

Yesterday, on the afternoon of August 2nd, Wild Bill was assassinated in cold blood only three weeks after he arrived in Deadwood, where he, like countless in attendance today, came in the hope of making his fortune in gold. But fate seemingly had other plans, while playing poker at the Nuttall & Mann's Saloon, a drunken fool known as Jack McCall, who the day previous had lost multiple hands of poker playing against the professional skills of Wild Bill; a day later, yet enraged over his losses, McCall entered the saloon, pointed a revolver at the back of Wild Bill's head, shot, and killed him—even though Wild Bill's final act of kindness in this world had been to offer to purchase a meal for McCall, whose indebtedness had reached the point that McCall could not afford to purchase even a meal to feed himself any longer.

This I promise will come to pass in the coming days: Wild Bill's death will be avenged, wherein Jack McCall, currently residing in the Deadwood jail, charged with the crime of murder, shall face a miner's court as soon as possible, and McCall will be tried for murder. If found guilty, he shall be hanged by the neck until dead.

James B. Hickok leaves to mourn his new bride, Agnes Lake Hickok—married nary six months earlier—who is currently occupied in the southern states on business. I've mailed his gold-cased Waltham watch as a final keepsake of James. And a note of condolence was sent by Pony Express to his mother Polly Hickok, residing in Illinois, to inform her of James' sudden departure from this world. Additionally, three brothers and two sisters survive. His father, Bill Hickok, died when James was a young man.

Preparations are underway, and hopefully, by early next year, Wild Bill's remains will be relocated to the Mount Moriah Cemetery.

One additional person, a young lad from our own Black Hills area, has requested the opportunity to give a few remarks, and I ask that you to

listen diligently to what he has to say about his heartfelt recollections of
Wild Bill, whom he met and spent a great deal of time with along the
banks of Deadwood Creek, where their friendship began. The boy is
accompanied by his father.

My name is Johnny E. Perrett and me and my pa, Thomas Perrett, wanted
to come today upon learnin' of the sudden death of Mr. Hickok, a man I
found to be a kind and generous man who only had patience and encoura-
gin' words for me, though a mere boy, as you can see, and one most folks
don't give a rat's arse to be around, much less address day to day.

Mr. Hickok was polite and listened to my instructin's on pannin' for
gold. I don't believe he found a lick's worth-a gold dust since he come to
Deadwood, but I believe he found the things in life of real value… He
spoke highly of his ma, Polly Hickock. He said she lived a godly life and
convict'on, such that he measured all he was and become by her example.
His life, like most of us, was part circum'stance, the rest of his own
makin'—some's his actions he said he sorely regretted—but at his core,
he knew right from wrong and tried to do what was right, much as he had
control o'er. I reckon there's great men in the world who commanded
many people, but I think Mr. Hickok's the greatest of 'em all. I believe he
were at peace and had done just 'bout everythin' he'd planned to do in
life. He said he longed to be reunited with his new wife, Agnes.

Mr. Utter—I petition you, that you give aid when the time comes—in
that, when I die I wish to be buried in a nice spot near the man I come to
call my dear friend, Mr. Hickok. I plans ta one day marry a girl I love
named Mollie B, and I reckon she'll out-live me, and will gladly give you
whatever fee is required.

Oh, and should any person here ta'day see in comin' days I'm in
possess'n of Black Nell, well that's cusin' Wild Bill told Mr. Utter, "If
anythin' happens to me, either by murder or from some freak accident,
please see to it my stallion goes to my new friend Johnny Perrett." Mr.
Utter informs me Black Nell does clever tricks…like "jumpn' on a bar and
dancin' with all four hooves like a ballerina"… Well, I have yet to see that
for my'sef, but I'm happy Wild Bill wanted me to get Black Nell.

·   ·   ·

Thank you, son, for your kind remarks about Wild Bill, truly a great man.

And this concludes the eulogy from me, Charlie Utter...though, I feel obliged to add one final brief remark, a word of caution, really: Some of you know Calamity Jane, who also requested the opportunity to speak today of her relationship with Wild Bill, but I deemed her remarks not permittable at this occasion, in that Wild Bill stated on numerous occasions he did not wish to associate with her beyond Buffalo Bill Cody's shows, wherein Calamity Jane was often associated. Now, quite boldly she asserts that she is the "Real Mrs. Hickok—not that old biddy and cake-faced Agnes Lake!" Moreover, she threatens, upon her burial, whenever her death should occur, her wish is to be buried alongside the gravesite of Wild Bill Hickok. Even more preposterous is her claim of the existence of a love child between the two of them, an assertion I appeal that you summarily dismiss, as well.

And now, I invite one and all to remain throughout the evening for food and drink and to tell stories in remembrance of Wild Bill. In closing I propose a toast and ask you to raise your glass: Rest in peace, my friend, J. B. Hickok. You shall be sorely missed.

AUTHOR NOTES

Jack McCall was acquitted of the murder by a miner's court (with no jurisdiction) the day after murdering Wild Bill Hickok. McCall fled Deadwood but was eventually captured, convicted, and hanged in March 1877 by legal authorities of Dakota Territory. He was buried in Mount Moriah Cemetery in Deadwood, Lawrence County, South Dakota.

Calamity Jane died in 1903 and was buried alongside Wild Bill Hickok.

Johnny E. Perrett eventually found a gold nugget that weighed over seven troy ounces, believed to be one of the largest nuggets taken from the Deadwood area. He married Mary "Mollie" B. Hamilton in 1907. He died in 1943 and was buried in Mount Moriah Cemetery.

ABOUT THE AUTHOR

I grew up in a small midwestern town where few people would expect the idea for a Gangster Series, yet this is where I drew inspiration for my premier historical crime novel, Gangster in Our Midst, Bookkeeper, Lieutenant, and Sometimes Hitman for Al Capone (2017), which won a Notable Indie Book award. I returned to "Oxbow" during the pandemic to write The Black Bag of Dr. Wiltse, Murder on the Prairie (2021), and it won a Notable Indie Book award. A third novel in the series will follow in summer 2024. The novels are loosely set in my hometown of Fairbank, Iowa.

My first two books were substantial memorials. My short stories, poetry, and novellas have appeared in numerous anthologies, magazines, and newspapers. I write a "Gangster Blog" and a column for my hometown newspaper, the Fairbank Islander, and am a member of several mystery crime writers' organizations. I'm also working on a children's book, and writing a play based on Gangster in Our Midst. A decade ago, after retiring from a Fortune 500 company, I launched my career as an author. My husband (my rock) and I reside in the Twin Cities. Together we have especially enjoyed rescuing Bichon Frise dogs…though, truth be told, they have rescued us.

More information on her works can be found on her website: BettyBrandtPassick.com.

BATTY FOR LOVE

TINA SUSEDIK

1

With her backpack holding her laptop and purse slung over her shoulders, Nella Cambien dragged her suitcase up the flight of stairs at the Deadwood Historic Brothel. Halfway up, she paused and glared at the gazillion stairs left to climb. She wiped away the sweat pouring down her face threatening to slide into her eyes.

All right. So maybe not a gazillion stairs, but at least thirty. Well, okay, probably twenty. Either way it was more than she'd bargained for. And this was the first trip of many. Food, books, things for the basket she needed to put together for the raffle at the Wild Deadwood Reads event in three days. In the past, the men who climbed these stairs to visit a lady of the evening were probably too tired to perform.

The suitcase clunking on each step echoed through the wide stairwell. Out of the ten people staying here, she was the first to arrive. Knowing this historical brothel was haunted shouldn't bother her. She enjoyed the paranormal. Things going bump in the night.

The caretaker of the building had told her the haunts were friendly.

Did silly things like knock newly washed and folded towels to the floor. Moved her coffee cup around, unplugged the vacuum cleaner as she was using it, and seemed to dislike the microwave as it would shut off halfway through a cycle. It had been replaced several times. There was no way every microwave could be defective, so it had to be the spirit still living here.

Nella paused at the top of the stairs to catch her breath. Maybe it hadn't been wise to dress in jeans, cowboy boots, long-sleeved shirt, and a western hat, but she hadn't expected it to be so hot for this early in June. She removed her hat and swiped her arm across her forehead, then proceeded down a short hallway to the end and stopped. To her right was a long corridor. A tall, antique-looking armoire at the end probably stored sheets and towels. Light filtered into the hallway from the right. Must be from two of the three bedrooms at the backside of the building. Both were assigned to models attending the event.

She set her laptop and purse on the floor, released the handle of her suitcase, and caught her breath. Maybe it was time she exercised more. She headed to the left. The first door immediately to her left was her and her friend, Teresa's, room. She peered through the open door. Sure enough, there was the long, claw-foot bathtub sitting in the bedroom. The attached bathroom held a shower, double sinks, and toilet.

The antique-looking furniture suited a building from the 1880s. Whether the furniture was authentic was up for debate. Since the fire of 1879 had wiped out the downtown, anything after then would be at least one-hundred-forty years old. Certainly, old enough to be considered antique.

Doilies covered the dressers, probably to protect them from careless visitors. With all the old touches in the room, the ceiling fan and pot lights appeared out of place. Did the rooms have tin ceilings in the 1880s?

A rustling noise came from behind her, like a swish of a skirt, then a clunk of a shoe. Probably the friendly ghost. Anyway, she hoped so. No one else was supposed to be here yet. Had someone arrived early without telling her? Her heart skipped a beat. Maybe it wasn't such a good idea to be here by herself after all. Ghosts she could handle, but an intruder? Not so much.

The sound came again. With her heart in her throat, she picked up a ceramic pitcher nestled in a matching bowl from the top of a dresser. As quietly as she could while wearing cowboy boots, she tiptoed from her room into the main, open living area. The room was long with a bank of windows across the front. Since she'd come in from the rear of the building, she assumed this room faced Main Street. The open kitchen on the left included the largest island she'd ever seen.

Clutching the pitcher in her hand, she took a step into the area and gasped. It was gorgeous. Like something out of a movie. A long, dark mahogany bar was on the other side of the room. A decadent picture of a nude woman reclining on a couch hung over it. A desk where a madam would likely take money from clients or do her books was by a small narrow wall set between the windows. Everywhere she looked were antiques.

There was even the slight scent of cigar smoke as if the gentlemen waiting for their entertainment of the night had recently left the room. It was hard to believe the lingering cigar odor would still be present after so many years. With the imagination of an author, she visualized men lounging on the flowered chairs and couches. Maybe playing a game of cards at a round table or spinning the small roulette wheel on the top of the bar.

Nella had written several historical romances set in Deadwood, called 'The Darlings of Deadwood.' Had done a lot of research, but this was the first time she was staying at such an historic and dubious place of pleasure. If only the walls could talk. The stories she could write. Instead, she would have to picture what had taken place here. Or at least use the multitude of pictures of women in various stages of undress in her books.

After poking her head in the bedroom nearest the kitchen, she tiptoed past the bar. There was supposed to be one more bedroom at the end of the room. Like the others, the door was open, but the room dark. More rustling came from inside. She swung the pitcher over her shoulder, preparing to attack anything or anyone who may emerge, ghost or not.

Nella took a deep breath and stepped closer to the room. Something squeaked, like a bird caught in netting or being chased by a predator. She sighed in relief. There must be a bird trapped inside the room. All she had to do was open a window and chase it out.

Since it wouldn't help a scared bird escape, she set the pitcher on a small table, stood in the doorway of the room, and reached for the light switch. As she did, something flew passed her head. Darn. Now she would have to catch it in the larger room. She spun on her heel as something else winged by, missing her face by a fraction of an inch. Great. Unless one bird followed the other, how was she going to get two birds free? Maybe she could open all the windows and they would naturally seek freedom.

Neither bird was in sight. Where had they gone? She walked across the room when something hit her on the head and fell to the floor. Two more birds flapped into the room and flittered around the space.

Whatever had landed on the floor crawled across her foot. Nella screamed. Oh. My. God. No. No. No. Her worst nightmare coming to life. The things she hated and was scared of the most. Those weren't birds but . . .

Bats! As if the hounds of hell and not innocent bats were chasing her, she skidded across the room, knocking over a small table and several chairs in front of the bar and into her room. She slammed the door behind her and leaned against the door trying to keep her stomach from revolting.

Something hit the other side of the door. Were they trying to get in? Had they morphed into humans set on attacking her? Good heavens. She had to get her wits about her. Her friends always said she had such a vivid imagination; she could take a banana and make it a murder weapon.

Taking a deep breath, she took a step away from the door and looked up. Bile filled her throat. She was going to die. Not from the bats themselves, but from fear.

Stuck in the door was a bat's wing. It must have tried to follow her and got caught when she slammed the door. The poor thing was squeaking and flapping on the other side. She bit a fingernail and blinked back tears. What should she do? If she opened the door to let it free, it could fly into her sanctuary. The brothel was on the second floor. There would be no way to escape if it, or others, would get in.

Wait. She could call the caretaker who would arrive to save the day – and her sanity. Nella slapped her hand against her forehead and dropped onto the edge of the bed furthest away from the door. She was an idiot. Her phone, laptop, and suitcase were in the hallway. She was stuck.

A friend had once said her reaction to bats was unrealistic. They ate mosquitos and other bugs. They were actually rather cute. *Cute* her behind. They were ugly, ugly, ugly. Besides, her friend hadn't spent time living in houses where bats routinely got inside. Lying beside her sister in bed at night, they'd cover their heads with blankets and scream for their father to come upstairs and either kill them or chase them out the window. She'd never get the sounds of bats squeaking and flapping their wings in their darkened room out of her memory.

Now what? The bat continued to flap against the door. As much as she hated the mammals, she felt sorry for the poor thing, but not bad enough to launch a rescue. She took a deep breath. It wasn't the bat's fault it got stuck. It was time to put her big-girl panties on and set it free. It would be better than listening to it squeaking and hitting the door until it died.

With another deep breath, a lump in her throat, and heart beating like a hummingbird's wings, she approached the door. If she opened it quickly, hopefully it would fly off and she wouldn't have to touch it. She closed her eyes to keep from seeing the brown membrane sticking out at her.

"C'mon, Nell. Don't be such a wuss. Get it over with." She opened her eyes, turned the doorknob, and with a screech rivaling a teenager at their favorite rock concert, creaked open the door. As soon as the bat hit the floor, Nella slammed the door closed, jabbed the lock button, ran to the bathroom, and locked the door behind her. She sat on the toilet seat, put her head between her knees, and swallowed the saliva pooling in her mouth. After a few moments, she sat up.

"You're being ridiculous." She filled a glass with water, downed it in several gulps, and glanced at herself in one of the oval mirrors over the sinks. Her face was pale. Perspiration beaded on her forehead and upper lips. She wet a washcloth and wiped her face.

Right about now, if he'd been here, her ex-boyfriend would be laughing his ass off at her. Never one to have sympathy for anyone's fears, he would have called her all sorts of names, like a little boy teasing someone on the playground. *Chicken. Fraidy Cat. Idiot. Coward. Lily-livered.*

Yellow-bellied. And he would be right, just as she had been right to dump the jerk.

"Okay, Nella." She patted her long, curly, auburn hair into place. "There is no way a bat can unlock the doors." She chuckled then froze. "But can they crawl through a crack beneath the door?" She grabbed a large bath towel from a shelf beneath the sink, unlocked the bathroom door, and tiptoed to the bedroom door. A bit of light leaked from the crack at the bottom of the door. Had the bat crawled through? There was only one way to find out.

Easing the door open, she peered through the slit and breathed a shuddering sigh of relief. The bat— she assumed it was the same one— was crawling across the floor away from her. Even though she hated them, she hoped he hadn't broken a wing or anything. She pushed the door closed, rolled up the towel, and placed it in front of the gap.

It seemed like hours since she'd entered the brothel, but how much time had actually passed? There were no clocks in the room. Since she used her phone for virtually everything, she didn't wear a watch and had no idea of the time. Maybe it was time to wean herself from relying so much on her phone.

Her stomach growled. Of course, her snacks were in her backpack. After turning on a red, Victorian-style lamp, she sat on the edge of the bed facing the windows. The wooden, plantation-style blinds were closed. She opened them letting in the blinding, afternoon western sun. With more light in the room, a picture of another 'working girl' hung to the right of the windows. What was different about this one was it included a written article.

In May of 1880, Ruby Prescott, one of the working girls, was murdered in this room. Her body was found draped over the side of the bathtub. Despite efforts to find the culprit, the murder was never solved.

"Oh, my. One of the working girls was murdered in this room?" Nella peered over shoulder as if expecting to find the murderer behind her. "The poor thing."

Throughout the century, murders in the wild town weren't unusual, but what could this woman have done to make someone take her life? Had she been married and her husband had taken umbrage at other men visiting her? Was one of her 'clients' unhappy with her service? Had she stolen money from one of the men?

Prostitutes were known to be on drugs, especially in the 'olden' days when men showed up drunk, smelly, and belligerent. The women had to survive their hell in some way. Had she stolen drugs? Nella shrugged. She'd never know.

Now what? At least she had a bathroom. If she drank enough water, maybe it would stem her hunger. And if she drank enough water, she had a toilet to relieve herself. Speaking of which . . .

Walking past the long, clawfoot bathtub, she ran her fingers over the edge, catching her boot on one of the feet.

A bright light flashed before her eyes, dimmed into sparkles of stars, then went dark. *What the hell* was her last thought as her body hit the floor.

2

"WHAT THE . . .?" NELLA LAY ON THE FLOOR BESIDE THE
bathtub. She rolled to her back and stared at the ceiling. Her head spun
and black dots swirled like snowflakes before her eyes. She blinked to
clear her vision, ran a hand under the back of her head, and let out a
breath. No lump. No blood. But what happened? She'd never ever
fainted, but one minute she was walking to the bathroom, and the next . .
.

After a moment to settle her head, she leaned up on her elbows, and
blinked several times. This was crazy. Where was the ceiling light? The
blinds? The only light coming into the room was through a crack at the
edge of a set of red, brocade drapes where dust motes danced through the
stream of sunlight.

Instead of dried flowers and lemon-scented dusting spray, the room
smelled musty or like unwashed bodies and dirty clothing. Rather like her
brother's unkempt room when they were growing up. There was also the
odor of the fuel oil her grandparents had used to heat their house.

Another underlying odor hit her nostrils. Metallic. A bit like . . .
Blood? But she hadn't cut her head. She checked her hands to see if she'd
cut them on the way to the floor. Nope. As clean as they were when she
entered the room.

She sat up. The sheets and blankets on the bed were in disarray. A white stocking hung over the bed's metal footboard. A shattered lamp lay on the floor. Along with lamp oil pooling across the floor, shards of green glass were scattered about.

Something to her left caught her attention. Her breath and pulse hitched. A body lay across the rim of the tub. A drab gray nightgown barely covered the lower body. A nearly shredded stocking hung down to one ankle. Was it a match to the one on the end of the bed?

Her body shaking, Nella rose to her knees for a closer inspection. Bent at the waist, the woman's upper body was draped over the tub. Her arms and head hung inside. Blood was splattered over the bottom and sides of the tub. Her long, brilliant red hair, a color not seen in nature, obscured the side of her face.

"Oh, my God. I think she's dead." Biting back a scream, she crab-walked across the floor toward the door, then clawed for the door handle. Wait. The bats. She couldn't leave the room with all those bats out there. She sat on the floor, leaned against the door, and rested her head on her bent knees. Where had the woman come from? Was this a bad dream? Maybe she'd been doing too much research on Deadwood for her books.

That was it. She'd fallen asleep at her desk and was dreaming about the upstairs brothels. She pinched her arm. Damn. Maybe she shouldn't have pinched herself so hard, but it wasn't hard enough to wake herself up. The woman was still draped over the tub. The curtains were still red brocade, and there were no electric lights.

Bats or no bats, the best thing to do would be to leave the room and find someone to help her. First, she should look out the window. Maybe there was a way to leave without going into the other room and sneaking around the bats. But it would mean going past the dead woman. She sucked in a breath. So be it. After all, a deceased person couldn't fly at her, get in her hair, bite her, or drop guano on her.

Nella stood. Instead of walking past the woman, she climbed over the bed; cowboy boots be damned. She'd pay for any damages they might cause. As she skittered across, the odor of the bedding stung her nose. Heavens, when was the last time this woman changed her sheets?

Along with the window blinds, the sign about the murdered prostitute was gone. She grabbed the drapes and yanked them open. Dust flew making her nose itch. After being in the darkened room, the bright light hurt her eyes. She blinked a few times and peered through the unwashed window into the empty lot behind the building.

Wait. Empty lot? Her car and everyone else's vehicles should have been there. Instead, there was nothing but muddy ground, a slope leading to a hill, and a sorrel horse tied to a rickety post. After several pushes, she managed to open the two sides of the window. She breathed in fresh air, then jerked back into the room. When had the leaders of Deadwood allowed the city to smell like something from a farm or outhouse? Deadwood was always clean and fresh.

A rickety shack barely clung to the hillside. Music from an out-of-tune piano came from her left. A gunshot sounded too close for comfort. The tinny music stopped, then started up again. Laughter, both male and female, came from the other side of her door behind her.

Goosebumps pebbled her arms. She never understood people saying the hair on the back of their neck rose, but now she did. Something was wrong. Terribly, horribly, scarily wrong. This had to be a dream where she wasn't where she was supposed to be.

"Ruby, someone is asking for you."

Who was Ruby?

Someone knocked on the bedroom door. "C'mon, girl. Your first client is waiting." The second knock was louder. "Ruby? Are you in there? It's going to be a busy night. Get your ass out here." The person rattled the doorknob.

She didn't dare answer the door. If they came in the room and saw the body, presumably Ruby, they would assume she'd killed the woman. She couldn't take a chance. Nella searched the room for a place to hide. Nothing where she could stuff her five-foot, eight-inch body. Crawling beneath the short bed would be impossible. There was no closet. The screen in the corner would be the first place someone looked.

The knocking grew louder and more persistent. Nella peered out the window again. The only place would be down. But how?

"Did anyone see Ruby leave her room?" The door handle rattled again.

Think, Nella. Think. The sheets. If she tied them together and then to the bedpost, would it be long enough to get her down from the second floor? There was only one way to find out.

Nella yanked back the patchwork quilt and wrinkled her nose at the exposed, dingy sheets.

A male voice joined the woman calling for Ruby. "Ruby. Answer the door. I paid fer you, so's you'd better come out."

There was no time to worry about bodily fluids and germs on the bedding. She removed the top and bottom sheets. She tied the ends together and pulled them tight, double tied one end to the metal foot-board, and tossed the other end out the window.

"Darn it." The end was about two feet shy of the ground.

"I'm gonna break this damn door in, Ruby, iff'n you don' answer." The entire door shook.

Grunting, Nella tugged the end of the bed until it was flush with the window, then climbed on the bed, and took hold of the sheet. Before heading down, she grabbed her hat and pressed it on her head, making sure it wouldn't fall off.

"Here goes nothing." She slid over the windowsill, clutched the end of the sheet then, hand-under-hand, slowly made her way down. Her boots hit the outside wall. Her hands sweated. Her heart pounded against her ribcage, and her lungs burned.

Nella glanced over her shoulder and shuddered. The ground was still too far away. And once she got to the bottom, what would she do? Obviously, she wasn't where she'd started out when arriving at the brothel. But where was she?

A crash came from the room. The door must have been bashed open. Someone screamed. The rope moved upward. She had to get to the ground before she was pulled back up. A man's head appeared in the window and the sheet slackened.

"Hey, you. Stop."

Like she was going to listen. The sheet grew taut again and rose about a foot. The man was hauling her back up.

"I said stop."

Without looking to see how close she was to the ground, and, instead of gripping hand-over-hand, she slid down the sheet. It was like trying to walk against the wind in a storm. She lowered herself two feet while she was hoisted up a foot. At least she was gaining ground. Speaking of ground, she was nearly there. Her tips of her shoes touched the mud, but before she could release her hands, she was jerked back up again.

The heck with it. She was close enough to the ground where she shouldn't break or sprain an ankle. Since the ground was muddy, if she fell, she wouldn't hurt herself. But, unfortunately, it was slippery enough to make her land on her rear end. Instantly, mud seeped through her jeans. Leaning back on her elbows, she glanced up at a man with a full, bushy beard. A blonde-haired woman stood beside him.

"You killed Ruby! You killed Ruby!" Her screams could probably be heard all the way to the front of the building.

"Don't you move an inch, mister." The dark-haired man raised a fist in the air. "I'm getting the cops."

Uh, no. Obviously, she somehow traveled to another time. What year was it? Now was not the time to figure it out. She needed to hightail it somewhere safe. Lord only knew where.

3

Stuart Adams walked down the raucous Deadwood Main Street, crossing a street dividing what was commonly known as 'The Badlands' and the 'good side of town.' Even though Sherriff Manning had hired him as a deputy after the 1879 fire, it was his day off and he was heading into the hills to search for wildlife. He hoisted his knapsack containing binoculars, beef jerky, cheese, bread, a pocket diary, and water higher up on his shoulders.

But old habits die hard. He was always on the lookout for trouble. As the town was rebuilding, an attempt was made to make the town safer, but it seemed no matter what they did, the rowdies and outlaws still managed to create havoc.

As fast as the town burned, rebuilding began, although this time citizens were made to use brick for their buildings. The businesses reconstructed the quickest were the saloons and brothels. Maybe, someday, there would be no more of either, but it probably wouldn't happen in his lifetime, nor his children's, if he were ever to marry.

He didn't begrudge men their drink and entertainment, but it was the way the painted ladies were treated. He'd seen plenty of supposedly upstanding citizens sneak into the back alley to enter the upstairs rooms. Other than breaking up fights or disputes, he'd never been in one for servicing. He'd been told there were hallways going across the second floors of each building from one end of the block to the other, all housing rooms.

A gunshot rang through the air, but since no others followed and no one yelled, he ignored it. Sometimes when men came in from their gold camps, they wanted to let off steam. As long as no one got hurt, they didn't follow up on gunfire.

What was difficult to ignore on were the screams of the ladies of the evening. It was hard to tell if they were really in danger or laughing and screeching with the men who frequented them. He couldn't count the number of times he'd run toward what he thought was a woman being accosted and found out it was one simply trying to get the attention of a customer. He believed there were times a woman, and sometimes men, could have been saved had there not been so many false alarms. It made for a frustrating job.

It was sad to say, if a woman screamed on the good side of Main Street, he would go running like a madman to save her. Those women weren't any better than the 'soiled doves,' but he'd know for sure someone was actually in trouble. Sometimes when the camp men came to town and had a few too many, they forgot which side to be on.

Even in the middle of the day, the Badlands were noisy. But beneath the pianos, girls calling from the balconies of the Gem, and other brothels, and men calling back to them, someone was yelling murder from what seemed to be from the rear of the buildings. He turned left on Wall Street, passed The Sideboard Saloon, and turned right onto the alley behind the saloons, brothels, and stores. Several buildings down, a man hung out a second-story window.

"Hey, deputy, someone done kilt one of the girls up here. The culprit climbed down dese sheets and got away."

From the corner of his eye came a flash of someone running down West Main Street. The person glanced over his shoulder before disappearing around a building. Should he make chase or check out the woman? Even if he went after the person, it didn't mean he was the murderer or if he'd even be able to catch him. From what he saw, the man was wearing a rounded, brown hat, dungarees, and a red plaid shirt.

Ah, hell. Dressed like about every other miner in Deadwood. What was different about this man was his clothes seemed clean and in good shape for a miner and a long, dark braid ran down his back. He shrugged. Best to check out the so-called murder. Probably was one of the girls too drunk on booze or on drugs to move.

"Someone open the door for me." Brothels usually kept their doors locked to keep out the worst of the men. He didn't blame them. Besides, some of the brothels had regular customers.

He stared down the alley waiting for the door to open. He tipped his hat when a woman opened the door. A lady was a lady no matter what she did. "Hey, Miss Edda. Where is she?"

"This way." Without making sure he was following her, the madam lifted her skirt and headed up the long flight of stairs.

Stuart followed her to a landing, then to a room on the left. He shoved his way through the scantily clad women gathered outside the door. "Move out of the way, people." The men were probably hiding from him or had scurried from the building.

The women made a path for him, several of them sniffling into hand-kerchiefs. "Where is she?"

"It's Ruby. She's lying over the tub."

The room was in disarray. For some reason, the foot of the bed was pushed up against the open window. A broken green lamp lay on the floor, the glass crunching beneath his feet as he walked to the tub.

Sure enough. There was a woman draped across the edge of the tub, her bright red hair covering her face giving him an idea where she got her name from. Blood was splattered in the tub and her hair. He squatted by the tub and felt the vein in her neck. Sure as shootin' she was dead.

"Does anyone know what happened?" His knees creaked when he stood up and looked at the group of women.

"No. When her customer arrived, I called for her, but she didn't answer. When I pounded on the door and got no response, Jack broke in the door. That's when we saw the open window and a man climbing down the sheets." She paused for a moment. "Jack was trying to pull him back up."

"Then what happened?"

"Well, Jack couldn't get him up fast enough, so the man got away. He was surely the person to murder poor Ruby. Then you showed up."

Stuart pulled his hat lower to observe the women in the room without them noticing who he was looking at. "When was the last time anyone saw Ruby?"

A few of the women shuffled their feet and wouldn't look up, which was strange. In his experience, brothel women tended to stick up for each other.

"Well? Doesn't anyone remember?" He placed a hand on his gun. Maybe it would put some fear in them. "Does anyone recall seeing a man enter Ruby's room this morning? Did anyone see her last customer leave last night?"

Clutching the neck of her robe together, a rather pretty brunette stepped forward. "I saw her last night or early this morning after her last customer left. She said she was going to sleep. But I didn't see anyone leave or come in."

"Anyone else?"

A few shook their heads, while others remained quiet. "All right. Have someone fetch Doc Morris and have him come up here."

Edda put a hand on one of the girls who turned to leave the room. "Call him. If he's not available, call Doc Von Wedelstaedt."

Would he ever get used to people having those telephones? They had one in the sheriff's office, but he didn't have one at his place. "Either one will work. Call Sheriff Manning and Undertaker Smith, too, and tell them what happened. And the rest of you get out of here." With all the people coming and going from the room, any evidence would be corrupted.

Edda shooed the women from the room. "What do you think happened?"

"From the large gash in the back of her head and the broken lamp, I'd say someone smashed it over her head." He took Edda's elbow. "Now, I need you and your girls to stay out of here."

"What are you going to do? Are you going after the murderer?"

"Since I don't know who it is, no sense in running after someone who is probably long gone. I'm going to stay here until the doctor and sheriff arrive." If there were still a door on its hinges, he'd close it. As it was, he'd have to stand in the doorway and keep guard. Since he wasn't sure who the culprit was, he would keep his back to the room. Not that he wanted to watch the goings on in the main room, but he figured with the murder of one of her girls, Edda would shut her place down or send the men down the hallway to another brothel.

The murmur of the girls' voices didn't stop until Edda halted their conversations. "Girls. Go to your rooms. We're closed for the night."

Stuart placed his knapsack in the hallway outside the door and stepped into the main room, surprised at the opulence. He expected something dingy and dark, not brocade curtains, a bar, floral-covered chairs and couches, and tables for gambling. Since there were still lit cigars in ashtrays, liquor glasses, and cards strewn about the tables, his assumption the men high-tailed it out of the premises was correct. "I believe the sheriff will want to question everyone, so why don't you all stay in this room. Maybe make tea or something."

His comment brought laughter.

"Tea?"

"Did he say tea?"

"Does he think that's what we drink up here?"

"Hey, deputy. Want us to make you a cup of *our* tea?"

Heat rose to his face. Okay, so maybe he was an idiot. Obviously, they don't drink tea. "Uh. No, thank you. I'll pass."

After a few more chuckles, the women went back to chatting, and he returned to leaning against the doorframe. Depending on where the sheriff and doctor were, they should be here soon. In the meantime, he could think about who would want to kill the young woman.

He glanced over his shoulder at the tub where the girl lay. Like so many prostitutes, she was young—maybe seventeen or eighteen. He always wondered what made a woman become a soiled dove. He firmly believed it was not a choice, but a necessity. Then there were men like Al Swearengen who tricked women into coming to Deadwood under the false assumption they would be waitresses, only to find out they would be upstairs girls instead.

What was taking those men so long? If he stood here any longer, he'd doze off on his feet. The girls' chitter-chatter had slowed. It was going on late morning. The women had probably been up until the wee hours of the morning.

Stuart repositioned his crossed legs and rested his head against the door frame. A yawn cracked his jaw. It wasn't from being tired, but because of boredom. It was his day off. He should be up in the hills looking for wildlife, and not the two-legged kind. At this rate, it would be too late to do any hiking, and he wouldn't have another day off until next week. Dammit. Why couldn't he have ignored Jack's yells?

Huh. Where had Jack gone? He'd disappeared into the hullabaloo. Stuart pushed from the doorway. "Miss Edda. Can you please come here?"

The bleary-eyed woman came around the corner. "Yes? Are you ready for some *tea* now?"

Stuart shook his head. "Very funny. Where did Jack go?"

Edda stared at the floor. "Now that you mention it, I don't rightly know."

"You wouldn't be lying to me, now. Would you? Maybe he's the one who killed Ruby and made up the story about a man tying bedsheets together to climb out the window. Maybe you caught him before he could get away."

"I'm not lying. Ruby was a friend of mine. I'd never let someone get away with killing her." She raised her chin in a sign of defiance. "Besides, he wasn't the first one in the room."

"Who was?"

"After he broke down the door, I was. And I can assure you, I didn't kill her."

Stuart raised an eyebrow. "You sure about that?"

"Yes. Not to sound crass, but besides being a friend, her death means a loss of income to me. Now I have to find someone to replace her."

Made sense in a rather greedy kind of way. "All right. You can go. Hopefully, the sheriff will get here soon." He pulled out his pocket watch and checked the time. He'd been here nearly two hours, giving the perpetrator plenty of time to leave Deadwood. Heck, he could be almost in Scooptown by now catching a stagecoach for parts unknown. He mentally corrected himself. It was now called Sturgis. Plus, there were plenty of woods and hills to hide in between here and there.

Deep voices and pounding of boots on the stairs signaled the arrival of at least the sheriff.

Followed by Doc Morris, Manning appeared. "What's going on here, Adams?"

"Someone murdered one of Edda's girls." Stuart stepped to the side to allow the men to enter the room.

"Has anyone touched anything?"

"Not while I was here. I don't know about before I arrived."

"How did you find her?"

While Doc Morris checked Ruby, Stuart filled him in on what happened.

"Did you get a good look at the man?"

"No. He got away before I could see his face. I was able to see what he was wearing, though."

Manning waved the undertaker into the room. "Anything distinguishing?"

"Unfortunately, no. He looked like any other miner in town."

"So, was she murdered, Doc?"

Morris stood and stared at the woman. "Unless she could smash the lamp on the back of her own head, I say yes. There's glass embedded in her scalp. Plus, there's a wicked stab wound in the side of her neck. That would account for all the blood."

"When do you think she was killed?"

"Hard to say, but some time yesterday."

Stuart nodded. "That would coincide with what Edda and some of the women said."

"Well, let's get her out of here." He signaled to the coroner who removed the bundled-up quilt from the bed and spread it on the floor.

Stuart would never get over how heavy a body could be. Even one as slight as Ruby. After wrapping the woman in the quilt, Morris and the coroner carried her down the stairs.

"You did a good job, Adams. I know it is your day off, but I would like you to join me in interviewing the women. Maybe someone saw something they didn't realize they'd seen."

Recalling the way some of them wouldn't look at him, he had an idea maybe they'd been involved. He could do a better job watching them while the sheriff did his interrogations. He withheld a sigh and followed Manning into the other room. Looked like his day off was ruined.

4

NELLA'S STOMACH RUMBLED. WHEN WAS THE LAST TIME SHE'D eaten? Based on what she'd seen while trying to hide, somehow, some-way, she'd been sent back a few years. After reading an old playbill flying across the muddy street, she was in 1880. So, essentially she hadn't eaten in a hundred and forty-four years. No wonder she was hungry.

From her hiding place in a deserted, ramshackle alley lean-to, she watched the comings and goings of Deadwood's less savory citizens provided by a door hanging on one hinge. Obviously, she was in the Badlands part of Main Street. She'd done enough research to recognize it.

The big question was now what? She had nothing but the clothes on her back. The few dollars with dates from the 2000s she had in her pocket would certainly raise eyebrows. Had the men from the brothel seen her face? Did they know she was a woman? Once she'd left the alley, she'd tucked her French-braided hair beneath her hat.

As it was, her favorite boots were covered in mud, as were her jeans. How long before a search party started hunting for her? Would they even look for the killer of a young prostitute, or were they treated as second or third-class citizens? Maybe they'd already figured it out. Any number of people could have killed the woman. How many men did she have to service a night? Had she cheated one of them? Robbed his wallet? Refused to do something he wanted?

Nella shuddered. Once when she had done a ghost tour of the Fairmont Hotel, they were given a brothel 'menu.' She couldn't believe some of the disgusting things the women were paid to do.

Her stomach growled its distress. Heavens, she needed something to eat and drink. Even the stink of the muddy, offal-filled streets couldn't curb her empty stomach. Sitting on the dirt floor with her back against an outside wall, her hat on the floor beside her, she sifted dirt through her fingers contemplating what to do next. Thinking about going into the past to see what it was really like was totally different than actually being here, all alone, with no money, and, on top of that, finding a corpse. Then having to climb out a brothel window and shimmy down a rope made from sheets. As an author, she couldn't begin to make this stuff up.

Nella scooped up a handful of dirt and poured it into her other hand, letting the dirt slip through her fingers. She stopped. There was something in the dirt. A pebble? A dried piece of . . . Well, she wasn't about to think about what it could be. She rubbed her thumb over it. It was thin and flat. Shiny through the dirt. Could it be? She spat on it and brushed it against her jeans.

Oh. My. God. Gold? Had she found a piece of gold or was this fool's gold? She'd read about people finding gold dust beneath buildings, but a piece of it? She couldn't tell what type of building this had been. A house? One of the many saloons lining Main Street? Except for coming up with a story about where she'd found it, it didn't matter. Now all she had to do was find an assayer's office.

Nella stood, put the piece of gold in her pocket, and plopped her hat back on her head, making sure to tuck her braid inside. Outside, after glancing both ways, she joined a group of men heading down the street. With each suck of mud on her boots, her worry grew. Would the assayer accept her gold? How much was it worth? Would he question where she got it? What should she tell him? Having grown up being told the truth was always best, she decided it was exactly what she'd do. Tell him how, but not where.

Who knew, maybe there was more buried in the dirt. And depending on how long she'd be stuck in 1880, she might need more. With no knowledge of gold and its actual worth – especially in 1880, would it be enough to survive? How she missed being able to look things up on the internet.

She stepped up on the wooden sidewalk and stomped the mud from her boots. How was she even going to get back to her time? Did she have to go back to the brothel and the room where the whole mess started?

Keeping with the flow of people, she tried to ignore the saloons and dance halls, especially The Gem Theatre. The last person she wanted to meet, even dressed as a man, was Al Swearengin.

There remained a slight scent of burned buildings from the fire which destroyed over three hundred buildings eight months previously. While it seemed most of the town had been rebuilt in such a short amount of time, a few empty lots were scattered about. And since there was more construction going on, more than likely, it wouldn't be long and those lots would be filled, probably with another saloon or three.

By the time she got to Lee Street and the end of the wooden sidewalks, she was ready to give up. The scent of food from various restaurants nearly had her begging for money. It was time to ask for help. But who? In this part of town, properly dressed women, accompanied by dapper-looking men, carried baskets over their arms, more than likely doing their shopping.

Finally, taking a deep breath, she approached a woman holding the hand of a tow-headed boy, practically dragging him down the sidewalk. The hem of her dress was caked with mud. How did anyone keep their clothes clean around here?

"Excuse me, ma'am, but could you please tell me where I can find the assayer's office?"

The woman gave her a frown, a huff, and her back.

"Well, that went well." She didn't actually blame the woman. She probably looked like someone dragged through the streets by a pair of oxen. Smelled like one, too.

"Excuse me, Miss. I couldn't help overhearing you asking where the assayer's office is."

The woman was dressed in a high-collared, white blouse with lace trim, and a dark blue skirt, which hid the mud at the hem. "Yes. Can you help me?"

"At first I thought you were Calamity Jane come back to town." Dimples showed when she smiled. "I mean, you're dressed like a man, but on closer inspection, you don't have her drunken look about you." She struck out her hand. "I'm Suzanna Lindstrom, I mean Winson. I'm the schoolteacher in Deadwood and recently married, so sometimes I mess up and use my maiden name."

Goosebumps ran up Nella's spine. Wait. This couldn't be right. Her name was one of her made-up characters in her book 'The School Marm.' She mentally shook her head. What the heck was going on? Suzanna stared at her. Darn, she hadn't taken the woman's hand. "I'm sorry. I'm new to town. I need to turn in some gold so I can get something to eat and a change of clothes." And maybe a new brain. This was crazy. "I'm Nella Cambien." Suzanna's gloved hand was warm and comforting. It was as if they'd been friends forever.

"Where are you from and what brings you to Deadwood?"

How did she answer? She couldn't very well say she was from the future, could she. For sure it would send her to jail and throw away the key. "I'm from Wisconsin." He stomach protested again, saving her from answering why she was here, since she didn't have a clue.

Suzanna giggled again. "Well, for food, I suggest King's. And I tend to favor Haywoods Dry Goods. Not only do they have a nice selection, but Sadie and Colin are two of my best friends."

A wave of dizziness overcame her. More names and places from her books. She had to be dreaming or else going crazy. Maybe she had a tumor or something. "Thank you. I'll take it into consideration." Her stomach growled loud enough to make Suzanna laugh. "I really must get to the assayer's so I can get something to eat before I faint."

Suzanna smiled. "Turn right here on Lee Street, then right again on West Main Street. I believe it's the second or third building on the left."

"Thank you so much, and I'll certainly try King's for dinner."

"By the way, if you'd care for a proper cleanup, I'd be happy to let you use our place. There are rooms above the restaurant you can use. My husband owns the hotel, so it won't be a problem."

"But you don't even know me. Why, I could be a murderer or something." Or at least be accused of being one.

Suzanna tapped her on the arm. "I trust you're not. I'm a pretty good judge of character. Or so I've been told."

Nella held back a giggle. Suzanna may be a good judge of character, but she was actually a character in one of Nella's books. A made-up person. One who didn't exist, except on paper. "Thank you." She glanced down at her dirty clothes. "I may take you up on it."

"Well, I hope to see you soon, Nella. Have a good day."

Following Suzanna's directions, she turned onto West Main, surprised to see the Lee Street stairs in place just as they were in her time. Horses whinnied from what must be corrals up the street. She stood in front of the assayer's office with a sign, Matthew Jones, swinging in the breeze. With a shaking hand, she knocked.

"Enter." The loud brusque voice rattled the glass in the door.

Should she? Would it be better to pay at the hotel with the gold? But then, how would she know if she were getting the correct change? She opened the door to an average sized room. A long, wooden counter ran across the middle of the room. Behind it were shelves filled with what she assumed were bottles of chemicals. Chunks of ore, a counterweight scale, a typewriter, and a small stove were on the countertop. Since she'd never written a story with an assayer in it, Nella had no idea what the other items were used for.

A tall, thin man stood behind the counter, a pair of spectacles resting on the end of his nose. The sleeves of his gray shirt were rolled up to his elbows, and a pair of black suspenders held up his pants. Even through his glasses, he squinted at something lying on a piece of black fabric.

"Be with you in a bit."

Nella took a seat on one of two wooden chairs placed on either side of the door. Heavens, she was tired, hungry, dirty, and her bladder was telling her it had been a while since she'd emptied it. There were probably no public toilets.

After what seemed an eternity to her bladder, the man removed the stone from the fabric, put it in a leather pouch, and looked at her. "Fool's gold."

"What?"

"Some fool brought in this piece claiming it to be real. Like I can't tell the difference."

Fingering the slice of gold in her pocket, Nella went to the counter. "How do you know the difference?"

Mr. Jones removed the rock from the pouch. "There are several tests I do." He picked up a U-shaped magnet. "First and foremost, I use a magnet. If the magnet sticks, it's not gold. I also use nitric acid. If it's gold, it won't react. The biggest one, though, is my eyes. I can tell real gold from a mile away." He put the rock back in the bag. "Now, what can I do for you, young lady?"

Humph. Young lady, indeed. She was twenty-four years old, and if she lived in this era and wasn't married, she'd be considered an old maid. "I have this piece of metal I think might be gold." She pulled the piece from her pocket, set it on the empty fabric, and crossed her fingers.

"Hmmm. I believe you're right." He picked up the magnet.

Nella held her breath. It didn't attach itself to it.

"Just to make sure." Mr. Jones opened one of the brown bottles and dipped a piping stick into it.

She leaned onto the counter for a better look and crossed her toes inside her boots. No reaction. She refrained from shouting.

"Yep. Gold." He looked at her over the top of his spectacles. "Where did you find it?"

Grandma Henny had always told her the truth was the best. Lies could snowball into real problems. "I was in one of the old buildings down the street and found it in the dirt floor."

He opened his mouth as if to ask which building, then closed it. "Since the fire, we're finding all sorts of things." He placed the gold on one side of a scale and a counterweight on the other. "If I were you, I wouldn't tell anyone about it and where you found the gold. Plenty of unscrupulous people about." Even through his glasses, he squinted at the numbers on the scale, then did a calculation on a piece of paper. "I can give you twenty-one dollars for it."

Twenty-one dollars? Ridiculous. It was barely enough for a decent meal. She opened her mouth to protest the small amount, then recalled a sign she'd seen in one of the restaurants advertising a full meal of roast, potatoes, beans and coffee for fifty cents. An extra ten cents if you wanted pie. Clothing certainly couldn't be much, either. In this day, she was practically rich.

"Miss? Do you want the money?"

"Oh. Of course." A few seconds later, with money in her pocket, she left the building and located King's. She took the stairs to the portico with its four pillars. Tall windows graced either side of the front door. More than a bit embarrassed by her appearance, she opened the door and let the mouth-watering aroma of food tease her empty stomach. She blinked. It was déjà vu all over again. She nearly slapped herself. Of course, this would seem familiar. For heaven's sake, she'd created the place, taking it from a tented restaurant after the fire to this magnificent hotel/restaurant.

"Good afternoon. Are you here for a meal, or do you need a room?" A tall woman, carrying a stack of what looked like menus in her arm, approached.

Nella did a double take at the woman's name tag: Leona Johnson. Leona Johnson? The name from the main character in 'The Proprietress?' It couldn't be. She was imagining things.

"Miss? May I help you?"

"Um. Yes. I would love to get something to eat, but I'm afraid I'm a bit of a mess."

"Oh, pishaw. We don't worry about things like that. If we did, we wouldn't get any customers." Leona waved a hand toward the dining room. "If you'll follow me."

Nella's head spun. The inside was the spitting image of what she'd created in the book, right down to the sconces made by Serenity Edelman in 'The Unconventional Blacksmith.' How was this possible? Had she somehow stepped into one of her books? But no. She'd never written a book about a prostitute being killed.

When she entered the room, everything and everyone froze. People held forks or spoons in midair. The flame from a man's match barely touched his cigar. A waiter, holding a tray on the palm of his hand, stopped in mid-step. Even while immobilized, it seemed everyone was eyeing her? What was going on? Had her clothes fallen off?

"Will this do?" Leona stood by a table in the far corner of the room.

"This will be fine." She took a seat with her back against the wall, so she could watch the silent room. The instant she sat down, activity resumed. The man waved the nearly burned match in the air. Silverware dropped to dishes. Someone spilled their water on the table. The waiter nearly dropped his tray, grasping it with both hands before it toppled to the floor. All the while, people whispered and stared at her.

Leona set a menu on the table. "Our special is roast beef, mashed potatoes with gravy, green beans, and biscuits. It comes with coffee or milk. Desert is extra."

Nella nodded. If she'd try to speak, drool will certainly run down her chin. She swallowed the extra saliva and glanced at her dirty hands. No way could she eat anything until she cleaned up. "Do you have a ladies' room where I can freshen up?" Even though she knew exactly where the room was, the way people were acting, it would be better to pretend she didn't know.

"Go through the dining room and take a left. It's at the end of the hallway on the right. I'll put your order in."

After taking care of her needs, she left the room and walked down the hallway to the dining room then stuttered to a stop. Standing at the reception desk was a tall, thin man wearing a badge on the black vest he wore over his light blue shirt.

The man paused his conversation with Leona and stared at her. Her heart skipped a beat. He was the man who had arrived at the brothel as she was running away. Did he recognize her? What should she do? She couldn't run past him. Didn't know if there was a back door. Besides, she hadn't done anything wrong and her food would be arriving.

An empty stomach trumped a scared one. Without looking at him, she walked past the reception desk, into the dining room, and to her table, ignoring comments ranging from: "I thought it was Calamity." "She's the one." "Will she write more?" "I wasn't in any of her books. I want to be." Were these people crazy?

A steaming cup of coffee and a plate of rolls were at her table. The coffee was black and hot and the rolls warm. Exactly the way she liked them. Over the rim of her cup, she eyed the room. Was that Bertha coming from the kitchen? The handsome man smoking the cigar was sitting with a woman who could only be Daniel Iverson and Julia Lindstrom, though if memory served her right, she had them get married a few months back. The couple sitting with them was Julia's sister,

Suzanna, and her husband, King. She shook her head. The more she looked around, the more she recognized the people from her books.

Except for the sheriff or deputy or whatever he was. He wasn't someone she'd conjured up from her imagination. Once again, he was staring at her. Ignore him. In her experience, the more she looked at a man, the more he'd be interested in her. And she had a feeling his interest would not be in a good way.

Her food arrived. The beef was so tender, she could cut it with her fork. The potatoes were real and smothered in dark brown gravy. While she didn't favor green beans, the cook had done something to make them the best she'd ever eaten. It could simply be she was so hungry, liver would taste good, but she doubted it. Tucking into the food, she didn't pay attention to her surroundings until a shadow crossed her table.

Afraid to look up, she swallowed around the lump forming in her throat. Leona had already asked her about the food, so it wouldn't be her. Plus, Leona wasn't wearing the pants she could see through her eyelashes. With trepidation, she set down her fork and raised her head. Damn. It was the man from the lobby.

"May I join you?"

Despite her fear, along with the deep timber of his voice, his handsome face sent a spark igniting through her body. If he recognized her, saying no would make her seem suspect. Inviting a man to a woman's table, even a lawman, would make tongues wag. She suppressed a giggle. She was in Deadwood in 1880, for heaven's sake. No one knew her or even cared about her. She nodded.

The man removed his cowboy hat and took a seat across from her. After setting his hat on the floor beside him, he raked his fingers through his thick, black hair, and leaned an elbow on the table. "Have we met before?"

Good grief. Men used this line on women over a hundred years ago? Was it ingrained in their brains when they were born? "I don't think so. I recently arrived in town."

"Leona said she's never seen you here before." He swept a finger over his thick mustache, narrowed his eyes, and grunted. "I believe I saw you running down the street behind Main Street a couple of hours ago. What were you doing there?"

How should she answer? Tell the truth? Lie? Somewhere in between? "What makes you think I was where you say?"

"Your clothes. Your long braid. At first I thought Calamity Jane had returned to town, but your clothing was too neat and clean. Also, too neat and clean for any miner. If you hadn't noticed, they tend to be a bit on the dirty side." He rested an elbow on the table and simply stared.

Think. Think, Nella. What would you have a character in your books do? But this wasn't one of her books. Was it?

———

Stuart swore he heard the gears in her brain grinding. What was this woman's response going to be? Would she lie? But how would he know if she did or not? One thing was for sure, she was the person he'd seen running down the street from the brothel.

Too bad she was so pretty and there was no blood on her or he'd arrest her on the spot for murder. In contrast to her black hair, her eyes were a brilliant blue. Like a summer sky. A few freckles dotted her nose, and her skin was like porcelain. His heart skittered. He was an idiot and a sucker for a pretty face, but pretty didn't mean she hadn't killed the prostitute. The reason was one he'd have to work out.

"What's your name?"

"Nella." She raised a pert eyebrow. "And yours?"

"Stuart Adams. Deputy Stuart Adams."

"Are you related to W.E. Adams?"

Did he catch her in a lie? "If you just arrived in Deadwood, how do you know W.E.?"

"Um."

Her hesitation said a lot.

"Actually, his reputation as a businessman is well known."

Well, it wasn't a lie. People around the territory seem to know the kind, gentle man. "Huh." He ran a fingertip over the white tablecloth. "What are *you* doing in Deadwood?"

"Visiting."

"Visiting who?" When she didn't say anything, he pressed on. "Look, a young woman was murdered at one of the brothels. It doesn't matter to me or the sheriff who the woman was or what she did for a living, a murder is a murder. I know I saw you running down the street outside the brothel. Now, what were you doing there?"

———

It appeared the deputy wasn't about to give up. Leona arrived at her table, giving her a chance to think of an answer.

"Deputy, would you like something to eat, or are you here to pester this young woman? Sitting and gabbing isn't free, you know." Leona scowled at Stuart and smiled at Nella.

"I was simply questioning Miss Nella about a murder this afternoon."

Leona gasped. "A murder? This lovely woman would never do such a thing." She patted Nella's hand. "Why, it would be the same as accusing me."

The room grew silent. Nella wanted to drop down and hide under the table. Everyone was staring.

"Now, Mrs. Johnson, I'm not accusing her of anything."

"Sounds like it to me, young man. Now order something or leave this establishment."

The man probably had a good four inches and fifty pounds on Leona, but he seemed to shrink before Leona's words. If memory served her right, she'd made Leona quite a harpy in the beginning of her story. Good thing, too.

"Well then, Mrs. Johnson, I'll have a piece of your famous apple pie."

"I will, too, Mrs. Johnson. And thank you for your kind concern. I believe Deputy Adams is simply doing his job." She raised an eyebrow at him. "Even if his accusation is uncalled for."

Before Leona left for the kitchen, she stopped at Julia and Suzanna's table. After a whispered conversation, she disappeared into the kitchen.

While the meal had been delicious, the pie was to die for. Licking her plate would be unseemly, but she was tempted. At least it kept the deputy from questioning her while they ate. In fact, the man had two pieces and for a moment thought *he* was going to lick his plate. Wouldn't that be a kicker?

After one last sip of her coffee, she pushed back her chair. "Well,

Deputy, while it's been a pleasure, I must be going." Where to, she had no idea.

He grabbed her arm. "Wait a minute. I'm not done asking you questions."

"Yes, you are, Adams." Daniel Iverson, along with Julia and the other couple approached. "As her lawyer, I insist I speak with her first."

Lawyer? She had a lawyer? Suzanna tugged on Nella's arm. "Come along, my dear. We have a room for you upstairs."

"Now, wait just a darn minute, Iverson. You can't take my suspect. I want the sheriff to talk to her."

Daniel poked a finger at Adams. "As you darn well know, she has a right to an attorney. She also has a right to be presentable when questioned, not attacked while enjoying a meal among the townsfolk."

"But . . ."

Before she had a chance to say a word, Julia and Suzanna whisked her through the room and up the grand staircase. Over her shoulder, she glimpsed Daniel, King, and the deputy arguing. Could this day get any stranger?

5

EVEN THOUGH THERE WERE PLENTY OF ROOMS ON THE second floor, Nella was nearly dragged up to the third floor where Leona and Asa's living quarters were located. At the top, she stopped.

"Wait. I need to catch my breath." Although they had practically run up several flights of stairs, she was the only one huffing and puffing. Maybe it was time to get into better shape.

Julia tugged on her arm. "Hurry. We need to get you presentable before the sheriff shows up."

"But I didn't do anything wrong."

Suzanna opened a door at the end of the hallway which Nella remembered led to a small bathroom. "We know you didn't but we have to make sure he understands it. We need more people from your books."

"Yes. We need a library." Julia turned on the tub's faucets.

Huh? How did they know she was working on a book about a traveling librarian? Nella rubbed her temples where a headache was starting. This was absolutely crazy. A dream. No, a nightmare.

"Now, get out of those filthy clothes and into the tub. Julia and I will find you something more suitable to wear."

Behind a silk screen, she removed her clothes and boots, cringing at the dried mud left on the hardwood floor. As she unwound her braid, flakes of dirt floated around her. How had she gotten so dirty in such a short amount of time?

When the door clicked closed, she came around the screen and tested the temperature of the water. Finding it comfortably warm, she eased in and sank to her chest.

Not wanting to be caught in the all-together, she ducked her head beneath the water, and washed her hair and body with a lavender-scented bar of soap. By the time she was done, the water was no longer clear, but a dark tan. Yuck. Showers were so much better, but beggars couldn't be choosers.

She eased from the tub, taking note of each scrape, each ache, each pain in her body. A nice, soothing massage would be great right about now. But as tired as she was, she'd probably fall asleep in the first few minutes.

A towel, big enough to wrap around herself two times over, lay across a table next to the tub. When the doorknob rattled, she scooted behind the screen and waited.

"Miss Cambien? May we come in?"

"Of course." She peered around the edge of the screen as Julia and Suzanna entered, arms overloaded with clothing.

"We brought you some clean clothes."

Her sarcastic vein wanted to say, *Well, duh. I can see that.* But since she was a guest and they were helping her, she kept her words to herself. If she turned snarky, they might decide to turn her over to the authorities. "Thank you."

Since she usually wrote historical romances, her knowledge of late 1800s clothing was extensive. But reading and wearing were different things. After a shift, they strapped her into a corset. And she'd thought bras were bad.

"Stop. I can't breathe."

Julia gave the strings in back one last tug. "Well, Miss Cambien, if you want to turn the deputy's head, you have to show your figure to its best advantage."

Was she kidding? "Why in heaven's name would I want to turn his head?"

Suzanna slipped a blouse over Nella's head. "For one thing, he's a good-looking man. For another, we all know you couldn't possibly kill anyone." She paused. "Well, except for a few in your stories. But, when he sees how pretty you are, he will forget all about trying to make you the killer."

Okay. So, number one, she wasn't pretty. At least not compared to these two sisters. Number two, the deputy seemed bright enough not to fall for a woman's charms. Number three, as far as she knew, she didn't have any charms, at least not according to the men in her time. And lastly, hopefully she wouldn't be sticking around 1880 for any length of time. Since she was the author of this story, it was up to her to solve it.

Nella looked in the cheval mirror. Even though she could barely breathe, she had to admit the corset gave her an hour-glass figure. The light blue, pristine, high-collar, high-necked blouse was a nice contrast to the full-length, dark blue skirt. She resisted the temptation to sway back and forth making the ruffles along the bottom flare.

Julia pressed her down on a chair. "Let me fix your hair. This red is such a beautiful color."

If they only knew the teasing she'd received as a child and teenager. Being the only redhead in a school full of blondes, brunettes, and those with black hair, she stood out like a seven-foot basketball player in a field of toddlers. Not to mention the curls she could never control.

In a matter of minutes, Julia had her curls under control in an upsweep, leaving several spiraling down her cheeks.

Julia stood back. "There. You look beautiful. Deputy Adams won't know what hit him."

"Look, ladies." Nella stood and brushed a wrinkle from her skirt. "I don't believe for a minute this will work. We'll have to come up with some other way to prove I didn't kill Ruby."

A knock at the door interrupted her.

"Julia? Suzanna?" A man's voice, one she didn't recognize, came through the door. She may create characters she could recognize, but not their voices. "Deputy Adams and the sheriff want to speak with Miss Cambien. They are waiting in the office."

Nella took a deep breath. This was going to be interesting. In a matter of minutes, she was going to have to explain her presence in Deadwood and in the street behind the brothel.

———

Feeling as if she were being escorted to the gallows, she walked down the stairs between Daniel Iverson and Kingston Winson. My, she'd done a good job creating these handsome men. Too bad she couldn't create them in her time. Or at least one like them. The sisters trailed behind them.

No matter how hard she tried to take the stairs quietly like the two women, her boots clunked on the hardwood stairs like a pair of Clydesdales. There had been no way she was going to try and fit her feet into the narrow, laced-up, pointed toe boots the sisters had offered her. Her cowboy boots were fine, thank you very much. And if the hooks on the boots were closed as tightly as the corset, she wouldn't be able to walk or breathe.

King opened the door to his office. Deputy Adams and a man who she presumed to be the sheriff stopped their discussion. Adams scanned her from head to toe and raised an eyebrow. Oh, yeah. He was nobody's fool to fall for her transformation.

The sheriff came forward. "Miss Cambien. We need to ask you the details of what transpired at the brothel."

"I'm acting as her counsel, Sheriff." Daniel swept a hand at three chairs lined up in a row and nodded for her and the sisters to take a seat. If he were acting as her lawyer, why did it feel like she was about to go under an inquisition? Well, probably because she was.

Adams set a chair in front of her, rested a foot on the seat, and leaned his elbow on his knee. "Now, Miss Cambien. What were you doing at the brothel?"

Nothing like getting right to the point. "What makes you think I was at the brothel? Do I look like one of those ladies?"

A corner of his lip lifted in a slight smirk. The movement sent a flutter in her stomach. A pleasant flutter, not one saying she was going to be hanged. More like *this was one cute guy* flutter.

"Seeing as you were dressed as a man, I'd say no." He leaned toward her. "Now, tell me what you were doing there. One of the men saw you shimmy down the rope you created but wasn't quick enough to stop you."

Daniel stood behind her. "Deputy, there are so many men coming and going in those places, you probably have a hundred suspects. Why focus on Miss Cambien?"

"Because she was seen fleeing the scene?"

"And why would she kill Ruby? What is her motive?"

Good question.

"Jealousy?"

Nella couldn't hold back a snort. "Jealousy? Why would I be jealous of the woman? I never was and never will be a part of a brothel."

Adams got into her face. "So why don't you tell me what you *were* doing there? And the sheriff and I want the truth."

The truth? What was the line from a movie? *You couldn't handle the truth.* They would never in a million years believe her.

"I've been in this town for a while, Miss Cambien. I've seen just about everything, so nothing you can say will surprise me."

Wanna bet? How about she was dreaming? How about, with the exception of Adams, everyone in this room, this building, were created from her imagination.

Suzanna patted her arm. "Tell him, Miss Cambien. We'll back you up."

Nella closed her eyes and sucked in as much breath as she could. Here went nothing. "I'm from the future."

No one said a word. Not good. Where were the displays of disbelief? "Did you hear me?"

Adams huffed a breath. "We heard you, Miss Cambien. And I must say, I haven't heard that one before."

"I'm sure you haven't, but it's the truth. Over one-hundred and forty years from now, the brothel will be a B&B."

How could six people frown at the exact same time? "It's like a small hotel." No response. "Anyway, I was staying there locked in the room where Ruby was killed."

Adams held up a hand. "Wait. Why were you locked in the room?"

"Bats."

"Bats?"

Was she imagining it, but had his voice raised an octave? Was he afraid of bats, too? "Bats had gotten into the building. I'm petrified of them, so I ran into the room and locked the door behind me."

His lip twitched. "You locked the door so the bats wouldn't get in? So, years from now, bats are able to open doors?"

"No. It was a reflex." Jerk. "Anyway, there is a sign on the wall explaining she had been murdered, but the incident was never solved. I was walking across the room when I slipped and fell. When I woke, this woman was lying across the tub. She was obviously dead. When people started pounding on the door calling for her, I panicked, made a rope from the bedsheets, and left."

Again, silence, but plenty of raised eyebrows, frowns, and outright disbelief.

Suzanna was the first to break the silence. "We like having our creator here."

"Creator?"

Leave it to Adams to jump on the word.

Julia grinned and patted Nella's arm. "Well, yes. Miss Cambien is an author who created all of us for her books."

This was absolutely the craziest thing she'd ever encountered. When she woke, she'd have quite a story to write. She nodded at Adams. "I didn't create him."

Adams dropped his foot to the floor. Was he pouting? "If what they are saying is true, why didn't you create me? What is wrong with me?"

Nella mentally rolled her eyes. Good grief. Next the Alice in Wonderland's King and Queen of Hearts would show up yelling to chop off her head. And why were these people so willing to believe she'd traveled from the future? Weren't the characters she created smarter?

"There is nothing wrong with you, deputy." Julia gave him a megawatt grin, garnering a glare from King. "You simply weren't needed in her stories."

"Huh." Adams raked his fingers through his hair. "I think this is all a cock-n'-bull story you're making up to hide the person you're in cahoots with."

Cahoots? Had she ever had a character say cahoots? It was a great word. Maybe one she could use in future historicals. "I can assure you, Deputy Adams, It's not a story. I am from the future. I did not kill Ruby. I wasn't jealous of her. I'd never met her. She was dead when I came to."

The sheriff leaned against the large, oak desk, crossed his legs at the ankles, and folded his arms over his chest. "I believe her."

"You do?" Nella bit back a laugh at the words spoken by her and Adams at the same time.

"Yes, I do. Don't ask me why, I simply believe her." The sheriff uncrossed his ankles. "The question now is who did? Miss Cambien, have any ideas? I mean you always got the bad guy in your books."

They wanted her to solve this problem? Why right now? She wouldn't be able to find her way back to the brothel, let alone back to her time.

Julia jumped up. "I have an idea. Remember how I helped Hattie with her problem at her brothel? I could . . ."

Daniel grabbed Julia's arm. "No. Never. There is no way I'll let you go into a brothel again. What if the killer comes after you?"

Julia pouted. "For one thing, I wouldn't be in the room by myself. We could hide one of you under the bed or something."

"No. Absolutely not."

Suzanna raised a finger. "I . . ."

This time King leapt from his chair. "No way. No how. If someone should see you . . ."

The room grew silent. Everyone's eyes were on her. Nella's stomach dropped. She had a bad feeling about this. "What? Why are you all staring at me like you expect me to do something?"

Julia knelt before her. "Because you can. No one knows you in Deadwood. You can create some kind of scenario."

Sure. Right. And how many times in her stories did her characters do something totally unexpected and she had to figure out how to save them. Or have the characters save themselves. These people were crazy. And she was probably crazy enough to go along with them.

"Who would be in the room? Everyone knows the deputy and sheriff."

Suzanna tapped her bottom lip. "And neither can Daniel nor King. They are too well known in town." She snapped her fingers. "I know. You can come up with a new person."

Don't they know how hard it is to do? Who was the person? What were their characteristics? What was the reason for him/her to be in the story? Besides, she usually had her female characters save themselves. Of course, they didn't know. All they had to do was follow her words on a page. And this was real. A real person who was murdered. At least she thought this was real. She hated stories where the main character went through all sorts of trials and tribulations, only to wake from a dream. She'd never done that and never would.

She created strong women, who fell in love with strong men, but were able to take care of themselves. Was she a strong person? Was she crazy to even consider pretending to be a prostitute?

"Couldn't we get the madam involved?"

Adams shook his head. "No. I don't trust her. I know she doesn't treat her girls well."

Great. And they wanted her to become part this woman's gaggle of girls? But the deputy was right. It would be easier if no one knew who she was. "But how will I keep from having to service anyone?"

Julie stood. "From my friendship with Hattie, I learned when a new girl comes into a brothel, she is given time to settle in. Since they are down one girl, she should welcome you into the fold."

"Who is this madam?"

"Edda Conrow."

Edda Conrow? This was crazy. Absolutely nuts. Positively ridiculous. But . . . she was going to do it. Especially if finding Ruby's murderer would send her back to her time.

"All right. Let's figure this out."

6

AFTER A SLEEPLESS NIGHT WHERE SHE TOSSED AND TURNED trying to convince herself she had the power over her own destiny, the next day Nella stood at the back door of the brothel, heart stuttering, satchel in hand. A satchel filled with several lacy, pink corsets with matching bottoms going to her knees. An off-the-shoulder red, brocade dress showed more skin than even her mother had seen. She did enjoy the soft slippers she was given. The bag also included a rather pretty, scrolled hairbrush, some hairpins, rouge, lipstick, and hair ribbons.

The plan had been for her to show up right after the noon hour. The brothel wouldn't be open and the girls would be awake. Anyway, they assumed Edda would be awake.

Today she wore the same blouse, skirt, and boots from yesterday. It wouldn't be good to show up in her jeans and shirt. With shaking hands, she rapped on the door. When no one arrived, she knocked harder. After all, there was a large set of stairs for the sound to travel. After a few minutes, the door was thrown open. Edda Conrow. From all her research, she'd recognize the madam's face anywhere. Nella locked her knees to keep from keeling over.

"Yeah? What d'ya want?"

"I'm new in town and heard you lost one of your girls. I'd like to take over her customers."

Edda stared at her red hair, then slowly perused her down to her boots. "Ya would, would ya?"

Nella's heart slammed in her chest. Surely the madame could hear it. Knew she was a fake. Knew she hadn't any thoughts of 'entertaining' men.

"Well, get yerself up here where we can talk."

The stairwell was not as wide as in the future. Dark, but with a hint of new wood. Of course, like everyone else in Deadwood, she would have had to rebuild after the fire. The main room was as large as in her time, but instead of a kitchen at one end, there was a bar lining a wall. Like before, brocade chairs, small couches, tables for cards, a roulette wheel, and pictures of nude women filled the room. Whomever had decorated the brothel in the future had been pretty darn accurate.

"Here," Edda pointed to a chair at one of the round tables. "Let's talk."

Her nerves were so bad, she wasn't sure she could remember the story they'd concocted last night or sit without missing the chair.

Edda lit what appeared to be a small cigar, took a puff, and blew the smoke into the air. Was that disdain in her exhale?

"Now, tell me about yerself. Where'd you come from? Who did you work for? Why are you in Deadwood?"

Last night they'd decided she had worked outside the area. Madams tended to know each other from town to town. Some even owned other places in different towns.

"I came from Minneapolis and worked for two years at Sarah Goodwin's establishment. When I heard about the gold rush out here, I thought it was time for a change of scenery. Get some of the gold my way. Besides, Minnesota is nothing but dirty farmers."

Edda chuckled. "And here you get nothing but dirty miners. Not much difference."

"I guess not, but I needed a change of scenery."

"And what do you think of our little town?"

"Other than the muddy streets, animals running rampant, and the men lounging around, I haven't had much of a chance to look around. I came here right from the stage."

Edda frowned. "I didn't know the stage had arrived. I thought it was later this afternoon."

Shoot. It was one thing they hadn't thought of. "Actually, I came in on yesterday's stagecoach and stayed at some place called King's."

"And they didn't question you? Those snooty folks always think they are better than the rest of us."

"No. No one said anything. Dressed like I am, I'm not sure they would know if I were an evening girl or not."

"How did you get my name?"

"One of my clients has been to Deadwood and mentioned you."

Edda raised an eyebrow. "And his name?"

Nella flipped a hand. "I don't remember. There have been so many, you know."

"Hey, Edda, who's this one?" Three girls, all blondes came into the room, all wearing silk-type robes.

Nella held back a cough at the cigarettes they each smoked. The odor of perfume covering unwashed bodies was worse than the smoke. She swallowed past her gag reflex. How could people stand each other? But then, if everyone smelled, no one would notice. The women draped their bodies over various pieces of furniture.

"This little gal would like to replace Ruby."

"Ruby? Why would you want to replace her? I can certainly take care of her men."

"Now, Sophie Rose. You know I have to replace her. The more girls I have, the more men who frequent our doors, the more money we all make. Now, be quiet and sit down."

"Is she gonna have Ruby's room, too?" Another glare and a shrug. "I guess it's all right with me. I wouldn't want no room where someone was murdered."

"Sophie Rose. One more time. Be quiet or go back to your room."

Sophie Rose gave Nella a glare sending shivers down her spine. This might be one woman to stay clear of.

"Are ya gonna make her dye her hair like the rest of us?"

"Sophie, I told you to shut up. Since Ruby had red hair," Edda lifted one of Nella's curls. "I believe we'll let Nella keep hers. Something different for our clientele."

"Hmph." Sophie Rose folded her arms over her ample chest. "Ya gonna call her Ruby, too?"

Guess Sophie Rose didn't listen. Did she have some type of hold over Edda? Otherwise, why did she keep letting the girl interrupt?

"No." Edda tapped a finger on her bottom lip. "I believe we'll call her Scarlett. Has a sultrier tone to it. Suits her."

Sultry? Never in her life had she been referred to as sultry. Tall. Thin. Boyish. But never sultry. Edda must be desperate.

Sophie Rose snorted. "Scarlett? That's a laugh. Sultry? Even funnier." She stuck out her chest. "Why, I can't see any man wanting her scrawny body."

And there it was. She frowned at Sophie Rose, but kept her mouth closed. Obviously, she'd already garnered the woman's distaste. No sense in making it worse.

"I see you have your belongings with you. I'll show you to your room. You'll have two nights to acclimate yourself to my place of business before you start entertaining. Tomorrow night, you'll spend time in the parlor so men can get a good look at you."

Nella suppressed a shiver. She had a strong hunch she wouldn't be serving tea and crumpets. She picked up her carpet bag and followed Edda.

"Hey, *Scarlett*."

Nella stopped and looked over her shoulder. "What?"

"I'd watch my step if I were you. Some of the men in this town can be downright dangerous." Sophie squinted her eyes. "You best be careful. You hear?"

Edda opened the door to Ruby's—or now her room. She set her bag on the floor. The bed had been moved back against the wall. From what she could tell, all the blood had been cleaned up.

"Is this the room where Ruby was killed?"

"Yes."

"Do they know who did it? I wouldn't want the same to happen to me."

"I believe they have someone in custody. I'm increasing my security during the working hours, though. Better screen who comes in here. The bouncers will check on the girls more often. We aren't sure what time she was killed." Edda shrugged as if the death of a young woman was no big deal. Or maybe it was her way of coming to grips with things.

"I'll let you get settled. You'll need to make the bed up. We washed everything to make sure there was no blood left behind."

At the foot of the bed was a stack of graying sheets, a quilt, two pillows, and equally gray pillowcases. Were those the same sheets she'd used to climb out the window? The sheets she was going to have to tie together again so Adams could climb into the room? If it were in her time, the CSI would use their black lights and probably find more than blood splattered all over the place. How was she ever going to be able to sleep on that bed.? Even with clean sheets?

"Join us in half an hour. We'll be having our meal. The doors open at four. I want you back in your room before then." Edda closed the door behind her.

The clicking latch was as loud as a bullet ricocheting through the room. She was really and truly in an active brothel, not simply staying in one used as a B&B. She took a deep breath. This was definitely one of the scariest things she'd ever done. Putting her characters into precarious positions was entirely different than being in one herself. Hopefully, she'll live through this, go back to her time, and use it in a story. Not knowing the policy of anyone coming into her room without permission, she placed a wooden chair beneath the lock.

Something hit the window. Deputy Adams said he'd be here around one. Having arrived at noon, and with the time she'd spent with Edda, it was probably one now. She pulled back the heavy drapes and pushed open the window.

"Psst. Throw down the sheets."

Through her fear, she snickered. Why didn't he say: *Rapunzel, Rapunzel. Let down your hair.* Good grief. She needed to get a grip. First Alice in Wonderland and now Rapunzel.

"Hold on. I have to tie them together." She tossed the pillows and quilt aside, and as she'd done yesterday, knotted two ends together, tied another end to the end bed frame, and pushed the bed to the window.

"Here." She tossed the sheet out the window. Adams tugged on it making sure it was secure.

"Scarlett? Is everything all right in there? I thought I heard some noises."

Great. "I'm fine, Edda. I just repositioned the bed to make it easier to make up."

"All right. See you in a few minutes."

Adams was halfway up the outside wall. "Hurry up," she whispered.

"I'm going as fast as I can. Move the bed back so I can climb over the windowsill."

Nella winced as the feet of the bed scraped across the floor. Hopefully, Edda would believe she was moving the bed back into place. She took Adams' hand to help him inside. The tingle of her hand at his contact traveled through her. What was that? She'd written about a spark between characters before, but never once experienced it firsthand. Weirder and weirder.

He removed a bag from his back and dropped it on the floor. Hand-over-hand, Adams brought the sheets into the room and handed them to her. "Here. I'm going to close the window and pull the curtains." As soon as he did, the room was enveloped in darkness.

Her throat closed. "Open the drapes. I can't see enough to light a lamp." Besides, she didn't care for the dark. Based on past experiences, and except for the time before transporting to 1880, darkness was what bats liked the best. She sat on the edge of the bed. "Now what?" she whispered.

"Now, we wait."

"For what?"

Adams shrugged. "For whatever happens."

"You can't stay in my room waiting for something that may or may not happen."

"It's my duty."

A strong rap came at the door. "Scarlett. Get your scrawny ass out here. We're ready to eat." Great. It would have to be Sophie Rose.

"Quick! Get under the bed."

He shook his head. "I'll just hide behind the door for now."

"Hey, Scar. Who ya talking to? Ya got someone in that room with you? I'm getting Edda."

"Under the bed. Now."

Nella kicked his bag after him. "Don't breathe." She removed the chair from beneath the door handle and opened the door. With Sophie Rose behind her, a smirk on her face, Edda stood with her arms akimbo.

"Sophie Rose said she heard you talking with someone. The rules are no men who haven't come in here properly are to be in the rooms."

Nella shook her head and gave Sophie Rose glare for glare. "I don't have anyone in my room. I have a habit of talking to myself." She sent Sophie Rose another scowl. "I find they are the best conversations." She swept her hand at the room. "Go ahead and check. I'm not sure how you think someone could have gotten in here, anyway."

Sophie Rose snorted and stomped off. She certainly was one person to keep an eye on.

"Never mind. Come join us and meet the other girls."

———

"Did you learn anything?" Adams lay on the floor, hands tucked beneath his head. He rolled to his side and propped his head in his hand when she entered the room and locked the door.

Nella sat on the edge of the windowsill and looked down at him. "I don't know how these women do it. They talk like it's no big deal to fulfill the needs of men, but I can see it in their eyes. I'm sure most of them are on drugs of some kind."

"It wouldn't be surprising. They have to have some way of surviving. I wouldn't wish their work on my worst enemy." He sat up and leaned against the bed. "Anything to help us?"

"Not so far. I met the girls. Besides Edda and me, there are eight of them. Then the guy they called Jack came in. He is one huge guy. Said he was the bouncer, but there's something off about him."

"Yeah. I met him the night of the murder. I don't believe his name is Jack, nor that he is a bouncer. I have a feeling he may have something to do with Ruby's death. He was also the one who watched you run off."

"He did give me a strange look, but there is no way he could recognize me."

Adams nodded at her. "Unless he managed to get a look at your hair. We don't see that color often around these parts."

"I had it in a braid and my hat on. I'm sure it would have been difficult to see." She shrugged. "Maybe he was wondering if I would be able to replace Ruby. Every time someone mentioned her name, his face grew white."

"Maybe he was in love with her."

"Do men fall in love with prostitutes?"

Adams brought a knee up to his chest and rested his wrist across his knee. "Stranger things have happened. Sometimes men, and I say foolish men, equate sex with love."

"Women, too."

After a moment of silence, Stuart glanced up at her. "I have to ask you something."

"Sure. I'm not sure I'll answer, but fire away."

"Yesterday you said you came from the future. Everyone else seemed to take your words at face value, but I'm not so gullible. Where are you really from?"

Nella clasped her hands in her lap. And here she'd thought she'd gotten away with something. "I'm from Wisconsin in the year 2024." When he opened his mouth to protest, she held up a hand. "I know. I know. Sounds like a crazy story, doesn't it? But it's the truth. I came to Deadwood for an annual event called Wild Bill Days. I'm an author. We have a big author signing each year."

"Wait. Wild Bill Days. Like Wild Bill Hickock?"

"Yes. It's a big celebration."

"You mean to tell me they celebrate a man's murder? A man who'd only been in Deadwood a few weeks before being shot? Ridiculous."

"Brings in tourists and a lot of money to Deadwood."

"I can't imagine more people in this town wandering the muddy streets. People with guns, shooting each other."

"Well, things have changed a bit. They don't carry guns, anyway most of them don't. The streets and sidewalks are paved, so there is no mud to wallow through."

"Let's say I believe you."

Nella opened her mouth to protest. "I . . ."

"Wait. I believe you didn't kill Ruby, but I have a hard time believing the rest of the stuff you're spouting. How did you get in the room?"

"I already told you. The story isn't going to change in the retelling."

Stuart sighed. "All right. Before I ask you more about the future, I want to know what the sheriff, the Iversons, and the Winsons were saying about you creating them."

How did one explain this? "I already said I am an author. A writer. I write mysteries. It seems not only have I been transported back in time, but to the time of my books. The people you mentioned, the Iversons, Winsons, and the sheriff are all characters I made up. Don't ask me how or why, but it's the truth. Now all I want to do is get back to my time."

"You don't care for the time you made up?"

"I didn't say I made up this time in Deadwood, just some of the people and stories. Don't worry, you're not a character in one of my books." Anyway, she didn't think he was or would be.

"This is crazy."

"Tell me about it."

While they were talking, the noise outside her room increased. "Sounds as if they've opened the doors." What was she going to do during the long hours she had to wait in the room? She doubted anyone would bring her supper. She didn't have anything to write with. No book to read.

All she had was the handsome man sitting on the floor. If this was one of her stories, she might be crazy enough to have them attracted to each other. Maybe have a little fun to pass the time.

Stuart opened his bag. "Cards?"

The thought of kissing him was fleeting. No way, no how was she going to kiss a man who essentially was old. Very old. Old. Old. Old. Like several times over great-grandfather old. "Poker?"

"Is there any other game?" He dealt them five cards each.

"I'll take two."

"The dealer takes three."

As the night wore on, he asked more and more questions about the future. Some she decided to skim over. After all, she didn't know Stuart.

Maybe she'd tell him something to change the future. She couldn't take the chance. So, she stuck with the basic improvements.

Along with a bottle of weak wine, they'd eaten the sandwiches he dug from his pack, and later a couple of sugar cookies he'd said Suzanna had made.

After losing more games than she won, she tried to stifle a yawn. "What time is it?"

He pulled a pocket watch out from his vest. "Nearly midnight."

"I need to get some sleep."

"You'll be able to sleep with all the noise going on?"

He had a point. Giggling. High-pitched laughed. Men's deep guffaws. With her room being in a far corner, at least they couldn't hear any of the more vigorous activities.

"I'll sleep on the floor."

Nella eyed the bed and winced. Even though the bedding had supposedly been washed, thoughts of bedbugs, bodily fluids, and bats crossed her mind. She removed her boots but left her clothes on as additional layer of protection. Thinking about possible fleas, her head already itched. But at least she wasn't sleeping in an old, abandoned building.

Before she'd wrapped the quilt around her, snores came from the floor. If only she could fall asleep as fast. Plus, the damn corset was digging into her ribs. She should have had Stuart loosen the ties for her. That would have been interesting. As a gentleman, he probably would have refused.

With thoughts of what tomorrow would bring, she rolled over trying to find a comfortable position. Even though she wouldn't have to entertain any men in her room, the idea of them gawking at her made her stomach roll. They'd better find out who killed Ruby before she had to perform her duties.

After a particularly loud snort, Stuart finally quieted down. She finally fell into a fitful sleep swearing at the tight corset digging into her ribs.

———

"Miss Cambien. Nella. Wake up."

Nella swatted at the hands jiggling her. "Leave me alone. Let me sleep."

"You have to wake up. I need to get out of here before it gets light."

She opened her eyes. Brothel. Bats. Murder. Ruby. It all came back in a rush. "All right." Sighing she rolled over the side of the mattress. "I'll tie the sheets, but at this rate, they're not going to last very much longer. I can almost see you through them."

"I'll bring a rope with me when I come back here later."

With everything he had taken from his bottomless satchel, it was surprising he didn't have a fifty-foot length of rope in there. "Good idea."

Once he was gone, she crawled back into bed and managed to get several more hours of sleep before nature called. Since it was light outside, it probably would be a good idea to get ready for the day. Whatever that would be.

She changed from yesterday's wrinkled clothes into another blouse and skirt, tried to subdue her curls into a semblance of order, and ate a sandwich left over from last night. When did the girls get a chance to eat? Even though she was confined to her room, one would think someone would have brought her something to fill her stomach. Did they get food only once a day?

"Hey, Scarlett. Get out here."

Nella dropped her brush on the dresser and opened the door. At least it wasn't Sophie Rose glaring at her. The girl was dressed in nothing more than white stockings attached to a garter belt and a pink, silk robe. Her hair was a mess, and, she had obviously not removed her makeup from last night.

"It's time for breakfast and for you to get geared up for tonight."

Nella followed the girl into the main living area. The air was still hazy, and the room reeked of cigars, booze, and bodies. She sniffed the air. Was she crazy or was that a tempting aroma of cooking bacon? Empty glasses, half-filled bottles, ashtrays filled to the brim littered every surface. If the girls didn't die from a venereal disease, they'd certainly would from lung or liver cancer.

"Ooh. Look how fancy the new girl is." A plump girl slouched in a chair, swinging her leg over the arm. "Hey, Scarlett. Why don't ya clean up this mess." She eyed her fingernails. "It's my turn, but I don't want to. What'd'ya say, girls? We let *Scarlett* clean up?"

She wasn't about to let them see her irritation. "Why, I'd love to clean up this mess. I live to clean up after you. First things first." She walked across the sticky floor, pulled back the drapes, and pushed open the windows. She swore the room sighed in relief at the fresh air.

"Hey. Watcha doin' that for?" Sophie Rose came up behind her. "We don't like those windows open."

"Well. Since I'm doing the cleaning, I'm opening them." She slapped her hands at her waist and, with a scowl, dared Sophie Rose to argue. Thankfully, the woman shrugged and poured herself some coffee from a pot on a pot-bellied stove Nella hadn't noticed the day before.

Someone had pulled away a tall screen revealing a cookstove, ice box, sink, and a cupboard filled with dishes, pots, and pans. Surprisingly, it was Edda at the stove, a frilly apron around her waist, cooking up a skillet of scrambled eggs and bacon.

Edda peered over her shoulder. "I know this doesn't seem like something a woman like me would do, but I love to cook for my girls. And," she sent a look around the room, "they, in return, love to clean up." She stabbed a fork in the air. "Get to work. You're not passing your chores to the new girl. She'll take over Ruby's jobs."

"Which is?"

Sophie Rose smirked and held up a large bucket, with chips of white paint revealing the black beneath it. "Why, I believe it was her job today to clean out the slop buckets. When it's full, you take it outside and dump it on the hill."

Seriously? She had to empty chamber pots? Nella yanked the pot from Sophie Rose's hand.

"Wait until we're done eating. Ladies, grab your plates and line up."

As with any new kid on the block, she was shoved to the end of the line. By the time she got to the stove, there was only a spoonful of eggs and one piece of bacon. Good thing she'd had the sandwich.

And after a half an hour of emptying pots and trying to ignore her gag reflexes, she was glad she hadn't eaten more. She unlocked the door at the bottom of the stairwell and sucked in a breath of fresh air, or as fresh as one reeking of animal and human offal could be.

A narrow, tallish building with a moon cut out on the door stood to her right. Why was she told to dump this bucket on the hillside when there was an outhouse right outside the back door? She set the bucket down, unhooked the latch, and gagged at the horrible odor. Hadn't anyone ever emptied the refuse?

She slammed the door closed and re-latched it. Against her better judgement and, swearing not to drink any water while in Deadwood, dumped the bucket's contents behind the stump of a burned-out tree.

The idea of going back upstairs didn't sit well with her. The temptation to run and hide was so strong, she took several steps down the back street.

"Where do you think you're going?"

A large, beefy hand grasped her upper arm. Darn. Busted. Jack loomed over her. "Nowhere. I needed a breath of fresh air."

He jerked her back to the brothel. "Pick up the bucket. No one leaves without Edda's permission." He pushed her through the door.

Somehow she pictured this man doing harm to the women if they disobeyed Edda. Had he been the one to kill Ruby? Maybe by accident? Or had she done something to make him so mad, he struck her hard enough to end her life?

At the top of the stairs, he pushed her into the main room. "I got her. She was ready to *take a breath of fresh air*."

Edda leaned against the sink. "Breath of fresh air, huh? You haven't even been here one day and you're already wanting to take off?"

"I'm telling the truth. I have no intention of leaving. It's such a beautiful day. I wanted to enjoy a brief moment of it." *Please let her believe me.* "It's the truth. I have nowhere else to go. Besides, all my belongings are here. If I were to leave, wouldn't I take them with me?"

"I suppose that's true. Just don't try it again."

Sophie Rose smirked. "I told ya she'd be trouble. Just like Ruby."

Wait? Ruby was trouble? Dare she ask what she'd done? "Why was Ruby trouble?"

"Takin' the best men. Thinkin' she was better'n the rest of us. Flauntin' her red hair, jest like you're doin.' Right, girls?"

Several of the other ladies nodded. Three in particular glared at Sophie

Rose behind her back. So, not everyone felt the same way Sophie Rose did. Interesting.

"I don't think I'm better than you or anyone else. I don't plan on taking the best men. At my last place, the men chose us, and we didn't have a choice but to go with them."

"Yeah. So, you say. Just don' be pushin' out your scrawny chest or flippin' your red hair to entice them or there'll be trouble."

Since she had no intention of getting so far in this place, it wasn't going to be a problem. Besides, she may not be the most well-endowed woman on the planet, but she certainly wasn't scrawny. It was time to move on.

"Is there anything else you'd like me to do, Edda?"

Sophie Rose jumped to her feet. "See. There she goes. Suckin' up to Edda."

"I wasn't— Never mind. I'm going to my room."

"Not so fast, Scarlett. We need to get you ready for tonight." She nodded to one of the girls who hadn't agreed with Sophie Rose. "Minnie, follow her and see what clothes she brought with her. Daisy, find Ruby's clothes and bring them out here."

Sophie Rose let out a screech. "But Ruby's things are mine."

Even though Edda was a good head shorter than her, Sophie Rose shrank back when Edda stood before her and poked her in the chest. "No one gave you permission to take Ruby's things. They are not yours. They belong to me. Now get them. I know what Ruby had, so don't even think about keeping any of them."

Nella followed Minnie into her room. "That was interesting. I take it Edda and Sophie Rose don't get along."

"No one gets along with that woman. She's been a pain in all our sides since she got here. Thinking because she came from Chicago, she is better than the rest of us." Minnie picked up the dance hall dress Nella had spread out on the bed. "She's nothing but a prostitute like the rest of us. You watch your step around her." She eyed the low-neck, off the shoulder, red and black dress. "Pretty fancy. Is this what you wore at your last place?"

"Yes. It was a dance hall, too, so we had to perform."

"Well, I can tell you right now, this won't work here." Carrying the dress over her arm, she left the room.

"That's probably the last time I'll see it." Not that she ever intended to wear it, but it was still better than those robes the girls wore.

———

The afternoon wore on. Ruby's clothes were too small for her, so, except for Sophie Rose who pouted in a corner chair, the girls scrambled to find something to fit. She had to admit, even though they were preparing her to meet and greet gawking men, it was rather fun. A bit like a slumber party. Giggling. Storytelling. Sharing their lives before ending up where they were. So many tragic stories.

Nella kept an eye on the grandfather clock ticking away the minutes. She needed to get back to her room for when Stuart came back. Since she hadn't slept much last night, she didn't need to pretend to yawn.

Edda clapped her hands. "Time to rest until we open. Get back to your rooms. It's the weekend, so we'll be busy with those miners coming to do their weekly shopping."

As she walked across the room, she couldn't miss Sophie Rose and Jack talking and looking at her. It had bothered her to have the man in the room as she'd undressed and tried on different robes. With his hat low over his eyes, it was difficult to see his expression, but the man gave her the creeps.

Nella closed her bedroom door, locked it, and propped the chair under the handle. A nap would be wonderful, but she needed to stay awake to listen for Stuart. Instead of lying on the bed, she waited on the windowsill until something tapped at the glass. She pushed open the window. Stuart stood below, his bag over his shoulders. After repeating the drill of the sheets, his head appeared, followed by his torso and legs.

"No one saw you, did they?"

"No. I made sure." He rolled his shoulders and winced. "I'll be glad when this is over. Pulling myself up makes my arms hurt."

She'd have more sympathy for him, except he wasn't the one who was going to parade her half-nude body in front of strangers.

"I brought a rope with me this time."

"Well, hopefully, we can catch the culprit tonight."

"Any leads?"

Nella relayed the events of the day. "If I had my guesses, it would be Sophie Rose who killed Ruby. The woman is so jealous, she probably hates her reflection in the mirror."

"Seems rather obvious, doesn't it?"

"That's what I thought. But I don't know who else could have done it." Nella sat on the edge of the bed and yawned. "I need to take a nap if I'm going to make it through the night."

"You go ahead and sleep. I'll keep watch."

———

Stuart sat on a chair by the window, making sure to keep out of sight, but still able to watch for movements down below. After a moment, Jack appeared, looking both ways down the street, before staring up at Nella's window. Stuart didn't dare peer out the window. What was Jack doing? Why was he focusing on Nella's window?

After a few seconds, the back door opened and closed. Had someone seen him or was Jack trying to decide how to get into the room? But then, from what Stuart knew, men like Jack didn't sneak into rooms, they simply entered without questions.

As he turned his attention to the woman on the bed, something caught his eye. There, below the sill. Was that a scratch? He knelt on the floor and ran a finger over it. An indentation similar to a hook. Had someone climbed into the room using a grappling hook? The murderer? Was that what Jack was investigating? Or was he deciding to get into the room again?

There was nothing he could do about it, so he sat back in the chair and returned to thinking about Nella. Strange person. Did he truly believe she'd come back from the future? More so, did she believe it, or should they cart her away someplace where she couldn't hurt anyone?

Surprisingly, his friends did. But he was more skeptical. Especially the part about them being characters in some books Nella wrote.

Admittedly, she was an attractive woman. Even dressed in men's clothing, dirty, and tired, she struck a chord within him. Then, when she showed up dressed as a lady, his heart nearly left his chest.

And, after spending time with her last night, he realized she was smart and funny, too. All those stories about things flying in the air. Vehicles moving without horses. Moving pictures. Telephones you carry in your hands. She'd pointedly left out his questions about more wars, which probably meant there would be.

The temptation to join her on the bed was more than the floor being hard. For some reason, he wanted to wrap her in his arms. Protect her. Kiss her. And . . .

Nella snuffled in her sleep. Having her greet men scantily clad went against everything he felt about women. If there were a way to stop prostitution, he'd be first in line to stop it. But where there were a lot of men, too few women, and unscrupulous men and women who prey on the weak, it was bound to happen.

"What time is it?" Nella leaned up on an elbow and squinted.

He bit back a laugh at her hair flying every which way reminding him of a wild orangutan he'd seen in a book. "Four thirty."

She swung her legs over the side of the bed revealing a pair of shapely calves and slender ankles. He averted his eyes. No gentleman would ogle a woman's bare body parts.

"I guess they will be opening soon. I need to get changed."

As she passed by, he took her arm. "You don't have to do this, you know."

"I do. I have a feeling I won't return to my time until Ruby's murder is solved. It has to be the reason why I was sent here." She patted his hand. "Edda said I'll only be introduced tonight. Give the men something new to come back to."

"I don't like it."

"Neither do I, but it's the only way."

He let go of her hand. "I could leave and come back as a customer."

Nella shook her head. "No. You've never been here before, have you?"

Was that a hopeful look in her eyes? If he said yes, would she be disappointed? "The only time I've been up here was when Ruby was found. Otherwise, I don't frequent the brothels."

Her smile made his heart hitch. "Good to hear. But since they've only seen you here as an officer of the law, wouldn't it raise questions? Wouldn't Jack want to know why you're here tonight?"

"You're right. But I'll be here in case something goes wrong."

When Nella stepped behind the screen, he let his mind wander to places it shouldn't. Was her skin soft? Was her backside as rounded as it looked, or was she wearing one of those stupid bustle things? Was it a corset making her waist look so tiny?

"Uh, Stuart?"

"Yes?"

"I need some help."

He gulped. "With what?" Please don't let her need help with her corset.

"I can't get my corset untied."

H swallowed around the lump in his throat. "You what?" Had his voice really come out sounding like a schoolboy?

"My corset. I'm not supposed to wear it tonight. I can't undo it."

"I . . . Uh . . ."

"Oh, for heaven's sake. Just get over here. I'll have my back to you. All you have to do is reach for the strings and untie them."

"I . . . Uh . . . Um . . ."

"I guess I'll ask Jack."

Stuart jumped to his feet. "All right. I'm coming." He tried not to look. Truly he did. But how could he untie the strings if he couldn't see them? She had her hair lifted in the air revealing a long, silky, sexy neck, just begging for his kisses.

Trying desperately not to touch her backside, which definitely was her own, he found the end of one ribbon and tugged. Nothing happened. He pulled again.

"I think the strings knotted."

"Well, then unknot them."

How could his mouth be so dry at the same time he was sweating? "All right." He couldn't avoid touching her warm back, the top of her luscious backside. He was getting . . . Well . . . he understood why men wanted to ravish women. He held his breath, and, with fumbling fingers, managed to untie the knot. Before the strings were loose, he was back in the chair, taking deep breaths, trying to get his mind from her body and on to something less savory. Like Ruby's murder. The cattle rustling going on the in the area. Illegal booze. Maybe just counting the metal tiles in the ceiling.

An audible sigh came from behind the screen. It sounded as if she muttered something about damn corsets being worse than bras. Didn't women like wearing corsets? And what was a bra?

He opened his eyes when she closed the screen. If he'd thought his mouth had been dry before, it was a desert now. A desert with no water for hundreds of miles. The red, silk robe she wore only came to her shapely knees. The tie around her waist accentuated her rounded hips. She held the top of the robe closed as if protecting herself. Her hair fell in soft curls over her shoulders. One side was held back with a red bow. What man in his right mind wouldn't want to spend time with her? He sure as hell did.

"Um. Do I look all right?" Her cheeks reddened. "I mean. I don't want to look all right, but I do. Doesn't make sense, does it?"

It didn't, but then he didn't understand woman in the least. His sisters were always saying nonsensical things to him. He simply ignored them, but ignoring Nella would be entirely different and difficult. "You are beautiful. I'm glad no man can be with you tonight."

"Good heavens, me too. I hope I don't have to put up with any groping. Edda said I only have to sit in a chair and look enticing. I guess the look, don't touch scenario is meant to increase men's interest."

If he were in the room, he would break every rule Edda had, but he wasn't about to tell Nella. For one thing, if he tried to speak, the words would get all jumbled up and he'd sound like he was a toddler learning to talk. A rambling, babbling, incoherent baby.

"Scarlett, it's time."

Her sigh was deep enough to wisp across his face. "Good luck."

"Thanks, I'm going to need it."

7

Nella opened the door to her room, locked it behind her, and groaned. How could sitting in a chair for hours on end be so tiring? It was probably from nerves. Having men stare at her, try to get her to go to her room with them, whisper disgusting things they wanted her to do to them. All the while not saying a word. Thank heavens Jack was behind her most of the night warding off the most enthusiastic ones.

Evidently there was a long list of men who would return tomorrow night to enjoy her 'charms,' as many of them so aptly put it. Huh. She'd charm them right out the bedroom window. Disgusting pieces of . . .

"How did it go?"

Her heart practically in her throat, she jumped. So lost in her thoughts, she'd forgotten Stuart was in the room.

"As one would imagine in a brothel. I guess word is out that Edda has a new redhead. They'll be lined up outside the door, or so Edda says." She removed a wrap draped over the screen, pulled it around her shoulders, dropped onto a chair, and propped her feet on the bed.

"We'd better get this solved before tomorrow. There is no way I'm going back out there. It was scary and creepy. There was one man who gave me more attention than the others. And with Edda and Sophie Rose's nasty glares, I have a feeling there was more to this man."

"What did he look like?"

"Tall. Rather thin. Dark hair. Dressed well."

"Did he wear a black coat and a top hat?"

"Yes. How did you know?"

"Word is there is a man who pays special attention to this brothel. I have a feeling he actually owns it."

"Interesting." Nella stretched her calves. It had been days since she'd gone for a run. Her body was tightening up. "How did it go here?"

"Quiet. I did find something earlier. Look." He pointed to the scratch in the windowsill. "I think someone got into the room using a grappling hook."

Nella dropped her feet to the floor, knelt on the floor, and fingered the indentation. "Interesting. It certainly would be easier than tying sheets together."

"Which means the person used it to get into and out of the room."

"Which means it couldn't be anyone from the brothel."

Stuart shook his head. "Not necessarily. If Ruby kept her door locked, someone could have snuck out of the building and climbed up here."

The faces of the soiled doves ran through her mind. With the exception of Sophie Rose, she couldn't see any of them going through the effort of shimmying up the side of a building. Not only would they not have the upper body strength, but they didn't seem the type. But one never knew. As in her books, she had no idea who the bad guy, or girl, was.

"I don't know, Stuart. There has to be someone else."

"Well, we aren't going to solve anything tonight. I'll take the floor again."

Nella opened the screen, and changed into a long, white nightgown Minnie had given her. It might be too warm, but it was better than sleeping in her clothes again. "Can we leave the window open? It's stuffy in here."

"Good idea." Stuart's voice was muffled.

Had he fallen asleep already? Jerk.

———

Roused from a dream of dancing with Stuart, Nella rolled over and stared at the open window.

"Shh." Stuart put a warm hand on her ankle. "I hear something. I'm going to get on the other side of the bed. You stay here. Pretend to be sleeping."

Where the heck would she go? Her heart skipped a beat. In another beat, something clanked against the wood. A thick rope draped over the ledge. Was this the killer?

Nella held her breath. No. Keep breathing. Deep breaths as if she were sleeping. She bit her bottom lip and rolled over so her back was to the window. Then she could keep her eyes open.

Time seemed to drag until there was a thud on the floor. Someone was in the room. A hand crept up her hip.

"Wakey, wakey, my lovely. I'm gonna have me a little fun before I take care of you. Jest like I did with Ruby." He ran his hand over her bare skin.

His odor was revolting. His touch nauseating.

"C'mon, girly. Wake up. Time for Benny boy to get some pleasure. Miss Edda said you could be mine for the night."

Edda? Edda knew this disgusting animal? Nella rolled over to face him. She didn't recognize him. "Edda sent you?"

He nodded. "It be my job to take care of them women who Edda believes will take her man away from her."

"Man? What man?'

"The bloke who owns this place. Edda hates anyone he pays attention to."

Sounded like the man who'd given her so much interest tonight. "How do you know?"

"'Cause she told me. She's my sister."

Ugh. She couldn't even imagine one of her brothers letting her be a prostitute, let alone kill anyone who might get in the way of being happy. "That's disgusting."

"It's the way of the world, sweetie." He yanked her upright. "Now, give me a little kiss."

What was Stuart waiting for? He needed to get his rear in gear. She turned her face away from the man's fetid breath.

"Don't fight me. There's nothing you can do to stop me." He tore her nightgown down the middle.

"Stop right there."

Finally. Benny let go of her. Her head hit the headboard. White dots filled her eyes. Like an echo chamber, the men's voices were hollow.

"Who are you?" Benny's voice rose an octave.

"Deputy Adams. Now get your hands up and sit in the chair."

Nella rose on her elbows. Stuart pointed a gun at Benny.

"Nella, get the rope from my bag."

With shaking hands, she handed him the rope. While she'd written characters who used guns, she'd never been this close to one pointed at a human being. It was quite disconcerting. On top of it, Stuart handed her the gun.

"Keep your finger off the trigger, but keep it aimed at him. I'll tie him up." He tied Benny's arms behind the chair and his ankles to the chair's legs.

"Wrap some around his waist, too."

Stuart raised an eyebrow at her.

"He was going to rape and kill me. Make the knots tight."

"Yes, ma'am."

"You're not going to get away with this." Even though he tried to look tough, his words had no bite.

"Well, Benny. That's where you're wrong. I heard everything you said." Stuart took the gun from Nella and leaned against a wall and crossed his ankles.

Nella kicked Benny in the shin. "And don't forget. I'm alive and will tell the sheriff everything you said." Too bad they didn't have tape recorders. "And the word of a deputy will hold more power than yours."

"Ha. Who is going to believe a whore?"

"I'm not a whore. I'm helping catch Ruby's killer."

"Now. This is what we're going to do, Benny. I'm going to have Nella scream. Scream loud enough to wake the entire town."

Benny stuck out his chin. "Sounds dumb to me."

"It should bring your sister running." Stuart nodded at Nella.

"Now?"

"Now."

She'd never had to scream before. Recalling how she was almost raped, she dug down deep, opened her mouth, and screeched for all she was worth. Then again. And once more for good measure.

In a matter of seconds someone pounded on the door. "Benny? You in there?" Edda must have been waiting outside the door. "Is it over?"

Stuart opened the door and stood behind it, letting Edda rush into the room. He shut it behind her.

Edda stopped at the end of the bed. "What? What's going on here?"

"Why don't you tell us, Edda." Nella folded her arms over her chest. "Tell us you don't know this man. Tell us you haven't had him kill women you want out of the way."

"Why, I don't know what you're talking about."

"Tie her to the other chair, Nella."

Did securing the knots tight enough to make Edda wince make her sadistic? Probably, but so be it. The woman had wanted her dead.

"Will you be all right here while I go for the sheriff?"

"Yes. But hurry. I want this over with." When he left, she sat on the edge of the bed. When Benny and Edda's yelling at each other got to be too much, she tore strips from the bottom of her nightgown, tied them around their mouths, then leaned against the tub.

So, Ruby's murder was solved. What did that mean for her? She was still here, wasn't she? No sooner had the words entered her head, then the room grew hazy. She closed her eyes. Her head spun. Her stomach pitched, and everything went black.

8

Nella lay on the floor. The ceiling light glared in her eyes. Ceiling light? She sat up and ran a hand over her face. Everything was as she'd left it, but not from 1880, but her time. Had this all been a dream? If so, it was an incredibly realistic one. Drawn to the sign on the wall, she pushed herself off the floor.

In May of 1880, Ruby Prescott, one of the working girls, was murdered in this room. Her body was found draped over the side of the bathtub. With the combined efforts of the local police, it was found the madam of the house, one Edda Conrow and her brother, Benny, conspired to kill any prostitutes she believed were after the man she loved. It isn't known how many women they disposed of, but there were as many as ten. Edda and Benny were hanged for their crimes. After her arrest, a soiled dove by the name of Sophie Rose took over the brothel, turning it into one of the most respected and prosperous establishments in Deadwood.

Huh. Sophie Rose. Who would have thought. She stuck her hand in her jeans pocket. What was this? She pulled her hand out. A small gold nugget. So, it hadn't been a dream after all. Nella's stomach growled loudly; she mistook it for a knock on the door. The knock came again.

"Is anyone in there? I don't know which room is mine."

Why did the voice sound familiar?

Not wanting a bat to fly in, Nella cracked open the door. Stuart? Or a man resembling Stuart stood outside the door. Her heart pounded in her chest. Had she slipped back into time again? But no. He was dressed in blue jeans and a T-shirt with a photo of a current rock band.

"Um. I'm Stuart Benson, one of the cover models. Do you happen to know which room is mine?"

Nella peered around him. "Did you see any bats?"

Stuart's face blanched. "Bats? Good grief, I hope not. I hate bats."

"Me, too." She opened the door wider. Behind him, something skittered across the floor. She grabbed his arm and pulled him into the room.

"Do I know you?"

Nella grinned. "No." But, she had a strong feeling that was about to change. She hated bats, but she was batty for love.

ABOUT THE AUTHOR

Tina Susedik is a multi-award-winning, multi-published, best-selling author who has been researching and writing books since 1997. She is published in non-fiction with military and local history books. She has also published children's books and romantic mysteries. She loves to add humor to her books, putting her characters in situations, and finding humorous ways to get them out of them. With forty-four books and short stories under her belt, she loves to use her knowledge of the writing craft to help other authors.

She lives in northwestern Wisconsin with her husband of fifty-one years and adores her five grandchildren. In the spare time she has, Tina loves to camp, hike, bike, garden, scrapbook, do jigsaw puzzles, and, of course, read, read, read.

Web: www.tina-susedik.com

Blog: tinasusedik.wordpress.com

Facebook: Tina Susedik, Author